The WIDOW'S CHOICE

Nancy Revell is the author of twelve titles in the bestselling Shipyard Girls series – which tells the story of a group of women who work together in a Sunderland shipyard during the Second World War. This new novel features some of the characters from the world of the Shipyard Girls series in a new County Durham setting. Her books have sold more than half a million copies across all editions.

Before that she was a journalist who worked for all the national newspapers, providing them with hard-hitting news stories and in-depth features. She also wrote amazing and inspirational true-life stories for just about every woman's magazine in the country.

Nancy was born and brought up in the north-east of England and she now lives in Oxfordshire with her husband, Paul.

Also by Nancy Revell

The Shipyard Girls
Shipyard Girls at War
Secrets of the Shipyard Girls
Shipyard Girls in Love
Victory for the Shipyard Girls
Courage of the Shipyard Girls
Christmas with the Shipyard Girls
Triumph of the Shipyard Girls
A Christmas Wish for the Shipyard Girls
The Shipyard Girls on the Home Front
Shipyard Girls Under the Mistletoe
Three Cheers for the Shipyard Girls

The WIDOW'S CHOICE

Nancy
REVELL

PENGUIN BOOKS

PENGUIN BOOKS

UK | USA | Canada | Ireland | Australia
India | New Zealand | South Africa

Penguin Books is part of the Penguin Random House group of companies
whose addresses can be found at global.penguinrandomhouse.com

First published in Penguin Books 2024
001

The image on p. 448 is courtesy of Alamy

Typeset in 10.4/15 pt Palatino LT Pro
by Integra Software Services Pvt. Ltd, Pondicherry

Printed and bound in Great Britain by Clays Ltd, Elcograf S.p.A.

The authorised representative in the EEA is Penguin Random House Ireland,
Morrison Chambers, 32 Nassau Street, Dublin D02 YH68

A CIP catalogue record for this book is available from the British Library

ISBN: 978–1–804–94507–0

www.greenpenguin.co.uk
Penguin Random House is committed to a sustainable future
for our business, our readers and our planet. This book is made
from Forest Stewardship Council® certified paper.

To My Wonderful Readers,

For it was your messages asking what would happen to the women after the war, which inspired me to write this new book. I hope you all love reading it just as much as I've loved writing it!

'To keep our faces toward change and behave like free spirits in the presence of fate is strength undefeatable.'

Helen Keller (1880–1968), author,
crusader and humanitarian

Acknowledgements

Very special and heartfelt thanks must go to Emily Griffin, Publishing Director of Century fiction, who has not only gifted me with her brilliant editorial guidance, but has also put such energy, time and enthusiasm into *The Widow's Choice*.

Writing a book – any book – is a team effort, and I count myself incredibly lucky to have such a sterling 'Team Nancy' across all departments – editorial, design, marketing, sales, PR and production. All experts in their field, all very professional and incredibly hardworking – as well as being genuinely lovely people.

Thank you all!

Cuthford Manor

The Residents

Angie Foxton-Clarke – the owner
Danny, Marlene, Bertie and Jemima – Angie's siblings
Bonnie Foxton-Clarke – her daughter
Lloyd Foxton-Clarke – her father-in-law
Evelyn Foxton-Clarke – her mother-in-law
Mrs Kwiatkowski – her old Polish neighbour

The Staff

Mrs Cora Jones – the housekeeper
Alberta – the cook
Wilfred – the butler
Thomas – the stablehand
Bill – the gardener
Jake – the chauffeur
Ted and Eugene – groundsmen
Stanislaw – the yard manager

The Animals

Winston and Bessie – Bullmastiffs
Ghost – a dapple grey gelding
Starling – a chestnut filly
Monty and Bomber – shire horses
Lucky – a rescued pit pony

Others

Clemmie Sinclair – Quentin's childhood friend

Dorothy Armstrong (née Williams) – Angie's best friend, living in America

Jeremy Fontaine-Smith and his mother Gertrude – neighbours

Dr Wright – the family doctor

Rebecca, Hilda and Jill – villagers

Prologue

Cuthford Manor, Cuthford, County Durham

Friday, 4 November 1949

Pulling open the oak door of Cuthford Manor, Angie brushed horsehair off her cashmere jumper and her jodhpurs as she watched Quentin's burgundy Morris Minor crunch its way down the long driveway. She hurried down the stone steps, bracing herself against the crisp autumn air, a smile already spreading across her face at the sight of her husband arriving home earlier than usual. The excitement she felt welcoming Quentin home each day had not dampened in the slightest during their four years of marriage.

Once out of the car, Quentin opened his arms to his wife, pulled her close and kissed her gently on the lips. 'You make me feel like the luckiest man alive,' he whispered as he kissed her neck and breathed in the smell of her skin – a mix of soap, perfume and the familiar scent of horses and hay.

Angie pulled back and looked into his piercing blue eyes. 'And you make me feel like the luckiest woman.'

The moment was interrupted by the sound of scrabbling on the gravel as their two sandy-coloured Bullmastiffs,

Winston and Bessie, raced around the side of the East Wing and charged towards them.

'Hello, you two scallywags!' Quentin chuckled as they vied for his attention.

'So . . .' He glanced up at Angie as he patted the dogs, their muscular back ends swinging from left to right. 'Is everyone excited about tomorrow's firework display?'

Angie bent down to stroke Bessie, who had been jostled out of the way by Winston. 'Oh, yes – very. I've just left Danny telling everybody the story behind "a penny for the guy", which he learnt at school today, and how poor old Guy Fawkes was sentenced to death by being hung, drawn and quartered.'

Quentin laughed. 'Which I'm sure horrified the younger ones.'

'I think that was the point of telling them,' said Angie.

They walked towards the manor.

'I'm guessing you've just been out.' Quentin knew how much his wife loved her daily horse rides in the surrounding countryside. The beauty of the rural landscape, she had told him, never failed to take her breath away.

Angie nodded and smiled.

'Ghost or Starling?' Quentin knew she liked to ride both horses.

'Starling. Your mother had already taken Ghost.' Angie had been relieved she had missed Evelyn, and was sure her mother-in-law felt the same.

As she and Quentin walked up the stone steps and into the warmth of the manor's huge, high-ceilinged entrance hall, the sound of footsteps could be heard hurrying towards them along the tiled corridor. Seconds later, the housekeeper, Mrs Cora Jones, appeared, pushing back a strand of hair that had come loose from her French twist.

'Oh, Master Quentin, you're home early.'

'A cancelled tutorial,' Quentin explained.

Mrs Jones turned her attention to Angie. 'Mrs Foxton-Clarke has just got out of the bath and is in a panic as she's left her favourite scarf in Ghost's stall. She's asked if you'd fetch it as she's worried the horse might decide to have a munch on it.'

'I think my dear mother's becoming as forgetful as Mrs Kwiatkowski,' Quentin joked.

'She was also concerned the scarf might go "walkies",' Mrs Jones added, keeping her tone level, even though it made her blood boil that Quentin's mother did not try to hide the fact that she didn't trust any of the staff.

Angie was about to carry out her mother-in-law's bidding when Mrs Kwiatkowski, who had become part of their family at Cuthford Manor, appeared at the top of the wide, carpeted staircase. She was clutching her handbag, her overcoat was buttoned up – and she was wearing just a pair of slippers. Her heavily lined face belied the childlike innocence that had come to her in her seventh decade.

Quentin squeezed Angie's hand, knowing the sadness she felt on seeing how her beloved old neighbour's mind was faltering.

'I'll get the scarf,' he said. 'You see to Mrs Kwiatkowski.'

*

Walking into the kitchen, Quentin was greeted by five excited faces. The three youngest children – their two-year-old daughter, Bonnie, plus Angie's siblings Bertie and Jemima – charged at him, flinging their arms open for their usual back-from-work embrace. Quentin grabbed the trio and managed to haul them into a communal bear hug – a well-practised manoeuvre. He looked across and smiled at Angie's other siblings, twelve-year-old Marlene and thirteen-year-old Danny, who now considered themselves too old for such public displays of affection.

'Where's Angie?' Marlene asked, sitting down at the kitchen table and pouring Quentin a cuppa.

'She's just seeing to Mrs Kwiatkowski,' Quentin said.

'Is Mrs K trying to make a run for it again?' Danny asked.

Quentin nodded and the pair exchanged sad looks.

Marlene pushed across the table a half-finished plate of the cook's oat and ginger biscuits, the reason the warm air in the kitchen was infused with a spicy sweetness. 'I'd grab one of these before Mr My-Eyes-Are-Bigger-Than-My-Belly over there polishes them off.' She glanced over at Danny, who had, in fact, been eyeing up the home-made biscuits.

'Thanks,' Quentin smiled. 'Just save me one. He's a growing lad.' He winked at Danny, who he and Angie had agreed really did have hollow legs.

After a quick sip of tea, Quentin headed towards the back door. 'I've just got to get something from Ghost's stall and I'll be back.'

*

As soon as Quentin stepped outside, he could feel the frost in the air. Autumn was fading rapidly and a little earlier than was expected, which was often the case in the elevated, hilly landscape of this part of the north-east.

Crossing the yard, he opened the door of the barn that housed the stables, letting it swing back. It was almost dark, but there was still just enough light to see where he was going.

Hearing the sound of swishing tails, a few snorts and stamping hooves as the horses sensed a visitor, Quentin headed for the stall of his dapple grey gelding, Ghost. He grabbed a handful of hay from the bag hanging by the side, putting it through the iron bars of the stable door as an apology for the disturbance.

'Here we go,' he murmured as Ghost chomped on the hay, his velvet lips tickling his master's hand.

'Sorry, boy. Won't be a jiffy.' Quentin unbolted the door and stepped into the stall. The door banged shut behind him. Neither Quentin nor Ghost flinched. The door of the stall had clashed shut for so many years, they would probably have reacted had it *not* done so.

As Quentin patted Ghost's perfectly groomed flank, he sensed the horse's ease and trust. Quentin had ridden most of his life, but he had never felt such a close bond with a horse as he did with Ghost.

Seeing his mother's silk scarf, which he knew to be very expensive as she had mentioned it often enough, he stepped to the back of the stall, where it was lying on the ground. The brown fabric with a light mustard pattern was well camouflaged.

He was just reaching down to grab it when there was a sudden loud bang.

A firework? A precursor to tomorrow's Bonfire Night celebrations?

These thoughts shot through Quentin's mind just as Ghost did what he always did whenever he was spooked by any kind of unexpected loud noise – he tossed his head in the air, neighing noisily, and reared up.

As his front legs lifted off the ground, he staggered back.

And as he did so, the heavy weight of his body slammed full on into Quentin, crushing him against the wall at the back of the stall.

There was a sharp, sickening crack as Quentin's head smashed against the whitewashed stone.

Chapter One

Three weeks later

Angie opened her eyes and gazed up at the ceiling, listening to the sounds of Cuthford Manor coming to life. Three weeks had passed since that unthinkable day and she'd barely left the bed she and Quentin had shared every night of their married life – but something felt different this morning.

Last night, tossing and turning through the darkness, as she had ever since Quentin's accident, a vision of the snowman the children had built after his funeral yesterday came to her, staying with her as she lay awake into the early hours.

She'd seen the snowman when she slipped away from the mourners who had come back to the manor for drinks and a small buffet. Walking into the kitchen, she'd heard the children's voices and had looked out of the window to see them building a snowman. Stepping out the back door into the freezing cold, she'd realised they had created their own memorial to the man they'd all loved and she had stood stock-still, taking in the sight. Quentin's wellington boots had been set into the snow and his favourite scarf wrapped around the snowman's neck. Twigs had been used for his arms and hands – positioned so that they were akimbo, something Quentin had had a habit of doing. The final touch was Quentin's well-worn tweed flat cap on top of his head.

She had blinked back tears as she'd told them how wonderful their snow statue was, forcing herself to smile even though her heart was aching so badly it hurt. Now, as she thought of the children standing proudly next to their memorial to Quentin, she realised how much she'd neglected them these past weeks and just how much they must be feeling the loss of the man they, too, had loved. A man who had been like a father to them all.

As the sun started to peak over the horizon, Angie was struck by life's unpredictability. When she was welding ships in one of the yards on the Wear as part of the war effort and had first met Quentin, never would she have guessed that within eighteen months she would go from being a single girl to a married woman, and from renting a small flat with her best friend Dorothy to lady of the manor, living with her husband, her four siblings and her old neighbour in a 'fairytale castle' surrounded by awe-inspiring countryside.

But just as her life had changed so dramatically after falling in love with Quentin, so had it changed again. Only this time, her life had been plunged into a deep, dark well of grief, and she'd been left nursing a heart so badly broken she was sure it would never heal.

Life had become a blur as she'd taken to her bed, exhausted by grief. But the inquest, which had ruled Quentin's death accidental, had now been held and she'd finally been allowed to bury her husband. It was time, Angie knew, to be strong – or at least to try to be – and for her to push back her own immeasurable grief for the sake of her siblings and her daughter, Bonnie. She had five young lives to nurture. Five children who needed her now more than ever.

As did Mrs Kwiatkowski. Angie couldn't abandon her old friend when she needed her most. Nor did she want to. Mrs Kwiatkowski had cared for Angie and Dorothy when they'd become neighbours at the start of the war. She had taken them under her wing, fed them the most delicious Polish stews and constantly nagged them to 'be careful' in the shipyard.

Angie owed it to all of them to put on a brave face and to start getting on with life again.

As she pulled on her clothes and plodded downstairs, she was glad she had given the staff the day off after their hard work organising yesterday's wake. Walking into the kitchen, she saw Winston and Bessie in their usual positions, splayed out on the floor in front of the Aga, their bulging bellies and a few random flakes of pastry stuck to their dry noses – evidence they'd snaffled plenty of leftovers from yesterday's buffet. The pair managed to haul themselves up to greet Angie, bringing a rare smile to her face.

Half an hour later, Angie had made a stack of pancakes and put lemon quarters, treacle and sugar on the table, along with five plates – two on the boys' side and three on the girls'. Hearing their chatter as they walked down the corridor and entered the kitchen, Angie saw their looks of surprise – and relief – at seeing her there. It gave Angie a stab of guilt that she had been so absent these past three weeks.

'Pancakes and hot chocolate for breakfast. Special treat after such a difficult day yesterday,' Angie announced, as the dogs pushed their way into the melee of children, their tails wagging nineteen to the dozen, strings of drool ending up on all of their dressing gowns.

Angie put the plate of pancakes on the table and watched as the children all clambered into their usual places on the benches on either side of the large kitchen table.

'Yummy!' Jemima, seven, beamed.

'Yummy!' Bonnie, two, copied.

Bertie, who was now eight, pushed his round wire-rimmed glasses up the bridge of his nose as he sat down at the table. 'Cor, it's been ages since you made us pancakes,' he said, his eyes feasting on their treat.

Marlene gave her sister a tentative smile. 'Thanks, Angie.' The words of gratitude were not for the breakfast, Angie knew, but for her return from her self-imposed exile from life.

A blast of icy-cold air pushed through the warmth of the kitchen as the heavy eighteenth-century oak door was tugged open and Danny came in from the yard, his rosy cheeks and dripping nose testimony to the dropping temperatures outside. His eyes lit up on seeing that Angie was there, causing her to experience another pang of guilt.

'Just in time . . . You're up bright and early?' Angie asked, pouring hot chocolate from the saucepan into five mugs.

'Thought I'd take Ghost out for an early-morning ride,' Danny said, nudging up to his younger brother.

Just the mention of Ghost shocked Angie back to a vision of Quentin lying on the straw-strewn stone floor, his head encircled by a halo of blood. Back to the feel of his rag-doll body and the stickiness of his blood on her hands.

Angie forced herself to focus on the here and now as she handed out the steaming mugs of hot chocolate.

She watched Bonnie copy her aunties and uncles as they squeezed lemons, drizzled treacle and sprinkled sugar onto their pancakes. The slight frown on her daughter's face as she concentrated on the task at hand reminded her so much of Quentin, it felt both a blessing and a curse.

Angie let them eat in peace while she made herself a fresh pot of tea, her mind drawn back to Ghost. Danny had adored Ghost since first setting eyes on him after Quentin had brought the gelding home from the stud farm near the Borders four years ago. Even though their chestnut filly, Starling, was smaller, Danny had persuaded Quentin to let him learn to ride on Ghost. It was a decision Quentin hadn't regretted as Ghost was incredibly calm and gentle with his novice charge. Thereafter, Ghost would always be Danny's first choice when going out for a ride.

Everyone had agreed that there was something different about Ghost. He was not only striking to look at, with his dappled white-grey coat and pewter-coloured mane, but he was intelligent and intuitive with whoever was riding him. There were times when Angie just wanted to go slowly and enjoy the countryside and he would adapt his pace without her having to pull back, just as he'd sense when she wanted to feel the pure rush of adrenalin and he would let loose, galloping as fast as he could.

Now, after what had happened, she knew that she could never ride him again.

Couldn't even lay eyes on him again.

Seeing that they'd all just about finished their pancakes, Angie sat down in her chair at the head of the table with her cup of tea.

'Bonnie, will you do me a favour and fetch Mrs Kwiatkowski, please? I think I might have enough mix left for one more pancake.'

Bonnie nodded, pushing herself along to the end of the bench, then heading for the kitchen door.

'Thank you, sweetie.' Angie gently ruffled her blonde hair as she passed, making her daughter giggle.

Once Bonnie had gone, Angie focused on her four siblings. Her guilt at neglecting them was compounded by knowing how much they'd already had to suffer during their young lives. Their own mother had abandoned them and run off with a man half her age, and their father hadn't even bothered to keep in touch after she and Quentin had brought them back to Cuthford Manor to live.

'I realise I've been a bit hopeless lately, but I want you to know that I'm back in the world of the living.' She took a deep breath. 'And I'm sorry I've not been here for you. But I am now – and will be from here on in.'

Seeing the relief on their faces, she herself felt relieved that she hadn't left it any later to come back to them, even if the pain of having to face the world again – to put on a mask to shield her grief – was almost unbearable.

'So, tell me, how are you all feeling?' she asked.

No one said anything.

Marlene broke the silence.

'We're all right. As all right as all right can be.' She looked at her two younger siblings. 'There's been some crying, but we've dried our eyes and soldiered on, haven't we?'

Bertie and Jemima nodded, their little faces serious.

Marlene turned her attention to her older brother.

'Danny hasn't cried – or at least we've not seen him cry – but he's been spending most of his free time with Thomas in the stables.'

Angie looked at Danny. It made sense he'd seek solace with the horses. Ghost might well be his favourite, but he loved them all: Starling, the chestnut filly, the two shires, Monty and Bomber, and Lucky, the little pit pony the children had begged Angie and Quentin to rescue from the knacker's yard. Horses were his passion. His love.

'And you?' Angie asked Marlene.

'I'm okay.' She thought for a moment. 'I can't believe I'm saying this, but going back to school has helped me take my mind off everything.'

Angie had the housekeeper to thank for that – Mrs Jones had been the one to convince the children to go back to school shortly after Angie had taken to her bed.

'Well,' said Angie, 'I fully intend to get us back to some semblance of normality, because I know for certain that

Quentin would hate it if I was miserable for any longer – and he would be upset if he thought you were all still feeling sad . . . He'd want you to be happy, you know? That's all he ever wished for you.' Angie tried to keep her voice steady and strong. She was determined to put on a convincing front for the children – and anyone else, for that matter – even if inside her heart was breaking.

Danny, Marlene, Bertie and Jemima nodded their understanding. Quentin had told them this many times.

Sensing there was something else that was bothering them, she asked, 'What's on your minds?'

'What about Ghost?' Bertie's eyes flicked over to Danny.

Angie caught the look. She knew her four siblings well and could tell by the resolute expressions on their faces that they'd all had a confab.

'What *about* Ghost?' Angie asked.

'Well, all the other horses are being taken out for rides and exercised, but not Ghost,' said Danny. He was quiet for a moment, thinking of the best way to express what he wanted to say. 'Now that Quentin's gone . . .' Another pause. 'And because of what happened, no one wants to ride him. I can take him out on a weekend and during the holidays, but he needs exercising twice a day, Monday to Friday.'

'Evelyn's refused point-blank to ride him,' Marlene stated. She'd forced herself to ask her on Danny's behalf. They were probably the most words they'd spoken to each other since Angie's mother-in-law had moved in less than a year ago. 'Every time Ghost's mentioned, she's like a broken record. *My darling son would still be here were it not for that bloody horse.*'

Angie sighed inwardly at the thought of Evelyn. Quentin had always been very candid about his mother, admitting that he might love her, but that did not mean he liked her. She could be charming, he'd said, but she also had another, far less attractive side. After Evelyn had moved back to the manor, it hadn't taken Angie long to see the verity of her husband's words, nor Evelyn's disapproval of her son's choice of wife – a disapproval born of the simple fact that Angie was the daughter of a coalminer.

'But it's not Ghost's fault that he's scared of loud bangs, is it?' Bertie implored.

Angie reached over and gave her youngest brother's arm a gentle squeeze and shook her head.

'And Lloyd's got a bad back, so he can't ride him,' Danny added.

Angie knew that her father-in-law had once been a keen horseman, but he had some kind of fusion of the lower spine that prevented him from riding or doing anything too physical.

'The only reason he's been exercised at all during the week is because Thomas takes him out,' Marlene told her. Angie noted the slight inflection in her sister's voice and wondered if she'd become close to – perhaps even a little sweet on – the stablehand.

'He was forced to by Lloyd,' Jemima chipped in.

'He said if Thomas wanted to keep his job, he'd best exercise Ghost once a day,' Marlene said, raising her eyebrows.

'But once a day's not enough,' Danny stated.

Angie could feel her head starting to throb. She had not expected to have a conversation about Ghost this morning.

Seeing Danny's face, she didn't have the heart to tell him that the problem about who would exercise Ghost would soon be resolved as she had decided during her weeks languishing in bed that the horse would have to go. Ghost would forever be inextricably linked with Quentin's death. Just the mention of his name had her falling back into the quicksand of grief.

She sighed and sat back in her chair.

'So, we thought,' Marlene said, 'that when you were feeling better, you could exercise Ghost?'

Angie felt her heart drop. 'Let's just see how it goes,' she said.

'What does that mean?' Danny demanded.

'Like I said, we'll have to see.'

'Ghost didn't mean it, you know?' Danny said. 'He'd never have hurt Quentin on purpose.'

'I know, I'm sorry,' Angie exhaled. 'I just can't ride him at the moment, but that's not to say that won't change in the future.' She knew, though, deep down, that her feelings would never change.

Just then, Bonnie toddled into the room, clutching her favourite book in one hand and holding Mrs Kwiatkowski's bony hand with the other. The old woman was happily chatting away to the little girl in Polish. Mrs Kwiatkowski, who had always been able to speak English well, now spoke solely in her native tongue, although thankfully she could still understand English. Knowing that the old woman who had been such a loving presence in her life for almost a decade was also leaving her – slowly but surely – added to Angie's heartache.

'Let's talk about Ghost later. Now go and get yourselves ready,' Angie said, getting up so that Mrs Kwiatkowski could sit in her chair, which was nearest to the warm Aga.

As her siblings trooped out of the kitchen, Angie breathed a sigh of relief. *She'd had a stay of execution, but for how long?*

As she poured Mrs Kwiatkowski a cup of tea, Angie knew that rebuilding her life was not going to be easy, but at least, she told herself, this morning she had taken the first step.

Chapter Two

After Mrs Kwiatkowski had enjoyed her pancake and had read Bonnie *The Tale of Two Bad Mice*, Angie took her old neighbour back up to her room in the East Wing, where she liked to spend the morning either looking out of the large sash windows, immersed in her own thoughts, or knitting. She had once been an avid reader, but not any more.

Angie had wanted Mrs Kwiatkowski to come and live with them at the manor since noticing, during the final few months of the war, that she'd often seemed confused and forgetful. It had been a kindness for which she had been repaid tenfold, as her old neighbour had become a doting stand-in grandmother to her brothers and sisters. The two youngest, Bertie and Jemima, had particularly gained so much from having 'Mrs K' in their lives. The love she gave them went some way to making up for the neglect they'd suffered in their formative years.

'I'll come and get you later,' Angie said, giving her a gentle hug. 'And we can go for a little walk in the garden – if it's not too cold, that is.'

Mrs Kwiatkowski settled herself in her armchair and replied in Polish. Angie told herself to be thankful that the old woman whom she loved so dearly still seemed happy. Dr

Wright in the village had warned Angie that the descent into senility often went hand in hand with feeling down, and with the propensity to suffer from mood swings.

Back in the kitchen, Angie got herself wrapped up, ready to take Winston and Bessie on a long overdue walk. Leaving with the dogs out the back door, she purposely took an immediate right to avoid passing the stables. She didn't want to see Ghost. Nor did she want to think about the desperate look on Danny's face when he'd asked her why she wouldn't exercise him.

An hour later, when Angie returned from a bracing walk, she found Mrs Jones waiting for her in the kitchen.

'Mrs Foxton-Clarke has asked if you would go and have a chat with her in the front reception room,' she told Angie over the noise of the dogs lapping at their bowls, getting just as much water on the flagstones as they were managing to drink.

'You're meant to be having a day off,' Angie said. 'She shouldn't be sending you on errands.'

'She caught me on my way here to make a cup of tea. I don't mind,' Mrs Jones appeased her.

'Well, if she asks you to do anything else, tell her no,' Angie stressed, pouring herself a glass of water.

'It's good to have you back,' Mrs Jones said as she got up and headed back to her little office-cum-snug next to the kitchen. Angie was sure she could pick up a sense of relief in Mrs Jones's tone.

Taking a deep breath, Angie headed off to the sitting room.

As soon as she got there, she was met by her mother-in-law's concerned expression.

'Oh dear, Angela, you look *dreadful*. Are you sure you haven't come back to us all too early?'

Catching a glimpse of herself in the mirror over the mantlepiece, Angie thought she did look washed out and windswept – but then again, she always looked pale.

'I'm fine,' Angie said, knowing her mother-in-law's concern was convincing but disingenuous. 'If I'd stayed moping around in bed for much longer, I'd have started to get bedsores.'

Angie caught Evelyn's look of distaste.

'Honestly, Angela, you do know how to paint a picture,' she sniped, her tone betraying her deep dislike of her daughter-in-law.

Angie sat down on the russet-coloured leather sofa and put her glass of water on the glass coffee table. It wasn't even midday and she felt exhausted.

'Anyway, how are *you* coping?' she asked, forcing herself to take into consideration that here was a woman who had just lost her only child.

'I got it all out in the space of a week,' Evelyn said stoically.

'Really?' Angie couldn't understand how anyone could do that. Not least when it came to the loss of their own son.

'Yes, really, Angela. I immersed myself in my grief – I raged against the cruelty and pain of having my son so viciously snatched from me. I sobbed my heart out. I gave in a few times when I just felt too overwhelmed by it all and took some of those pills Dr Wright had left for me, but I'm a believer in expunging one's grief, not subduing it with pills. So, on the whole, that's what I did.'

Angie listened, doubting very much that she herself would ever succeed in 'expunging' her own grief.

'I've been holding the fort ever since,' Evelyn said with undisguised self-satisfaction. 'Which is the reason I've asked you to come here for a little tête-à-tête.'

Angie looked at her mother-in-law and part of her felt jealous that she could overcome her grief so effectively. Angie might be up and dressed and able to make pancakes, but she still felt her own grief in every moment.

'So, Angela, I'll get straight to it. I'd like to make a suggestion. And looking at you now – well, it makes me all the more certain that this is the right thing to do.'

Angie gave her a puzzled look. 'Which is?'

'Which is,' Evelyn said, straightening her back and shuffling in the chair, 'that I think it would be a good idea – best for everyone – if *I* took over Cuthford Manor, just until you're feeling a bit better – stronger – more yourself.'

Angie felt herself stiffen. When Evelyn had decided that she'd had enough of York and that she and Lloyd were coming back here to live, Quentin had not opposed their return as he'd promised his grandfather, Leonard, that his mother and father could live at Cuthford Manor, if that was what they wanted. It had been Leonard's concession to his son and daughter-in-law on leaving the manor to his grandson.

Angie had been a little worried that her mother-in-law's far from congenial nature might chill the warm and loving atmosphere of her marital home, but she needn't have been concerned as the place was huge. Evelyn and Lloyd moved into rooms in the West Wing, enabling Evelyn and Angie to live their own separate lives. A relationship of mutual avoidance was established, and if there *had* to be contact, then a strained civility was played out, which suited Angie just fine.

'Oh, that's all right, Evelyn, I can manage. But thanks for the offer.' Angie tried to be diplomatic. This had been her home for the past four and a half years; she had always been in charge. Quentin had worked full-time at the university, so the general day-to-day running of the place had naturally fallen to her. And she did not want that to change.

'Mmm, well, I suggest you think on it, my dear,' Evelyn pushed. 'I think you'll struggle to cope.'

'I'm fine,' Angie insisted, biting back her annoyance.

Evelyn looked at her gold Cartier wristwatch and stood up. 'Dearie me, is that the time? I must dash. I'm off to Durham to meet up with an old friend.'

She walked to the door, stopped and turned around.

'Just remember, Angela, Cuthford Manor was mine – or should I say mine and Lloyd's – for almost thirty years, so I can run the place with my eyes closed. It'll be no bother.'

Before Angie had time to reply, Evelyn had turned and sashayed her way into the hallway and out of the front door, where Jake the chauffeur was waiting.

Chapter Three

December

Over the following weeks it soon became very clear to Angie that Evelyn was loathe to hand back the reins of control. Without Quentin in the picture, Evelyn seemed to feel she could interfere more and more in the running of the manor, telling Angie how she thought things should or should not be done, and regularly showing her disapproval of the staff calling Angie by her first name, something Angie had insisted they do the first day she'd arrived at Cuthford Manor.

'It's blurring the boundaries,' Evelyn would say.

Evelyn was also vocal about her concerns that the traditional upstairs-downstairs divide was being 'blurred' still further by Angie and the children preferring to gather in the kitchen in the old servants' quarters, despite there being two plush reception rooms, a drawing room, a dining room, a library, a back parlour, a billiard room and a large music room.

But it was Angie's friendship with the housekeeper that really irked Evelyn. It was something she'd kept to herself when Quentin had been alive, but not any more.

'You shouldn't fraternise with the help. It's simply not *done* in our circles' had become Evelyn's frequent rebuke to Angie whenever she saw the two chatting.

Similar diatribes about 'breaching the social divide' were made about the children's closeness with Alberta the cook, and Danny's with Thomas and the other workers on the estate.

As if to make her point, Evelyn had the staff running about accommodating her every want and need. Angie had lost count of the number of times she'd needed one of the maids to do something, or Wilfred, the butler, to run a quick errand, only to find they weren't free because her mother-in-law had tasked them to do something for her.

Angie tired of Evelyn pointing out whenever the chance arose that she and Lloyd would still be in possession of the manor had her father-in-law not 'lost his marbles' and bypassed his own son, leaving everything to Quentin.

'Sometimes I wish he *had* left all this to them,' Angie confided to Mrs Jones one day when they were walking through the rooms in the East Wing, discussing the mammoth task of restoring it. 'We'd never have come here, and Quentin would still be alive.'

On top of Evelyn's antagonism, Angie was also having to deal with Danny regularly pushing her to ride Ghost, as Thomas was complaining of having too much to do to exercise him. The school holidays couldn't come soon enough – in just a few weeks, Danny would be on his Christmas break and would be able to exercise Ghost himself. Angie knew, though, that she was just buying herself time and putting off the inevitable.

Making sure she caught Mrs Kwiatkowski before she headed out for her teatime walks – usually in her slippers and a cardigan – was also a daily concern. Thankfully, Mrs Kwiatkowski always left by the back door, so there was usually someone in the kitchen to stop her if Angie hadn't arrived in time to take her out for a stroll around the gardens – clothed in some proper outdoor wear.

Although Angie's litany of problems showed no signs of resolving themselves, they did drag her mind away from her grief. As did running the manor and looking after the children and Mrs Kwiatkowski. The more she had to do, the less she had to feel. Whenever her grief broke through, she forced it back, sternly reminding herself there were many other women out there who had also suffered the loss of husbands and loved ones.

The approach of Christmas brought the usual festivities, which were both a distraction and a heart-wrenching reminder of her loss. Quentin was not there to see Jemima's first nativity, or to smile through Marlene's painful recorder recital of 'Jingle Bells', or to savour their excited anticipation of what Santa might bring.

Angie tried her utmost to make the Yuletide a fun and happy occasion for the sake of the children, but it was hard – at times almost unbearably so. It felt wrong signing her Christmas cards with just her own name – not the usual 'Quentin and Angie'. And the cheer she normally experienced going into Durham city centre to scour the quaint shops in Silver Street or the stalls dotted along the medieval

Elvet Bridge for presents now felt like a direct affront to her grief.

It was at times like these she felt particularly alone. She'd also noticed that *being* on her own – without her husband – made many of their old acquaintances feel uncomfortable. People, she realised, treated her differently now she was a widow. Some even seemed to deliberately avoid her, as though Quentin's death was somehow catching. Others struggled with what to say and how to act.

On Christmas Day, as the children opened their presents from Father Christmas, Angie forced herself to smile and appear joyful, all the while wanting simply to curl up in bed and cry. Evelyn and Lloyd joined Angie, the children and Mrs Kwiatkowski for Christmas dinner, which was still a grand affair despite the ongoing rationing. Although the children weren't keen on Evelyn, nor she on them, they did like Lloyd – particularly Danny and Bertie, who seemed to have a never-ending list of questions for him about cars, trains, aeroplanes – anything with an engine. Questions Lloyd was able to answer in detail as he had spent much of his working life on the Continent as a mechanical engineer for an oil company.

The day after Boxing Day, their nearest neighbours, Gertrude and her son Jeremy Fontaine-Smith, who lived in a manor house a half a mile away, came calling. The pair were adamant that Angie could not break with tradition and insisted that Cuthford Manor's New Year Eve's party still went ahead.

'My darling Angela, the show must go on. It simply *must*,' Gertrude insisted. Gertrude was also a widow and had told Angie that she just had to keep 'a stiff upper lip' and 'carry on'. 'This New Year heralds the starts of a new decade!' Gertrude continued. A vast amount of newsprint was being given over to reflecting on the tumultuous war-torn decade and just about every radio broadcast made references to what the new era might hold. To Angie it seemed like the start of a marathon she did not feel she was in any way capable of completing.

'You won't have to worry about a thing – I will organise it all,' Jeremy declared. 'Your only requirement will be to put on a frock and join in the celebrations!' As he issued his orders, he took hold of Angie's hand and squeezed it gently.

Angie barely noticed, her mind too preoccupied with the thought of having a load of partygoers revelling under her roof when all she wanted to do was to go to bed as soon as she'd got the children settled and try to blot out the prospect of entering a new decade without Quentin by her side.

'All right,' Angie acquiesced. 'As long as the children can have their own little party.'

Jeremy and his mother shot each other a look. But if catering for the children meant Cuthford Manor's much-lauded New Year's Eve party could go ahead, then so be it. Not only would it be a great shindig, it would also present Jeremy with an opportunity to ingratiate himself with the young widow, for they were determined Angie would be wooed and won over. Their only worry was that someone else might beat them to the finishing line.

With Quentin gone, the gates of opportunity had suddenly been thrown open for those who wanted Cuthford Manor for themselves.

Chapter Four

Friday, 30 December

'Sorry to bother you, Mrs Foxton-Clarke . . .'

Answering the phone, Angie immediately recognised the voice of the family solicitor, Mr Conway. His voice had become familiar to her over the past eight weeks since Quentin's death. She'd given up trying to get him to address her by her first name.

'That's all right,' Angie said, looking out into the main hallway, where Evelyn and Gertrude were trying to decide where to put an elaborate floral display ready for tomorrow's dreaded party. 'How can I help you?'

'I've been chatting with the other partners and we have agreed that, as your legal representatives, we really should be advising you to update your will.'

Angie sighed. Was there no escaping talk of death?

'As I'm sure you are aware, your will is very detailed and clear about what should happen in regard to the children if you were to die first.'

'Yes,' Angie said, remembering how she and Quentin had thought long and hard, discussing in depth what would be the best thing to do if something were to happen to her. Quentin had been adamant that he would not be able to remain at Cuthford Manor if she was not there. And so, after a lengthy chat over the phone with Liz, her elder sister, who had emigrated to Australia shortly after the end of the war, it had been decided in the very unlikely event that Angie should die when the children were still young, then Quentin would take them – and Mrs Kwiatkowski if she was still with them – to Australia, to live near Liz and her family in Sydney. They'd buy a house over there and leave his mother and father in charge of Cuthford Manor.

'As your husband is tragically no longer with us,' Mr Conway continued, 'I think we would be negligent were we not to point out that there are now no longer any instructions for the future care of the children, or for Mrs Kwiatkowski, should, God forbid, you die.'

Angie digested his words. 'Yes, you're right.'

'This being the case,' Mr Conway said, 'we think it is best that we draw up a new will.'

Angie felt her heart sink.

'I was wondering if perhaps we could put a date in the diary, say next week, to discuss this?' Mr Conway asked. 'Obviously, I will come to Cuthford Manor – unless you'd prefer to come to us?'

'No, come here,' Angie said. She still couldn't face going beyond the boundaries of the estate unless it was imperative.

As they agreed a time and date, Angie again looked out at Evelyn and Gertrude. Evelyn was smoking a cigarette.

Quentin had told Angie that his mother had never smoked, but she seemed to have taken it up when she was living in York.

'Hopefully,' Mr Conway said, 'this will give you time to consider what you would want your will to stipulate.'

'Yes, it will,' Angie said. 'And thank you, Mr Conway. It's good you've brought this to my attention. It's something I know Quentin would encourage me to do.'

After Angie rang off, she sat in the leather swivel chair, turning slightly so she was looking out at the front lawn, which was hard with frost. Quietness had fallen, as Evelyn and Gertrude had agreed on the perfect spot for the floral arrangement and had retired to the front living room.

Staring out at the white-tipped shards of grass, Angie spotted a robin redbreast. She remembered the saying she'd learnt as a child: Robins appear when loved ones are near.

If only that were really the case.

Chapter Five

New Year's Eve

As Angie came hurrying down the stairs on the hunt for Bonnie's favourite teddy bear, the grandfather clock started to chime. It was six o'clock. Angie needed to find Mr Grizzly before the New Year's Eve party guests started to arrive, otherwise her daughter would fast become her bear's namesake.

Angie was wearing a pair of slacks designed by her old friend Kate, an up-and-coming haute couture designer in London. Jeremy's suggestion that she put on a 'frock' had rankled her for some reason, which was not unusual as she was easily irritated of late. She'd confided her feelings to Mrs Jones, who had told her not to worry – it was one of the after-effects of grief and would eventually pass.

Angie knew that her housekeeper spoke from experience as she had also lost her husband after being married for only a short time. Unlike Angie, though, she had not had the comfort of having a child with her husband. It made Angie appreciate that she did at least have part of Quentin still with her in Bonnie.

Chatting to Mrs Jones helped, as the housekeeper understood how she felt. Although Angie had her old workmates from J.L. Thompson's shipyard, none of them, thankfully, had lost their husbands. And as Dorothy lived in America now, it wasn't so easy to pick up the phone for a quick chat, as her best friend worked long hours for a magazine called the *New Yorker*, and there was the five-hour time difference to contend with. Still, what Angie loved most about her chats to Dorothy was hearing her best friend's voice, so familiar, so vibrant, so passionate – and for the duration of their calls, she would forget her own misery.

Walking across the foyer, past the elaborate winter floral display of white roses, ferns and holly, Angie was just about to open the door to the front reception room to see if Bonnie had left her teddy there, but on hearing Evelyn's sharp, distinctive voice, she stopped.

'. . . and why she refuses to get a nanny for Bonnie is beyond me. It's something she should have done a long time ago. *Quentin* had a nanny. All families of our standing have nannies. It's just what we do.'

Angie presumed Bonnie had been getting on Evelyn's nerves. She always brought up the subject of nannies whenever her granddaughter tried to get her 'Nana' to play or go somewhere with her.

'I know you think I'm always finding fault with her, but, *darling,* I just can't forgive her. If it wasn't for her, our son would still be alive.'

Angie stopped still by the door, which was slightly ajar.

'Can't forgive who?' Lloyd asked absent-mindedly. He had not been listening to a word his wife had said, which was not uncommon.

'Honestly, Lloyd, I might as well talk to the bloody wall,' Evelyn gasped.

Lloyd had been thinking about the party and how he planned to retire upstairs early. He knew Angie wouldn't mind. She'd probably love to do the same herself were she not the host, even if she was host in name only. The party had been organised by the Fontaine-Smiths, and Evelyn had also put in her two pennyworth, insisting she oversee the guest list. He knew she was trying to downplay her involvement as it would not be seemly to be too excited about having a good knees-up so soon after her son's death.

'Who do you think I'm talking about, Lloyd? *Angela, of course!*'

Lloyd sighed and got up from his chair.

'Not this again,' he said wearily.

Angie heard the chink of the glass stopper being removed from the decanter and guessed he was pouring himself a drink.

'Yes, *this again*,' Evelyn hissed. 'If *she* had gone to get my scarf as she'd been asked to do, we'd still have our son.'

'And if you hadn't left the bloody scarf there in the first place, *no one* would have died!' Lloyd snapped.

Evelyn ignored her husband's words and changed tack.

'She'll never belong here, you know that, don't you? She might have while our son was still alive – but that was only by proxy. By marriage. Now Quentin's gone, she's nothing but an outsider. In all honesty, I'm surprised *Angie* and her street urchins have chosen to stay!'

'Angie and her *siblings* belong here. As does our granddaughter. It's their *home*. Why wouldn't they still be here?' Lloyd demanded, his voice betraying his disbelief that his wife would even think to ask such a question.

Evelyn tutted. 'Because, Lloyd, *they don't belong*! How many times do I have to say it. And despite what your father's will stipulated, Cuthford Manor should be ours – *yours*,' Evelyn corrected herself quickly.

'Well, it's not!' Lloyd did nothing to hide his sheer exasperation. 'It was Quentin's. Now it is Angie's. And it will no doubt pass to Bonnie when the time comes.'

'Oh, come on, Lloyd! Listen to yourself. This manor. This beautiful, historical, unique manor – in the hands of a *miner's daughter*!'

'Well, get used to it, Evelyn, because there's absolutely nothing you can do about it,' Lloyd retorted.

There was a pause as Evelyn mumbled something Angie couldn't hear.

'What's that?' Lloyd asked.

Angie sensed another argument brewing.

'Nothing,' Evelyn said dismissively.

They were quiet for a moment.

'You've changed, Lloyd,' Evelyn said, her tone full of reproach.

'Having a son die in his prime can do that to a parent,' Lloyd said bitterly.

Angie quietly backed away from the door, tiptoed across the entrance hall and headed down the corridor to continue her search for Mr Grizzly.

Angie had not been as quiet as she'd thought by the living-room door. Evelyn had heard the soft tapping of her daughter-in-law's footsteps approaching the room.

Just as she heard them tiptoeing away.

Hopefully, her words would give her son's widow food for thought.

Evelyn had not come this far in life to simply let this woman welder and a load of waifs and strays take over the manor.

Cuthford Manor had been hers from the day she had arrived here with her new husband twenty-nine years ago. Lloyd's father, Leonard, might have owned it, but he liked to travel, and when he was home, he tended to keep himself to himself. When he'd finally breathed his last, Evelyn fully expected to be lady of the manor in name too. But to her shock and disbelief, that was not to be.

When the probate solicitor read Leonard's will to her and Lloyd as they'd sat in the dining room, drinking tea and nibbling on biscuits, she'd nearly choked on hearing that Leonard had written a clause into his will stating that both his housekeeper and his trusted valet, Wilfred, be allowed to live at the manor rent-free for as long as they wished.

But then when they'd been informed that Leonard had decided to leave Cuthford Manor to Quentin – who was only sixteen years old – she'd nearly screamed the place down;

had only refrained from doing so by storming out of the room. *How could he do that?* If the old man wasn't already dead, she'd have killed him herself.

She should have realised Leonard didn't like her. She'd wondered, and over time had become convinced that he had somehow got to know the whole truth about her, and her background, and that was why he'd done what he'd done.

She just wished she had somehow been able to check her father-in-law's will before he'd died. She might have been able to do something about it. She'd tried to convince Lloyd to contest it, claiming the old man was 'as nutty as a fruitcake', but Lloyd had refused, saying his father must have had his reasons.

When life started to settle back down, Evelyn had realised it was not such a tragedy. Cuthford Manor was, for all intents and purposes, hers. She was lady of the manor. She bossed the staff around, organised parties, continued discreetly taking lovers and lived the life she jolly well deserved.

But all that had changed when her soft-headed son fell in love with the daughter of a coalminer. Evelyn had always presumed that when Quentin did get married, he'd want to set up home in London. He had worked there for the duration of the war and clearly enjoyed living there, despite it becoming a bomb site. But Quentin had decided to take his inheritance and move his wife as well as her *four* siblings *and* an old Polish woman into Cuthford Manor.

Evelyn would never forget that day as long as she lived. Unable to bear the thought of another woman coming and taking over *her* manor, she'd packed her bags, demanded that Lloyd do the same and they'd left for York.

She thought she might be able to settle in the plush Georgian town house they had rented, but it was no good. She had tried to forget Cuthford Manor, but on returning there for visits to see her son and his new bride, and then to see Bonnie, her granddaughter, it was too much. She had fallen in love with the place when Lloyd had first taken her there and, like any great love, she could not bear to be parted from it. It had a hold on her, and one she did not want to loosen.

And so she told Lloyd that she wanted to return – 'so the family can be together'.

Evelyn knew it would be hard, very hard, to endure the everyday reminder that this woman welder was the mistress of the manor. But she had tolerated it. Which was quite some feat, as Evelyn didn't think she had ever hated anyone as much as she hated her son's wife – apart from her own parents, of course, but she'd been lucky that they had died just days after her fifteenth birthday. A case of good riddance to bad rubbish if ever there was one.

The hatred Evelyn felt for her daughter-in-law had been further stoked up by the constant reminder that Cuthford Manor had just landed in Angie's lap. The miner's daughter had not had to work as Evelyn had, to become lady of the manor. Now *former* lady of the manor.

And so, from the moment Evelyn had returned from York, she had tried her damnedest to find a way to reclaim what was hers.

But then her son had died.

Her plans had been ruined.

Evelyn would never admit it to anyone, but she did blame herself for her son's death.

If only he'd not gone to get her scarf.

After her week of wailing, she'd decided to draw a curtain over what had happened. It was her only way of coping. All the crying, anger, guilt and regret in the world would not bring him back.

But the anger and hatred she felt towards her daughter-in-law only intensified.

It should have been *Angela* – not her son – whose life had been cut short.

And it was that feeling of fury and injustice that now fired Evelyn on as she vowed to get back what was rightfully hers.

Chapter Six

After fetching Mrs Kwiatkowski, Angie finally forced herself to join the New Year's Eve party. She surveyed the front living room, which had been exquisitely decorated, like all the rooms in Cuthford Manor, to complement the amazingly ornate ceiling and intricately carved marble fireplace. Now, balloons and streamers had been artfully added to create the perfect party setting for welcoming in the new decade.

It rankled Angie to see that most of the guests were local landed gentry or professionals from Durham. There were lawyers, financiers and, of course, the local Conservative parliamentary candidate. She hardly knew any of them and immediately felt like an outsider in her own home. She admonished herself for giving Evelyn carte blanche with the guest list as not a single person from Cuthford village had been invited – other than the vicar and Dr Wright and his wife – which seemed such a snub, given that the village was only a short walk from the manor.

She looked at Lloyd and thought his weary demeanour mirrored her own, and then at Evelyn, who looked younger than her fifty years. She had coiffured her naturally blonde hair into victory rolls and her make-up was minimal, though still applied so as to make the most of her startling blue eyes and sharp cheekbones.

As Angie took Mrs Kwiatkowski over to the makeshift bar manned by Jake, who had swapped driving for bartending this evening, she watched Evelyn move gracefully around the room in her fashionable little black dress. Angie thought she looked in her element, the perfect hostess, the perfect lady of the manor, which, Angie was now sure, she believed she should be.

Handing Mrs Kwiatkowski her vodka and tonic, Angie smiled as her old neighbour chatted away in Polish, her milky blue eyes alert and full of curiosity as she surveyed the guests in their fancy clothes and smart DJs.

As the guests came for the obligatory small talk and to thank her for putting on such a fabulous party, Angie's mind kept wandering back to what her mother-in-law had said earlier. How it should have been Angie who had died that day. Another woman might have felt guilty that fate had saved her and not her husband, but Angie understood that guilt was often grief's bedfellow. She did not blame herself, or anyone else, for her husband's death. What good would it do? It wouldn't bring him back.

What had bothered her, though, was Evelyn's rant about her not belonging here at the manor. Angie had always known that Evelyn had never approved of their marriage – Quentin had even been convinced that his mother had faked being ill to avoid having to go to their wedding.

The problem was – and Angie hated to admit it – Evelyn was right. *She didn't belong*. Had only belonged, like Evelyn said, because of Quentin. Now he had gone, so too had her sense of belonging. She'd started to feel that way shortly after the funeral. Just as she'd also started to feel that people's attitudes towards her were changing. She couldn't quite put her finger on it, but she felt that those she came in contact with were starting to treat her a little differently.

On the other extreme, though, some of the county's eligible bachelors, like her neighbour, Jeremy Fontaine-Smith, had started to treat her like royalty. And Angie was under no illusions as to why.

Seeing Jeremy pat down his slicked-back hair and straighten his perfectly tailored dinner jacket, Angie braced herself as he made a beeline for her and Mrs Kwiatkowski. Manufacturing a smile as Jeremy theatrically held out his arms and complimented them both on how they looked, Angie made a pretence of listening while her hopeful suitor pontificated about rationing and how it was becoming 'quite the political football', and how even 'the socialists' were totally fed up with Labour as there were still shortages. All Angie could really hear, however, was her mother-in-law's voice in her head, saying, 'She'll never belong here!'

Seeing Mrs Kwiatkowski was tiring gave Angie the opportunity to excuse herself. Taking her old neighbour upstairs to her room, Angie was glad of the respite from having to keep up the charade of being in the party spirit.

When she returned, she was immediately cornered by Evelyn.

'Wonderful party, isn't it, Angela?' she said.

Angie nodded, not wanting to give her mother-in-law the praise she was looking for.

There was an awkward silence.

'Oh,' Evelyn suddenly perked up. 'I've just been chatting to some of the local landowners and heard that the wretched gypsies are back. For a few weeks, it sounded as though they'd gone away, but unfortunately they have returned to blight our lovely landscape. And they've set up camp not far from here. So, I'm afraid we'll have to be extra vigilant. There have already been whispers they've been poaching.' Evelyn took a sip of her champagne. 'And obviously, it goes without saying that the children must be warned to steer well clear – they're not to mix with them.'

As Angie forced back her anger, she again wondered how Quentin, who had been such a gentle, kind-hearted and unprejudiced man, had been born of such an abominably shallow and snobby woman.

As they inched towards the midnight hour, Angie felt thankful that it was all nearly over with, but also irked that everyone's excitement was notching up a gear as they neared the start of the new decade.

At quarter to twelve, Angie clapped her hands to get everyone's attention. When no one responded, she felt a rush of annoyance and put her thumb and finger in her mouth and whistled. She had perfected the skill during her four years of welding at Thompson's. The ear-splitting sound had the desired effect, and everyone immediately fell silent. Most of the guests looked baffled, not thinking that such a mannish whistle could come from the small, slightly built woman in cream slacks and a delicate silk blouse.

'As it is now nearly midnight, it's time for "the tall, dark and handsome man" to first foot,' Angie declared, manufacturing a wide smile. She took a lungful of air and imagined that Quentin was right there next to her, supporting her as he had always done.

The northern tradition of 'first footing' to welcome in the New Year involved a man, preferably with dark hair, going out of the house just before the clock struck twelve and stepping back over the threshold a few minutes after midnight with gifts – a piece of coal, bread, salt, a coin and a dram of whisky. In this way, the household would be guaranteed a year of warmth, food, flavour, prosperity and good cheer.

The guests bristled with anticipation to see who Angie would pick. Jeremy was adjusting his black tie and buttoning up his double-breasted dinner jacket. Angie also noticed a few of the other men who had spent longer than normal talking to her during the evening pushing back their hair and preening themselves in anticipation of being the chosen one. For the man tasked with bringing luck into the house was also rewarded with a hug and a kiss from the hostess.

Scanning her audience for Evelyn, as she wanted to see her expression when she named this year's first footer, Angie spotted her mother-in-law standing close to 'Dashing Desmond' Pyburn, a solicitor in the family's law firm.

'This year,' Angie said loudly, so everyone could hear, 'in place of my husband, who would always be the one to do the honours – ' she had to swallow hard to hold it together ' – I have chosen as first footer . . .' she paused for effect '. . .

my tall, dark and, I have to add, very handsome younger brother, Danny!'

Angie turned towards the open doorway of the front reception room and gave a little clap as Danny appeared, dressed in his best suit. It was the one he had worn for Quentin's funeral, but Danny had just had another growth spurt and now the arms were a little short. He blushed as everyone stared at him. There were some motherly 'aahs' from the women guests and some guffaws from the older men, who clearly approved of Angie's choice. Jeremy and the bachelors looked crestfallen. Evelyn was furious, which heartened Angie no end.

As Danny entered the room, Angie noted grey horse-hair on his sleeves. He'd obviously been to the stables to see Ghost. Again, she pushed back her anxiety about getting shot of Quentin's horse. She wished she'd just bitten the bullet and sold him straight away. The more she put it off, the harder it would be.

Handing Danny the wicker basket containing the gifts, she brushed off some of the more visible horsehair.

Glancing at her watch, Angie walked out of the smoky room, across the grand reception hallway and opened the front door.

'See you in a few minutes,' she told Danny, who looked as proud as Punch to have been chosen for such an important job. All the more so because it was one that Quentin had done.

Once the door had been closed, the wireless was switched on and everyone listened to the BBC presenter before silence fell and only the sound of Big Ben could be heard. On the twelfth chime, everyone threw up streamers and hats, and a cascade of balloons were released from the ceiling, where they had been kept at bay by a length of netting. Seeing that Jeremy was heading over to her, Angie clapped her hands loudly.

'Let's welcome the first footer!' she shouted. Everyone spilled out into the foyer and watched as Angie opened the front door. Danny was standing on the driveway, looking up at the night sky.

'Time to come in!' Angie called.

Turning, Danny hurried in with his basket of New Year good fortune and was given a big hug and a kiss on the cheek by his sister. Angie turned to see Marlene, Bertie, Jemima and Bonnie hurry down the stairs. The three youngest were in their pyjamas, but Marlene had put on her party dress and, Angie noted, had obviously been rooting around in her dressing room and pilfered some lipstick. Their happy, excited faces brought an instant smile to her own and at that moment she felt her heart and spirits lift. The emptiness she felt seeing in the New Year without Quentin by her side was suddenly filled by her love for her family – and their love for her.

By the time Angie had fussed over the children, wished them a Happy New Year and introduced them to some of the guests, it was time for 'Auld Lang Syne'. After which, Angie packed them off to bed, then snuck off to bed herself to avoid any drunken, amorous advances from Jeremy, or any of the other eligible bachelors. She might have only just lost her husband, but she was now clearly fair game, despite it being glaringly obvious she felt not a flicker of attraction to any of them.

Angie knew that what was driving these potential suitors was not a genuine attraction to her, but to what she owned.

Cuthford Manor was the jewel in the crown of this side of Durham and it seemed it was now up for grabs.

Chapter Seven

Lloyd had managed to escape the party just after eleven and had gone in search of Mrs Jones, who he had guessed correctly was in the kitchen. She'd told him that she hadn't felt much like celebrating this year and had turned down her friend Izzy's invitation to a party in Durham.

Seeing Lloyd enter the kitchen, Mrs Jones smiled, shifting slightly in her chair by the Aga to look at him. They were both in their early fifties, but Lloyd had aged since his son's death.

Winston and Bessie were too sleepy to get up, but showed their welcome with a few sweeps of their thick tails.

'Fancy a cuppa?' she asked.

'No thanks, Cora,' Lloyd said, raising his tumbler of Scotch as he pulled up a chair.

Lloyd always called Mrs Jones by her first name as they'd known each other since they were youngsters, his father never having objected to him playing with the children from the village, something frowned upon by their wealthier neighbours. Lloyd's father, who was described as 'eccentric' by his kindlier associates, didn't give two hoots what anyone might say or think about how he conducted his life. 'It's my life to lead and of no concern to anyone else – and that's the end of the matter,' he would often declare, drink in one hand, cigarette in the other. Leonard had not been a man for moderation.

The young Lloyd had got to know Cora better still when, aged fourteen, she'd come to Cuthford Manor to work as a scullery maid, shortly after Lloyd's mother had died of tuberculosis. They'd meet up when Cora had breaks, and when she finished work they'd often go for walks in the countryside.

'Will Evelyn not throw a fit if she knows you're down here with the hoi polloi and not up there, mingling with the *important people*?' Mrs Jones asked, taking a sip of her tea, to which she had added a splash of brandy.

Lloyd shook his head. 'No. She's always happy to see the back of me at parties as it gives her the chance to flirt. I told her I was going to bed.'

Mrs Jones knew that since they'd moved back to the manor, Evelyn and Lloyd not only had separate beds but separate bedrooms too. The West Wing had plenty of space should a couple not want to spend much time with one another. She'd heard the maids gossiping that Lloyd didn't even pay Evelyn any 'nocturnal visits'.

Mrs Jones had always thought they would stay in York, knowing how much Evelyn would hate living at Cuthford Manor if she was not Queen Bee. So, when she'd returned with Lloyd in tow, Mrs Jones had been intrigued.

'You know, Lloyd, I've always been curious why Evelyn wanted to come back here.'

'It took me by surprise too,' Lloyd said, taking a drink of his whisky. 'Especially after her reaction to the news that

Quentin was marrying Angie. It was awful. I'll never forget it.'

'Which makes her return all the more curious,' Mrs Jones mused.

'She said we should be nearer our son and his family, but I don't think that was the real reason – her interest in her only son was always minimal,' he said, welcoming the ease he always felt when chatting to Cora. 'To be honest, I just think she missed living here. And I was just happy to come back, to spend time with Quentin, get to know Angie, and Bonnie. It's been an added bonus getting to know Angie's siblings – I like them an awful lot.'

Lloyd smiled at Cora and wondered if she knew what he wanted to say but couldn't. That there was another reason he'd been keen to come back – and that was the woman sitting right here with him now. But how could he? When he'd already told her how he'd felt all those years ago when she was sixteen and he was just a year older; when what had passed between them had put a halt to what could have been.

'You know,' Lloyd said, breaking the silence, 'I really do wonder about Evelyn.'

'In what way?' Mrs Jones asked.

'This is going to sound awful,' Lloyd confided, 'but in darker moments, I've wondered just how upset she's really been about Quentin's death. She's made the usual sounds, she's cried, ranted and raved against the injustice of losing a son so young. But something just doesn't ring true.'

'She's not really *feeling* that grief?' Mrs Jones suggested.

'Exactly! I'd know it if she was. I'd be able to sense it. Like I can with Angie.' Lloyd's own grief still felt all-consuming, although he tried to behave in a way that would lead people to believe he was coping with his son's death. The immense pain of his loss had been compounded, if that were possible, by the fact that, since his move back to the manor, he and Quentin had bonded more than they'd ever done before.

He took a sip of his single malt. 'God, I feel awful claiming that my own wife hasn't been that affected by the death of her only child.'

'I think you're just being honest,' Mrs Jones said. 'And it might well be true that Evelyn isn't *that* affected – or certainly not as affected as you. Like you say, she wasn't really close to Quentin, was she?'

Lloyd nodded. They both knew that Quentin had been brought up by a string of nannies, then packed off to boarding school. It was something else Lloyd regretted – he should have taken more control of rearing his own son.

At that moment, a loud cheer sounded from upstairs, where the guests were celebrating the start of a new year. A new decade. The pair looked at each other.

Lloyd stood and reached out to Mrs Jones, who took his hand and stood up too.

'Happy New Year, Cora,' he said softly.

Mrs Jones smiled a little sadly as she thought of the year they had just left behind.

'I hope so,' she said. 'I really do.'

Lloyd gave her a chaste kiss on the cheek.

'Well, I'd better go and get my beauty sleep,' she said.

Lloyd looked at her and knew his eyes must surely betray his feelings.

After Mrs Jones had gone, Lloyd took a mouthful of whisky, pushing down the torment he always felt when it came to Cora. Their lives could have been so different. *If only he'd had the courage to follow his feelings.*

Many years had passed, but the memory of the time they had spent together when they were young was still crystal clear – the time when their friendship had become more than that and they had shared the most wonderfully romantic and passionate of kisses, and he had told Cora how he felt. But she had pulled away, declaring that it would 'all end in tragedy', that 'the future lord of the manor doesn't marry the hired help'. He was still a little dazed from the feeling of their kiss when she had said she would not be one of those maids who are loved and then cast aside when it was the lord's time to marry someone more appropriate. She hadn't come out and said it directly, but she'd made it quite clear – it had to be marriage, or nothing at all.

Lloyd had been taken aback. He hadn't been thinking so far into the future. He had just wanted to be with her. To hold her in his arms and kiss her. Looking back, which he had done too many times over the years, he realised that Cora had wanted him to tell her that she *was* 'appropriate' for him, that he loved her and that was all that mattered – he would marry her, regardless of the confines of class. But he hadn't. He'd stuttered that they were 'still very young' and 'marriage seems such a long way off'.

He'd never forget the look on her face. The hurt and disappointment.

A year later, when he was more mature, it was too late to rectify his mistake as Cora had become engaged to the son of the village blacksmith.

Thirty years had passed, during which time their friendship had remained strong. As had his deeper feelings of love for her.

God, how he wished *he* had been stronger.

As he finished off his drink, he felt, more than ever, overwhelmed by regret.

Chapter Eight

As Angie lay in bed listening to the final stragglers driving off down the gravelled driveway, her mind was churning. Evelyn's words kept coming to the fore, as well as the nuanced changes she had detected in those who had only known her because of her marriage to Quentin.

The New Year was about change, wasn't it? About wiping the slate clean and starting again. At least, that was how she had always viewed it.

As she lay in her bed, which still felt too big for her – too empty – she thought about her home, which also felt too big for them all. How different Cuthford Manor felt now to when she'd first arrived the day after her wedding to Quentin on VE Day in May 1945. As they had driven through the bespoke cast-iron gates and down the curved gravel driveway to their new home, her brothers and sisters – along with Mrs Kwiatkowski – had fallen unusually quiet in the back and Angie had shuffled round in the passenger seat to see five awestruck faces. Turning back, mesmerised herself by the manor's castellated Gothic grandeur and tapered towers, Angie remembered declaring that she had never seen such a magnificent building. Marlene, who was then just eight, had shouted out that it was a 'fairy castle' and Quentin had laughed and agreed that their new home did indeed have 'aspirations of being a castle'.

When she walked through the large arched front door, opened by the elderly butler, Wilfred, Angie hadn't known where to look first – at the crystal chandelier hanging from the ceiling or the mammoth sandstone fireplace with two medieval suits of armour on either side.

This was now *her* home. *Their* home. Their *family* home.

But now that Quentin was gone, all colour had left her life and Cuthford Manor. The surrounding estate, which she had once loved so much, felt overshadowed by darkness.

Giving up on sleep, Angie got out of bed and pulled on her dressing gown. She went to sit in the window seat and looked out at the waning moon and bruised sky. She'd been given no choice about the life she'd had foisted upon her following Quentin's accident. The reins had been snatched from her the moment he'd been killed. But perhaps now it was time to take control of the life she'd been saddled with.

She thought about her elder sister, whom she'd called to wish a Happy New Year this afternoon. Liz had sounded cheerful and contented. She and her husband had made a huge change to their lives when they'd decided to emigrate. As had Dorothy, who had changed the course of her life by staying in New York with her husband, Bobby, after their travels.

It must have been hard, leaving behind everyone they knew and starting afresh, but it had turned out well for them.

And the more she thought about it, the more an idea began to take shape.

An idea for change.

Chapter Nine

On the afternoon of New Year's Day, Angie rang Dorothy in New York to wish her lots of health, wealth and happiness, but more than that, to tell her about the thoughts she'd had while lying in bed listening to all the revellers finally going home.

'I had an idea last night,' Angie said, 'which I feel quite excited about, but I don't want to tell anyone until I've had a chance to work out if I can do it.'

'Really?' Dorothy said, her throat raspy. They'd had quite a knees-up the night before. She'd drunk and smoked too much and was paying for it. 'Sounds intriguing. Give me a second while I grab my coffee and then I'm all ears.'

Angie heard Dorothy clattering around in her kitchen.

'Right. I'm back!'

As she listened to Angie outline her plan, Dorothy's excitement at hearing her friend sound almost happy waned.

There was silence down the phone.

'Hello, you still there, Dor?'

'Sorry, Ange, yes, I'm here, I'm just surprised – this all seems like a bolt from the blue. It's a lot to take on board.' Dorothy tried for once to be diplomatic. 'It's quite some plan.' She also didn't want to let her friend hear her concern. 'Tell me from the start – what initially gave you the idea?'

While Dorothy drank her black coffee, Angie told her about the call from the family solicitor and how they'd advised her to write a new will.

'And just explain to me,' Dorothy asked tentatively, 'why you want to do something so extreme?'

'Because, Dor, I've realised that I don't belong here. Never have done!' Angie tried not to show her annoyance that her best friend wasn't squealing down the phone with excitement.

'Really?' Dorothy couldn't hold back her surprise. In all the time Angie had lived at Cuthford Manor, she had never once complained about feeling as though she didn't belong. She'd actually told Dorothy that since first stepping over the threshold, she had never felt at odds or as if she didn't belong in such a grandiose place, despite it being a far cry from where she'd grown up.

'Yes, *really*,' Angie said. 'Lately, Evelyn's always going on about how "we" do things. And every single time, I feel myself getting vexed. But I've realised why it gets to me.'

'Why's that?' Dorothy asked.

'Because I know she's right! It's crystal clear that Evelyn – and others that live around here – don't see me and the children as part of "their" world now Quentin's gone.'

Angie heard Dorothy light up a cigarette, a habit she'd started shortly after getting her job on the magazine.

'Well, I can understand how you're going to feel differently without Quentin—'

'*Exactly*,' Angie said, becoming less zealous and more sombre. 'I do feel *differently* about this place since Quentin died.'

'In what way?' Dorothy asked, still struggling to take in her friend's plans.

'For starters, I feel like I'm stuck in the middle of nowhere. And during the winter, we're more or less cut off from the outside world.'

'But it's never bothered you before,' Dorothy said, hearing the return of the fanaticism in her friend's voice.

'That was before Quentin died!' Angie wanted to bellow the words down the phone, but instead she had to hiss them quietly into the receiver as she was trying to keep her voice down. She had a feeling Evelyn eavesdropped on her conversations. 'I'm starting to feel incarcerated within these four walls.'

Dorothy burst out laughing. 'Ange, I think you're becoming more of a drama queen than me. The manor has far more than four walls. How on earth can you feel hemmed in?'

'You know what I mean,' Angie groused. 'Besides, since Quentin's gone, I've realised that I haven't really got any friends here. I just feel such an outsider, Dor . . . I miss *belonging* somewhere. I don't feel like I belong where I was born and brought up because I live in a manor and have money, but then I don't belong here either as I'm a *miner's daughter*.'

Angie let out a long exhalation.

'And that's the other thing,' she confessed. 'I don't want Bonnie or my brothers and sisters to turn out like the people round here. Marlene's already showing signs of getting uppity. I don't want them to become arrogant snobs.'

'You mean like the Fontaine-Smiths?' Dorothy probed.

'Exactly. *And Evelyn*. They're awful,' Angie said, no longer caring if her mother-in-law could hear her.

'But they're not *all* like that,' Dorothy said, knowing she needed to play devil's advocate. 'Lloyd doesn't sound like a snob, and remember, you thought I was a snob just because my mum and stepdad lived in a big house in The Cedars.'

'That's different. *You're* different.'

Dorothy laughed. 'I'll take that as a compliment . . . Seriously, though, there will be other people who are like you – you just need to find them.'

'I've tried, Dor. I haven't met anyone I really get on with. It didn't matter when Quentin was alive, but it does now. The people in the village I *could* get on with treat me differently because I live here – they kowtow to me. Honestly, Dor, I swear some of the older folk practically curtsy when they see me, and then when I'm nice to them, they seem even more eager to please.'

'Because they love the fact you're not all snooty. They'll relax with you in time, when they get more used to you being on your own . . . And the people who work at the manor, they all think the world of you.'

'Yes, but I'm still their boss at the end of the day. That's the whole irony of my life here. I'm more comfortable with the workers and the people from the village, but because I'm "lady of the manor", they can never become friends.'

'I think you might be wrong there,' Dorothy argued.

'Mmm.' Angie didn't sound convinced.

'But what about being out in the country?' Dorothy said, now feeling as if she was grasping at straws. 'You've always loved it. The fresh air. Nature.'

'That was when being out in the country meant being with Quentin,' Angie said, her tone quiet and sad.

Dorothy's heart went out to her friend. Everything about where she lived was a constant reminder to Angie of the love she had lost. Which was why her friend had concocted what could only be described as an escape plan.

'I just don't think you should do anything rash,' Dorothy said gently. 'Especially so soon after . . . everything.'

Out of the corner of her eye, Angie saw the flash of a white broderie anglaise dress.

'Oh God, sorry, Dor – just hang on a moment.'

'Mrs Kwiatkowski . . .' Angie shouted out into the hallway.

The old woman stopped in her tracks just as she reached the corridor that led to the kitchen. Hearing Angie's voice, she turned and hurried back to the study. As soon as she saw Angie, she started chatting away in Polish.

'Let me say hello,' Dorothy shouted down the phone to Angie.

'Okay,' Angie said. 'Mrs Kwiatkowski – guess who I've got on the phone? It's Dorothy – you know, Dorothy from the flat in Foyle Street?'

As soon as Mrs Kwiatkowski put her ear to the receiver, her face lit up.

'Ah, Dorothee!' she exclaimed, before chatting away in her native tongue for a short while and then handing back the phone.

'I'd better go,' Angie told Dorothy.

'Just don't be too hasty—'

Angie had already hung up before Dorothy had finished speaking.

Putting out her cigarette and heading back to the coffee maker for some more caffeine, Dorothy felt a niggle of anxiety – her best friend did not sound at all herself.

Half an hour later, after Angie had cajoled Mrs Kwiatkowski into some appropriate outdoor wear, they were walking around what Angie called the Italian gardens, with their stone statues of naked men and women.

Dorothy was right. Angie had once loved living here. Loved every inch of Cuthford Manor and its grounds. But not any more. She actually felt as though the manor itself had changed – which she knew was ridiculous as it was bricks and mortar and not a living being – but still, she no longer felt as though it was a place of comfort and security.

Painful memories continued to fill Angie's mind. Everywhere she looked, every room in the manor, every blade of bloody grass in the grounds, reminded her of Quentin – of a conversation in the library that had ended up in a fit of giggles, the billiards they'd played in the games room. The rides out they'd had, Quentin on Ghost and Angie on Starling. Walks around the vegetable patch, digging up carrots and potatoes and picking tomatoes from the greenhouse, then getting told off by Bill the gardener as that was his job.

Her entire life had been turned upside down. Everything had changed, including how she saw things. The skies no longer reminded Angie of an artist's pallet heavy with the swirl of colourful oils, but were instead dark, grey and gloomy.

Even the landscape had lost its enchantment and now merely looked vast and barren.

Chapter Ten

Over the following weeks, Angie's idea began to germinate. For the first time since Quentin's death, she started to feel empowered, knowing that she had choices.

With the start of the new decade, it seemed the whole world was undergoing a change alongside her. Fashion was changing, music was changing, women were changing – or trying to – people's attitudes and opinions on just about everything were changing.

There was one change, however, that Angie knew she couldn't put off any longer. And every time she thought about it, she felt sick to the pit of her stomach.

It was time for Ghost to go.

Much as she dreaded telling Danny and the rest of the children, Angie could not move on with life if Ghost was there. She knew this was not how the children felt, knew they loved Ghost unconditioally, and they saw the handsome gelding as a reminder of the man they'd lost. By keeping Ghost near, they were keeping Quentin close by. But having Ghost around was just too painful for Angie.

She had promised herself she would do what she had to do before January was out, and now it was the last weekend of the month. Taking her coat from the stand by the back door, Angie felt a wave of nausea.

'Good luck,' Alberta said as she came out of the pantry and saw her. The cook and Mrs Jones knew of Angie's intentions – and how difficult it was going to be to tell the children.

'Thanks, I'll need it,' Angie said ominously.

Stepping outside, Angie was dazzled by the winter sun. Despite the cold, she knew the children would be outside. As she had guessed, they were by the paddock just beyond the barn. When she saw that Danny was on Ghost, her heart dropped. He was riding him around the paddock bareback.

Bertie was sitting in the shade under the centuries-old oak with Winston and Bessie sprawled out next to him. He was reading a book, living up to his new nickname, 'Bertie the bookworm'. Jemima was being led round the middle of the paddock on Lucky the pit pony by Marlene and Thomas, who were deep in conversation. When he saw Jemima pointing over to Angie, Thomas quickly headed back to the stables.

Putting her hand to her forehead to shield her eyes from the sun, Angie shouted, 'Can I have a word?'

Danny turned Ghost, pressing his flank with his left leg, and pushed him into a relaxed canter.

Bertie put his bookmark to keep his place in *The Adventures of Tom Sawyer* and clambered up. Winston and Bessie followed suit and the three made their way towards Angie.

Marlene held Lucky while Jemima dismounted, and they walked the little pony over to their older sister.

As soon as they'd all gathered, Angie got right to it.

'I'm just going to spit it out,' she said. 'I'm really sorry, as I know how you all feel, but Ghost is going to have to go.'

'Where?' Marlene asked, her pretty face a replica of their mother's.

'Not to the knacker's yard?' Bertie panicked, swinging his attention to Ghost, who was chomping on some grass.

'*No*, of course *not* to the knacker's yard – I'd never do that,' Angie said, glancing at Danny, who was stroking Ghost's long, muscular neck as he grazed.

Danny didn't say anything but just stared at Angie as though she were the devil incarnate.

'Ghost's got to go to another owner.' Angie tried her hardest to sound convincing. 'He needs someone who will ride him. It's not fair to keep him here. He needs exercising twice a day, every day, and we simply don't have anyone who can do that here. It's better for him.'

'*You* could ride him,' Bertie said.

Danny, Marlene, Bertie and Jemima fell silent and waited for their big sister to speak.

'I can't ride Ghost,' Angie said eventually.

'Why not?' Danny demanded, even though deep down he knew why. But he just couldn't understand how Ghost could be blamed for what had happened to Quentin. It wasn't his fault. It was unfair to punish the horse, and that was exactly what he felt Angie was doing.

'Danny, I haven't got time to ride him. I've got my hands full with the manor, with Bonnie, the grounds – the list goes on.' Angie purposely did not say that much of her time was spent looking after them – that she was, in effect, a single mum of five children. She and Quentin had made a resolution when they had become their guardians that they would never *ever* make her siblings feel as though they were a burden.

'I'll ride him,' Danny said. 'I'll ride him before I go to school and when I come home.'

Angie could see the desperation in his eyes and hear it in his voice, which was starting to break as he began his transition from boy to man.

'That's just not going to happen, Danny. Your schoolwork will suffer. And you've got all those clubs you go to.' Danny was in the hockey team and the football team, which meant lots of practice during the week and tournaments at the weekends.

'I'm sorry, my mind's made up,' Angie said, feeling Winston nudge up to her, having heard the change in her voice and becoming concerned.

'You won't keep him' – Danny's voice was growing louder – 'because he was Quentin's!' His voice cracked.

Angie saw the tears in her brother's eyes before his anger brought them to a halt and he blinked them away.

'I hate you!' he shouted before turning Ghost and walking him out of the paddock.

Angie wanted to explain to Danny the other reason they needed to find a new home for Ghost – but this was not the right time.

Besides which, there was still much to sort out.

Chapter Eleven

As arranged, at nine o'clock the following morning the local horse dealer turned up at Cuthford Manor with a horsebox in tow.

Danny had taken Ghost out for an early ride and stayed with him in his stall, grooming and talking to him.

'It's just not fair,' he said, brushing his dark grey mane for the umpteenth time. 'You belong here with us. I'd have given up the football and the hockey.'

Seeing the horse merchant's old mud-splattered Land Rover pull into the yard, Danny's heart pounded. 'I'm sorry, Ghost. I never blamed you, you know that, don't you?'

Ghost responded by nuzzling his broad grey-speckled head into Danny's neck.

Tears pricked Danny's eyes. He tried to keep them at bay, rubbing his face against Ghost's, breathing in his smell for the last time.

Having heard the dreaded arrival of the horse trader, Marlene, Bertie and Jemima came trooping out of the kitchen. They had been waiting, giving Danny as much time as possible with Ghost before he was taken away.

As Danny walked Ghost out of his stall for the last time, the wooden stable door slammed shut behind him.

'Bye-bye . . .' Bertie walked over to Ghost. The horse dipped his head low so that Bertie could kiss his forehead, then did the same for Jemima, who gently stroked the sides of his face.

'Don't forget us,' Marlene said, putting her arms around his neck and giving him a cuddle. Ghost bent his neck around to encircle her.

Angie was watching them from afar, trying hard to push away a wave of guilt that felt as if it was about to drag her down and drown her. Taking a deep breath, she marched over to the horse dealer.

'Make sure he goes to a good home,' she said.

'Aye, I will,' he said, handing over the payment. The dealer would likely make a decent profit on this one – fifteen hands high, only six years old and a lovely-looking horse into the bargain. Providing, that was, it didn't come out about what had happened to his previous master. Horsey folk in these parts were known for their superstitions.

Having watched Ghost being led into the horsebox, Evelyn left the leaded window on the first-floor landing overlooking the yard and hurried down the wide staircase. The door of the study was open and, seeing Lloyd sitting at his desk, she strode in and made for the art deco fan mirror above the fireplace. She stopped and admired her hair, which she'd just had coiffed into a new style called the 'poodle cut' – tight permed curls stacked on top of her head, with the sides pinned close. She patted her hair, moving her head left, then right, to check nothing was out of place.

'Thank goodness for that,' she said to her reflection. 'That bloody horse has finally gone. I thought Angela would never do it. Better late than never. Gone is the constant reminder of our son's death.'

Lloyd wanted to say that just living was a constant reminder of their son's death, but didn't. Instead, he watched as she turned and sashayed out of the study.

'I'm off to meet the girls,' she said, raising her hand and giving a wave of farewell as she walked across the foyer as though she were on a catwalk.

Lloyd heard Wilfred's shoes on the tiles and his muffled voice wishing her 'Good day, ma'am.' And with that she was gone. Seeing Evelyn so perky on a day like this made Lloyd hate her even more and, in turn, himself. How had he allowed so much of his life to be consumed by her? Perhaps there had been an excuse when he was younger and oblivious to her manipulative ways. Especially as during their early courtship he had needed to convince himself that he could be in love with someone other than Cora. And Evelyn had been very good at creating a persona that drew him in. Perhaps, deep down, he had known there was another side to her, but he'd pushed those thoughts back because, by then, they had a child – and Lloyd knew they would be forever bound together by their son. Was this why he now felt so differently towards Evelyn? Had his son's death severed the final tie to a wife he no longer loved?

Lloyd turned in his mahogany swivel desk chair and looked through the sash windows as Evelyn walked down the stone steps to the Bentley. God only knew how long Jake had been waiting for her, standing to attention with the car door open. He continued watching as Evelyn positioned herself on the red leather seat and swung her legs in before Jake closed the door, climbed into the driver's seat and pulled away.

The Bentley was halfway up the gravel drive when the horse dealer's muddy Land Rover appeared and followed at a slower pace, the horsebox hitched to the back. Lloyd got up and walked over to the window to watch as it made its slow passage away from Cuthford Manor. Ghost's head was looking out the back. Lloyd thought his eyes were sad, or was that his imagination?

He had purposely come to the study to avoid saying goodbye to Ghost. Seeing the handsome gelding had reminded him of Quentin and how happy he'd been whenever he was out for a ride. It didn't seem right to let go of the beautiful animal that had been so loved by his son.

A part of Lloyd had wanted to go out and say goodbye to Ghost – to see him for one last time. Quentin had bought Ghost as a two-year-old just a few months after moving into the manor. He'd been well looked after, with everything a horse should have – but most of all he'd been well loved. Not just by Quentin, but by everyone at the manor, especially Danny. And as much as Lloyd hoped Ghost would end up in an equally loving and caring home, he doubted it was possible.

Lloyd had not trusted himself to say goodbye to Ghost, knowing there'd be a good chance he would break down, but also because he could not bear to see the faces of the children saying their farewells. They were losing yet another being they loved. He just wished Angie had been able to see that. But it was not his place to meddle.

He turned away from the window and went to pour himself a Scotch, knowing it was far too early for a drink. He sat back at his desk and slowly turned the glass round on the brown leather inlay of the desktop, watching the amber alcohol leave a blurred tidemark on the side of the glass as he thought of Quentin and his beloved horse.

The distant sound of an engine pulled him from his thoughts and he looked out of the window to see the manor's small green van making its way up the gravelled driveway and crunch to a halt. Thomas got out of the driver's side and helped Cora with her shopping.

Of course, it was Saturday. Market day. Even as a young girl, Cora had loved Durham's bustling market, full of stalls selling everything from meat, fish and vegetables to pots and pans and clothes. Looking at the clock, Lloyd saw that she'd gone earlier than normal. She'd obviously timed it to miss Ghost's departure.

Watching Cora checking over the parcels she was handing to Thomas, Lloyd wondered what their lives together might have been.

Soon after, as though conjured by his thoughts, Mrs Jones appeared in the study's open doorway.

'Do you fancy a snack before lunch?' she asked, clutching a large brown paper bag to her chest. 'To soak up some of that liquor?' She eyed the cut-glass tumbler.

Lloyd smiled, as Cora always seemed able to make him do.

'Go on, then.' He got up, leaving his glass of Scotch, and strode across the worn Turkish rug.

'And let me take this,' he said, taking the shopping bag from the woman he loved.

Chapter Twelve

A week of sour faces and bad tempers followed Ghost's departure. *Five* sour faces and bad-tempered children, as even though Bonnie was not mourning the loss of Ghost, she was at that stage of her young life when she was copying her older uncles and aunties – and if they were in a mood, then so was she. It was at times like this that Angie really felt the pressure of being a lone parent. And to add to it all, Lloyd had been unusually quiet, which made Angie feel both angry and even more guilty that her decision to sell Ghost had caused so much heartache.

'What's done is done,' she said to Dorothy over the phone. 'They'll have to just get on with life.'

Dorothy listened. She understood her best friend well enough to know that Angie was really telling *herself* to 'get on with life'; that underneath her seemingly hard exterior was a glut of sorrow and remorse. She had known Angie would feel bad about selling Ghost, despite her best friend's claim that she simply couldn't live with a daily reminder of her husband's death. The irony was that Dorothy was sure her friend would continue to suffer a daily reminder of Quentin's demise in the sad and resentful faces of her siblings – especially Danny.

'Anyway, enough about Ghost. That's in the past now,' Angie said. 'I've decided it's time to tell them my plan. It might take their minds off things.'

'You don't think it's all a bit soon?' Dorothy asked. She didn't think this would take their minds off Ghost but merely compound their misery. 'It's a big change for them. What if they want to stay where they are?'

'They'll love it! They're young – they'll adapt,' Angie declared.

'And Mrs Kwiatkowski?'

'As long as she's with us, she'll be happy.'

Dorothy wasn't about to give up. 'It's still not that long since you lost Quentin. Why not hold back until the summer? I read an article the other day about how you shouldn't make any changes until *at least* six months after you've suffered a bereavement.'

'Rubbish,' Angie said. 'Typical American twaddle.'

Dorothy knew there was no arguing with her best friend when she was in this mood. Knowing that Angie was seeing their old workmates a little later in the day, she simply had to hope they might have more success changing her mind – or at least in persuading her to hold back for a while. For Dorothy was sure that if Angie were to go ahead with her 'escape plan', she would live to regret her actions – and would realise too late that the pain of grief could not be left behind, no matter where you might make your home.

Later on that afternoon, Angie made the ten-mile trip to Sunderland to catch up with her old friends from Thompson's

– Rosie, Gloria, Polly and Martha. They tried to meet up every month in their old local, the Tatham Inn, in Hendon. Martha would bring any letters sent by Hannah and her husband, Olly, who'd both been employed in the drawing office and now worked for the Red Cross. And Angie would regale them with stories about Dorothy in New York.

After they'd all settled down, Angie told them her plan.

'It's time for pastures new,' she declared.

'The children and I don't belong there any more,' she said. 'Honestly, I feel like an imposter in my own home.'

'But that's just cos of yer awful mother-in-law,' said Gloria, who had always been the mother hen of their squad. 'Yer've gorra show her who's boss.'

The rest of the women voiced their agreement.

'Put yourself in my shoes,' Angie said. 'It doesn't seem right that I've got this great big manor just because I fell in love with Quentin and then he died on me. His bloody mother's right – it should have gone to Lloyd.'

'Well, it didn't,' said Polly, now pregnant with her third child. 'And there was a reason for that. Whatever that reason was.'

Angie sighed. 'But it's not just that. It's the attitude and the snobbery.'

'But surely they're all not like that?' Rosie asked. Like Dorothy, she believed their former workmate was about to make a huge mistake.

Angie eyed her old boss, who had recently been promoted to head welder at Thompson's. 'That's what Dor says – you two been talking?'

'Come on,' Martha said, distracting Angie. 'Let's get another round in.'

As they walked over to the bar, Angie asked Martha about her work. Their squad's gentle giant had swapped her welding rod for a riveter's gun and was one of the few women left working in the Wearside yards after the end of the war. While they waited to be served, Martha asked after Bonnie and the rest of the children.

Angie huffed. 'God, don't let Danny and Marlene hear you call them *children*.' She raised her hand to try and catch the barmaid's eye. 'They're both growing up fast. Danny's already on at me to ask his school if he can leave early. And Marlene is more like eighteen than thirteen.'

'What can I get yer both?' the barmaid asked, having finally dragged herself away from the young bloke who was chatting her up.

As soon as Angie opened her mouth and gave her their order, she saw the smile drop from the young woman's face. Angie sighed inwardly. She had experienced this before. After almost five years living at Cuthford Manor, her broad Sunderland accent had naturally softened and she now said 'yes' instead of 'aye', and 'didn't' instead of 'dinnit', although the rhythmic lilt of her home town could still be heard. To those who came from where she did, though, she sounded posh. Which, in turn, made people judge her and presume she was a snob.

Angie had come to realise that the unfriendliness she experienced from people like the barmaid was different to the kind of snobbery she had encountered from the likes of

Evelyn. It was an inverted snobbery she herself had been guilty of when she was younger and knew nothing other than life within a half-mile radius of her home.

It was another reason why she was certain that her plan for change was for the best. She didn't fit in anywhere. Not even in her home town.

Arriving back at the manor, Angie made it just in time to join everyone for their evening meal in the dining room. Evelyn seemed in particularly good spirits as she regaled them all about her day, most of which seemed to have been spent lunching with 'Gertrude and the girls'.

'Oh my goodness,' she spluttered suddenly, putting down her knife and fork. 'How could I forget to tell you! You'll never believe what I heard today?'

Angie was only half listening as she was making sure Marlene ate some of the food on her plate. The subjects Evelyn and Gertrude talked about at their luncheons held no interest for Angie – or anyone else at the table.

As Lloyd seemed in another world, Angie forced out the expected response.

'I can't guess, Evelyn, what did you hear?' she asked, catching Marlene's eye and mouthing 'Eat' at her. Marlene responded by putting a small piece of venison in her mouth and making a show of swallowing.

'Everyone's up in arms,' Evelyn said.

'About what?' Angie asked.

'About the refugees who have suddenly been dumped on us,' Evelyn explained.

Lloyd suddenly scraped back his chair. 'Damn it. Sorry, everyone, I forgot I've got a call coming through . . .' he looked at his watch '. . . just about now.' He uttered another apology and said to tell Cook the meal was delicious, and then he was gone.

'What refugees?' asked Angie.

'The Polish refugees,' Evelyn said, pushing her plate away and lighting up a cigarette. 'Although don't get me going about all the others pouring into the country from all four corners of the world.'

'People from Poland are coming here?' Bertie asked with an expression of wonder on his face. He'd been learning about all the countries of the world at school, and now anything beyond the shores of Britain drew his interest.

'Yes, Bertie, they are indeed, and we are not happy about it. Not happy about it at all.'

'Why?' Angie asked as one of the maids came in to clear the table in anticipation of dessert.

'Because they don't belong here,' Evelyn said. 'We don't want to be overrun. My God, Angela, most of them can't even speak English. The country's in a state as it is. We've still got rationing, for heaven's sake.' Evelyn gasped to punctuate her point.

Angie felt ready to explode. She was just glad Mrs Kwiatkowski had not joined them for dinner that evening.

'We're thinking of getting a petition together. There's already been graffiti in the city telling them to "go home",' Evelyn added somewhat triumphantly.

'So, are you suggesting Mrs Kwiatkowski also goes home?' Angie sniped.

Evelyn looked shocked. 'Of course not. She's an old woman. And from what you've told me, she came over here years ago – well before the war.'

'Ah, so that makes it all right?' Angie could feel an argument brewing.

'Honestly, Angela, you're not understanding what I'm trying to say – we don't want foreigners here en masse. Not in our country – and certainly not in our county.'

Angie looked at the children, who for once were listening to the conversation.

'Even though those *foreigners* fought on our side,' she argued, 'and now can't go back to their own countries because they'll either get thrown into prison or killed?' Angie knew more than most about what had happened in Poland both during the war and after, as it was something that had affected Quentin deeply, and was the reason he'd resigned from the War Office and taken a teaching job at the university.

'Poland was basically handed over to Stalin by us and the Americans as a *reward* for swapping sides at the start of the war,' Angie continued. 'And then, to add insult to injury, our government, for all intents and purposes *banned* the Polish Armed Forces from taking part in the post-war Victory Parade to avoid offending Russia.

'We should be welcoming them with open arms after we basically shafted them big time. I'm surprised they even want to come here.'

Evelyn's face curled at Angie's use of the word 'shafted'. *So uncouth.*

'I think you're being a bit dramatic,' she countered.

'I'm not being dramatic.' Angie gasped in disbelief. 'It's well known that Stalin is either executing those he sees as traitors or putting them in labour camps. Just like he was when he was fighting on Hitler's side at the start of the war.'

'Angela, I can see this is going to lead to us falling out, so I'm afraid we're going to have to agree to disagree,' Evelyn said. 'But I stand fast in my belief that these Poles who are swamping our green and pleasant land don't belong here. And I think you'll find that's what most people round here believe.'

Most people you know, Angie refrained from saying.

Later that evening, as Angie put Bonnie to bed and read her the story of the Lambton Worm, her mind kept wandering back to Evelyn's belief that the Polish refugees should 'go home'.

It strengthened her resolve. She did not want Bonnie or her own siblings growing up with this kind of entitled, prejudiced and self-serving attitude.

She thought of the daffodils that had started to appear. It was almost spring. It was the right time for new beginnings.

It was time, Angie decided, to do more than just think about her idea for change.

It was now time to put all those plans that had been swirling around in her head into action.

Chapter Thirteen

The following day, Lloyd woke with a heavy heart, which was not unusual. Every morning since his son's death, the burden of grief had made it a struggle for him to get up and get on with another day. That weight had felt greater since Ghost had been taken away by the horse trader last Saturday. After breakfast, he went to his study and worked for a short while on the bookkeeping, but his concentration was lacking and he found himself instinctively heading down the corridor to see Mrs Jones in her office-cum-snug next to the kitchen.

As he knocked on the partly open door of the box room, Lloyd realised that lately he had been feeling the need to be with Cora more and more. A need only matched by his desire to be with Evelyn less and less.

'Only me,' he said, peeking his head round the door.

Mrs Jones smiled on seeing Lloyd. She was sitting behind a small but solid desk made of English oak. It was probably one of the few traditional pieces of furniture in the house.

'Come in. Sit down,' she said, pouring him a cuppa from the little tea tray on her desk. She, too, was aware that they were spending more and more time in each other's company. Before Quentin's death that might have made her feel a little uncomfortable, but so much had changed since then, and the amount of time they might or might not be spending with each other didn't seem important. Death had a way of putting life's trivialities into perspective.

'Thank you,' Lloyd said as he took the china cup and saucer from Mrs Jones's outstretched hand.

'Is everything all right?' she asked, seeing straight away that something was troubling him.

'You know me too well.' Lloyd gave the woman he loved a sad smile as he lowered himself into the chair opposite.

'Ghost?' Mrs Jones guessed.

Lloyd nodded. 'It was this time last week the horse trader took him.'

'I was just thinking that myself,' Mrs Jones said. 'I couldn't bear to see him go.'

'And that's why you went to the market early—'

'And *you* know *me* so well,' said Mrs Jones.

She looked at Lloyd.

'But,' she probed, 'I sense there's something else bothering you?'

Lloyd nodded. 'I feel like Angie's up to something – planning something.'

'Why's that?' Mrs Jones asked.

'She just seems as though her mind's elsewhere,' Lloyd mused.

'I know what you mean,' Mrs Jones agreed. 'She's definitely seemed a bit distracted lately.'

'She's been squirrelling herself away in the library, and when I've gone in, she's been at pains to cover up what she's reading. And she's been ringing Dorothy in New York and Liz in Australia more frequently. I know this because of the huge telephone bills we've been getting.' Lloyd took a sip of his tea. 'And she's still not riding, which seems such a shame – she used to love taking the horses out when Quentin was alive.' An image of Quentin with Ghost flashed across his mind, as it often did, dragging his mood still lower. 'And then, the other day, she asked me in a roundabout way if I could afford to buy Cuthford Manor.'

'Oh dear,' Mrs Jones sighed. 'That doesn't sound good.' She put her teacup back on its saucer.

They were both quiet, both thinking the same thought – that they would be distraught if Angie and her family were to leave.

'Did you tell her – about your financial situation?'

'Oh, yes. I think she was quite surprised that I couldn't buy the place outright. I told her that my father had left me a good amount but not good enough to be able to afford this place – and keep it up.'

'It'd be a mistake if she decided to go. She belongs here now,' Mrs Jones said.

'I couldn't agree more,' said Lloyd. 'And bloody Evelyn's not helping matters. I keep hearing her go on about "this is how *we* do things".'

'Do you think it's getting to Angie?' Mrs Jones asked.

'Angie just ignores her, but I can tell by her face that it bothers her.' Lloyd had got to know Angie much better since he'd moved back, and even more since taking over the financial management of the estate, something his son had always done. 'There's something going on and my gut feeling is that it's not good. I've asked her, but you know Angie. She's very good at keeping her thoughts and feelings to herself.'

'She is,' Mrs Jones agreed. 'You know, she's going to feel as though she's had the rug pulled out from under her for a while yet. She just has to ride this storm of grief and wait for the calm to come, which it will.'

Lloyd wondered if this was how Cora had felt after her husband died, but he didn't feel it was appropriate to ask. If he *had* asked, and Mrs Jones had spoken with complete candour, she would have told him that she had grieved Joshua's death, but it was the pain of not being able to have her own family that had caused her the most heartache.

'The thing is,' Lloyd continued, bringing his concerns about his wife's behaviour back to the fore, 'Evelyn's barbed comments really aren't helping matters.'

'And have you told her to stop?' Mrs Jones felt annoyed. She had been unaware this was happening, which wasn't surprising. Evelyn wouldn't want others to hear.

'I've tried.' Lloyd sighed. 'God knows I've tried. But all Evelyn comes back with is that I'm going "funny in the head" like my father and I'm imagining it all.'

Mrs Jones shook her head. Leonard had been eccentric, that was for sure, different and unconventional, but he had most definitely been of sound mind.

Lloyd finished his tea. Pushing himself out of the chair, reluctant as always to leave the woman he wanted by his side day and night, he offered up a smile that only managed to show how sad and helpless he felt.

'Thank you for the tea and the company,' he said, before turning and leaving the room.

Heading back to his study, Lloyd's thoughts were again filled with an image of Ghost looking out of the back of the trailer as it trundled down the driveway. There was no getting over it. Ghost leaving had deepened his grief. God only knew how Danny was feeling.

He just wished he'd tried to convince Angie to keep Ghost.

He should have at least tried.

Lloyd sat at his desk deep in thought for a good ten minutes until he was brought out of his reverie by the chiming of the French Boulle grandfather clock in the entrance hall.

'Sod it!' he exclaimed.

Standing up and taking a deep breath, he headed out of the study, across the brightly coloured mosaic-tiled foyer and yanked open the front door.

He'd had just about enough of regrets.

Chapter Fourteen

Angie watched Lloyd drive off in Quentin's old Morris Minor, wondering where he was going. He usually told her if he was going out in case she wanted anything bringing back.

Hearing the chatter of her siblings approaching the sitting room, she took a deep breath, fighting back a burst of nerves. She hoped they'd be as excited as she was.

'Angie's got something up her sleeve,' Marlene said under her breath to her older brother as they walked into the room.

'Yeah, and I've a feeling it's something we're not going to like,' Danny muttered back.

'Where's Bonnie?' Jemima asked as they trooped over to the sofa.

'She's helping Cook in the kitchen,' Angie said.

'Making a cake?' Bertie asked.

When Angie nodded, there was, as expected, outrage from the two youngest that they hadn't been involved.

'Don't worry, you can go and join her as soon as we've had our little meeting.'

Angie smiled at them all and was met by a collective look of wariness. Danny was still viewing her as though she was the devil's cohort for selling Ghost.

Once they'd all squashed onto the settee, Angie forced herself to sit down on the armchair, despite her nervous excitement making her feel as though she needed to move around.

She leant forward, her hands clasped.

'I've got some exciting news,' she said, scanning the four worried faces. She laughed, a little too loudly. 'Don't worry, you're not getting told off about anything. This is *good* news.'

Angie's slight fanaticism was not making any of them feel any more reassured.

'So, go on,' Danny said, his tone surly. 'Tell us what this "exciting" news is.' The only exciting news for Danny would be that Ghost was coming home.

'Don't keep us in suspense,' Marlene said, her tone heavy with sarcasm.

Bertie and Jemima were quiet, waiting to see what their big sister had to tell them.

There had been a time when they could all probably have guessed what their older sister had planned, but not any more.

Angie took another deep breath.

'We're going to emigrate!' she declared. 'To Australia!'

Chapter Fifteen

Sensing that something was up, Evelyn had quietly tiptoed to the door of the sitting room, which had been left ever so slightly ajar. She stood as still as the two knights in shining armour standing guard by the fireplace in the hall as Angie started to tell the children that she had some 'exciting news'.

Hearing the words 'emigrate' and 'Australia', Evelyn felt like jumping for joy; she would have if she could have done so without making a noise.

Instead, a wide, slightly maniacal smile spread across her face.

Her plan had worked! At last! And better than she could have imagined.

Not only was the miner's daughter going to move out – she was going to the other side of the world. And she was taking her motley crew with her.

She would finally reclaim her rightful position as lady of the manor.

'Of course . . .' she murmured to herself as she quietly left the doorway. She should have guessed that Angie might consider going to live with her sister and her family down under. She recalled her daughter-in-law's last will and testament, to which she had been privy, along with her son's, when she'd been living in York. Her clandestine affair with one of the family solicitors, Desmond Pyburn, had certainly paid dividends. Her daughter-in-law's will had stipulated that if she were to die first, then Quentin would take over sole guardianship of the children and they would move to Australia to be close to their older sister and cousins. It made sense that Angie would consider doing the same now that Quentin was no longer here with her.

Evelyn felt like skipping down the corridor. She knew Angie would not go against her husband's wish to leave Cuthford Manor in the care of his parents, who would be deemed sitting tenants.

Cuthford Manor would be hers once again.

And so it damn well should be. It was only right. The miner's daughter and her 'tribe', as her son had been so fond of calling them, did not belong here. She'd put enough time, energy and effort into making her son's widow realise that.

Opening the kitchen door, Evelyn saw that the cook was making a cake. The wireless was on, and Bonnie was helping her by cracking an egg into the mixture.

'Morning!' Evelyn's voice sang out.

The cook looked up, amazed that Mrs Foxton-Clarke had even acknowledged her.

'It's such a lovely day now that the wretched fog has lifted,' Evelyn said, walking over to the back door and reaching down for the wicker basket that was kept there. 'I thought

I'd go and pick some flowers for the dining table. And then I'll go out for a ride.'

The cook nodded and smiled. Mrs Foxton-Clarke was lucky Bonnie was engrossed in making a cake, otherwise she would have had to deal with her granddaughter begging to go with her. And all the staff knew that any kind of attention from Bonnie irked her. This went for any child. The older workers had seen her act the same way when Quentin was a boy.

As Evelyn walked to the walled garden to pick some daffodils, she looked around at the beautiful grounds and then at the magnificent manor house bathed in the late-morning sun.

Admiring the stonework and the cone-shaped towers that made the manor unique, Evelyn's thoughts went to her father-in-law, Leonard Foxton-Clarke.

'I hope you're turning in your grave, old man,' she said out loud. 'I *will* have Cuthford Manor and there's nothing you can do about it.'

Evelyn now firmly believed that Leonard had found out about her past and guessed that the only reason she had married his son was this place – and everything that went with it. Leonard might not have disclosed her past to Lloyd, but the old man had safeguarded the family home by bequeathing it to his grandson.

But now Cuthford Manor would be hers.

Perhaps not in name, but she would once again be in charge – and rid of the interloper and her raggle-taggle children.

She congratulated herself on her powers of manipulation and her skills of coercion.

Feeling the warmth of the sun on her face, Evelyn smiled.

Life was good. Life was *very* good.

Chapter Sixteen

Angie tried to keep up her enthusiasm as she answered the slew of questions her siblings were angrily chucking at her.

'Why would you want to emigrate?' Marlene asked.

'And to Australia?' Danny added.

'Because,' Angie said, 'unless it's slipped your mind, your sister lives in Australia.'

'A sister,' Marlene practically spat out the words, 'we can hardly remember.'

'Just because you can barely remember her doesn't mean she's not your sister – and that she doesn't love you all,' Angie argued back.

'What?' Danny sniped. 'She loves us all so much that we didn't see hide nor hair of her after she ran off and joined the lumberjills?'

'Yeah,' Marlene jumped in. 'A sister who never even came to see us before she moved to the other side of the world.'

Angie stalled. It was true. As soon as Liz had left the house in Dundas Street, she'd never looked back. It had been Angie who had made the effort to keep in touch.

'You've got cousins you've not met.' Angie looked at Bertie and Jemima, who had been very quiet. Their little faces didn't show a flicker of excitement at the prospect of moving or having relatives they'd never met.

'Blood's thicker than water,' she said, but as soon as she spoke the words she realised that the proverb did not really apply to their family. It was something Danny immediately seized upon.

'Is it?' Danny demanded, his anger and bitterness clear.

'Yeah, is it?' Marlene backed her brother. 'It's so thick our mam ran off and left us, our dad can't be bothered with us even though he lives in the same county, and Liz didn't even give us a backward glance when she left.' Marlene remembered Liz's departure only too well as she had inherited all her sister's chores, as well as having to look after the two young ones.

'Okay,' Angie placated them, 'just mull it over for the time being. I've still got a lot to sort out before we go. But honestly, I think you'll like it once you see what's over there – the sun and the beaches, and Sydney's just like London, by all accounts.' Angie looked at Marlene, who was obsessed with the capital.

'No, it's not,' Marlene said. 'It's nothing like it. We studied it in geography.'

'What about Mrs K?' Jemima asked, her face full of concern.

'Of course Mrs Kwiatkowski will come with us – she goes wherever we go,' Angie reassured them.

'Bet you she'll love the sweltering hot weather over there,' Marlene said, deadpan.

'Is it really hot over there?' Bertie blurted out.

Angie looked at her younger brother's pale, angst-ridden face. Bertie didn't like being out in the sun or getting too hot. Angie sighed inwardly. She must have the only brothers and sisters who didn't want to move somewhere there was sun, sea and sand.

'It's not hot all the time,' she tried to reassure them.

The room was quiet. No one seemed convinced.

'This is going to be a great adventure,' Angie said, lifting her voice, hoping she sounded convincing.

'I don't want an adventure,' Jemima said, leaning into Bertie, who put his arm around his younger sister.

'It'll be *fun*,' Angie argued. She'd forgotten just how anxious her little sister could get about change. 'A *good* adventure.'

'This is all about you!' Marlene stood up. 'You want to leave here because of Quentin.'

The room went silent.

Angie looked at her brothers and sisters. She wanted to tell them that there was another reason she wanted to move near to Liz and her family. Should anything happen to her, then she needed to know that they would be looked after. But there was no way she was going to tell them that. The last thing she wanted was for them to be worrying that something might happen to her. Everyone they knew and loved, or who was meant to care for them, had bailed on them, either intentionally or otherwise – their mam, their dad, Liz and Quentin.

She didn't want them even thinking of the possibility that she might be taken from them too.

Chapter Seventeen

Angie had asked her siblings to keep her plan to themselves – she wanted to tell Lloyd, Evelyn, Mrs Jones and the rest of the staff herself. They had done as they'd been told, but a week had now passed and she knew the time had come. She would tell everyone today – after she'd had her chat with Jeremy.

'Thanks for coming over.' Angie stood up and smiled as Wilfred showed Jeremy into the front reception room.

'Angela, how lovely to see you,' Jeremy said. Seeing that she was still wearing what was becoming her trademark black slacks and black cashmere jumper, he held back from suggesting it was time to ditch the mourning attire. They were no longer in the Victorian era. This was 1950. A time for moving forward – not looking back at the past.

Angie bristled at being called Angela. Why couldn't people like Jeremy and Evelyn call her Angie, as she had repeatedly asked them to? Did they think it too common? *Another reason she was doing the right thing*. Australia, she had read, was known to be classless – or as classless as a society could be.

'Lovely to see you too, Jeremy. Please, sit down.' She motioned to the armchair by the fire, which was stacked up but had not been lit as it was unseasonably warm today.

'What a surprise to be invited over,' Jeremy said, which was true. Angie had never invited him over. Not once. 'Although it has to be said, a *lovely* surprise.' He settled himself into the chair. 'So, how are you?' He put on a suitably serious face and paused for sombre effect. 'Really? Under that veneer? How long's it been now? Three months?'

'About that,' Angie said. It had been three months and ten days, to be exact. In some ways, Angie felt it had been so much longer. At other times, it felt nothing at all. There was still that moment every day around teatime when – just for a split second – she expected Quentin to walk into the kitchen full of life and chatter after a day at the university.

Hearing Mrs Jones's footsteps tapping across the main hallway, Angie turned to see that, as planned, she was bringing in tea for two.

Placing the silver tray on the glass coffee table, Mrs Jones wondered yet again why Angie had invited the Fontaine-Smith boy round. As she left the room, she cast Angie a look. Lloyd was right. She was definitely up to something – but what?

'I have to say you look lovely today,' Jeremy said. 'Am I allowed to say that to a widow?'

'You can say whatever you want, Jeremy. As long as it's the truth.'

They both knew it wasn't. Angie had lost weight since Quentin had died, and as much as she'd tried to force herself to eat and keep her strength up, as Mrs Jones kept nagging her to do, it was hard when she simply didn't have any semblance of an appetite. Her strawberry-blonde hair was straggly and her eyes now seemed to have a shade of blue-grey permanently underneath them.

As soon as Mrs Jones had pulled the door to, Jeremy leant forward and grasped Angie's hands.

'How are you *really* feeling?' He adopted the most puppy-dog look he could. Angie pulled her hands away a bit too sharply.

'I've got you here today, Jeremy, to talk about what I am *planning* – rather than what I am feeling.'

'Oh, this sounds interesting,' Jeremy said, trying not to look crestfallen.

'I've been doing a lot of thinking since Quentin died,' Angie began. 'And I've decided to leave Cuthford Manor. Leave the area, actually.'

Jeremy couldn't hide his shock. 'Really? Are you sure? But you belong here.' He looked around at the beautiful lemon and blue Willian Morris wallpaper.

Angie let out a short burst of laughter. 'Really? You honestly believe I belong here?'

'Of course. Why wouldn't I?'

'Mmm,' Angie said, not hiding her scepticism. 'Well, anyway, I've decided to sell up.' She had to sell up if she wanted to buy a big enough property in Sydney, maintain a decent standard of living – and pay for the children's education.

Jeremy couldn't hold back his distress. 'No, no, Angela, you can't! You simply can't! You need to stay here. You really can't sell!'

Angie looked at Jeremy, amazed at the sudden change in his manner. 'Why?' she asked.

Jeremy straightened himself up, put his cup and saucer on the coffee table, took a deep breath, and then dropped down on one knee.

'Angela Foxton-Clarke,' he asked with aplomb, 'will you do me the honour of becoming my wife?'

Angie stared at Jeremy for a moment taking in his proposal. She should, of course, be feeling incredulous at his insensitivity. She'd only been widowed a matter of months, after all. But she didn't. She felt too sad to be angry as a vision came to her of Quentin proposing in the middle of the dance floor at the Christmas Extravaganza her workmates had organised for the wounded soldiers at the Ryhope hospital. It had all gone terribly wrong, with the diamond ring he had bought for her going flying and being almost trampled underfoot by those dancing. It had been the most disastrous, most comical, most romantic declaration of love ever. She remembered thinking that she had never felt happier in her entire life. The antithesis of how she was feeling now.

'Oh, Jeremy, no, of course I can't marry you.' Angie took his hand and patted it as though he were a child. 'Please, sit back down.'

Jeremy did as he was told.

'But why?' he asked, his tone almost a whine. He wanted to inform Angie of his credentials – that he was a good-looking man, well educated, in his prime, from good stock.

'Where do I start, Jeremy? Because I've only just lost my husband? Because we don't love each other. Because we don't even find each other attractive? Shall I go on?' Angie exhaled.

'But I *do* love you . . . do find you attractive,' Jeremy said, trying his utmost to sound genuine.

'Stop it, Jeremy!' Angie felt as if she was reprimanding one of the children. She wanted to say that women were clearly not Jeremy's preference, but knew that would be improper.

'Let's be honest with each other,' she said. 'The only reason you want me as your wife is because I come with this place.' She looked around the room to demonstrate her point.

Jeremy started to object. Angie silenced him with a look.

'Which brings me back to why I asked you here today. I know how much you love Cuthford Manor, and also how much you would love to own it, so I'm giving you first dibs on buying the place.'

Angie expected his face to light up with the prospect of acquiring the manor, imagining all the parties he and his mother could throw. But it didn't. Instead, he looked completely downtrodden.

'Oh Angela, I would love to – would probably have already offered to buy it before now – if I could.'

'You can't?' Now it was Angie who could not hide her shock and surprise. *Jeremy and his mother lived in a beautiful mansion just half a mile from Cuthford Manor. They were loaded, weren't they?*

'I'm afraid I can't. Can't afford it,' Jeremy admitted.

'And your mother?' Angie asked, feeling more disappointed by the second that this was not turning out to be as straightforward as she had anticipated.

'No, nor Mother,' Jeremy confirmed.

Angie and Jeremy sat, neither of them knowing what to say. Both feeling a huge sense of disappointment.

Chapter Eighteen

By the time Jeremy was driving through the gates at the top of the driveway, Angie was in the study, asking the operator to put her through to the only property agency she knew, a long-established firm called Durham Estates, based in the city centre.

After speaking with their top man and negotiating terms and the commission rate, she went down to the kitchen and asked Mrs Jones to get everyone together in the library as she had something important to tell them all.

'Mr and Mrs Foxton-Clarke too?' she asked.

Angie nodded.

'And the children?'

'And the children,' Angie agreed. 'And Mrs Kwiatkowski. This involves her too.'

Half an hour later, everyone had been shepherded into the large oak-panelled library. The children, Mrs Kwiatkowski, Evelyn, Lloyd, Mrs Jones, Alberta, Wilfred, Thomas, Bill, Ted and Eugene – even Winston and Bessie had managed to sneak in and were trying to avoid detection by squashing up next to Jemima and Bertie.

'I've got you all together as what I've got to tell you affects everyone.' She glanced at Evelyn, who was clearly appalled that she should be summoned along with the children and the 'servants'.

Everyone was quiet. Angie looked around. This was the first time everyone had been in the same room together. It was also the first time that Angie realised how ridiculous it was to have nearly as many employees as those who lived there. Another of the many reasons that selling was the right thing to do – even if they weren't emigrating. This place was just too big for them all. There were rooms she hadn't been into for months.

'There's no easy way to say this, so I'll just come straight out with it. I've decided to take the children – and, of course, Mrs Kwiatkowski – to live in Sydney.'

There were gasps of surprise and a few mumblings.

'In Australia?' Lloyd asked, even though he knew of no other Sydney in the world. This was shocking news. Much worse than he'd anticipated.

Angie smiled sadly. 'Yes, to be near our sister Liz and her family.'

A stunned silence fell on the room. No one, bar Evelyn, had expected this. Angie hardly ever mentioned her sister down under.

'And because of that, I'm going to have to sell the manor.'

Angie heard Evelyn gasp, and saw her mother-in-law's hand go to her mouth. For a moment, she thought Evelyn was going to scream.

'I know this means many of you are going to be worried about your jobs, which I can totally understand,' Angie empathised. 'So I will endeavour to see if it can be written into the contract of sale that you continue working here for a minimum of six months, with the hope that whoever buys Cuthford Manor will see how priceless you all are and keep you on.'

There was a smattering of smiles. Bill tipped an imaginary cap to show his appreciation.

Angie forced herself to look at the children, who appeared forlorn. Even the dogs' dark brown eyes looked more sorrowful than normal.

'I've just spoken to the estate agent, who told me that they will be ringing round all their clients and spreading the word, so as soon as we have anyone who wants to buy, I will keep you all informed.' She looked around. 'Has anyone got any questions?'

No-one spoke.

'Okay, well, I'll let you all get back to what you were doing. Any worries or concerns, you know where to find me.'

As everyone started to leave, Angie grabbed Mrs Jones.

'I know what your answer will be, but would you please at least consider coming with us?'

Mrs Jones put her hand on Angie's arm and squeezed it gently. 'That's such a lovely compliment, but my home is here.' As she spoke, she tried to hold back her heartbreak that Angie and her family, whom she had come to care for and love dearly, were going to leave – and not just move from the manor, but relocate halfway round the world.

As she left, Angie turned to see that Evelyn and Lloyd were still standing. Danny and Marlene, who had Bonnie on her knee, were sitting on the cushioned window seat, and Bertie and Jemima were cross-legged on the rug with Winston and Bessie.

'We can take the dogs, can't we?' Bertie asked.

'Of course,' Angie said.

'And what about Starling, and Monty and Bomber – and Lucky – we can take them too, can't we?' Danny asked sarcastically.

Seeing Jemima's face light up at the thought of being able to keep Lucky, Angie panicked. 'No, sorry, Jemima.' She threw Danny a dark sidelong look. 'Lucky and the rest of the horses will have to find new homes.'

Seeing that Evelyn wasn't going to leave until she'd said her piece, Angie turned her attention to the children. 'Go on, off you all go. I'm sure you've all got homework to do.'

The five youngsters and two dogs got up and trudged off. Words weren't needed; their body language spoke volumes.

'Why, Angela? Why sell?' Evelyn demanded as soon as they'd gone.

Angie thought that Evelyn sounded as traumatised as Jeremy. Although she'd have thought her mother-in-law would be overjoyed that they were emigrating.

'Because, Evelyn, I have to sell this place in order to afford to move to Australia.'

Angie had been astounded by the amount of money she was having to pay the government in Estate Duty following Quentin's death.

'Really?' Evelyn asked, working out how to say what she wanted without letting on that she had seen Angie's will prior to Quentin's death. 'It's just I know my son would want us to stay here, look after the place—'

Angie looked at her mother-in-law. Quentin, she presumed, must have told his mother what was in their wills, which was odd.

'That's right,' Angie said, glancing at Lloyd, 'he would have wanted that, but so much of the money Quentin left in his will has to be paid out in taxes. I'll be honest, it surprised me when I was told – nearly eighty per cent.'

Evelyn was momentarily speechless. She put her hands on her hips. 'But you can't *sell* this place, Angela. It belongs to the family. It should be kept in the family.' She looked at Lloyd for backup and was met by a blank look.

'I'm happy to sell it to you and Lloyd,' Angie said to her father-in-law, giving him an apologetic look. 'Sorry, Lloyd, I know this was your father's, but we really won't be able to afford to move if we don't sell.'

Lloyd nodded. 'This is yours, Angie. It's up to you to decide what's best for yourself and the children,' he said, straightening his back and glaring at his wife. 'We'll leave you in peace.'

Evelyn opened her mouth to speak, but seeing the way her husband was staring at her, decided against it.

Evelyn followed her husband into the study. She was furious. 'She can't sell the place!'

'I'm afraid she can,' Lloyd said. 'Legally, it's hers to do with as she wishes.'

This was not what Evelyn had planned. She felt as though she'd been cheated. All that hard work trying to get Angie to leave – and now this! It had never occurred to her that

Angie would *sell* Cuthford Manor. *How the hell could Angie even consider it?*

Of course, Evelyn did not blame herself – nor see it as an oversight on her part.

She looked daggers at Lloyd. *This was his fault*. He should have told her about the financial situation. About all these death duties.

'You've got to stop her,' Evelyn told Lloyd. 'She'll listen to you. Tell her she can't do something so drastic. The manor has been in the family for centuries.'

'Well, that's not strictly true,' Lloyd said, pouring himself a drink. 'Father bought it from his uncle, who bought it from the son of a colliery owner.'

'Oh, for God's sake, stop nit-picking,' Evelyn snapped. 'I think you should get a lawyer involved. There must be something they can do to stop her selling.'

'Why would it be such a catastrophe if it was sold?' Lloyd asked. The only tragedy in what he'd just learnt was that those he had come to see as his family were moving to the other side of the world.

Evelyn opened her mouth, but nothing came out other than a disbelieving gasp.

She stomped out of the room. She had to rectify the situation and she had to do so quickly. Especially as it was clear that Lloyd was going to do absolutely nothing to save what should be theirs.

Hers.

*

'So, what are we going to do?' Danny asked his younger brothers and sisters.

After leaving the library, they'd all agreed to put their heads together and so they'd gone to their favourite spot under the large oak tree next to the paddock.

Bertie and Jemima looked at Danny and then at Marlene. They were the eldest. They usually knew what to do.

'I'm not sure there's anything we can do,' Marlene said. 'We've tried to talk her out of it, and that's done us no good whatsoever.' This was true. This past week they had argued, pleaded, sulked and attempted to bribe her with promises to do whatever she wanted them to do for the foreseeable. Nothing had worked.

'She's determined to go,' Danny mused. 'She's always been like this. Once she's made up her mind about something, there's no changing it.'

Marlene muttered her agreement.

'We could run away?' Jemima suggested.

'Where to?' Bertie asked.

'Bertie's got a point, Jemima – where would we go?' said Marlene.

'Yeah, we'd be lucky to make it to Durham without anyone recognising us and marching us straight back here,' Danny said. 'Besides, that kind of defeats the object, doesn't it? Running away from the place we want to stay.'

They fell silent.

A silence that was broken by Marlene.

'We've tried to argue our case and it's got us nowhere – let's try and pull on her heartstrings. Angie can be a hard nut to crack when she wants to be, but she's really a big softie on the inside.'

'I beg to differ,' Danny said, thinking of Ghost and how heartless his sister had been in selling him.

'It's worth a try,' Marlene said, exasperated by her brother's negativity. 'Nothing else is working, is it?'

Mrs Jones, Alberta and Wilfred sat round the kitchen table, supping cups of tea. No one spoke for a while. It was as though everyone had been temporarily struck dumb by Angie's revelation.

Alberta was the first to break the silence.

'Well, I'll say it if no one else will . . .' She put her cup back down on its saucer. 'That lass is making a big mistake. It's as clear as the day is long.'

Wilfred mumbled his agreement.

'I agree. She can't outrun her grief,' said Mrs Jones.

'Well, if she's trying to run away, she couldn't find anywhere further to go,' Alberta huffed.

'I've also picked up,' Mrs Jones continued, 'that since Quentin's gone, Angie doesn't feel like she belongs here.'

'Never heard such nonsense,' Wilfred mumbled.

'Ridiculous!' Alberta said, nearly choking on her tea. The dogs lifted their heads at the sound of the cook's sudden outburst. 'If anyone belongs here, it's Angie a' t'family.'

'I know,' Mrs Jones said sadly.

'It's the bairns ma heart bleeds fer.' Alberta continued her rant, her Yorkshire accent thickening alongside her anger. 'Yer don't have ta be a mind reader ta see none o' them wants ta move to Australia. I've never heard 'em mention this sister o' theirs the once.'

'The problem is,' Wilfred mused, 'it's not our place to say anything.'

They were quiet for a moment as they drank their tea.

'Couldn't someone else talk some sense into the lass?' Alberta looked at Mrs Jones.

After she'd finished her tea, Mrs Jones went to find Lloyd. Her first port of call was the study, guessing he'd have gone there after Angie's news. She knew it would have blindsided him and he'd be upset. He had grown close to Angie and the children – especially since Quentin's death.

She was right. Lloyd was in the study, nursing a Scotch and looking as despondent as the children.

His face brightened a fraction on seeing Mrs Jones.

'Sit down. Sit down. Do you want a drink?' He nodded over to the decanter of brandy.

Mrs Jones shook her head. 'I've just been chatting to Alberta and Wilfred. We're all agreed that Angie is trying to run away from her grief – and that moving to Australia is not the wisest decision.'

'I agree one hundred per cent – if only Angie could see that,' Lloyd lamented.

'We thought you could try and change her mind?' Mrs Jones suggested.

'I can certainly try,' Lloyd said. 'But I have a feeling it won't do any good. Angie seems set in her resolve to leave here by hook or by crook.'

Chapter Nineteen

Over the following week, Lloyd and Dorothy tried to dissuade Angie from making such a huge change. Both in their own way tried to coax Angie to reconsider, or at the very least to hold off for a little while longer as she might not realise it at the moment, but she was still grieving.

'I've done my grieving' seemed to be Angie's stock reply.

'Perhaps you can go there for a holiday?' Lloyd suggested. A brilliant idea, he thought, which had been Mrs Jones's, but she had felt it would be better coming from him. Despite the friendship Mrs Jones and Angie shared, they were still employee and employer, and Mrs Jones didn't want to 'overstep the mark'.

Angie, though, had batted away the idea, saying she 'just had to get on with life'. Her mind was made up.

Dorothy had been upfront, telling Angie she thought she was making a mistake, but she also knew that the more she pushed, the more her best friend would push back. She had called Lloyd and was relieved to hear that he and Mrs Jones were desperately trying to keep Angie at the manor, but not so relieved when she heard their attempts had met without success.

'When Angie gets something into her head, she can be as stubborn as a mule,' she said.

The children, on the other hand, had been uncannily quiet and were being very secretive. As soon as they arrived home after school, and the cook had given them a glass of her home-made lemonade and a slice of quince tart, they would all march purposefully over to the oak tree, accompanied by their co-conspirators, Winston and Bessie.

Angie had been curious about what they were up to and had watched them from the kitchen window a few times, thinking that they looked like they were practising for some kind of play or recital, performing to the dogs as if they were their audience.

Her curiosity was satiated on Friday after school, when Danny asked everyone to meet them all in the sitting room.

Claiming her place on the three-seater leather chesterfield, Evelyn threw Lloyd a look that told him to do the same. She bristled when Angie sat down next to him. The two of them had become far too chummy. Although, she mused, that might work to her advantage if Lloyd could persuade Angie against emigrating – and to rent a house instead of buying one. It would mean they could revert to the original plan in the will, leaving her and Lloyd in charge of the manor.

Angie waved Mrs Kwiatkowski over to sit on the adjacent armchair. Mrs Jones, Wilfred and Alberta stood behind the sofa, waiting with bated breath.

'We all wanted to say something,' Danny said, his voice deep and serious.

'It's what we all feel,' Bertie added, looking at Danny, Marlene, who had Bonnie on her hip, and then finally at Jemima, who was wringing her hands with nerves.

'It's called "Home Is Where the Heart Is", by Mrs Mary Lambert,' Bertie announced.

The room fell silent.

Angie looked at Jemima with wide eyes and a broad, encouraging smile across her face. Jemima was notoriously shy when it came to public speaking.

Jemima took a step forward, as she had been coached. She then pulled a folded-up piece of paper from her skirt pocket and straightened it out.

The room was so silent you could hear a pin drop.

Jemima looked up nervously at her audience, then back at her siblings, who all nodded their encouragement.

She gave a little cough.

'*Home is where the heart is, that's where we should be . . .*' Her voice was quiet and a little croaky.

'*Home is where the heart is, for all the world to see . . .*' Now a little louder and less croaky.

'*Families together, friends are welcome too. Home is where the heart is, for me and yes, for you . . .*' A deep breath.

'*There'll be times there will be laughter, and times there will be tears . . .*' Her big blue eyes looked up and found her oldest sister. Then she looked back down at the poem, which Bertie had written out for her in large capital letters.

'*But when we're altogether, we'll . . .*' her little face scrunched up '*. . . conquer all our fears.*' A little smile. '*Home is where the* *heart is, that's where we should be . . . Home is where the heart is, for you and yes, for me.'*

Jemima turned her head to look at Danny, Marlene, Bonnie and Bertie behind her. They all took a collective breath and recited the last few lines of the poem together.

> 'Let us stand together, let's all get along.
> We can make it happen,
> We'll show them we are strong –
> We'll show them we belong –
> Home is where the heart is!'

'Bravo!' Wilfred called out, unable to hold back.

Mrs Kwiatkowski stood up and clapped, her eyes shining with tears.

Everyone started clapping.

'That was brilliant!' Lloyd exclaimed.

'Well done!' Mrs Jones raised her hands in the air so they could see her enthusiastic applause.

Alberta was alternating between clapping and using her apron to wipe her eyes.

Suddenly, Winston and Bessie appeared, having heard the rumpus. Pushing the door open with their bulk, their wagging tails hitting furniture, they forged their way into the room. Everyone chuckled as the dogs caused chaos with their sheer size and innate clumsiness.

'Oh, Jemima.' Angie opened her arms and beckoned Jemima over for a hug. 'That was amazing. Wonderful. Thank you.' She gave her little sister a big hug and held her tight.

Jemima was beaming from ear to ear.

'I reckon Jemima and the rest of her travelling troubadours deserve a treat, don't you?' Angie looked over to Mrs Jones and Alberta.

The cook nodded. 'Oh, aye, ah think there just might well be a bit o' chocolate stashed away fer special occasions,' she said.

Jemima's eyes widened. Chocolate was still rationed and therefore seen as the best treat in the entire universe by the children. She skipped over to the cook.

Marlene put Bonnie down and watched her scamper across to join Jemima and Mrs Kwiatkowski. 'We'll be through in a minute,' she told them. The dogs followed, knowing to go where the cook went for fear of missing out on any treats.

Seeing Danny's serious face, Lloyd and Evelyn also left the room.

After everyone had gone, Danny, Marlene and Bertie looked at Angie expectantly.

Angie felt her heart drop at seeing their hopeful faces. She sat back down on the sofa. She was just about to open her mouth to speak when Danny beat her to it.

'You're *still* not going to change your mind, are you?' he said, his voice hard and angry. He knew his sister better than anyone.

'No, I'm not,' Angie said, her tone genuinely apologetic. It had filled her heart with such joy to see how they had all planned this, just as it broke her heart to let them down.

'Why?' Bertie was almost in tears.

'You know why, Bertie. Because I want us to have a fresh start. This is going to be exciting – a new chapter in all our lives,' Angie said with all the conviction she could muster.

'But we don't *want* a new start.' Marlene glowered at Angie.

'It's for the best, trust me,' Angie argued, standing up.

The three children looked at her with anger in their eyes. All three mouths were pursed shut.

As they made to leave, Marlene stopped and stared at her big sister, who was now not so big, as they were almost the same height.

'God, you're hard, Angie. You've devastated Danny by selling Ghost – I'd never have thought you could be so cruel. Don't you see how miserable he's been? And now you're dragging us to live somewhere we don't want to go! You never used to be like this!' Marlene spat the words out, before turning on her heel and stomping out of the room.

Angie stood rooted to the spot. Her sister's words stung. All the more because she knew in her heart of hearts that what Marlene had said was right.

'Well, if that's not going to change Angie's mind, I don't know what is,' Lloyd said as he walked into Mrs Jones's office. His voice expressed the despondence displayed on his face.

'I know,' Mrs Jones agreed, pouring him a cup of tea as he sat down. She thought he looked weary.

'There's been three viewings this week,' Lloyd said. 'It's just a matter of time before a buyer is found. And the way Angie is at the moment, she'll be on her way before the ink on the contracts has dried.'

Mrs Jones nodded.

'Is there anyone you can think of who might be able to at least get her to hold off for a while – someone who can convince her that she *does* belong here?' she asked. She had seen with her own eyes how Angie had fallen in love not just with Cuthford Manor, but with the beauty of her surroundings as soon as she'd moved there.

'There must be *someone* who might be able to persuade her. Make her see sense?'

Lloyd took a sip of his tea.

'Someone Angie could relate to,' Mrs Jones added. 'Someone who belongs here but is also a bit different. And someone who is not frightened of saying the truth, no matter what the reaction might be.'

Suddenly, Lloyd's face brightened.

'There just might be . . .' he said, looking up at the wall clock and checking the time.

'It's a long shot, but any port in a storm and all that.'

He reached for the phone.

'Leave it with me,' Dorothy said.

'Well, good luck,' Lloyd said. 'It's safe to say we're all feeling jolly wretched about the whole idea. I think this might be our last chance saloon. Not to put any pressure on you. But strength in numbers and all that.'

'I'll do my very best. We'll keep in touch,' Dorothy promised before hanging up.

Lighting up a cigarette, she dialled the operator.

Having spoken to Lloyd, Dorothy was even more convinced that Angie was making a huge mistake. Couldn't she see that she had a loving and caring family already around her? It might not be what was considered the norm, but all those at Cuthford Manor – apart from Evelyn – really loved and cared about Angie and the children.

Grief, she thought as a tally of clicks and beeps sounded down the phone, could make a person as blind as a bloody bat.

Hearing the voice of the British switchboard operator as she was finally put through, Dorothy exhaled smoke.

'Durham University. Which department would you like?' The receptionist spoke perfect King's English.

'Can I speak to your head of languages, please?' Dorothy requested.

'One moment . . .'

The line clicked one last time before a voice boomed down the phone, causing Dorothy to hold the receiver ever so slightly away from her ear.

'Hello! Clemmie Sinclair speaking!'

'Hello, there. I'm Dorothy Armstrong – I'm Angie Foxton-Clarke's best friend. I heard you've just returned back home after a stint in Berlin, and I wanted to chat to you about something – something very important – something I'm hoping you'll be able to help with . . .'

Chapter Twenty

The following day, Angie was feeling hopeful. She'd just had a call from the estate agent informing her that he had another couple interested in Cuthford Manor and would it be convenient for him to show them the property tomorrow? Angie would have said yes even if they'd wanted to come within the hour.

Finding herself with a little free time before the children came back from school, she headed to the study with her stack of documents. It was time to make a start on all the forms she needed to fill in to obtain their official emigration papers.

She'd just sat down when she heard a car pulling up abruptly on the gravelled driveway. Leaning over to see who was visiting, she caught a glimpse of a woman, but it was her car that drew her attention. It was a sleek, pillar-box-red, two-door sports car with a cream-coloured soft top. The distinctive grille at the front told Angie it was a Jaguar.

She heard the car door slam shut, followed by hurried footsteps on the gravel before the front doorbell rang. Angie automatically got up to answer, a lifetime's habit that she couldn't break.

Wilfred, of course, beat her to it, as he usually did, giving her his glare of disapproval for yet again trying to make him redundant.

'Ah,' he said, pulling the door open, a little out of puff. 'Miss Sinclair. Welcome!' He stood aside as Angie's visitor strode purposefully through the open doorway.

'Good to see you, Wilfred,' she said, full of gusto. 'It's been a long time.'

'It has,' Wilfred said. 'A long time indeed.'

Having been beaten to the door, Angie was standing a little self-consciously in the middle of the foyer. She looked at the short, slightly stocky woman with her mop of dark brown hair, wearing a skirt and jacket which looked more uniform than casual wear, and racked her brain as to who Miss Sinclair was. The name was familiar.

'Apologies, miss. This is Clemence Sinclair. *Miss Clemence Sinclair*. She is – was – Master Quentin's old friend.' Wilfred stumbled through the introduction. Miss Sinclair had always entered the house this way, even as a child. He knew it wasn't discourteous, merely overexuberant.

Quentin had mentioned his old childhood friend a few times over the years, and that they had both worked in the War Office. Angie remembered being told that Clemmie couldn't make it to the funeral because bad weather had grounded her flight.

'Well, at long last!' Miss Clemence Sinclair exclaimed, looking at Angie with a smile spreading across her face. Before Angie had a chance to say anything, Clemmie strode across the hall and wrapped her arms around her friend's widow in a big bear hug.

'It is so, *so* good to finally meet you, Angie,' she said, releasing her hold but keeping her hands on Angie's shoulders and inspecting her, as though a treasure to behold. 'I'm guessing you still prefer to be addressed as Angie – not Ange or Angela?'

'Yes, that's right,' Angie said, more than a little flummoxed by this strange woman's sudden appearance in her home. 'I like Angie. Hate Angela. And only my best friend calls me Ange.' Fragments of information from Quentin were drifting back into her consciousness. How Clemmie was 'quite the character' and 'bloody good at her job'. Quentin hadn't been able to tell her much about either his own job or Clemmie's due to the secret nature of their war work, but he had mentioned that Clemmie had taken a position over in Germany at the end of the war.

'Good that we've got that sorted – I'm Clemmie,' she informed. 'And like your good self, I don't like being called by my full name, Clemence . . .' she grimaced dramatically '. . . or by a shortened version of just one syllable – Clem.' She smiled. 'See, we have something in common already.'

Angie thought this was likely to be the only thing they'd have in common.

'Right.' Clemmie looked around. 'First stop – the kitchen.'

Angie didn't know whether to laugh or object to the barefaced audacity of this woman who had just barged into her home, nearly squashed the living daylights out of her and was now marching off to the kitchen. In the end, she did neither, but instead followed her husband's larger-than-life friend down the corridor.

On entering the kitchen, Angie watched the cook's face light up as Clemmie strode over and subjected her to the same robust bear hug. As the dogs scrambled to their feet and pushed their faces between the two women, Angie noticed that Alberta didn't seem all that surprised by Clemmie's visit.

'Oh, and who do we have here!' Clemmie exclaimed.

'That's Winston and Bessie,' Angie said, watching as Clemmie gave them both energetic pats. She seemed unfazed by their size, or by the fact they had manged to leave their slobber on her skirt.

'Ha! Let me guess,' Clemmie said, giving them both a good scratch behind their ears. 'It was Quentin's idea to name them after Churchill and the formidable Liverpudlian Labour politician Bessie Braddock – fearless campaigner for better health, housing and education for the poor.'

'That's right,' Angie conceded.

'Coffee and cake?' Alberta asked.

'Yes, please,' Clemmie said. 'Or *Kaffee und Kuchen*, as they say in Deutschland.'

Seeing the alarm on Angie's face, Clemmie laughed.

'I've been over in West Berlin these past four and a half years, working. Only just returned to Blighty. Got a job at the uni,' Clemmie explained. 'Modern languages department.'

She smiled as Alberta placed a pot of tea, milk and sugar on the table, and then returned with two thick slices of cake for them.

'Oh, date and walnut cake! My favourite!' Clemmie exclaimed.

Angie caught Clemmie giving Alberta a wink and was now sure that the cook had been told of Clemmie's 'surprise' visit, which only made her feel even more irked.

'There's more on t'side, if yer want.' Alberta nodded over to the cake stand. 'Right, then, I'll leave yer to it.' She smiled at Angie and headed out the back door. Angie knew she would be going to see Bill to have a smoke and a chat and see what vegetables she could plunder for the evening meal.

Through mouthfuls of cake and tea, Clemmie told Angie that she had been a regular visitor to Cuthford Manor as a child, as her father, 'God rest his soul,' had been good friends with Leonard.

'My dear father was much older than most of my friends' fathers – most people thought he was my grandfather. Anyway, that's how I got to know Quentin, and this place.' She waved an arm around. 'We remained friends, and it was thanks to Quentin that I got the job at Whitehall.'

'Yes, Quentin told me,' Angie said, her tone flat and purposely unfriendly. She supped her tea.

'Now, I'm not going to get all moribund about your husband – my friend,' Clemmie said, putting her teacup down, 'but I have to say that I honestly didn't know a gentler, kinder man. And so blummin' intelligent!'

Angie felt her heart constrict. She took another sip of her tea to swallow back her emotions.

'You know, when I was growing up, I was pretty much ostracised by all the other children because the way I looked was – ' she glanced down at herself ' – more like a boy than a girl. But not Quentin. He never treated me any differently. I loved him most of all for that.'

It was one of the traits that Angie also loved about Quentin. His total lack of judgement or any kind of prejudice. Angie could feel the tears coming. *God, this woman had railroaded her way into her home, and now thanks to her she was on the verge of crying.*

'Right, come on,' Clemmie said, fighting back her own tears, 'otherwise we'll both be blubbering and we won't be able to stop, and I know Quentin wouldn't want that. He'd be happy as Larry that I was here with you and wouldn't want us crying like a baby.' Draining her cup of tea, Clemmie put her hands on her knees, leant forward in her chair and stared at Angie intently. 'Now, what's all this nonsense I hear about you wanting to sell Cuthford Manor?'

Again, Angie felt herself stunned by this woman and her forthrightness, which bordered on rudeness. She wondered briefly if Clemmie had been some sort of interrogator during the war.

'How did you hear?' Angie asked. 'It's only just gone on the market.' *If Alberta had been given a heads-up about Clemmie's arrival, it must have been Lloyd.*

Clemmie tapped her nose. 'A little birdie.' She then sat back and took a deep, rather dramatic breath. 'Righty-ho, I'll just come straight out and say it, Angie.'

A pause.

'I think you're making a mistake. A *huge* mistake. This place is yours – you belong here.'

Angie spluttered into her tea.

'Well!' she said, aghast. 'Don't beat about the bush on my behalf!'

'Ha!' Clemmie slapped her thigh.

'I don't want to be rude,' Angie said, 'but as we've never met before, I don't think you're able to make any comment at all about what's in my best interests or where I belong.'

'Ah, but I *do* know you,' Clemmie said. 'I have got to know you by proxy – and I know for certain that this is where you belong!'

'I'm guessing that "by proxy" – ' Angie eyed Clemmie as she lifted a piece of cake to her mouth and took a big bite ' – means Quentin.'

Clemmie shook her head and swallowed hard.

'There are others,' she said, drawing an imaginary zip along her lips to show Angie that she would not divulge her sources.

'Well, you and your "by proxy" informants are wrong, Clemmie. *Very wrong.*'

'Poppycock!' Clemmie blustered. 'Sometimes those who know and love you know best.'

Angie shook her head. 'I know what I want, Clemmie. It's time for pastures new. This place is too full of memories.'

'Then make some new ones,' Clemmie retorted. 'You can't run away from memories – that's the very nature of them.'

'It's not *just* that,' Angie said, trying to hold back her vexation. 'Not that I owe you any kind of explanation, but seeing as we are being so upfront, I'm leaving because I don't *belong* here, and never will. I only ever fitted in because of Quentin and now he's gone—'

'At the risk of sounding like a Yank, what a load of baloney!' Clemmie declared. 'If Quentin's grandfather were alive now, he'd be clicking his heels you're queen of the castle.'

The mention of Leonard threw Angie.

Seeing the look of bemusement on Angie's face, Clemmie explained. 'Leonard was a liberal. As I'm sure you know. Some called him eccentric, but he was just ahead of his time, in my opinion. Leonard would be proud to see a woman in command – a woman who took on the most arduous war work and spent nine hours a day, six days a week, either operating cranes or welding ships.' Clemmie didn't try and hide her own admiration. 'Dear Leonard would have been absolutely over the moon to have you living here with the children and your dear Mrs Kwiatkowski – and his great-grandchild.'

Angie looked at Clemmie and was stuck for words.

'Just because you're not the same as some of the people who inhabit great houses like this doesn't mean you don't belong. Just because you're different, that doesn't equate to not belonging. Look at me – I'm different, but I don't feel as though I don't belong because of it. I have as much right as anyone to be here.'

'Yes, but you were born and bred here,' Angie countered.

Clemmie sighed. 'But, Angie, even if you won't agree with me that you belong here, I have to remind you that right up until Quentin passed, you loved it here. You loved everything about the place – the manor itself, the countryside. Your grief is skewering your judgement. You must not sell this place.

It's your home. The home of the children. *You simply cannot emigrate to Australia.*'

'I don't mean to be rude, Clemmie, but I really don't think you can march into my home and tell me how I should live my life,' Angie said.

Clemmie opened her mouth to argue her case, but was prevented from doing by the children bursting through the back door.

Seeing a stranger in the kitchen, they ground to a halt and stared.

'Hi there!' Clemmie greeted the children. She stood up. 'I'm Clemmie – a good friend of Quentin's. I knew him from being about – ' she pointed to Bertie ' – about your age.'

Bertie blushed at suddenly finding himself the centre of attention.

'Quentin told me all about you!' She smiled. 'All good,' she reassured them. 'So then, go on, tell me who's who!' Clemmie spoke loudly and with enthusiasm, which seemed to put the children at ease.

Angie watched as they each told Clemmie their name. She wished she'd asked Quentin more about his old work colleague.

Clemmie looked across at Angie. 'I can't tell if Bonnie looks more like Quentin or you.'

'Yes,' Angie said, her tone still showing her annoyance at this blunt and rather bossy woman. 'People used to say that Quentin and I looked alike, so that would make sense.' Which was true – Angie and Quentin had shared the same colour hair and pale, slightly freckled skin.

After dumping their school satchels and hanging up their blazers, Danny asked if Clemmie wanted to meet the horses, which she did.

'Angie sold our best horse, Ghost,' he told her when they were walking over to the barn. Clemmie caught the resentment in his voice, as well as the friction between Angie and her younger brother. Knowing the circumstances of Quentin's death, she wasn't at all surprised that Angie had not wanted the horse around, but as she listened to Danny's description of the dapple grey gelding, the love the boy had for the horse, as well as for the horse's master, came across loud and clear. As did his feeling of sadness for having lost another being he'd loved dearly.

When they returned to the kitchen, Angie had brought Mrs Kwiatkowski down from her room to say hello to Clemmie.

'Oh, how lovely to meet you, Mrs Kwiatkowski – my good friend Quentin often mentioned you to me.'

Mrs Kwiatkowski smiled and said something in Polish.

Clemmie nodded as though she understood and took a seat at the kitchen table. She looked over to the side, where the cook had left the cake. 'I'm wondering if Mrs Kwiatkowski would like a slice of Alberta's delicious date and walnut?'

Angie widened her eyes. Quentin's friend was certainly not backwards at coming forwards. 'I'm going to interpret that as meaning *you* would like another cuppa and some more cake.' Angie walked over to the Aga and put the kettle on. 'Cake all round?' The children nodded vigorously and sat down at the table.

'So, Mrs Kwiatkowski, I understand you hail from Poland – you must tell us all what it was like back then,' Clemmie said. She nodded and smiled as Mrs Kwiatkowski chatted away and they all ate cake and drank tea or lemonade.

'Can you speak Polish?' Bertie asked, slightly in awe of their unexpected visitor.

'Sometimes, dear chap, it's all about listening,' Clemmie said cryptically.

'And Quentin told me,' she said to Mrs Kwiatkowski, 'how wonderful you've been with the children, and how you nursed Jemima through the chickenpox when Angie was expecting Bonnie and couldn't go anywhere near the little mite for fear of causing problems with her pregnancy.'

Mrs Kwiatkowski nodded and they both looked at Jemima, who sat up and smiled, crumbs in the corners of her mouth.

When the cake had been devoured and the teapot was empty, Clemmie sighed. 'Righty-ho, time for me to go back to my own modest abode in Durham.' She looked at Angie. 'But I shall return, if that's okay?'

Before Angie had a chance to answer, Danny perked up. 'Is that your car out the front?'

'It is indeed,' Clemmie said, widening her eyes. 'Would you all like to come and have a look and wave me off?'

All five children nodded.

A few minutes later, they were standing around the red Jaguar roadster, which Clemmie told them was a model XK120. She had just popped the bonnet to show Danny the engine while the other children took it in turns to sit in the driver's seat, when the Bentley crunched up the driveway.

It pulled up next to Clemmie's Jaguar. After waiting for Jake to hurry round to open the Bentley's passenger door, Evelyn got out.

'Oh, *Clemence*, this is a surprise,' she said, her tone clearly indicating that it was not a particularly nice surprise.

'Hello, Evelyn. You're *still* here?' Clemmie didn't crack a smile.

Everyone fell silent and stared at the two women. You could have cut the atmosphere with a knife.

'I thought you might have gone back to York,' Clemmie said.

Evelyn stretched her mouth into a smile. 'And *I* thought you might have gone back to Berlin?' *Touché.*

'No, I'm here for good,' Clemmie said. 'There's *no* getting rid of *me*.'

Evelyn started to walk towards the house. 'Same here, my dear Clemence. Same here.'

Angie watched the exchange and felt herself start to warm a little to Quentin's childhood friend.

When Clemmie arrived back at her little cottage on Dun Cow Lane, just a stone's throw away from the city's famous cathedral, she kicked off her shoes, made herself a martini and sat down in her armchair. Picking up her phone, she dialled the operator and gave the international number she wanted to be put through to. She waited as the call went through a slew of operators before she was eventually connected.

'Hello, the *New Yorker*. Dorothy Armstrong speaking.'

'Dorothy! Hi there! It's Clemmie!'

'Clemmie! Hi! Have you been?'

'I have indeed.' Clemmie sat back and took a quick sip of her martini. 'I have just returned, having met with your "Ange", and I made the arguments as discussed and have told her in no uncertain terms that it would be a huge mistake to sell and an even bigger one to move! So fear not, I'm on the case.'

Clemmie smiled on hearing Dorothy's reply.

'I have to say,' Clemmie gushed, 'I don't think I've ever met another woman like her. Angie is quite an anomaly, don't you think?'

Dorothy agreed, at the same time feeling sure that Angie would be thinking the same about Clemmie. She was quite a character too.

'She's worked in a shipyard, now she's managing Cuthford Manor and its estate,' Clemmie continued, 'she's got five children and a Polish granny to look after, and two huge dogs that are almost as big as Lucky the pit pony. Never mind having to deal with The Wicked Witch of the West lurking about in the background.'

Dorothy laughed at the description of Evelyn.

'Your best friend is a tour de force!' Clemmie paused to take another sip of her martini. 'You know, I do believe she's more of a feminist than most of the feminists I know – and she has no idea!' Clemmie looked at her watch. 'Sorry, old gal, I've just realised this is your lunchtime. Go and get one of those American hot dogs I've heard all about. We'll stay in touch, and I'll let you know of any developments.'

Dorothy hoped their plan would work, but, as Clemmie had just said, Angie was an anomaly – and an anomaly who could also be incredibly obstinate.

After hanging up, Clemmie got up and went over to her record collection and picked out one of her favourites – *Salut d'amour* by Edward Elgar. As it crackled into life and 'Love's Greeting' filled the room, its heady mix of joyfulness laced with a slightly contradictory, mournful undercurrent moved her as it always did.

But it wasn't just the music that was affecting her and making her heart soar one moment and drop the next.

'Oh, no . . .' She sighed heavily. She'd had this feeling before – enough to recognise it immediately.

Angie was everything she'd ever wanted in a woman. She was unconventional and outspoken, but under that tough veneer there was a gentle soul. And, *so* attractive – and so unaware of how attractive she was.

Clemmie sighed again.

She could feel herself falling. And – yet again – it was with someone she was pretty sure would not be able to reciprocate her feelings.

Not in the way she wanted, anyway.

Chapter Twenty-One

Clemmie's initial attempt to persuade Angie to change her mind – to make her see that she did, in fact, belong at Cuthford Manor – might have been as earnest as the children's attempt to make her stay put, but it was just as unsuccessful.

Clemmie, however, was not one to accept failure; her determination strengthened as she was now part of a team working to keep her childhood friend's wife at the manor. And so Clemmie became a regular visitor to Cuthford Manor.

Each time she was there, as well as giving Angie support and a friendly ear, she would try to find different ways of helping her realise that this was her home. It was usually done during long walks out in the country with Angie and the dogs, when Clemmie would have the chance to enthuse about 'our green and pleasant land', which was 'beautiful and so different to the scorched earth of Australia' – and did Angie know Sydney was presently experiencing temperatures touching eighty degrees Fahrenheit?

The children were over the moon that they had a new and very forthright ally in their battle to persuade Angie to remain, although they had to concede that after a few weeks, Clemmie, like just about everyone else who had tried, was getting nowhere.

Even so, the children loved Clemmie's visits. Danny because she let him drive the Jaguar up and down the driveway, Marlene because she always brought her the latest edition of *Vogue*, Bertie because she had read all the books he had read or was reading, and Jemima and Bonnie because she would play whatever game they wanted and would also give them both piggybacks – something Quentin used to do.

In spite of her initial feelings of irritation towards her husband's old friend, Angie also found herself enjoying Clemmie's company. In many ways, she reminded her of Dorothy. Like Dor, Clemmie didn't give two hoots what anyone thought of her. She would ignore Evelyn's disparaging looks and was quick to retort to her subtly derogatory comments with something equally subtle and equally insulting. It was exactly what Dorothy would do.

With the world changing so rapidly, Angie found Clemmie's in-depth understanding of politics particularly interesting – especially the global divide that had developed between communists and capitalists, now evident in the war between North and South Korea. The Second World War might be over, but hostilities between China and the Soviet Union dominated the news.

It disturbed Angie that young British men in the regular army and those doing national service were also being called to arms to fight alongside the Americans and South Koreans. Hadn't this country suffered enough loss of life? Her heart was naturally with the wives and loved ones of the men in combat. She would never wish the kind of grief she was experiencing on anyone.

Besides their informed chats, Angie was pleased that Clemmie always insisted on seeing Mrs Kwiatkowski whenever she visited. Despite not understanding Polish, Clemmie was willing to learn and brought a dictionary on her visits, pointing to words that would prompt the old woman to chat away.

Evelyn, meanwhile, had become even more vocal, if that was possible, about how she felt Cuthford Manor should be run. Lately, she had been on about entertaining more. Her desire for more social events was disguised as a duty to raise money for some local charity or something similar. But she couldn't fool Angie.

'People in our social sphere use their properties to help the less fortunate,' Evelyn tried to explain one day when Angie had pushed back a request to hold a spring ball at the house.

'By inviting them to a ball?' Angie had asked.

'Those with money will dig deeper if they think they can come somewhere like this to enjoy themselves,' Evelyn explained, waving her arm around the drawing room to prove her point.

It was only her plans to emigrate that enabled Angie to bite her tongue and not get embroiled in an argument.

When the summer holidays started, Angie began to feel the first niggles of despondency that although the property was known throughout the county and beyond for its uniqueness and Gothic-like grandeur, and although there'd been a good few viewings, no offers had been forthcoming. The feedback she was receiving from Mr Day was that although it was undoubtedly an amazing property, and most of those who had viewed Cuthford Manor had fallen in love with it, they'd had to put their 'sensible heads' on and admit it was just too big for the needs of their families. The other drawback was the money needed for the maintenance of a place this size, coupled with how much it would cost to fix a large section of the roof on the East Wing.

The only upside was that the children's moods were improving with each passing week that Cuthford Manor remained unsold, although Danny was still talking about Ghost and was clearly still missing him terribly. It prodded Angie's guilt, but as she'd told herself numerous times before, it was done, the horse was gone and that was that. There was no turning the clock back. And yet the removal of Ghost's physical presence had not helped to erase the memory of finding Quentin in the stable that day. All the more reason why she had to get away. Away from the memories.

On the twelfth of August, which was also the start of the grouse-shooting season, Angie headed to the study to make her weekly call to the estate agents. Dialling the number she now knew by heart, she crossed her fingers that this time she'd hear some positive news. When the receptionist put her through to Mr Day, the head honcho at Durham Estates, her heart lifted when, instead of hearing the usual 'Sorry, Mrs Foxton-Clarke, but I'm afraid there are still no takers,' Mr Day asked if he could pop by for a chat. Angie agreed, hoping it was because he wanted to tell her the good news face to face.

An hour later, hearing the jangle of the front doorbell and knowing that it would be Mr Day, as arranged, Angie let

Wilfred do his job. For once. After Mr Day had been shown to the study, Angie followed polite protocol and asked the estate agent if he would like some tea – or something stronger. A Scotch or brandy, perhaps? She was surprised when he said he would appreciate a Scotch. Something told Angie it was either to celebrate or because he needed Dutch courage.

'So, Mr Day,' Angie said when the drink had arrived and they had discussed the lovely weather they had been having of late, 'I'm interested to know what you have to tell me in person rather than over the phone.' Angie guessed Mr Day to be around the same age as Lloyd, but he looked as though life had treated him more kindly; she might go as far as to say with kid gloves.

'I'm afraid, I don't come bearing good news,' Mr Day said. 'We have exhausted all possible channels in the hunt for a buyer. We've had our offices in Newcastle and York approach all their clients and put out advertisements. We've even sent the details to our London office so they could see if there were any potential buyers looking to relocate up north. But sadly, there has been nothing.'

Taking in Mr Day's words, it was now Angie's turn to feel the need for a strong drink. 'I don't understand,' she said. 'I thought you'd have people beating down your door to make an offer.'

'I'm afraid we're living in unprecedented times – certainly when it comes to the property market. More people than ever are buying houses, but they want new houses – affordable houses. And credit is being extended to those whose wages allow it. Which is good news for your average working Joe, but the downside is that homes like this are just too big, too grand – they cost too much money to buy, but more than anything, they cost too much to keep up. And as you are aware, there is the question of the roof.'

Angie didn't say anything, not wanting to admit that actually, she was not really 'aware' of the cost of maintaining the house, as she had only really paid a cursory interest in the manor's outgoings. Quentin had always taken charge of the financial side of their lives and Lloyd had taken over the responsibility of the manor's running immediately after Quentin's death. Angie knew the upkeep was a lot, but not how much.

'There are relatively few people who have the money necessary to buy and maintain a manor like this, I'm afraid.'

Mr Day took a sip of his drink as now it was time to impart the second part of the bad news, which also could not be sugar-coated.

'I've had a chat with the other partners and I think it might be a good idea to take Cuthford Manor off the market – just for the rest of the year. Once a property has been on the market for a while, it can become stigmatised.

'Our strategy,' he continued, 'would be to put Cuthford Manor back on the market in the spring – say March. That's always the best time of year to start marketing a house.'

Angie felt she couldn't breathe and got up and walked over to the window to open it. She was trapped. Trapped in her memories. Trapped in a world that would forever remind her of what she had lost. What she could never have again.

For the first time in a long time, she felt the sudden need to go out for a ride. She needed to breathe fresh air. Feel the wind on her face. To feel anything other than this suffocating sensation of being confined.

She walked over and pulled the bell cord behind the desk. She forced herself to offer up a polite smile.

'Thank you, Mr Day, for coming here and informing me of the situation.'

'I'm sorry I couldn't bring you better news,' Mr Day said, quickly finishing his whisky.

Wilfred had been eavesdropping on the conversation, having learnt the art of making it seem as though the door was closed when in fact it was ever so slightly ajar. He was presently having to hold back his elation. What he'd just heard meant that he would be in gainful employment for a while longer – something he doubted would be so with new owners.

Feeling a tap on his shoulder, he turned to see Mrs Jones scowling at him.

'She's just pulled the bell,' she hissed into his ear.

Wilfred's eyes widened. Mistress Angie rarely pulled the bell. Mrs Jones often got him to test it to make sure it still worked as it was used so infrequently.

Wilfred knocked on the study door.

'Come in, Wilfred,' Angie called.

Wilfred entered and made out he was a little out of puff, having just hurried from the servants' quarters. He still called them servants' quarters. A lifetime's habit.

'Can you see Mr Day out, please?'

Wilfred nodded and held the door wide open for the estate agent's departure.

'And, Wilfred, can you get Thomas to saddle up Starling, please. I'm taking her out for a ride. I just need to change and I'll be right there.'

While Angie was out on her ride, Wilfred regaled Mrs Jones and Alberta with the good news over a celebratory glass of brandy, which was kept at the back of the pantry for just such occasions.

'It *is* a relief,' Mrs Jones said. 'But I really do feel it for Angie. She's going to be gutted. I just hope she's not going to feel like she's trapped here.'

'She'll be all right,' Alberta said. 'She's got us watching out for her.'

'Aye,' Wilfred agreed, 'and I think this'll give her the time she needs to realise that she's making a mistake – and she *does* belong here.'

Wilfred raised his glass. Mrs Jones and the cook raised their china teacups, which also contained a good drop of cognac. 'Here's to wonderful old manor houses that are unsellable.'

'And 'ere's ta it staying that way,' Alberta added.

Mrs Jones thought about how everyone had unsuccessfully tried to 'turn' Angie. But, in the end, it was fate that had led to Angie staying put. For now, anyway.

'To fate,' Mrs Jones declared. 'May she continue to show her rule over all our lives.'

'But only if it's for the best,' Wilfred chuckled.

'Here, here!' they chorused, chinking china and glass.

Alberta looked at the clock on the wall above the Aga. It was two o'clock. 'I think I'll bake a cake for when the children get back from their trip to Durham . . .'

Angie had just returned from her ride when she saw Danny, Marlene, Bertie, Jemima and Bonnie come round the corner of the house and head across the cobbled backyard. Thomas appeared and offered to take Starling on her walk around the paddock to cool down. Normally Angie would have done so herself, but she wanted the children to hear the news about the manor from her own lips. She knew that walls had ears, and if there was one bit of joy to be had from the depressing news she'd been given by Mr Day earlier, she wanted to be the one to convey it.

Before reaching the open doorway of the kitchen, Angie could smell that the cook had been baking. Walking into the kitchen, she saw five hungry faces watching Alberta slice up what looked like a chocolate cake, which told her she'd been right – the staff knew. Anything with chocolate in it equated to a celebration.

'That smells delicious,' Angie said, eyeing Alberta with a look that said she knew exactly why she had used up the rest of the month's rations on the one cake. 'And very timely, as the children have something to celebrate.'

Five pairs of eyes immediately focused on her.

'What? What have we got to celebrate?' Danny asked, forcing himself to sound as surly as possible.

'I've got some good news,' Angie said, pulling up a chair.

'Oh God, you've got a buyer for the house!' Marlene's voice was sodden with defeat.

'Actually,' Angie said, 'quite the reverse.'

The children looked puzzled.

'I've just been told today that they can't sell the manor – and they're taking it off the market.'

'Really?' Bertie said. 'Why can't they sell it?'

Angie, always one for being honest and straight-up with them, explained the situation.

'So,' she ended, 'it looks as though we're staying put until March next year – if not longer.'

'That's fantastic news!' Danny jumped up from the table. 'I'm going to tell Thomas.'

''Ere.' Alberta put two slices of cake onto a sheet of grease-proof paper and handed it to Danny. 'Don't drop it!' she warned.

'No chance. Thanks!'

'Oh, my goodness,' Marlene said, scraping back her chair. 'This is so exciting! Can I use the phone to tell Belinda?' Belinda was Marlene's best friend at school.

'Yes, you can,' Angie allowed.

The cook was ready with a slice of cake on a plate.

'Mmm, thanks, Alberta. Looks lovely,' Marlene said with a wide smile, for once not worrying about her weight or having a twenty-inch waist.

Bertie celebrated by taking his slice of cake off to his room so he could finish his English homework, which left Jemima and Bonnie. Both were in high excitement and despite her own feelings about having to stay put, Angie's consolation prize was seeing the happiness her own entrapment had brought to others.

Angie went to find Mrs Kwiatkowski to tell her the news. On her way, she stopped off and told Lloyd. She knew he would ring Clemmie as soon as Marlene was off the phone. And that Clemmie would then ring Dorothy.

Evelyn had already heard the news from Wilfred, who received special favours for feeding Mrs Foxton-Clarke with information and gossip. She was presently celebrating with Gertrude Fontaine-Smith and a bottle of champagne in Durham's most exclusive cocktail bar, housed in the Royal Hotel.

Gertrude was still under the delusion that her son might win Angie over and become the new owner of Cuthford Manor.

Evelyn, on the other hand, was letting her mind wander as to how she could get shot of Angela and her clan and reclaim her crown as lady of the manor.

She rated her chances far, far higher than Jeremy's.

When Angie had changed out of her riding clothes and was back in the study, checking over some correspondence, she could still smell Starling on her. The ride, she mused, had done her good. She resolved to go out more often, as it had cleared her head.

She might not be able to leave Cuthford Manor behind just yet – but she hadn't given up. She *would* find a buyer. It was just going to take longer than she'd initially anticipated.

Still feeling the adrenalin of her ride out, and recalling the joy on everyone's faces on hearing the news, Angie decided she would make the most of this temporary hiccup.

Chapter Twenty-Two

The atmosphere was brighter in the days and weeks that followed. Angie enjoyed the general feeling of lightness that had returned to the manor and resolved to live with her grief as best she could – a task made all the more bearable because she could see that a weight had been lifted from everyone's shoulders. The children were obviously cock-a-hoop because they were staying in the place they loved, in an area they loved, with the animals they loved. Minus Ghost, of course.

Angie had hoped that, over time, Danny's feelings about Ghost's departure would soften – but his resentment over his beloved gelding being sent away still held fast. As did her own guilt. Angie had to admit to herself that she might have made a mistake.

Lloyd was very happy at the unexpected turn of events because it meant not only that he got to keep those he loved close by, but he could remain living under the same roof as the woman he was in love with.

And Evelyn was happy because the threat of losing the inheritance that 'should' have been hers (and Lloyd's) had been put on hold for the foreseeable future.

Clemmie, naturally, was also jubilant. With no students to lecture as it was the summer break, she'd become an almost daily visitor to Cuthford Manor, barrelling her way into the house, finding Angie for a quick chat, then going in search of the children. Marlene loved Clemmie as she allowed her to be her hair and make-up model, which always caused much hilarity and which Danny said left 'poor Clemmie' looking like a circus clown. Angie had to agree with her brother, although she would never say so. Marlene also loved nothing better than quizzing Clemmie about London, where she had worked and still visited for the occasional weekend. *Had she seen Buckingham Palace? Was Soho as wild as she'd read in the magazines?* The questions were endless.

During her visits, Clemmie would always make sure she spent time with Bertie to discuss whatever it was he was reading. Clemmie had told Angie that he was well above the average reading level for his age. 'He's reading Orwell!' she exclaimed one day. Seeing the lack of comprehension in Angie's face, she instead told her to keep encouraging him with his schoolwork.

'That's his teacher's job,' Angie huffed. 'The school gets paid enough!'

'Undoubtedly,' Clemmie said cautiously. 'But it's still good to keep an eye on him – keep him on track.' Angie was happy when Clemmie volunteered to go with her to the next parents and teachers meeting. She felt it would be helpful to have someone who knew – as Quentin had – all about maths and English and all the other subjects the children were learning. There was also a part of Angie that mischievously wanted to see the faces of the more uppity parents and teachers when she turned up to events with Clemmie, who was not one for hiding what she called her 'tomboy' nature.

'It'll certainly get the tongues wagging,' Angie chuckled.

Clemmie let out one of her characteristic guffaws of laughter.

'It will that!'

When the children went back to school, Angie breathed a sigh of relief. And as Bonnie now had no one to play with during the day, she decided to start her at the village nursery. The bonus being that it gave Angie the free time to start working out exactly how she could make Cuthford Manor attractive to potential buyers. She wanted to chat to Lloyd about getting the roof fixed, and perhaps, if their finances allowed, they could renovate the East Wing and generally spruce up the place. Give it a lick of paint. Work on the gardens to show off their beauty and colour, especially if it was to be put back on the market in March next year when everything would be starting to blossom.

Realising she needed help, Angie asked Lloyd, Evelyn and Mrs Jones to meet up for what she called a 'powwow'.

'Honestly, a "powwow",' Evelyn muttered to Lloyd as they made their way downstairs to the meeting. 'Makes it sound as though we'll all be performing some kind of tribal dance around a fire.'

Lloyd bit his tongue. Evelyn had been pushing his patience to the absolute limit of late, obsessing over finding ways they could legitimately take over the ownership of

Cuthford Manor and making out it was 'to keep it in the family, where it belonged'.

Angie was waiting in the dining room, where there was a large tray of tea and biscuits in the middle of the table. Winston and Bessie were lying sprawled out on either side of her at the head of the table. She had a notebook and pencil in front of her, and she'd placed more where Mrs Jones, Evelyn and Lloyd were to sit. Angie had wanted to invite Clemmie, but had decided against it as she knew she and Evelyn would spend the whole time sniping at each other.

When Mrs Jones bustled in, Angie noticed she had changed from her usual workwear of black skirt and white starched blouse to what Angie knew to be her best day dress, a copy of a Jacques Fath design that the village seamstress had done an excellent job of recreating. It was made from an unusual bluish-green tartan wool, and complemented Mrs Jones's figure with its high neck, long sleeves, nipped-in waist and two pleats down either side. Angie had often said to Quentin that she hoped she aged as well as their housekeeper.

Hearing Evelyn lecturing Lloyd about something or other as they approached the dining room, Angie and Mrs Jones exchanged looks.

'Oh!' Evelyn exclaimed on seeing Mrs Jones. 'Why are you here?'

Angie couldn't believe her mother-in-law's rudeness.

'Mrs Jones is here,' Angie said, 'because she has worked at Cuthford Manor since she was fourteen years old and therefore knows the place better than any of us – well, apart from Lloyd, obviously.'

Seeing the look Lloyd was giving his wife, Angie decided to charge on.

'So, as you all know,' she said, sitting up straight in her chair, 'I have not given up on selling this place, but I need to work out how to make it more attractive to potential buyers.'

'And how will you do that?' Evelyn asked, looking at the two dogs and showing her disapproval. If she had her way, they'd both be in kennels out in the yard.

'Well,' Angie gave a short laugh, 'that's why I've got you three here, to see if anyone's got any suggestions.'

'Oh,' Evelyn said, immediately losing interest. The only ideas she wanted to hear were those that would help her gain possession of Cuthford Manor. She'd be damned if she was going to help Angie sell the bloody place.

Angie got up and poured the tea. Mrs Jones was visibly uncomfortable at having her do so, but she was also wise enough to know why she'd done it. Angie wanted them all to be seen as equals.

'So, any thoughts?' Angie asked, sitting back down and taking a sip of her tea.

'Well, all I'm thinking at the moment, Angela, is that you need to be careful in your rush to sell this place,' Evelyn said.

'Why's that?' Angie asked, genuinely interested in what her cantankerous mother-in-law was going to come out with next.

'Well, you might end up selling to some nouveau riche Neanderthal who knows nothing of the manor's history and ends up demolishing it and building a load of those so-called housing estates on the plot, or worse still, prefabs. There's certainly enough acreage. And if that happened, you would be guilty of destroying a piece of British history.'

She paused. 'Did you know, there have been nearly one thousand four hundred country homes like ours demolished in the past fifty years!'

Angie noted Evelyn's use of 'ours' – no wonder she herself struggled to see Cuthford Manor as her own. It was as if this place was one of those 'collectives' that communists seemed so keen on.

'That may be so,' Lloyd butted in, 'but owners of these manorial homes have been demolishing their houses since the early sixteen hundreds.'

'That was because they wanted to rebuild something grander!' Evelyn's voice was raised. Angie prayed they wouldn't start arguing – again.

'And I have to say that our son,' Evelyn looked at Lloyd, 'would turn in his grave if this place were ever to be demolished.'

Lloyd felt his ire grow. Evelyn only ever mentioned their son when there was something to be gained from it.

'That's not going to happen. I shall make sure Cuthford Manor is sold to a family,' Angie reassured her mother-in-law. 'To someone who does not want to raze it to the ground and build a housing estate – not that I have anything against housing estates.' Angie thought of her friend Gloria, who had moved to one with her family and said she'd never been happier.

'Good,' Evelyn said.

'Actually . . .' Lloyd changed the subject, knowing that Evelyn would go on for ever now she had everyone's attention. 'This is probably a good time to talk about the manor's financial situation.' He pulled out a sheet of paper from his inside jacket pocket and spread it out in front of him.

'I've got a copy of the latest accounts and it's clear that we need to do something to bring money in, otherwise it will be *this* manor that falls into disrepair.'

'Why didn't you say anything about this before now?' Evelyn demanded.

'Because, Evelyn, I've only just had a chance to go through the accounts myself.'

An uncomfortable silence fell over the room.

'Shall I make us some more tea?' Mrs Jones asked.

'No, Cora,' Lloyd said. 'You're here as an important part of this "powwow".' He turned his head and glared at Evelyn. 'If we need more tea, we can ask one of the maids to bring us a tray.'

Hearing his tone of voice, Winston and Bessie both immediately got up and positioned themselves so that they were standing close to Angie. Their ears had pricked up and their heads were tilting slightly to one side. Angie gave them a reassuring pat and pointed her finger to the floor to tell them to settle, she did not need protecting – although she thought Lloyd might, judging by the way Evelyn was glowering at him.

'I'm afraid, Angie, as you've had to pay such steep death duties there's not an awful lot left in the pot.'

'I should have been more involved in the finances,' Angie reprimanded herself, frustrated at having left the fiscal housekeeping to Quentin. And then to his father.

'No, my dear, business and finance are a man's domain,' Evelyn retorted.

This annoyed Angie further still, because she had been guilty of this way of thinking herself – and only now did she realise just how wrong that was.

'So,' Lloyd quickly continued, seeing Angie's growing irritation, 'I think our problem is not so much about making Cuthford Manor a more attractive property to sell, it's about us being able to pay for the upkeep moving forward.'

Angie sat back and listened as Lloyd explained in more detail about the income and outgoings and gave what he called a 'trajectory' of the next financial year, which did not look at all good.

She felt her mood plummet. What had begun as a constructive meeting had quickly turned into a conversation to work out how they were going to prevent themselves from slowly drowning in debt while living in a house that would gradually become run-down and dilapidated if more money could not be found.

When Mrs Jones, Evelyn and Lloyd left, Angie put her head in her hands in despair.

God, her life just seemed to trail from one disaster to the next.

She'd lost her husband and had felt as though she had also lost part of herself.

Money was the one security she thought she had, enabling her to give her siblings and her daughter a good life and a good education.

Now not only did it seem nigh on impossible to sell the place, it also looked as though it would be nigh on impossible to keep it up and running if they didn't take action.

But how were they going to bring in the kind of money Lloyd had said they needed to stop Cuthford Manor from becoming derelict – to stop her and the children from becoming destitute?

Selling the manor was now the least of her worries.

She had to ditch her plans to emigrate to the other side of the world.

Now she had no choice but to simply focus on her fight for survival.

Chapter Twenty-Three

Every day over the next couple of weeks, Angie would walk the children to the village, wave them off on the school bus and then take Bonnie to the nursery before hurrying the half mile back home to meet with Lloyd in the study. It was the start of her education on how Cuthford Manor ran financially. For someone who had left school at fourteen and had never had any need to be particularly good at maths, other than to make sure her wages equalled the number of hours she'd worked, it was tough going. But Angie was determined. Everything was new to her. There were outgoings on taxes, heating, wages, general repairs, food and fuel, plus the upkeep of the Bentley, the other vehicles and the horses. It was certainly a steep learning curve.

Angie had asked the maids to help her convert the back parlour room into a 'proper office'. The study was small compared to other rooms in the manor and there was only one desk. They needed a bigger room with two desks and a table where they could put the tea tray and sandwiches Mrs Jones brought them.

Evelyn observed all this from afar, thankful that something was being done to keep the roof over their heads while she worked on her own solution as to how to make Cuthford Manor hers.

The more Lloyd saw how hard Angie was working – and how supportive Clemmie, Mrs Jones and the rest of the staff were being – the more he avoided Evelyn, who clearly did not think she should help and believed doing so was beneath her.

Since their son's death, Lloyd had taken off the blinkers he had worn for many years when it came to his wife. He no longer dodged the truth that the woman he had married was totally self-centred, caring about no one but herself.

'I've come to realise I've never really known Evelyn – nor what goes on in that head of hers,' Lloyd confided in Mrs Jones. In darker moments, he wondered if his wife had ever really cared about him or their son. If she was even capable of care or love.

And just as he felt the need to be honest with himself about Evelyn – he also had to be honest with himself *about himself* and his own motivations for marrying her.

His mind kept going back to his youth, and how devastated he'd been on hearing Cora was to marry the local blacksmith. He'd gone to London to escape, and it had been there that he'd met Evelyn at a party. She had been the belle of the ball. Perfect. And despite the amorous advances of some very eligible and very handsome young men, it appeared that she only had eyes for him. It had been a huge confidence boost. And they'd got on well. They were interested in the same subjects, had the same sense of humour. And there was an obvious attraction there. They'd had a whirlwind romance, got engaged within just two months and were married eight months later.

Only now could he understand, or admit, that their relationship had been founded on need rather than love. He'd needed Evelyn – needed the illusion that he had fallen in love with her and was over Cora. Evelyn, meanwhile, had needed a rich husband and a grand estate. But when they arrived back at the manor after their honeymoon, Lloyd had been sick to the stomach to hear that Cora had been widowed. How could he have been so impetuous?

He'd not been able to stop thinking about Cora, about those early days of playing tag with the other children from the village, and about when they were older and Cora came to work at the manor – when he'd realised he was in love with her and they'd begun a courtship of kinds, spending time together and going for long walks out in the country.

Following the news of Cora's husband's death, all of the feelings Lloyd had pushed down came rushing back. After just a few months, he decided he would tell Evelyn that he'd made a massive mistake – that he was in love with another woman. But he kept putting it off. Evelyn was so happy. Married life suited her. As did living here in Cuthford Manor.

But just when he'd resolved it was time – that he *had* to tell Evelyn, there was no more putting it off – Evelyn announced that she was pregnant.

And that was that.

And so Lloyd had once again forced himself to switch off his feelings for Cora. He would have to live with his mistake. When his father asked Cora to return to her role of housekeeper after she'd been widowed and she agreed to do so, Lloyd did not think he could bear it. To be so near the person he desperately wanted would surely be torture. But he'd been surprised, after a while, that it actually made him happy. They had always been close friends – and that friendship continued.

He'd felt guilty, of course, for harbouring feelings for Cora – a guilt compounded by Evelyn being the perfect wife. It wasn't until his father died that he saw a crack in what he now knew to be her carefully crafted veneer. Anger at his father's will was understandable, but what he saw in his wife was pure venom. The way she slated his father for his actions. It was the first time he had seen this darker, nastier side, just as it was also, he realised, the first time his wife had not got what she wanted. He'd never said no to her about anything. If she asked for something, he bought it for her. He allowed her free rein with Cuthford Manor. And with how they brought up Quentin. This was the first time she hadn't got something she wanted. And by God, did she want Cuthford Manor.

Evelyn had calmed down in the weeks following her father-in-law's death once she realised that she was still in charge of the manor, probably more so as she no longer had Leonard to contend with. But having borne witness to this vitriolic side of her personality, Lloyd started to see an outline of the real Evelyn.

He only saw the complete picture when their son announced his intention of making the manor home for him and his new wife.

Lloyd had only survived the four years of living in York after Quentin and his new family moved into Cuthford Manor because he'd made frequent trips back – many on his own. Many without Evelyn's knowledge.

By this time, any guilt he'd had about his feelings for Cora had completely disappeared.

Evelyn, he realised, was a master manipulator, driven by her own wants and needs.

And the more he realised what kind of a woman Evelyn was, the more he gravitated towards Cora.

Chapter Twenty-Four

October

Walking into the village with Bonnie, Angie thought about Clemmie and how like Dorothy she was – full of life and chatter. She'd become a real friend and a huge support, helping her with the children, and Mrs Kwiatkowski, who she was now in the habit of taking out for a walk at teatime, thus preventing her from going on one of her walkabouts alone.

Reaching the village hall, Angie saw the 'nursery mams' gathered round, chatting animatedly. Their expressions were serious.

'Off you go, sweetie. I'll pick you up later,' Angie told Bonnie, crouching down to give her daughter a hug and a kiss on the cheek. She watched her scamper through the main entrance.

She walked over to the women she always made an effort to talk to, even though they still seemed rather strained with her. 'Morning, everyone,' she said, rubbing her hands together. The temperature had dropped these past few days.

'All reet there, Mrs Foxton-Clarke,' one of the mams said. Angie could never quite work out if the accent in these parts was more Geordie or Yorkshire.

'Hi, Angie,' said Rebecca, who had twin boys at the nursery. Angie was eternally grateful that Rebecca always called her by her first name. She had repeatedly asked the women to do the same, but most of them seemed unable. Dorothy had told her to persevere, that they would accept her, despite her position. But it would take time.

Moving aside to let Angie into their gaggle, Rebecca looked at Hilda, who seemed to be the one doing most of the talking. 'Tell her, Hilda – tell Angie what yer've heard.'

Angie looked expectantly at Hilda, who was a little older than most of them and, perhaps because of that, seemed more of a head teacher, or rather, head mother.

'All reet,' she conceded, 'but this dinnit come from me, okay?'

'Yes, of course,' Angie assured her, now more intrigued than ever.

'Well,' Hilda began, her tone sombre, 'I've heard from a very reliable source that next year the county council in their great wisdom are gonna make Cuthford what is knarn as a "Category D" village.'

Angie had no idea what this was.

'D for dunce,' one of the mums explained, seeing Angie's puzzled look.

'D for dead end,' another chipped in.

'D for destroy,' said Rebecca.

'Aye,' Hilda agreed, 'I think the D stands fer all those things. The council have graded the villages in the county from A to D – A being those they see as the most prosperous, with D the ones they see as the least prosperous. And we've been given a D.' She looked at Angie. 'Durham County Council are gonna "initiate" a plan early next year whereby they'll no longer invest in Cat D villages.'

Angie's eyes widened, her mind clicking into gear. This wasn't some inconsequential village gossip. This was serious.

'Which means,' Rebecca said, 'if they're not gonna invest, this place will gan to rack 'n ruin.'

'And Cuthford has definitely been named one of these Category D villages?' Angie asked, now looking as worried as the other women.

Hilda nodded.

'Oh my goodness,' Angie said, visibly shocked.

One of the mams mumbled something Angie didn't catch.

Rebecca turned on the woman. 'Jill, that's not fair. Cuthford Manor will be affected too.' She wrapped her coat around herself. 'I dinnit knar about you lot, but I'm parched – let's gan 'n have a cuppa at the café.'

Everyone agreed and five minutes later they had taken over the small tea shop owned by a middle-aged woman called Nora. Angie felt the familiar lurch in her stomach when she realised that the last time she'd been in the little café was with Quentin. It had been a day like today – cold, with a bitter wind – and they'd treated themselves to a big pot of tea and one of Nora's home-made mince pies, which always reminded Angie of the pies she and her workmates had practically lived off when they were at Thompson's.

Angie forced herself into the here and now. This was the first time she'd had a cuppa with the mams from the nursery. She guessed they came here often after they'd dropped off their little ones. Needless to say, they had never invited Angie. This, however, was the least of her worries and she listened intently while Hilda told them everything she knew – and the women speculated on the consequences.

'Just so I understand this right,' Angie said, 'the council aren't going to invest in villages where they think the population is going to drop.'

Hilda nodded.

'And they reckon the population of these villages is going to drop because of the mines – or rather the lack of?'

'Yes, most of the small mines in the area have closed down as they're no longer making money – or they've worked the coal.'

'And it's rumoured that another seven are gonna close next year,' Jill added.

'Blimey,' Angie said, genuinely shocked.

'So,' Hilda continued, 'those in the council have decided that when existing houses become uninhabitable, families should be rehoused elsewhere. In other words, they're just gonna let villages like ours slowly deteriorate 'n become derelict.'

'The buggers are gonna strangle us financially, until our village withers 'n dies.' Jill spat out the words.

Angie thought again of Cuthford Manor and how this would also be its future if it continued to be starved of cash.

The women chatted on, full of outrage and condemnation of the council's plan, as well as mourning for the slow diminution of the local mining industry. The future did not look good for anyone.

*

As soon as Angie got back to the manor, she flung off her coat and headed straight for the newly converted office. She was surprised to see Lloyd pouring himself a Scotch. She raised her eyebrows.

'Oh, don't worry, just another marital spat,' he explained.

Angie sat down. It seemed as though everything was falling apart: the manor, literally; the village, economically; and her mother- and father-in-law's marriage. Although perhaps the latter was not such a bad thing.

'I think you'll be having another when I tell you what I've just heard,' Angie said, her tone full of doom and gloom.

By lunchtime, Angie had exhausted herself and Lloyd discussing how they could possibly survive this latest blow, as well as lamenting the fate of Cuthford and the other one hundred and thirteen villages that had been given Category D status. Lloyd had been incensed when Angie had told him and had snatched up the phone and asked the operator to put him through to the council's chief executive, who, he told her while he was waiting to be connected, was an old school friend.

Angie had watched as Lloyd listened with growing fury to what he was hearing.

'The village has been in existence since AD 600!' Lloyd had said, raking his fingers through his greying hair. 'Dear God, it was in the Boldon Book!'

Angie had no idea what the Boldon Book was, but knew it must be important.

'Well, I have to say, Charles, I think you're making a terrible mistake!' were Lloyd's final words before slamming down the receiver.

When Angie went to pick up Bonnie from the nursery, she and the other mams chatted some more. None of them could understand why Cuthford was on the D list, as, unlike the rest of the villages, it had never had its own pit. It had always been a farming village, and so economically hadn't suffered as badly as others from the gradual closure of the local mines. Hilary was set on petitioning the council when the D list was made public, but the other women didn't think that would do much good.

Walking back home, Angie could empathise with Lloyd and the women – and everyone else who had lived here all their lives. It was totally unjust. How awful and upsetting to be faced with the prospect of their village gradually disappearing. But Angie was also thinking about herself – how fate seemed determined to keep her here. The council's plan would be announced at around the time Cuthford Manor would be going back on the open market. Who was going to buy a home in a village that was going to be financially choked to death by the powers that be?

Even if she became so desperate that she had to consider selling the house to developers, that too would be highly unlikely to happen. No developer in their right mind would buy land where the council had ruled they would not grant permission to build housing.

When Danny, Marlene, Bertie and Jemima returned from school, they didn't hang around in the kitchen as they usually did. Danny wanted to catch the rest of the light and take Starling out for a quick ride; Marlene said she had homework to do, which meant she wanted to sit in her room, play records and try styling her hair to look like some Hollywood starlet; Bertie had homework too, which he did, and would actually do; and Jemima wanted to play with Bonnie in the music room.

Mrs Jones was in her little office with Alberta, trying to work out ways of saving money on the cooking and housekeeping.

Clemmie had told Angie that she wouldn't drive over, but would instead pay a visit to a few 'old chums' to find out more about the council's list of Cat D villages, and if there was any way of getting Cuthford taken off it. 'Which means I won't be over to take Mrs Kwiatkowski out for her teatime walk,' she said.

'Don't worry, I'll take her,' Angie said, and rang off.

Her mind swinging back to the problem at hand, Angie decided to walk around the entire manor in the hope that inspiration might strike and she would suddenly be hit by a brilliant idea that would have people queuing up to buy 'a manor that had aspirations of being a castle'. Quentin's description of Cuthford Manor had stayed with her since her first day here. She had liked it, as it had made the place seem almost like a living being that wanted to be more than it was.

Now it felt like a living being that would not let her go. And had somehow conspired with to keep her here – even if the place crumbled around her ears.

At five o'clock, Mrs Kwiatkowski wandered into the kitchen and was surprised to see it was empty – even the dogs weren't in front of the Aga – which must have been a first.

Looking up at the wall clock above the cooker, she saw it was time.

She walked across the kitchen in her carpet slippers, wrapping her cardigan around her wiry frame, and opened the back door.

When she stepped out into the yard, she was no longer in the north-east of England, but in her home town of Pułtusk in the north-east of Poland. And it was time for her to go and meet her husband, Janusz, on his way back from work.

She did love to see his face when he spotted her.

Chapter Twenty-Five

Hearing the chink of the plates being set in the dining room, Angie froze.

When she heard the first chime of the grandfather clock, she looked at her watch.

It was seven o'clock.

She felt as though she'd been punched in the stomach. She'd completely forgotten that Clemmie wasn't taking Mrs Kwiatkowski out for her five o'clock walk.

Please, please, please let someone have stopped her.

Angie ran to the East Wing to see if Mrs Kwiatkowski was in her room. She would usually come back from her walk and sit there, knitting, until it was time for dinner. Angie could feel her heart thumping in her ears as she ran. *Alberta would have been in the kitchen and stopped her, wouldn't she? Or the children. There was always someone about—*

As soon as Angie reached Mrs Kwiatkowski's bedroom, she flung open the door.

No, no, no!

Sprinting down the long corridor, she shouted out Mrs Kwiatkowski's name, and continued shouting it as she checked the sitting room and the dining room. Empty.

Running to the kitchen, she found it empty too. There was no one there – *not even Winston and Bessie.*

Hearing the latch on the back door rattle, she turned and stared at the oak door. It hadn't been shut properly.

And that was when the panic really set in.

'No! Please God! No!'

She ran out the back and stood in the middle of the yard, scanning the area for movement, hoping against hope that by some miraculous chance, Mrs Kwiatkowski had only just left the house.

Suddenly, she caught movement out of the corner of her eye. Her head snapped round.

Damn! It was only Thomas.

'Mrs Kwiatkowski's missing!' she shouted across. Only then did she see that Winston and Bessie were with him. Both dogs came charging over.

'Take the dogs,' she said. 'Check every nook and cranny in case she's holed up somewhere.' She knew it was unlikely, as Mrs Kwiatkowski always seemed as though she had a purpose when she went on her walkabouts, but it was worth a try.

Bending down to both dogs, who had sensed their mistress's distress, she cupped her hands around Winston's head. 'Go find Mrs Kwiatkowski!' she commanded, with the stress on 'Go find'. She did the same with Bessie. It was a game they had played since they were pups, and although they might not know exactly what or who they were looking for, they knew they were searching for something – and that if they found it, there'd be a reward.

Thomas whistled and the dogs charged over to him.

Angie heard Thomas calling out Mrs Kwiatkowski's name as she herself hurried back to the house. Stepping into the kitchen, she saw that Alberta was now there, checking on the shepherd's pie she had made for their evening meal. The children were sitting around the table, chatting.

'Mrs Kwiatkowski's gone missing!' Angie declared. 'Go and check all the rooms – just in case.'

Danny was the first up. 'You two do the East Wing,' he told Jemima and Bertie. 'You do the West Wing – ' he looked over to Marlene ' – and I'll do the ground floor. Meet back in the hallway after.'

Alberta took off her apron. 'I'll go 'n tell Missus Jones.' She put her hand out to Bonnie, who took it, sensing this was no time to argue about being allowed to go with her aunties and uncles.

Angie ran to the study, knowing Lloyd usually stayed there until he was called for dinner.

'Mrs Kwiatkowski . . .' Angie said breathlessly. 'She's gone walkabouts!'

Lloyd got up and hurried over to her. 'Okay, get your breath back. Breathe,' he commanded, putting his hands on her shoulders.

Angie did as she was told and inhaled deeply, then exhaled.

'You've checked inside and outside?' Lloyd asked.

'Thomas is checking the grounds – the children have split up and are checking the house.'

Lloyd looked out of the window – it was now pitch-black. If Mrs Kwiatkowski had gone AWOL and had made it further than the perimeter of the estate, it was going to be like looking for a needle in a haystack.

Reading his thoughts, Angie panicked even more. 'It's dark and it's bitterly cold out there – she'll not survive for long, and there's nothing to her. Oh God, this is all my fault. I forgot – forgot Clemmie wasn't coming over . . .'

Ignoring Angie's self-recriminations, Lloyd stood for a moment.

'Let's think,' he mumbled. 'Work out the best way of finding her.'

They heard footsteps in the hallway, then more coming down the stairs. Looking through the doorway, they saw Danny first, then Marlene, Bertie and Jemima arriving at the bottom of the wide, sweeping staircase.

'She's not here,' Danny said, looking from Angie to Lloyd.

Wilfred appeared, looking a little dishevelled. He'd just got wind of what was happening.

'We need to get a search party organised, and quickly,' Lloyd said. 'Angie, you take the Austin and check all the main roads and any of the minor roads you can get down. Take Danny with you – an extra pair of eyes.'

Spotting Thomas with the dogs out the front, Lloyd looked at Wilfred. 'Let them in.'

Winston and Bessie came bounding in first, their claws scratching and skidding on the tiled floor. Thomas stood in the entrance, his face flushed with exertion and cold. He shook his head dejectedly.

'Nowt,' he said simply.

'Keep looking,' Lloyd commanded. 'I'm going to make some phone calls. I know someone who can help, who knows the area well. Then I'll head into the village and rally the troops.'

He looked at Angie and Danny. 'You two, go!' *God help his daughter-in-law if the worst happened. He didn't know if she would be able to deal with another death.*

Heading out the front door with Danny, Angie turned back and shouted at Lloyd.

'Ring Clemmie! She's got a car – and she knows the area.'

As Angie and her brother hurried out to the Austin, she heard Lloyd telling Wilfred to put every light in the house on and get as many fires going as possible. A good idea. If Mrs Kwiatkowski was trying to get back, she might see the lights and the smoke coming out the chimneys.

As she crunched the car into gear, a few blobs of rain started to splatter the windscreen. Angie cursed.

'Great! That's all we need.' She spat out the words while turning on the wipers.

'I think we should head north to Pittington,' Danny suggested. 'We can stop every quarter of a mile and look for her. It's mainly farmland, so with any luck she will have taken the road.'

'I wouldn't bet on it,' Angie mumbled. She'd seen Mrs Kwiatkowski on one of her walkabouts and it was like she was in a trance – walking in a straight line to wherever it was she thought she was going.

In her rear-view mirror, Angie saw the lights of the manor go on, one after the other. Wilfred must have got the children to help out, as there was no way he was that quick on his feet. *God, if anything happened to Mrs Kwiatkowski, the children would be devastated.*

Looking up at the sky, Angie berated the waning moon. *Typical.* A full moon would have improved their chances of picking out Mrs Kwiatkowski in the dark.

God, she hated this place. If they'd been back in civilisation, Mrs Kwiatkowski probably wouldn't have got to the end of the street without someone stopping her and bringing her home.

Lloyd asked Bertie to find Jake and tell him to get the Bentley ready. He'd have preferred to take the Morris Minor, but it was low on petrol. Failing to get through to the person he knew could be a good scout, he rang Clemmie, who said she'd go straight to where she usually walked with Mrs Kwiatkowski. After that, Lloyd called Jeremy Fontaine-Smith, who told him he'd take the Land Rover. If they had to go off-road, it would cope with the rough terrain. Jeremy hoped that if he was the hero who found the old woman, it might change Angie's view of him.

Evelyn came down from the West Wing to find out what the commotion was. Lloyd told her that Mrs Kwiatkowski had gone missing and asked if she could man the phone – ring anyone she knew who might be able to help with the search.

Evelyn said, 'Of course,' but it irritated Lloyd that she hadn't shown much concern. If anything, she seemed annoyed. She was dressed up to the nines, which meant she'd obviously planned an evening out.

When the Bentley pulled up at the front door, Lloyd hurried outside and jumped in. Their first stop was the village pub, the Farmer's Arms. Within minutes of their arriving, a search party was organised and the licensee, Donald Grey, started to ring all the other pubs in the vicinity to tell them that an elderly woman had gone missing.

After that, Lloyd told Jake to drive to Coxhoe Hall. 'There's a bloke there who knows the area better than most. As does his horse.'

It didn't take long for the countryside within a one-mile radius of Cuthford Manor to become speckled with bobbing orbs of light from those walking with torches and with vehicle headlights on full beam as people patrolled the country roads. There were whistles and shouts into the darkness of 'Mrs K – are you there!' The talk amongst those out searching was that the dropping temperatures would not do the old woman any favours. There was speculation that she'd become exhausted and would hunker down somewhere. It wouldn't take long for hypothermia to set in with someone so old.

All of this also went through Angie's mind. Repeatedly. And with each minute that passed, she became more and more fraught.

'If she's been out in the cold all this time . . .' she worried.

Danny didn't say anything. He had been thinking the same.

As they drove around, stopping every now and again for Danny to jump out and shine the torch across the dark landscape, they debated just how far she could have walked in the time she'd been missing. Danny would look at the map kept in the car's glove compartment and see if there were any areas they hadn't checked before going back to where they had started looking. Passing through the village of Hilton, he wound down his window. 'Any sightings?' he shouted out to an old man who was sitting outside the pub, watching and waiting for news.

'Sorry, lad,' came the reply. 'They'll keep looking till they find her.'

Every village they drove through, they stopped at the local pub or social club to ask if anyone had found 'the old Polish woman', which was how Mrs Kwiatkowski was now known. Each time, they had the same response. No. But they would keep looking until they did.

After they'd driven through the pit village of Littletown, Danny looked at the dashboard. And at the petrol gauge.

'We're almost out of fuel,' he said.

'Damn!' Angie swerved over to the side of the road and braked hard, causing the tyres to skid on the wet country road. She turned off the engine and with her clenched fist started bashing the steering wheel in frustration.

'This is not happening!' she shouted, tears welling up in her tired, bloodshot eyes. 'This is all my fault!' she said, before the anger and self-recrimination dissolved into heaving sobs.

Danny looked at his sister, his resentment about her selling Ghost forgotten – for now, at least. 'This isn't your fault, Angie. You can't save everyone all the time. It was bad luck there was no one there when Mrs K left.' His words fell on deaf ears, though, as Angie cried gut-wrenching tears, gripping the steering wheel so tightly her knuckles went white.

Eventually, he put his hand on her arm. 'Let's go back to the manor,' he said. 'We've just got enough petrol – and you never know, Mrs K might be there. Someone might have found her.'

Angie released her grip on the steering wheel, wiped her nose and dried her eyes with the cuff of her wool jumper. She turned to her younger brother, who suddenly didn't seem that much younger any more, and nodded.

Many of those out searching on foot were now also heading home, chilled to the bone and exhausted after trudging through fields, their shoes heavy with mud made worse by the light rainfall.

Like Angie, the handful of searchers who had been driving around in their trucks, cars or motorbikes were having to limp back with tanks nearly empty of fuel. Their sacrifice for someone they hadn't even met was particularly great as petrol was still rationed, and the vehicles out looking for Mrs Kwiatkowski were needed for work.

Back at Cuthford Manor, everyone had been out with torches, walking around the grounds, hoping that Mrs Kwiatkowski might have seen the lights and the smoke billowing from the chimneys and headed back home. Alberta was keeping everyone stoked up with hot Bovril and cups of tea. She had tried to get them to eat some shepherd's pie to keep their strength up, but they'd refused.

'We'll 'ave it when we've found 'er,' Thomas had said.

Marlene had agreed.

Wilfred had taken up his post on the second floor with a pair of binoculars, his old eyes straining, hoping, willing the image of Mrs Kwiatkowski to come into view.

He'd been joined by Jemima and Bonnie after Mrs Jones had told them they had to come in from the cold.

At nine o'clock, Alberta sighed and sat down with a cup of tea. There was no way the old woman would survive being out in the elements for this long.

Chapter Twenty-Six

Seeing the headlights of the Austin at the top of the driveway, Wilfred, Jemima and Bonnie hurried down the stairs, hoping against hope that Mrs Kwiatkowski was being returned to them.

Wilfred pulled open the heavy oak front door, and the old man and the two young children scrutinised the car as it pulled up. Seeing that there were just two figures in the car – a very sombre Angie and a desolate-looking Danny – all hopes were dashed.

Sister and brother stayed in the car for a moment – neither speaking. What was there to say?

Eventually, Danny opened the passenger door.

'Come on, sis,' he coaxed.

Angie hauled herself out of the driver's side and slammed the door.

'Any news?' she called out as she trooped towards the house.

Wilfred shook his head.

'Afraid not.'

And with those words, any last vestiges of hope left Angie. It was now past nine – if Mrs Kwiatkowski had gone out at five o'clock, as she was wont to do, she'd have been walking in the freezing cold, probably with just her cardigan for warmth, for *four* hours.

Angie walked through the door, followed by an equally crestfallen Danny, and slumped against the high-backed, wood bench. Guilt and self-recrimination sluiced through her body. As she started to pull off her muddy boots, Bonnie toddled over to her and put her arms around Angie's neck. Angie gave her daughter a hug, swallowing back tears.

Jemima walked over to Danny, her arms out, showing him that she too needed comfort, tears rolling silently down her cheeks.

'Come here,' he said, bending over and giving her a cuddle. He wanted to say something of comfort, but felt it would be wrong to feed his younger sister false hope. So, he said nothing. Just squeezed her hard.

Wilfred tried to keep his emotions in check, but it was difficult. Very difficult.

Shivering as a burst of cold wind blew through the open doorway, he gripped the polished brass knob and started to close the door, but as he did so, something caught his eye and he stopped.

Some kind of movement at the top of the driveway.

He shook his head. He'd been staring through those damned binoculars for too long. Putting it down to the shifting shadows of the trees as the wind forced the bare branches to dance to its tune, he continued to close the door on the dark, godforsaken night.

But, again, he stopped.

This time he thought he heard something. The sound of heavy footsteps on gravel. He stood transfixed, trying to make out exactly what it was.

And then he saw a patch of light grey.

'What is it, Wilfred?' Danny asked, seeing the old man squinting, a puzzled look on his face.

'I don't know,' he muttered. 'Can't quite make it out.'

Jemima let go of her brother and the two went to stand next to Wilfred.

'What are you looking at?' Angie asked, standing up and swinging Bonnie onto her hip.

She joined the others in the doorway.

'It looks like a horse . . .' Wilfred said, his brow furrowed as he stared out into the pitch-black.

'It is,' Danny confirmed, walking out of the house. 'A horse and rider.'

Angie stood, momentarily unable to move as a terrible feeling of dread seeped through her.

Forcing herself to take a deep breath, she put Bonnie down and followed Danny out onto the gravelled driveway, part of which had been illuminated by the lights from the manor.

As a dapple grey gelding appeared, Danny stopped dead in his tracks.

'Ghost? Is that you?' He strode towards the handsome but tired-looking horse.

'It *is* you!' he said, not quite believing his eyes.

Angie was caught between the shock and confusion of seeing Ghost and a sickening foreboding at what the rider might be here to tell her.

The man brought his charge to a halt and watched as the dark-haired boy patted the horse's neck and nuzzled his face. Ghost blew noisily through his nostrils, tossed his head and then rubbed his forehead against Danny's chest, almost knocking him over.

Angie was staring at the rider, trying desperately to read his face.

Her eyes flicked to Ghost. They both looked shattered. More confusion. *They must have been involved in the search.*

She suddenly felt as though everything was in slow motion as she watched the tall man dismount and walk towards her, his gait that of a soldier – or former soldier. Straight back. Head held high. Her guess was confirmed when he stopped in front of her and saluted.

'I am Stanislaw Nowak . . . Are you Mrs Angie Foxton-Clarke?' The man spoke good English, but there was still a hint of an accent.

'Yes, I'm Angie!' *He looks serious. It's bad news. Oh God, please don't let it be bad news. Please.*

'I have come with news about a woman who lives here – Mrs Magdalena Kwiatkowski.'

Angie felt Wilfred's hand on her shoulder. She put her own on top of it and squeezed.

'Yes?' she said. The word came out as a whisper, as though she dared not ask it for fear of what the answer might be.

'Don't worry,' he said immediately. 'She is fine. She is found.'

'You've found her? You've really found her?' Angie said, her tone more a plea than a question.

'Yes, she's been found,' the man reassured her, nodding at the same time.

Angie stared up at the lean, slightly weathered-looking man with cropped hair. 'And she's all right?' She looked imploringly into his eyes, seeking more reassurance.

'She is well,' the man said with a smile he hoped would convince her. 'She has come to no harm.'

'Oh, thank God!' Angie exhaled.

'That's brilliant news!' Danny turned to look at Angie.

'Yeah!' Jemima and Bonnie shouted out in unison, clapping their hands in excitement. The two ran over to Ghost and started petting him.

Stanislaw smiled at the children's joy – and at Ghost being made a fuss of. The horse had earned it.

'I'll go and tell everyone the good news,' said Wilfred.

'Yes, yes, please, Wilfred. We'll come round the back,' Angie said.

'I'll walk Ghost to the stables and give him some water and a feed,' Danny said.

'Yes, of course,' Angie said distractedly.

'Mrs K is safe! And Ghost is back!' Jemima sang the words as she and Bonnie ran ahead.

Suddenly, Angie sank down onto her haunches. She felt as though she was going to be sick.

'Are you all right?' Stanislaw asked. 'Shall I get you some water?'

'No, no, I'm fine.' She took a deep breath and stood up, her hands on her hips. 'I'm just relieved.' She forced herself to breathe – in through the nose and out through the mouth. 'And she's not unwell?'

'She appears absolutely fine,' said Stanislaw.

'So, where is she? Tell me, what happened?' Angie asked as they started to walk round to the stables.

'Mrs Kwiatkowski was taken in by the Irish Travellers up near Sherburn Hill. One of the women from the camp was coming back from the market in Durham and she saw the old woman walking across one of the fields. So she took her back to the camp.'

'Thank goodness she did.' Angie breathed a sigh of relief. She recalled Evelyn warning her about the 'wretched gypsies' during the New Year's Eve party. She'd gone on about the importance of everyone staying well away from them and how they were always up to no good. Well, thank goodness they *had* set up camp not far from here.

'So, how did you know Mrs Kwiatkowski lives here?' Angie asked as they walked down the side of the manor, passing the Tuscan-inspired terraced gardens, which were dimly illuminated by the light coming from the living-room windows.

'I am also Polish.' Stanislaw smiled. 'You pronounce her name perfectly. Like a true Pole.'

Angie nodded, thinking back to how she and Dorothy had made Mrs Kwiatkowski teach them how to say it properly. It had taken them a while and had caused their old neighbour much amusement.

'Your Mrs Kwiatkowski is quite a character, isn't she? But also a little confused, I think?'

'She is,' Angie admitted sadly.

'But she is happy,' Stanislaw said. 'She was telling me all about her life here. She loves you all very much.'

'As we do her,' Angie said, feeling a lump in her throat. Thank God Mrs Kwiatkowski was alive and well. She could feel the tears of relief and joy waiting to be unleashed. But not in front of a stranger.

When they turned the corner into the backyard, Angie saw Marlene, Bertie and Jemima crowding around Danny and Ghost. Winston and Bessie were pushing their way in between the children, trying to get in on the action. It seemed they too wanted to welcome Ghost back. Mrs Jones was watching the reunion from the kitchen doorway with Bonnie on her hip. Alberta stood next to her, a big smile on her round face as she watched the happy scene.

'I told the woman looking after Mrs Kwiatkowski that I'd find someone from her home to come and get her,' Stanislaw said.

'Of course, of course,' Angie said. 'I'll go and get her.'

Stanislaw looked a little puzzled.

'You drive?' he asked.

'Yes, of course,' Angie said. Knowing what he was thinking, she added, 'Not everyone who lives in a manor wants to be driven about by a chauffeur.'

Stanislaw nodded. If he had met this young woman in the street, he would never have guessed she owned a manor house, let alone had a car that she could drive.

'Right.' Angie clapped her hands to get everyone's attention. 'I'm going to go and get Mrs Kwiatkowski – so, Marlene, can you call Dr Wright and get him to come here so he can check her over when we get back – I want him here by the time we return.'

She turned to Danny.

'I'll get Ghost settled for the night!' he said.

Angie made to object. *Ghost was no longer theirs. She hadn't realised he had been sold to someone nearby. Strange she hadn't heard.*

'Ghost can't go back to his own stables, Angie – he's exhausted!' Danny exclaimed, looking at the man.

Stanislaw nodded his agreement. 'We have covered many miles. The horse needs to rest.'

Danny gave his sister a triumphant look.

'Okay,' she acquiesced.

'Bertie,' she commanded, making him stop in his tracks, 'look after your sister and Bonnie. They can say hello to Ghost, but then I want you all changed and ready for bed by the time I get back.'

Bertie nodded and continued to hurry after Danny, with Jemima and Bonnie hot on his heels.

Angie looked at Stanislaw. 'Will you be able to show me where the camp is?'

Chapter Twenty-Seven

After Thomas had fed the Austin a gallon of petrol, which had been put aside for emergencies like this, Angie and Stanislaw set off to collect Mrs Kwiatkowski from the Travellers' campsite, which she knew to be a couple of miles north of Cuthford.

They drove in silence for a while, Angie concentrating on the road and Stanislaw's directions. Slowly, she found herself starting to relax.

'I'm guessing you fought in the war, and that's what's brought you over here?' she asked.

'Yes, the 22nd Artillery Supply Company. The 2nd Polish Corps,' Stanislaw said proudly.

'And now you're a refugee?'

'I am,' he said, this time with resignation.

'I read a little bit about how you can't go back to your homeland because of Stalin.'

'That is right,' Stanislaw agreed.

'So, I'm guessing you work around here?' Angie asked. Out of the corner of her eye, she saw Stanislaw nod as he concentrated on their route.

'Is that why you went out looking for Mrs Kwiatkowski? Your employer asked if you'd help with the search?'

She noted a slight hesitation on his part.

'Yes, that's right,' he said, staring into the darkness. 'Turn right here – then in a few hundred yards you'll come to a dirt track.'

Angie fell silent while she concentrated on driving – and avoiding potholes.

As she parked a short walk away from the main camp, she glanced at Stanislaw.

'What made you come here to look for Mrs Kwiatkowski?' she asked.

'I've worked with a few of the Travellers over the past year. I knew they'd help when they heard an old woman was in trouble. Also, they have horses.'

Angie pulled the handbrake on and switched off the engine.

'Although I have to admit that I didn't expect her to be *here*,' said Stanislaw.

'Thank God they took her in,' said Angie. 'I can't even think of the consequences had they not.'

As soon as they got out of the car, they were accosted by three dogs, who immediately started sniffing them. Angie knew they'd be able to smell Winston and Bessie on her and put out her hand to show she was friend, not foe.

As they walked towards the camp, the dogs dancing around them and letting out the occasional bark, Angie looked ahead, fascinated. She had always wanted to see how the Travellers lived. As they neared, she could see there was a large fire, which seemed to be the focal point of their camp, and about half a dozen caravans facing the warmth. Most looked like grey boxes with covered windows and a small steel chimney coming out of the roof.

Two young children ran up to them and started chatting away. Angie could barely make out what they were saying. Their Irish accents were thick. She looked at Stanislaw, but he shrugged his shoulders to show he also had not understood. As they walked across the muddy grass, the door of one of the caravans opened and Mrs Kwiatkowski appeared. As soon as she spotted Angie, her face lit up and she started to chat away in Polish.

'She says she's very, very happy to see you,' Stanislaw translated.

Angie hurried over and wrapped her arms around Mrs Kwiatkowski. 'Eee, you gave me such a shock, you did.' She hugged her hard, only releasing her when she saw a middle-aged woman come out of the caravan. She had two plaits resting on the front of the tunic she was wearing, and her skin was leathery and heavily lined. As the woman stepped out of her caravan, she pulled on a heavy woollen coat.

Angie strode over and put out her hand. 'Thank you. Thank you so much for taking Mrs Kwiatkowski in.'

The woman eyed her suspiciously before pulling her coat tightly around her with one hand and hesitantly shaking Angie's with the other. Angie cursed herself for not bringing something to show her thanks. The woman didn't say anything, just nodded and continued to eye Angie.

Not knowing what else to say, Angie again thanked the woman. She looked around to see that she, Stanislaw and Mrs

Kwiatkowski were now the focus of attention. Other Travellers had come out of the caravans and were sitting on their steps, some with babes in arms, all staring at the three curiosities – the tall man they'd seen earlier, the small strawberry-blonde woman and the old woman they'd taken in.

'Well, we'd better get going. Get this one back home. Thanks again,' Angie said to the woman with plaits.

Guiding Mrs Kwiatkowski back to the car, Angie gave what she hoped was a friendly and thankful smile to their audience. After getting Mrs Kwiatkowski into the back seat and putting a blanket around her, Angie and Stanislaw waved their farewells and climbed into the car. Some of the children waved tentatively back; a couple of the men, wearing suits and mufflers, lifted their battered trilbies a fraction off their heads.

Glancing into the rear-view mirror as she turned the ignition and slowly pulled away, Angie saw that everyone was going back to what they'd been doing before – apart from a pregnant woman and her young son.

The flickering flames of the fire allowed Angie a glimpse of their pale, dirty faces.

But it was their sombre expressions that struck Angie the most.

And the feeling that they knew her.

Chapter Twenty-Eight

As soon as he'd spotted the headlights of the Austin driving through the main gates at the top of the long driveway, Wilfred had rung the handbell, which was kept on the marble console next to the front door, and announced – as he promised he would – the arrival of Mrs Kwiatkowski.

By the time the car had reached the manor, everyone had piled on to the front steps. The children were standing on the bottom step, with Lloyd, Evelyn, Clemmie, Mrs Jones, Wilfred and Alberta behind them.

As Mrs Kwiatkowski climbed out of the car, the children ran to greet her. She chatted away to them, putting her bony hands on the heads of the smaller ones as they wrapped their arms around her waist and hugged her. Accepting an embrace from a relieved Marlene, she was admonished for nearly leaving Marlene without a model to practise on. This made Mrs Kwiatkowski chuckle and touch her long grey hair, which definitely needed, at the very least, a comb through it. Danny stood nearby with a big smile on his face. He was now at that awkward age when he felt hugging and kissing were not the done thing.

'Right, let poor Mrs Kwiatkowski go – it's freezing out here,' Angie said, but her words were spoken with softness, her voice a little croaky after swallowing a swell of tears.

Watching Mrs Kwiatkowski walk up the steps, being greeted by all the people who loved her dearly, Angie smiled. The old woman accepted handshakes and hugs with dignity and a regal demeanour – despite looking as though she had been out in the wilds all night, which she had. Any outsider looking in, Angie mused, would assume without a shadow of a doubt that Mrs Kwiatkowski was the real lady of the manor.

Angie followed the children up the steps to the house and saw Wilfred escorting Mrs Kwiatkowski into the sitting room, where she knew Dr Wright would have been asked to wait.

'Right, why don't you all head to the kitchen? Mrs Jones and I will join you after Mrs Kwiatkowski has been checked over.' Seeing everyone's happy, relieved and also exhausted faces, Angie was suddenly struck by an incredible lightness of being. Something she had not felt since before Quentin had died.

'Danny, can you introduce Stanislaw to anyone he hasn't already met, please?'

Danny nodded. He'd do anything for the man who had brought Mrs Kwiatkowski home and Ghost back into his life.

'And, Alberta, can you feed everyone, please? Marlene will help you.' Angie looked over at her sister, who rolled her eyes.

The cook was about to object, but seeing the look on Angie's face, stopped herself. She knew why. Marlene was a lovely girl, but she could be a bit of a madam when she wanted to be.

Ten minutes later, Mrs Kwiatkowski was given a clean bill of health, but told she must rest.

When Angie opened the lounge door, she found all the children together, sitting on the stairs. They jumped up.

Marlene picked up a plate of sandwiches and a mug of hot milk from the foot of the medieval suit of armour. 'We thought Mrs K would need a little something to eat before she went to bed.'

Angie interpreted that as meaning Alberta had suggested it, and probably made it as well.

'Ah, that's very thoughtful,' she said. 'Now, why don't you say goodnight to Mrs Kwiatkowski, and I'll be down in a minute.'

Bertie looked at his brothers and sisters. 'One, two, three . . .'

'*Kochamy cię*, Mrs Kwiatkowski!' they said in unison.

Mrs Kwiatkowski's face broke into a big smile.

'*Ja też cię kocham.*'

Angie smiled, tears once again threatening. She had a feeling she knew what had been said – and who had taught them how to say it.

When Angie walked into the kitchen after seeing to Mrs Kwiatkowski, the atmosphere was celebratory – full of chatter, sweet-smelling cigar smoke and warmed-up shepherd's pie. She could not help but think of the camp. Cold, wet and muddy. The caravans were so small, there must be hardly room to turn around. Angie glanced at the cream Aga and thought of the solitary pot hanging over the Travellers' open fire. She looked at Marlene, Bertie, Jemima and Bonnie all sipping their Horlicks. They looked so clean and rosy-cheeked.

Lloyd, who was the one responsible for the smoky room and was puffing away on a Corona, was talking animatedly to Stanislaw. It was obvious the pair knew each other well, but Angie had no idea how. Clemmie was chatting to Mrs Jones at the kitchen table, and Alberta and Wilfred were in the chairs next to the cooker, where the dogs now lay flat out after all the excitement.

There was an empty oven dish and plates of crusts and crumbs on the table, telling Angie that everyone had been fed.

As soon as Bertie spotted his big sister, he shouted out, 'Angie! Angie! There was a bear – a real live bear – that fought in the war. On our side. Stanislaw knew him!'

'A bear!' Jemima shouted out.

Bonnie lifted Mr Grizzly in the air. On hearing about the soldier bear, she'd run like the clappers to her bedroom to get her own bear to show Stanislaw.

Angie looked from the children's excited, flushed faces to Stanislaw's slightly embarrassed one from having the attention drawn to him.

'Really?' Angie said, not believing a word. She'd heard of dogs and messenger pigeons being used to help the Allies, but not a bear.

'Yes, Mummy, a bear!' Bonnie told her sternly.

Angie looked at Stanislaw, who had clearly already won the children over.

'Well, you can tell me all about it tomorrow – now it's time for bed!' she ordered.

The kitchen filled with a collective moan.

Angie headed towards the back door.

'When I'm back, I don't want to see a single child still up,' she said.

'I'm not a child,' Marlene huffed.

'How old are you?' Angie asked.

'Thirteen,' Marlene mumbled.

'Point made,' Angie quipped. 'Now, off to bed! All of you!'

Walking out into the backyard, Angie saw that Danny had put Ghost back into his old stall, which hadn't been used since the day he had been sold to the horse dealer. Spotting his sister, Danny raised his arm to show her he was coming in. As he left the stall, the door clashed behind him, as was its habit, and Danny turned to give Ghost one final stroke on his grey-flecked forehead before drawing the bolt.

Angie saw the exchange of love between boy and horse.

She'd have to ask Stanislaw if he was Ghost's owner, and if not, who was. She had a feeling that Danny would not let the horse leave Cuthford Manor a second time. And she wasn't sure she wanted him to leave either. If only because she could not stand the guilt.

After Alberta had been taken back to her home in the village, and Wilfred had retired to his bedroom down the corridor from the kitchen, only Lloyd, Mrs Jones, Clemmie, Stanislaw and Angie were left sitting round the wooden table.

They were all listening intently as Stanislaw told them the reason Mrs Kwiatkowski liked to go walkabout around teatime.

'It is because this was the time she would go to meet her husband, Janusz, from work,' he explained.

'He died more than thirty years ago,' Angie said. 'It was his death – and the war between the Polish and the Russians – which made Mrs Kwiatkowski move to England.'

'Ah, that's interesting,' Stanislaw said. 'So, her mind is going way back.'

Angie nodded sadly.

'When we were chatting,' Stanislaw added, 'her mind seems to – what's the word? – *fluctuate*, that's it. It fluctuates. It seems that sometimes she knows exactly where she is and understands that she lives here with you all, and then the next moment, she is back in Poland.'

'Going to meet her Janusz,' Clemmie mused. She knew a little about the problems some old people suffered due to a decline in the brain's function – her father had suffered similarly in his dotage.

'We'll have to sort something out,' Angie said. 'Perhaps keep the back door locked. I can't handle another night like tonight.'

Everyone mumbled their agreement.

'Don't you worry, there won't be another night like tonight – we'll all make sure of it. Mrs Kwiatkowski is everyone's responsibility,' Lloyd said.

'Exactly,' Mrs Jones said. 'We all love her and want to care for her too.'

'We'll make sure there's always someone in the kitchen from four o'clock – just in case Mrs Kwiatkowski decides to go out a little earlier,' Lloyd decided.

Seeing the relief on Angie's face, everyone relaxed.

'So,' Clemmie turned her attention to Stanislaw, 'do *you* own Ghost?'

He shook his head.

'Who does then?' Angie asked, curious.

'Well . . . that's a difficult question to answer,' he said, running his hand across the top of his light brown hair and glancing nervously across to Lloyd.

Angie laughed. 'What's *difficult* about it?'

Everyone looked at Angie and then at Stanislaw.

Even the dogs shifted, as though sensing the slight tension in the air.

Lloyd coughed. 'Actually, it's me. *I'm* Ghost's owner.'

Angie looked at Lloyd, puzzled. The large shot of brandy she had sloshed into her tea was making her brain sluggish.

Now everyone was looking at Lloyd.

'I'm sorry, Angie,' Lloyd began, 'it was just that the children were so upset when you sold Ghost to that horse dealer. Danny in particular.' He took a deep breath. 'And I must admit that I was too. I could understand why you wanted Ghost gone.' He leant forward and patted her hand. 'But, well, you see, I could see how hurt Danny was – and I have to admit, when I watched Ghost leaving that day, I felt like I was losing part of Quentin all over again. Ghost gives me happy memories of Quentin – he loved that horse.'

Tears had started to well in Angie's eyes. She wanted to say something but couldn't, for fear she'd lose control and burst out crying – and she'd already done that once this evening.

'Oh, Lloyd, I wish you'd told me how you felt,' Angie said, her lower lip trembling, fighting so hard to keep herself in check.

Lloyd squeezed her hand. 'It all worked out in the end, didn't it?'

Angie gave him a weak smile and wiped away a tear that was just about to make its escape.

If she was honest, she felt a sense of relief. She had fought against the guilt of selling Ghost, but it had been hard, and the aftertaste of watching Quentin's much-loved horse being put into the back of the horsebox had not gone away.

'So, how did you get Ghost back?' Clemmie asked.

'I managed to get to the horse trader before he sold him. He was just about to take him out of the area. I don't think anyone round these parts wanted him – because of what happened.'

Everyone looked at Angie. It had been big news at the time. And the locals had long memories.

'I got the chap to take him to Coxhoe Hall, where I met Stanislaw, who'd been employed to look after the horses. I had a word with Roger, who runs the estate, and he was happy for me to rent a stable from him. It all worked out very well, actually, as Roger was just on the verge of letting Stanislaw go—'

'Not enough work,' Stanislaw interjected, fearful that they would think he had been sacked.

'Exactly,' Lloyd agreed. 'So, me paying Stanislaw to look after and exercise Ghost meant Roger could keep him on part-time.'

Angie sat back. *So that was how they knew each other.*

'Is that how Stanislaw came to be involved in the search?' Clemmie asked.

'Yes, I drove over to see Stanislaw and asked him to join the search,' Lloyd said.

Angie remembered hearing that Lloyd had got someone who knew the area 'like the back of his hand' looking for Mrs Kwiatkowski on horseback.

She glanced across at Stanislaw, who appeared embarrassed at having been caught out with his white lie.

'Looks like there's been quite a lot of subterfuge going on,' she said, looking from Lloyd to Stanislaw.

'Sorry, Angie, we didn't mean to deceive.' Lloyd offered up a sincere apology.

Angie glanced at Mrs Jones and thought she saw a shadow of guilt. Lloyd, she guessed, had confided in her. Angie thought the pair had become closer since Quentin's death. Or had they been as close before, but she just hadn't noticed?

'Well,' Stanislaw said, standing up and breaking Angie's thoughts, 'it is time for me to go. But thank you for your kind hospitality.'

Angie smiled. 'And thank you for finding our Mrs Kwiatkowski.'

Lloyd looked at Angie, surprised she was just going to let him go – with no horse and therefore no transport – to walk the five miles back to his lodging in the freezing cold.

'No, Stanislaw,' Lloyd said. 'You must stay here tonight. Not only did you bring Mrs Kwiatkowski back to us, but it's the least we can do for a former Allied soldier.' He looked expectantly at Angie.

'Yes, of course,' she agreed. *God, the brandy tea really had gone to her head.*

'Are you sure? I don't want to be any trouble,' Stanislaw checked.

'Of course we're sure,' Lloyd said, again looking to Angie for confirmation.

'Yes, of course, it's no trouble,' she said.

'Good,' said Mrs Jones. 'Stanislaw, if you can follow me, I'll show you to the guest room.'

'Good night.' Stanislaw stood up straight and gave the smallest of bows.

'Good night, Stanislaw,' they chorused, watching as their guest ducked slightly to miss hitting his head on the beam of the kitchen doorway.

Lloyd, Clemmie and Angie were quiet for a moment, the gentle snoring of Winston and Bessie the only background noise.

It was Lloyd who spoke first.

'Are you thinking what I'm thinking?' he asked Angie.

Angie looked back at him. 'I don't know what I'm thinking at the moment, Lloyd. Should I be thinking something?' *God, her head felt like it was swimming.*

Clemmie gave Angie a sympathetic look. She looked completely wiped out.

'I think Lloyd might be suggesting we keep Ghost – and we also keep our tall Polish soldier, who, I have to add, has the most interesting accent,' Clemmie said.

'That'll be because he's been living in Scotland the past few years – since he was decommissioned in '47,' Lloyd said. It was the 1947 Polish Resettlement Act that had allowed Poles like Stanislaw who'd served in the armed forces to stay and work. It had been big news, as it was the first time the government had passed a law to settle such a large number of migrants – estimated to be around 150,000.

'So, what do you think, Angie?' Clemmie asked. 'Are you going to keep Ghost?'

Angie sighed. 'I can't believe I'm saying this, but, yes, Ghost stays. I don't *want* to keep him, but I can honestly say, hand on heart, that I couldn't deal with the guilt if I didn't. Or any more downcast faces.'

'And what about the tall Pole?' Clemmie asked, enjoying her play on words and secretly wondering if she could also get him to teach her Polish. She could afford to pay him for proper lessons.

'Mmm . . .' Angie hesitated.

'It makes sense,' Lloyd said. 'He could look after Ghost, ride him twice a day, help out with the other horses – and, of course, it would be a huge bonus to have someone to help care for Mrs Kwiatkowski.'

'A live-in translator,' Clemmie chipped in.

Angie still looked undecided.

'I think we'd be foolish not to,' Lloyd pushed, feeling as if he was pulling teeth.

'Okay,' Angie said, with less enthusiasm than Lloyd would have liked.

'So that's a definite yes?' Lloyd checked.

'Yes,' Angie said. 'A definite yes.'

'Great. Let me square it with Roger, though I doubt very much it will be a problem. Like everyone at the moment, he's really having to tighten the purse strings.'

'Do you think *we* can afford it?' Angie asked, suddenly worried. 'We were just discussing whether or not we'd have to let Jake go the other day, when we were looking at where we could make cutbacks.'

'Ah, well, this is where I can help out a little. I can simply carry on paying Stanislaw out of my own pocket, like I've been doing, which means the manor will only really be paying for his board and lodging.'

'Which would be next to nothing,' Clemmie stated.

Angie didn't say anything.

'It's going to make looking after Mrs Kwiatkowski so much easier,' said Lloyd.

'And we'll actually be able to know what she's saying!' Clemmie pushed.

'Yes, you're right,' Angie said, unsure why she felt a little anxious.

Chapter Twenty-Nine

As Lloyd waited for Stanislaw to arrive for a chat about working at Cuthford Manor, he thought back to yesterday's drama – and in particular to his wife's reaction to the news that Mrs Kwiatkowski had gone missing. She had not shown any distress. Nor had she shown any real joy when Mrs Kwiatkowski had turned up safe and well. If anything, he thought he'd detected Evelyn's slight disappointment that she'd been found.

Lloyd immediately admonished himself. *His wife wasn't that heartless. Was she?*

Hearing Stanislaw walking across the hallway, Lloyd forced his mind back to the here and now. To a happier scenario.

'Morning!' he greeted Stanislaw, waving him into the study and gesturing for him to take the chair opposite.

As Stanislaw pulled back the chair and sat down, Lloyd got straight to it. 'How do you fancy coming here to work? As our live-in yard manager?'

Stanislaw's face lit up. 'I would like that very much!'

Lloyd explained that he'd spoken to Roger, who was happy to let him go with immediate effect and wished him well. He'd even offered to drop off Stanislaw's belongings, along with any wages he was still owed.

Lloyd had heard the relief in Roger's voice that his employee had found another job just in the nick of time. The house had been bought by the East Hetton Colliery Company in 1938 and had then been used to house Italian and German prisoners of war. There had been attempts to return it to its former glory, but it was a losing battle and Roger had heard it might not just be Stanislaw's job on the line, but everyone's. There had been whispers that the once glorious country mansion, like many others requisitioned during the war, would be demolished.

'Like most of the big houses around here,' Lloyd told Stanislaw, wanting to be upfront about the situation, 'it's a struggle financially, but Angie is working hard to find a way to keep this place going, and to pay for some costly repairs – namely the damn roof. It really is a case of working out how to keep a roof over our heads.' Lloyd raised his eyes to the ceiling to indicate he was speaking literally.

'I am just happy for a job,' Stanislaw said.

Lloyd knew a little of Stanislaw's background, how he had suffered his own personal tragedy at the very start of the war, and the bravery he had shown by joining the Polish Armed Forces, led by the famous commander Władysław Anders. It was why Lloyd was keen to keep Stanislaw in employment. On top of which, having got to know him while he'd been caring for Ghost at Coxhoe Hall, and having chatted with Roger, he knew Stanislaw was a hard worker who was not only good with horses, but could also turn his hand to most things.

As they discussed wages and hours, Lloyd was surprised that Angie didn't want to be there. He'd asked her, but she'd declined. She was normally so keen to be involved in everything to do with the manor. Still, after yesterday's drama, she was probably shattered.

'Right then,' Lloyd said, extending his hand to their new employee. 'I do believe we have a deal.'

The two men shook on it.

'Come on, then. Let's tell everyone the good news,' Lloyd said, pushing himself out of his chair.

The children were all in the kitchen, having just finished their breakfast, when Lloyd arrived with Stanislaw in tow. Mrs Kwiatkowski was also sitting at the table, nibbling a piece of toast with marmalade. Angie was pouring them a top-up of tea. Alberta was in the pantry, perusing the shelves for inspiration as to what to cook for dinner, humming a song she kept hearing on the wireless about 'baking a cake'. The maid had just been to tell her that Evelyn would not be having breakfast this morning, which meant she could get on with the rest of her day and not worry about whether the egg had been boiled and the bread toasted to Mrs Foxton-Clarke's exact requirements.

Winston and Bessie hauled themselves up from their spot in front of the Aga and went to greet Lloyd and Stanislaw.

'I come bearing good news!' Lloyd said, bending slightly to pat the dogs and looking at Angie, who was nursing a cup of tea, and the children, who looked in a state of high excitement. 'Actually, *two* lots of good news.'

Danny, who had already been to see Ghost before breakfast, was just on his way out again. He stopped, his heart in his mouth. *Please let them be keeping Ghost.*

'The first piece of good news,' Lloyd said turning to Stanislaw, 'is that we have a new yard manager.'

Mrs Kwiatkowski clapped her hands and said something in Polish, to which Stanislaw replied. Everyone else welcomed Stanislaw on board with words and big smiles.

'And the second lot of good news?' Marlene asked, keeping her fingers crossed for her brother.

'Do you want to tell them?' Lloyd asked Angie.

She shook her head, glancing at Stanislaw, who was smiling broadly, then looked away when he caught her eye.

'Well,' Lloyd said, enjoying being the bearer of good news, 'I know you will all be very happy – especially you, Danny – to hear that we will be keeping Ghost for good!'

The kitchen erupted in shouts and cheers. Alberta came bustling out of the pantry and stood, arms akimbo, savouring the joyful atmosphere.

Angie looked at Danny and saw his eyes were wet with emotion.

'Thanks, Angie!'

'Don't thank me,' she said, turning to look at Lloyd. 'It was all down to Ghost's secret owner.'

Danny looked puzzled.

'Come on. I'll explain later,' said Lloyd. 'Let's go and say hello to the old fella. Welcome him back properly.'

Angie stayed behind with Mrs Kwiatkowski, but watched as they all bustled out, the children firing questions at Lloyd and Stanislaw. Bonnie, Angie noted, was holding on to Mr Grizzly, who had lost favour of late but had clearly regained his position of importance since the tale of the soldier bear.

She could still hear them after the door had shut as they walked over to the stables. Danny was telling Stanislaw it was great that he was staying. There was a happiness in her brother's voice she had not heard in a long time.

'Well, Mrs Kwiatkowski,' Angie said, 'isn't this a turn-up for the books?'

The old woman nodded and replied. In Polish, naturally.

'And I will finally be able to know what you're saying to me,' she said. 'When Stanislaw isn't out working, that is.'

Angie could hear a slight hesitancy in her own voice. *Why?* She no longer had to feel bad about selling Ghost. And she would be forever thankful that Mrs Kwiatkowski had been found – on top of which, she would now be able to talk properly to her old neighbour. *There it was again.* Just thinking about having their new employee on hand to translate unsettled her. Which was ridiculous. Stanislaw seemed like a genuinely nice man. And it wasn't as though he was a total stranger. Lloyd had clearly got to know him and was a good judge of character. He would not have suggested taking Stanislaw on if he wasn't one hundred per cent sure about him – *so the last thing she should be feeling was uneasy.*

As she got up to make a fresh brew for herself and Mrs Kwiatkowski, she wished she could put her finger on what it was that was making her feel this way.

Chapter Thirty

It was clear that no one else at Cuthford Manor shared Angie's feelings about their new employee. By early afternoon, Bill had given Stanislaw a tour of the Tuscan-inspired flower gardens, his personal pride and joy; Ted and Eugene had shown him around the estate and even given him a quick lesson on how to drive the tractor, which ordinarily they were very precious about; and Thomas was clearly as pleased as punch to have someone older to take charge of the stables – especially with Ghost back. Even the maids, who were usually quite sniffy with the men who worked outdoors, had a smile and a few words of welcome for the new yard manager.

But as the day went on, Angie still didn't seem able to shake her unease. As she approached Stanislaw and Thomas, who were chatting in the stables, she heard them discussing Monty and Bomber and whether they needed more exercise now that the tractor was doing a lot of the work they normally did.

'I guess it's much quicker just to jump on the tractor and turn a key than get the horses harnessed up,' Stanislaw mused.

'If it weren't fer petrol rationing,' Thomas said, 'Mistress Angie might think o' gettin' shot.'

He blushed when he saw Angie appear in the stable doorway.

'I don't think I'd dare to get rid of any of our horses ever again,' Angie said, deadpan. 'I'd have an all-out rebellion on my hands.'

'I'm guessing you're going out for a ride?' Stanislaw asked.

Angie looked down at her jodhpurs and the black velvet riding hat she was holding. 'You guessed right.'

'Ghost or Starling?' Stanislaw asked, looking at the two horses. Both tossed their heads on hearing their names.

Thomas turned pale. His face said it all. *Did Stanislaw not know?*

Stunned at the audacity of the question, or rather the inference that she *should* ride Ghost, Angie did not give him an answer. Instead, she threw him a look more thunderous than the stormiest of winter days before heading over to Starling's stall.

When she returned from her ride, Stanislaw was sitting on Ghost, adjusting the stirrups to accommodate his long legs.

'Good ride?' he asked.

'Yes, thank you,' she said, keeping it cold and courteous.

'Oh, and just so you know,' she added, 'I don't ride Ghost – although I have a feeling you already know that – so I'd appreciate it if you didn't suggest I might like to ride the horse that killed my husband.'

Stanislaw's face went ashen. 'I'm sorry,' he said, his tone full of contrition. 'I promise you I won't. And please accept my apologies for overstepping the mark. I did not think. Sometimes I speak before thinking. It is a fault of mine.'

He then tipped his cap and looked at Angie in a way that showed her his words were genuine.

'Apology accepted,' Angie said with a taut smile.

Stanislaw urged Ghost to walk on with a gentle squeeze of his legs and a slight flick of the reins.

Angie found herself watching as Ghost obediently clip-clopped across the cobbled yard, only breaking into a trot when they reached the paddock. She knew it would be hard to have Ghost back. But she had learnt too late after selling Quentin's horse that she had merely swapped one kind of pain for another, as all it had done was bring more heartbreak and sorrow to her brother and added guilt to her grief.

Watching Stanislaw push Ghost into a canter as they approached the fence, beyond which lay hilly countryside, Angie held her breath. Man and horse seemed to blend together as they cleared the jump and galloped off.

Even when they were out of sight, Angie continued staring into the distance.

On Sunday, Lloyd rang around to thank those who had helped with the search. Angie asked to speak to a few in person to show just how much it had meant that they had all dropped everything to look for Mrs Kwiatkowski. The locals had stopped whatever they were doing to search for her, just like those in her own home town would have done if someone had gone missing. Where she lived might be very different to where she'd been born and brought up, but the sense of community was the same. And it wasn't just the villagers who had shown her this, but the wealthy families who lived nearby in the other big country houses.

That evening, they all gathered for a particularly grand Sunday dinner – the first attended by Stanislaw, who was there as Mrs Kwiatkowski's translator. Clemmie also joined them, her desire to start learning Polish overriding her dislike of being anywhere near Evelyn.

Angie had to admit to herself, it was worth enduring her own discomfort around Stanislaw to see how furious it made her mother-in-law to have 'staff' at the table, and to witness the new lease of life Stanislaw's arrival had given Mrs Kwiatkowski. The joy of being able to communicate in her mother tongue was clear to all. As was her delight in talking about her homeland.

'Mrs Kwiatkowski was just telling me,' Stanislaw said, 'that she too used to live in a very big house. Like this one.' Stanislaw looked around at the spacious dining room with its dark oak-panelled walls, and then up at the gold-leaf chandelier that emitted a warm white light, giving the room a wonderful ambience.

Everyone looked at Mrs Kwiatkowski, who was taking delicate sips of the fish bouillon. She was sitting at the head of the table, opposite Angie.

'Really?' Angie said. 'Eee, Mrs Kwiatkowski, you are a dark horse.'

Mrs Kwiatkowski's eyes glistened as she nodded. She spoke and Stanislaw translated.

'She says it was all a very long time ago. But it is true.'

'Wow!' Marlene said. It was her new word.

Evelyn was gobsmacked and didn't try to hide it. 'Oh, how fascinating!' Her voice went up an octave. 'Tell us more!'

The attention of all those at the long oval dinner table was trained on Mrs Kwiatkowski as Stanislaw translated that she had once been extremely wealthy and had lived in a house as large as Cuthford Manor but different in style. Those with money and living in such big, affluent homes had been run out of their homeland in the 1920s. Mrs Kwiatkowski, who preferred to wear cardigans and sensible shoes, and who for many years had lived in a modest one-bedroom flat in Sunderland, had once been akin to Polish nobility.

Somehow, Angie was not so surprised. She and Dorothy had always thought there was something effortlessly elegant about their old neighbour.

After dinner, Angie and Clemmie went to sit in the lounge. Angie was glad of Clemmie's company, for Dorothy was away on holiday in some place on Long Island where 'you can eat your body weight in lobster'. Dorothy would always be Angie's *best* friend, but Clemmie was fast becoming a close friend whom she could talk to and confide in, including about the rollercoaster of the past few days.

'Did you see Evelyn's reaction?' Clemmie said, referring to the moment Mrs Kwiatkowski's aristocratic roots had been revealed. 'God, that was priceless. If I didn't despise the woman so much, I would be inclined to say it was almost comical.

'But enough about that,' she continued, producing a cigar from her inside pocket and lighting up. 'How are you dealing with the new *male* addition to the household?' The way she asked the question implied she already knew the answer.

Angie shuffled a little uncomfortably in her chair. Sometimes Clemmie was so like Dorothy. Not just straight-talking – she could also read her like a book.

'Mmm.' Angie frowned. 'I'm a bit uneasy, if I'm honest. I think it's just gonna take some time to adapt to having another person around. And, you know, it's not the same as simply having a new employee, because Stanislaw is going to be here permanently, so I guess it just feels a bit . . .' Angie's voice trailed off.

'A bit much?' Clemmie suggested.

'Yeah, a bit much,' Angie agreed. 'He'll be about all the time.'

'I'm wondering,' Clemmie suggested tentatively, 'if you might see Stanislaw as stepping into Quentin's shoes?'

'Perhaps,' Angie mused. 'It does feel like he's stepped into Quentin's shoes.' Her face clouded over. 'And no one's allowed to do that!'

'Of course not,' Clemmie placated her. She thought for a moment. This, she knew, was an important conversation as Angie rarely talked about her feelings and even less about her feelings around Quentin. 'Well, I can see why you might feel that way. Stanislaw is about the same age as Quentin, and overnight he has become part of life here. You might feel angry that his physical presence is replacing Quentin's invisible presence.'

'Yes, that's exactly it,' Angie said, glad of the understanding.

'And also, you might feel as though he is taking on Quentin's role with the children,' Clemmie mused. 'There's no doubt they all adore him.'

'Yes, they do don't they?' Angie said. 'These past two days, Bonnie and Jemima have been constantly vying for his attention. Bertie clearly wants to drain him of everything and anything he can tell him about Poland and every place he fought. And Marlene has taken to wearing lipstick for dinner.' Angie shook her head. 'God knows what I'm going to do with that girl. And Danny clearly sees him as his saviour for bringing Ghost back, and a role model when it comes to all things "manly".'

'Well, he's certainly manly,' Clemmie said, eyeing Angie. 'The question is, do you notice such things?'

'What? Like Stanislaw being "manly"?' Angie asked, feeling herself flush. This conversation had suddenly become uncomfortable.

Clemmie nodded and took a sip of her brandy.

'Well, I don't know. I guess he is a man. And I can see why Danny would look up to him.'

'I'm just wondering if you feel a little uneasy *because he is a man,*' Clemmie said. 'A manly man?'

Angie furrowed her brow.

'Oh, I don't know,' she said, getting up and giving the log fire a poke. 'It's just strange having another bloke around, that's all.'

*

Clemmie decided not to push it, but felt a little relieved that Angie didn't seem as enamoured of Stanislaw as everyone else was.

She knew it was unlikely that she herself would be a future contender for Angie's feelings, but she didn't want anyone else to be either. Which she knew was not a kindly thought, but still, it was just the way she was.

And there was always the tiniest of hopes that circumstances – and Angie's feelings – might just change. You never knew.

Chapter Thirty-One

When Angie took Bonnie to the nursery on Monday, she insisted on treating Rebecca, Jill, Hilda and the rest of the nursery mams to tea and scones at the café to show how truly thankful she was that the village had jumped in to help when they'd heard Mrs Kwiatkowski had gone missing.

'And can you also tell everyone else you know that everyone at Cuthford Manor can't thank them all enough. That we're truly grateful,' Angie stressed as they tucked into their cream tea.

They shrugged it off as nothing.

'Gans without saying we'd help,' Jill said, biting into her scone.

'Wouldn't think twice,' said Hilda, who was also clearly enjoying eating something she hadn't had to bake herself.

The rest of the mams agreed. 'It's just what yer dee when someone needs help,' Rebecca said.

Angie smiled at everyone and found herself feeling unusually emotional.

Walking home, Angie thought about the Irish Travellers. She also wanted to go and thank them properly, but was unsure how to do it. She considered giving them money, but that didn't feel right.

By the time she was back at the manor, she knew what to do.

First off, she went to see Alberta in the kitchen, then she took a couple of cardboard boxes upstairs, where she set about raiding her own wardrobe of unwanted clothes, before moving on to the children's for garments they had either outgrown or didn't wear, making sure there were plenty of warm jumpers, woollen skirts and trousers.

Catching Evelyn before she headed out for the day, she asked her for any clothes she didn't want and was given two old evening dresses that were totally impractical, but which Angie knew the Travellers would sell.

'What do you want them for? Is the village having yet another fête and asking for more donations?' Evelyn asked.

'No, it's for the Travellers. My way of saying thank you for rescuing Mrs Kwiatkowski.'

'God, Angela, you're not going back there, are you?' Evelyn snapped.

'Well, the clothes aren't going to take themselves,' Angie said, surprised at Evelyn's change in mood and seriousness.

'Honestly, it's not right for you to go up there, fraternising with them. You already thanked them when you and the Pole went to fetch the old woman.'

Evelyn, Angie noted, seemed determined not to call Stanislaw by name.

'I want to give them something to show my gratitude.'

'You're so naive, Angela.' Evelyn's tone was now derisory. 'They were probably going to keep her for slave labour or make money from her somehow. You probably got there just in time, before they carted her off somewhere.'

Angie laughed. 'Blimey, Evelyn, you've got some imagination.'

Evelyn gave her daughter-in-law the daggers. 'Quentin wouldn't want you going up there,' she said.

Angie felt as though she'd been slapped in the face. Evelyn rarely mentioned her son. How dare she speak on his behalf. She had no idea what Quentin had really been like, never mind what he would want Angie to do or not do.

Angie forced herself not to react and simply turned on her heels and headed back to her own bedroom. Once there, she took a deep breath.

'It's time,' she said aloud.

Walking over to the polished mahogany wardrobe next to her own, Angie turned the small key and opened both doors wide. As she did so, she inhaled. The last time she'd opened the wardrobe, she'd been immersed in Quentin's scent. It had felt as though he was there, right next to her. It had broken her heart all over again. She'd not gone into his wardrobe since. This time, though, the scent was different. There was the faint hint of her husband, but it was overridden by a stale, musty malodour, making her feel more like she was being doused in the aftermath of death.

Forcing herself into action, she started stripping the wardrobe bare, tossing suits, shirts, ties, jumpers and jackets onto the floor until there was only a row of swinging hangers left on the brass pole. She left the wardrobe doors open, then marched over to the bedroom's large sash window, pushed the latch to release the lock and yanked up the lower panel. A gust of cold, damp air billowed into the room.

Angie slumped onto the chaise longue at the end of the four-poster bed. The sudden rush of adrenalin had passed and she felt depleted of energy.

She looked at the pile of clothes on the floor. For a moment, she didn't think she could do it. Couldn't bear to throw out the things Quentin had worn when he had held her in his arms, kissed her, walked with her, ridden with her.

'Well, I'll be damned if I'm going to hang them all back up there,' she said aloud.

Hardening her heart, she stood up, walked over to the pile of clothes, folded them all up and put them in an old suitcase she dragged out of the bottom of the wardrobe.

Half an hour later, she had heaved the leather suitcase down the stairs and across the entrance hall to join the rest of the boxes and bags ready to take to the Travellers' camp.

Looking into the wooden crate the cook had left, Angie saw she had done as asked and had put together ingredients for a broth – home-grown vegetables and some beef brisket – as well as some bones and offcuts for the dogs, a home-made apple pie and two malted loaves.

Angie stood and wondered if it would all fit in the Austin.

'Only one way of finding out,' she muttered.

Half an hour later, after a great deal of precision packing, Angie had almost filled the car when Stanislaw came trotting down the driveway on Ghost, returning from his morning ride. Smoky breath billowed from both horse and rider.

'Bloody typical,' Angie grumbled.

'You look like you're off on holiday,' Stanislaw said as he drew Ghost to a stop a few yards away from the car. He eyed the back passenger seat, which was full to bursting, and the boot, which was open. 'Either that or you're running away.'

Angie tried to force a laugh, but it didn't work and instead came out as a gargled noise.

'Very funny. I'm going to the Travellers' camp. I wanted to thank them for rescuing Mrs Kwiatkowski,' Angie explained.

When she saw the change in Stanislaw's face, she immediately regretted telling him.

'I must come with you,' he said.

'No, Stanislaw, there's no need.'

Stanislaw shook his head. 'No, I'll come.'

'I'll be fine on my own.'

But before Angie had time to argue, he'd pushed Ghost into a trot and headed off to the stables.

In a panic, Angie jogged back to the house and grabbed the last two boxes. Hurrying out to the car, she stuffed the clothes into the boot, but when she tried to close it, she couldn't. Cursing, she grabbed one of the boxes and tipped it upside down; then she ran back into the house to dump it, determined to get away before Stanislaw had time to see to Ghost and head back to the front of the manor.

Stanislaw, meanwhile, knowing exactly what Angie would be doing and determined she wouldn't go without him, jumped off Ghost at the stables, asked Thomas to take care of him and then ran back round just in time to catch Angie getting into the driver's side. She had tipped the last of the clothes into the boot with such haste that the sleeve of an expensive-looking blouse was peeking out.

Stanislaw ran round to the passenger side, flung open the door and jumped in just as Angie was turning the ignition.

Both were red-faced from rushing.

'Thanks for waiting,' Stanislaw said, poker-faced.

'I didn't,' Angie said, crunching the Austin into first gear. 'Honestly, no one ever listens to a word I say – or does what I want.'

'Only when it's in your best interests,' Stanislaw said.

Angie mumbled something under her breath.

'Pardon?' he asked.

'Nothing. Nothing at all.' Angie sighed.

They drove the first part of the journey in silence, which was only broken when Angie had to ask for directions.

'Glad I came?' Stanislaw asked, unable to suppress a smile.

Angie gave her best withering look, then panicked as the gearstick slipped into neutral, something it kept doing of late. The engine revved.

'Damn it!' Angie said, forcing the gearstick back into fourth. 'Even the bloody car won't do what I want.'

Stanislaw laughed.

Angie scowled. 'That was not a joke.'

Changing down to third gear as they approached the turn-off to the camp, the car suddenly stalled. Never before had Angie experienced so much trouble with the gears. She turned the ignition and slammed the car into first.

Stanislaw tried to suppress another chuckle. The tense atmosphere in the car was making him want to laugh even more.

'I hope you were a better crane operator than you are a car driver,' Stanislaw said, trying to keep a straight face. Danny had told him that his big sister had worked in a shipyard during the war. 'I would not have wanted to have worked under you . . .' He made a movement as though he was ducking to miss a falling object.

Angie looked at him.

'I was a very good crane operator, I'll have you know!' Hearing herself, Angie realised how ridiculous she sounded. She burst out laughing. All the tension and stress of making a fast getaway was suddenly transformed into sheer mirth.

They both laughed. Big, gutsy bellows of laughter that made their sides ache and their eyes water.

'Stop it!' Angie demanded. 'Or I won't be able to see where I'm going.'

Halfway along the potholed drive to the camp, they managed to calm down. It was the first time, Angie realised, that she had laughed – properly laughed – since before Quentin had died. And it shocked her. A feeling of guilt hit her like a brick. Guilt which quickly morphed into anger that another man had made her laugh.

'It's hard, isn't it?' Stanislaw said.

'What's hard?' Angie asked, frowning as she concentrated on the rough track.

'To feel happy.'

'What do you mean?' Angie was becoming concerned that the conversation had turned too personal.

'You felt bad after you laughed just then. I could see it in your face,' Stanislaw explained.

Angie was quiet. Partly because she didn't know what to say and also because he had read her mind. Known how she felt.

'What makes you such an expert?' she sniped.

'Because I also lost someone I loved – my wife,' Stanislaw said.

'Oh, I'm sorry,' Angie said, more than a little stunned. 'I didn't know.'

She drove a short while.

'Yes, but it was ten years ago . . . At the start of the war. I have adapted, but I have not forgotten how it feels when the grief is still raw.'

Seeing the camp in the distance, Stanislaw changed his tone. 'There it is! I think the Travellers are going to be very happy to see you today.'

As they drove along the end of the track towards the caravans, Angie looked at the camp. When she had picked up Mrs Kwiatkowski, it had been at night. In daylight, she could see there were more vehicles and horses on the periphery and some bushes and a few trees around the camp. A young girl about Jemima's age was hanging out washing on the branches of one of the smaller trees. The traditional gypsy caravans looked, she thought, more like the wagons she'd seen in cowboy films, with wooden wheels and an arched canopy. The horses were untethered and grazing in the field nearby.

The camp was busy. Young children and dogs were running around, playing tag; a man was chopping wood; another man, older and more grizzled, wearing a woollen waistcoat and flat cap, was sorting out a pile of scrap metal; two younger women, their dark, almost black hair piled high, were peeling potatoes; a grandmother was tugging a comb through a young lad's hair as he howled his objections.

Seeing the car approach, they all stopped what they were doing and watched as Angie and Stanislaw got out.

One of the men shouted out, 'Clodagh!' as he looked over to the bow-top caravan that had sheltered Mrs Kwiatkowski. In the light of day, Angie could see its beautiful, vibrant paintwork, which made it stand out against the surrounding grey. *This must be the one used for the markets and fairs.* The one that had been returning from Durham on the evening Mrs Kwiatkowski went missing.

The top half of the red door was already open, but an old mauve curtain was covering the entrance. It twitched, then was pulled back with an energetic tug, revealing the woman who had rescued Mrs Kwiatkowski, and who Angie now knew to be called Clodagh. She was smoking a slim hand-rolled cigarette. She eyed them before opening the bottom part of the painted door and carefully making her way down the caravan's wooden steps to greet them. Her gait showed Angie that she was older than she'd initially thought.

'Hello again,' Angie said, a little nervous as she felt the entire camp's attention on her. She could feel Stanislaw's presence behind her. Was glad he'd come.

'Good day to ya,' Clodagh said through a swirl of cigarette smoke, her Irish accent thick.

'I wanted to come and thank you properly for taking in Mrs Kwiatkowski and looking after her for us,' Angie explained. She glanced over to the car and suddenly felt worried that her way of thanking them might seem like charity. 'I brought some clothes and a little food to show our appreciation.' She watched the woman, taking in her heavily lined face, trying to gauge her reaction.

''Tis kind,' Clodagh said, nodding.

Angie pointed to the Austin. 'Everything's in the car.'

Clodagh turned her attention to their audience.

'Aiden, Findley, Patric, Shan – go 'n fetch what's in ta vehicle,' she ordered.

Three of the boys ran over to the car.

'Shan – you too!' Clodagh glared at the boy. He was standing in front of his ma, whose arms were wrapped around him. The young woman with the curly red hair, which today had been freed of its headscarf, eyed Angie with suspicion before letting her son go.

Turning, she walked away, disappearing into one of the large canvas tents pitched next to a caravan.

Noticing that she was pregnant, Angie immediately recognised her and the boy as the pair who had watched her leave with Mrs Kwiatkowski. Who had looked at her as though they knew her. It was the same look they had today.

Within minutes, the car had been cleared out.

'Well, then,' Angie said, realising she was not going to get a look inside Clodagh's caravan. 'Thank you once again.'

Clodagh nodded, but Angie caught something in her eye. She couldn't tell what it was. A natural suspicion born of a lifetime of enduring the prejudices of others? Or something else?

As Angie and Stanislaw walked back to the car, a few of the women who were pulling out some of her siblings' old clothes from a box smiled their thanks. One of the young lads was carrying Alberta's pie over to Clodagh as though it were the crown jewels. All he needed was a red cushion. A ginger-haired girl was peering into the bag of vegetables and had already picked out the beef, which had been wrapped in greaseproof paper. Her eyes were like saucers.

As they reached the car, Angie caught sight of one of the younger men putting on one of Quentin's coats. She forced herself to turn away and get in the car. As soon as Stanislaw had bent his lanky frame into the passenger seat, she pulled away. This time not looking in her rear-view mirror. She couldn't bear to see any other man in her husband's clothes. It had been hard enough to give them away, but seeing them on someone else the same age – and so full of life – well, that was too much.

'I think what you did was very brave,' Stanislaw said. 'It can't have been easy. Especially seeing another man wearing your husband's clothes.'

Angie was quiet. It had been harder than she had imagined it would be. She desperately wanted to turn round and go back to reclaim what had once belonged to Quentin. *But why?* she argued with herself. *So she could magic Quentin back to life and he could wear them again?*

They drove in silence.

Part of Angie wanted to talk to Stanislaw about his loss. She had no idea how his wife had died. *Did he also have to give clothes away?* But she couldn't trust herself to talk. Her struggle with her emotions was all-consuming. She kept thinking of Quentin. *What would he think?* It had felt as though she was throwing him away. *Would he think that?* Of course not. He'd be glad. But still, it felt like she had given up on him. Which was so nonsensical. Illogical. *How could she give up on him when he was dead?*

Angie slowed down as they approached Cuthford village. Suddenly, she started to shake. An image came to her mind of Quentin wearing that bloody coat, walking, the dogs either side of him, a smile on his face when he saw her. Tears started to roll down her cheeks. And then she started to sob. Her shakes turned to shudders. The dormant volcano of grief inside her was starting to erupt. She managed to pull over on the roadside before her vision became totally blurred.

Stanislaw sat quietly while Angie cried. Her lungs didn't seem to have enough air as she heaved great sobs. The occasional words she uttered were completely unintelligible, even for a native speaker. Stanislaw simply sat and waited. And Angie continued to allow herself to purge her deep sorrow without any inhibitions.

When she finally stopped, she felt as though she would collapse with exhaustion. Stanislaw looked at her. He checked the road, opened his door and got out, then cocked his head over to the building they were parked outside. It was the Farmer's Arms.

Angie wound down her window.

'If ever there was a need for a midday drink, then this is it,' Stanislaw said.

Angie saw him bend down and open the car door. She didn't have the strength to argue, so she wound the window back up, pulled the keys out of the ignition and clambered out.

Chapter Thirty-Two

They were both hit by the warmth of the pub, their attention immediately going to the open fire to the right of the bar. The lounge was empty save for a few miners from one of the local pits who were enjoying an end-of-shift pint before heading home.

'Go and sit down,' Stanislaw said. 'I'll get us a drink.'

The lure of the flickering coal fire naturally drew Angie towards it. Sitting on a cushioned wooden chair to the side of the flagstone hearth, she let her gaze fix on the glowing red coals and quivering amber flames. She had no idea how long she had been lost in her own world when she sensed movement to her side and reluctantly drew her gaze away.

'The barmaid made you a nice cup of tea,' Stanislaw said. 'And there's a brandy to go in it if you want.' He put down two mugs of tea and a bulbous glass of cognac.

'Thank you,' Angie said, taking a sip of the brandy and then pouring it into her tea. They were quiet for a moment before she turned her attention to Stanislaw. It was as though she was looking at him for the first time. She could see a scar partly camouflaged by his short light brown hair; his skin was tanned but weathered, making him look older than she knew him to be. But it was his hazel eyes that drew her attention. There was a kindness there, yet also a deep sadness.

'Do you mind me asking how your wife died?' She kept her focus on his face, needing to know if she was overstepping the mark.

'I don't mind,' Stanislaw said, before taking a deep breath. 'It was in the September of 1939, when the Russians invaded Poland. My wife, Adrianna, and I lived in a village called Grabowiec, in the south-east of Poland. She was six months pregnant. She was sure it would be a boy. I was sure it was a girl.' He smiled at the memory. 'We were very happy. But then the Germans invaded the west and sixteen days later the Russians the east. They had decided they would take our country, halve it and share the spoils.'

Angie could hear bitterness and anger and a sense of injustice in his voice.

'I had joined the army, of course, and Adrianna, who was a nurse, was tending the injured in the military hospital in our village.' Stanislaw paused. He was clearly trying hard to keep his emotions under control. 'One week after the Soviet invasion – on the twenty-fourth of September – Russian soldiers came to our village, stormed the hospital and shot dead forty-two nurses, doctors and patients.'

Angie did not take her eyes off Stanislaw.

'I came back and found Adrianna. Her arms were wrapped around her belly, as though still trying to save our child, even in death. She had been shot twice. Once in the head. The other in her stomach.'

Angie gasped, her hand automatically going to her mouth.

'You see, I understand what it is to lose someone you love, so suddenly, and so unjustly. And to see the full horror of it.'

Angie nodded, tears trickling down her cheeks. She had heard about such mass executions – massacres – during the war, but had never met anyone who'd not only had a loved one who had been killed, but had also witnessed the aftermath of the killings. She thought of her former workmate, Hannah, whose parents were now believed to have been killed in gas chambers shortly after arriving at the German concentration camp in Auschwitz.

'How did you manage to keep going?' Angie asked, pulling out a hankie from the pocket of her cardigan and wiping it under her eyes.

'I had to,' Stanislaw said simply. 'I had to do whatever I could to stop this . . . this . . .' He struggled to find the right word.

'*Inhumanity*?' Angie said.

Stanislaw gave a sad smile. 'Yes, it was not human what I saw. Even the word evil does not suffice.'

Angie nodded. 'It doesn't, does it.'

They looked into the fire.

'The deaths of your wife and your unborn child were truly unjust,' Angie said. 'Whereas my husband's death felt so, so . . . so *bloody unlucky*.'

'Because he was in the stall when Ghost was spooked?' Stanislaw asked.

'Yes,' Angie said. 'All of it. Quentin getting his mother's scarf at the exact time a firework went off – it would have been hard to have timed it better.'

Stanislaw sat back. He knew that Lloyd blamed his wife for his son's death; had she not left her scarf in the stall, Quentin would still be alive. But he wondered if Angie felt it should have been her who'd died, as she had been the one who was meant to fetch the scarf.

'You don't blame yourself, do you?' Stanislaw ventured.

'No,' Angie said honestly. 'I don't. There is no one to blame.' She looked at Stanislaw. 'It was, like I say, bad bloody luck. Although not that unusual. The coroner at the inquest said that there'd been a jockey the previous year who'd died after being crushed in the starting stalls when his horse had got spooked.

'Quentin's death was a terrible, terrible accident.' Angie sighed. 'Whereas your wife's death was *cold-blooded murder*.'

'That might be so,' Stanislaw said. 'But either way, both their deaths have left holes in our lives which will never be filled. But you will learn to live with the emptiness that grief leaves. I have – and I think you will too.'

Angie could feel tears stinging her eyes again, but she didn't stop them, just let them roll down her face. She cried, only this time it was softly.

'Sometimes I just feel so sad,' she said through the tears.

Stanislaw nodded slowly. 'I do too. But the amount you feel that sadness will lessen. I promise you.'

Angie took a juddering breath and exhaled slowly. She looked at him and offered up a wan smile.

'You promise?'

He returned her smile with one he felt was hopeful.

'I promise.'

Angie blew her nose and stuffed her hankie back into her pocket.

'I'll hold you to it.'

As they drove back in the car, the atmosphere between them felt relaxed for the first time. They chatted a little about Poland and Angie was surprised to learn that although the country was mainly associated with farming due to its good soil and climate, it was also known for mining and shipbuilding.

'See, our countries have much in common,' Stanislaw said.

'Do you miss Poland?' Angie asked. She tutted. 'Silly question, really. I know you must miss it terribly.'

'I do,' Stanislaw said, 'but I've been away for such a long time now. I hope to go back there one day. I hope I live long enough to see Stalin gone – not just so *I* can go back, but for my people.'

'You must feel very . . .' Angie hesitated '. . . very, I can't think of the right word – like you've been cut adrift – like you don't belong?'

'Mmm, perhaps. I haven't really thought of it like that.'

He was quiet for a moment.

'Is that how you feel? That you don't belong here?'

Angie sighed. 'I don't think I know what I feel any more. But, yes, I think it's fair to say that I don't feel like I belong at the manor – not now that Quentin's gone.'

'That surprises me,' Stanislaw said.

Angie looked at him. 'You really think I *belong* here? Me being a *miner's* daughter?'

'Yes, I really *do* think you belong here. I don't think our past dictates where we belong, like we're led to believe.'

Angie was going to joke and ask if Danny and Lloyd had coerced him into arguing the case for her to stay, but she didn't. She could see that he was speaking from the heart. His words had been spoken with sincerity.

They drove in a comfortable silence. Their minds wandering.

'So,' Angie said with a half-smile, 'I've been wanting to ask you if your soldier bear story is true?'

Angie watched as a smile stretched across Stanislaw's face. His eyes sparkled with happy memories. And love.

'Ah, Wojtek is indeed real. It is a true story.'

Angie eyed him with suspicion. Stanislaw caught the look.

'You have to trust me,' he said as they turned off the main road and through the gates of Cuthford Manor. 'I will tell you about it another time. It is quite a story.'

'It sounds it,' Angie said. 'I look forward to it.'

And much to her surprise, she realised she meant it.

That evening, after dinner, when everyone had wished each other goodnight, Angie stayed downstairs. After making herself a cup of tea in the kitchen, she allowed Winston and Bessie to follow her into the sitting room, where the log fire was still glowing and the room was warm and cosy. She curled up in the cushioned armchair while Bessie settled by her side and Winston thudded his heavy weight down in front of the marble hearth.

As she sipped her tea, she realised that this was the first time since Quentin had died that she did not feel quite so alone in her grief. Stanislaw was the first person who had really understood the way she felt. It had been cathartic to talk to someone who had suffered the same loss, especially as she could tell that Stanislaw had loved his wife with the intensity that she had Quentin. It was clear he, too, would never love again in the same way.

How could you when you'd lost the one great love of your life?

Angie's own feelings seemed to pale in comparison to the suffering and displacement that Stanislaw had endured. How must he feel knowing that the very people who had invaded his country and had so brutally killed his wife and unborn child were now in charge of his homeland? How unjust. He had risked his life for his country – only then to know that he would risk his life again if he returned. Whereas Angie was not only living in her homeland, but in the same county she'd grown up in, and she not only had her family around her, but friends too. People like Mrs Jones and Lloyd, who she had become close to. And Clemmie. And if she wanted to go back to Sunderland, she just needed to get in her car and drive there. Which she did, often. And it was where she also had friends. Good friends. Lifelong friends.

She stretched out her hand to stroke Bessie, feeling ashamed of herself for complaining. How pitiful it now sounded. Especially after the whole community had come to her aid in the search for Mrs Kwiatkowski.

As she continued to stroke Bessie, Angie realised for the first time in almost a year that she had much to be thankful for.

And for the first time, she started to question the wisdom of her plan to emigrate to Australia.

Chapter Thirty-Three

In the weeks that followed, Angie felt her mind less cluttered by her grief. It was almost as if the day she physically packed up Quentin's clothes, she had also packed up a good amount of her sorrow, which, in turn, freed up space to think and reflect. Cuthford Manor had now been her home for over five years. Years during which she had been insular – apart from the obligatory attendance at various fêtes and at services at St Cuthbert's. Mrs Jones and Alberta did all the shopping, so it wasn't as if Angie had got to know any of the shop owners or tradespeople. And because she had no need to go into the village, she'd not had a lot of contact with the villagers themselves. She'd only just begun to get to know a few of the women because of Bonnie starting nursery.

And so Angie resolved to ask the cook to tell her when she was going into the village to get provisions so she could tag along. Alberta was extremely uncomfortable about shopping with Angie. It was simply not the done thing. And there were more than a few raised eyebrows initially, but that concern soon evaporated.

Angie even chatted to Evelyn over dinner more, quizzing her about the local gentry and their country houses, prodding her for information about their financial situations, particularly how they were able to afford the upkeep of their huge properties. She listened intently as Evelyn waxed lyrical about the upper classes, but it was with a sinking heart that Angie learnt most of them had 'family money' left in trusts for them by their forebears.

Despite uncertainty over the financial future, there was no mistaking that a lightness had started to illuminate the manor. The return of Ghost had infused everyone with joy. Well, almost everyone. Angie still felt the pain of remembrance every time she set eyes on the dapple grey, but she told herself that it would fade. In time.

Danny, especially, was on a high and spent every spare minute he had in the stables. Angie knew Stanislaw often stayed late to chat to him about the horses or rose early to go riding with him before school. Bertie, Jemima and Bonnie were also the happiest she'd seen them in a long while. They now had not only Clemmie but also Stanislaw tied around their little fingers, indulging them in their need for games of tag, hide and seek and skipping – as well as stories about their lives in foreign lands, of which they had plenty.

Stanislaw and Clemmie had brought a wholesome breath of fresh air to the place with their naturally cheerful and positive dispositions. And it was catching. Much to Angie's surprise, it was now not unusual to hear Thomas, Ted and Eugene having a laugh while they worked; even Bill, who was not known for his sociability, occasionally joined in with the banter.

Although Angie hadn't chatted much to Stanislaw since their afternoon in the pub, the ease between them continued.

She often thought of their conversation and about what he had said about how he'd learnt to 'adapt'. She started to believe that she could survive the loss of Quentin, not by battling or trying to conquer it, but by adjusting. In a funny kind of way, it was a compromise. As though she was allowing herself to keep Quentin with her as she slowly started to move on.

Mrs Kwiatkowski had also gained a new lease of life now that she could make herself understood. And since Stanislaw had translated the ingredients of some typical Polish food, she and Alberta had become a team in the kitchen, making hearty stews like *gulasz* and *forszmak lubelski*, a rich meat casserole perfect for the cold late-autumn weather.

One evening after they'd all just enjoyed a traditional Polish dinner, Angie said it would be a perfect end to their meal if Stanislaw would relate the tale of Wojtek the soldier bear, as he had promised. She did so knowing the children would also want to hear it again.

'Would you?' Angie asked.

Stanislaw looked round the table at Lloyd, Evelyn, Clemmie, Mrs Kwiatkowski and the children. 'I will, of course, but does everyone else want to hear it? I'm sure most of you have heard it already?'

'Yes, yes!' Jemima exclaimed.

'Again. Again!' Bonnie shouted out, encouraged by Jemima, before clambering off her chair and running off to fetch Mr Grizzly.

'Most definitely!' Clemmie exclaimed. 'I have only heard it second-hand from the children!'

'Same here,' Lloyd said, pulling out a cigar from his jacket.

'Okay, if you're all sure,' Stanislaw said. He spoke to Mrs Kwiatkowski, who had heard the story previously, but her blank expression told him she had now forgotten.

'I hope you'll all forgive me,' said Evelyn, unusually politely. She scraped back her chair. 'But I've got to go and see an old girlfriend who is having a few marital problems and needs some advice and a shoulder to cry on this evening.'

The words 'the blind leading the blind' came to mind, but Angie didn't say anything. Instead, she watched as Evelyn walked out of the room. Her mother-in-law, she thought, had been going out more and more of late. If she wasn't having luncheons with 'the girls', there was more often than not something else or some*one* else demanding her attention.

Once Bonnie had returned with Mr Grizzly and Lloyd had lit up his cigar, Stanislaw began.

'It was 1942 and I had joined the 22nd Artillery Supply Company. We were travelling across Iran on our way to Palestine to train with the British Army—'

'Sorry to interrupt,' Clemmie said. 'But where were you before then?'

Angie saw a shadow fall across Stanislaw's face. She had wondered this herself, but had not wanted to pry.

'I was a prisoner of war in a gulag in Siberia,' Stanislaw said, hoping his face had not shown the torment of remembrance. The images of all the dead bodies he'd seen, tossed out like rubbish and left in the snow for weeks before being buried.

Mrs Kwiatkowski, who had heard about the notorious Soviet gulags and how no one was expected to survive more than one winter, scowled and angrily muttered something in Polish.

'What's a gulag?' Marlene asked.

'It's a Russian forced labour camp,' Bertie informed them.

Knowing that Stanislaw would not want to talk about his time in Siberia, the atrocities committed there being akin to those in the German concentration camps, Lloyd spoke up.

'When the Soviets invaded Poland, they put their prisoners of war into these gulags, but when Germany tried to invade Russia, the Red Army joined the Allies and released all their prisoners of war – which is how Stanislaw ended up in Iran with a soldier bear.'

Stanislaw smiled his thanks to Lloyd, while also wondering if he'd ever be able to talk about that time.

'So,' he continued, 'we were in Iran when a little boy asked us soldiers if we had any food. One of the men went off to get him some tins of meat we had in the lorry when the sack the boy had put on the ground started to move. Then we heard some whimpering noises. My friend Dymitr bent down and loosened the top of the sack.' Stanislaw paused for dramatic effect. Angie thought him a natural storyteller. 'And then a little black nose poked out!'

'A baby bear!' Bertie, Jemima and Bonnie shouted out in unison.

Angie sat back and smiled, thinking how wonderful it was to see them so happy. She glanced at Mrs Kwiatkowski, who smiled and nodded, as though she had read her thoughts and was showing she agreed.

'That's right.' Stanislaw laughed. 'A baby brown bear, who had been orphaned when his mother was killed by hunters.'

He looked at Bonnie, who had placed Mr Grizzly on the tabletop in front of her so he could have a front-row seat. 'A bear which at that time was not much bigger than Mr Grizzly here.'

Bonnie smiled proudly at having her toy made part of the story.

As Stanislaw continued his tale about Wojtek the bear and how he grew to be huge and learnt to stand on two feet and salute like a human, the dining room filled with cigar smoke and cries of laughter or disbelief, interspersed with the odd question.

'We would often find him in the kitchen area. He was always on the lookout for food, even though we fed him well. Just like Danny.' Everyone laughed.

'And he drank beer out of a bottle and ate cigarettes!' Danny chipped in. 'He would take one puff of a lit cigarette and then swallow it!'

'Ugh!' Marlene pulled a face.

'He was with us during the battle for Monte Cassino. He carried our ammunition. He displayed great courage. And strength,' Stanislaw said.

Clemmie whistled. Everyone knew that battle in the Italian theatre of war had been particularly bloody and hard-won.

'After the battle, the official badge of the 22nd Company became a likeness of Wojtek holding a shell. And he was promoted to corporal!'

'And then what happened to him?' Angie asked. She could understand why the children wanted to hear the story again as it was so life-affirming. An orphaned bear bringing laughter and happiness in the midst of the death and darkness of war.

'Well, when we were demobilised in 1947, he was resettled in Edinburgh Zoo. Lots of my old unit still go and visit him,' Stanislaw said. This was something he hadn't told the children.

'Can we go?' they all shouted out in unison. As he knew they would. He looked apologetically at Angie.

'Please! Please! Please!' Jemima and Bonnie chorused.

'Oh, me too, please!' Clemmie added. Angie had to laugh. Sometimes Clemmie was like one of the children, only in an adult body.

'If,' Angie said, looking at her watch and seeing how late it was, 'you all get off to bed now, without any palaver or any moans or groans, I will consider it.'

'Come on,' Danny told his siblings and Bonnie. They all got up without any fuss.

'If we hold our side of the bargain, you have to hold yours,' Danny said.

'Okay,' Angie agreed.

And with that, Danny cocked his head and with the commanding air of a corporal, led his unit away, a tired Bonnie at the rear, dragging Mr Grizzly behind her.

Chapter Thirty-Four

Despite the new energy at Cuthford Manor, there was no ignoring the dark clouds looming in the distance, threatening its survival and that of the village – as well as all who lived there. Most of Angie's days were spent with Lloyd, going over the accounts and looking at ways to keep the manor afloat.

On the last Friday in October, Angie drove to Sunderland for her monthly meet-up with her old workmates. She was particularly keen to see them as she had so much to tell them all, and also so much she wanted to ask. They were good at finding solutions to each other's problems.

Once they'd all settled around a corner table at the Tatham Inn, they exchanged gossip and updates, and Martha told them that Hannah and Olly, who were still working for the Red Cross, had recently been sent to Korea. When Angie told them about her worries for the future of Cuthford Manor – and therefore the future of her family – the women started to bandy around ideas. Angie was so excited about one particular suggestion, she didn't stay as long as she'd normally have done, but jumped in her car and tried to keep her speed down as she travelled the ten miles home. A trip made longer by the dark and uneven country roads.

When she pulled up outside the manor, she bustled up the steps and into the main foyer, then headed straight to the kitchen, where she knew everyone would be.

'I want you all to come to the living room – I've got something to tell you!' she said breathlessly.

They looked at Angie. She seemed wild, her eyes slightly manic, her cheeks flushed. As they made their way from the kitchen, the two dogs pressed up against Mrs Kwiatkowski in the hope of getting into the warm sitting room unnoticed. Angie was standing in front of the fireplace. She waved everyone in impatiently.

'Right, now that you're all here,' she began, surveying everyone, 'I think I might just have the perfect solution to our money woes!'

Bonnie clapped, not because she really understood what her mum was saying, but she sensed her excitement and wanted to mirror it. Angie smiled at her daughter. She had really come out of her shell since going to the nursery, and she was sure the other children had become more pally with her since Angie herself had become more friendly with their mams.

'As most of you know, I see my old workmates every month or so,' Angie began. 'This evening, when we were chatting, I was telling them about our situation – ' she pulled a face and the two youngest chuckled ' – and Rosie started telling me about a manor house where her husband Peter did his training during the war.'

Clemmie immediately perked up. She knew that Peter had been in the French division of the Special Operations Executive, and that he and all the others who'd been sent over the Channel as covert operatives had been trained at Wanborough Manor, near Guildford in Surrey.

'Anyway, it sounds like this manor house was left a little worse for wear, but was done up and is now a B&B. Rosie said it's lovely, some of the locals even go there to play bridge in the lounge area. She said the rooms were very nice too. And there's an amazing dining room serving up "fine wine and food".'

Evelyn snorted. 'I can hardly see any of the villagers here coming to play bridge and enjoy fine wine.'

'No, I'm guessing they'll have better things to do,' Angie hit back, giving Evelyn one of her scathing looks. 'I wasn't going to suggest that.' She inhaled to quell her irritation. 'What is this area known for? Apart from mining and the university?'

Thomas nervously raised a hand.

Angie rolled her eyes. 'Thomas, I'm not your schoolteacher – go on . . .'

'Hunting,' he said quietly.

Evelyn turned round and stared at him. She couldn't believe that Angie had allowed the stablehand to come into the sitting room.

'Shooting,' Thomas continued, wanting the ground to swallow him up. 'Grouse shooting, mainly.'

'Well done, Thomas!' Despite not wanting to be treated like a schoolteacher, Angie was doing a good job of sounding like one.

'Raby Moors!' she declared. 'We give them a place to stay, a hearty breakfast before they head out, a packed lunch, and then, when they return, they've got the good food and wine – if that's what they want – but if not, we've got plenty of locally brewed ale.' Angie looked at everyone. '*And* we will be buying goods from the local shopkeepers – and the pub will no doubt get some extra trade as well. So, we might even be able to get the village taken off the "Doomsday list".' Everyone knew this was Angie's new name for the council's Category D list of soon-to-be-derelict villages.

'Yes, but the shooting season is only from mid-August to mid-December,' Evelyn butted in. 'That's four months. What will we do for the other eight months of the year?'

Angie eyed her mother-in-law. She seemed determined to pour water on Angie's entrepreneurial fire.

'Well, regardless of it only being four months, I think that's a brilliant idea,' Clemmie piped up from the back row. 'And hearing about this manor house down south has brought to mind a place I know, an incredibly grand fisherman's lodge called Sharrow Bay, which overlooks Lake Ullswater and the nearby fells.' Seeing a few blank faces, she went on, 'Which is in the Lake District.'.

'Anyway, a good friend of mine is very good friends with a chap called Francis Coulson.' If Clemmie had just been chatting to Angie, she would have confided that the two men were partners – and not in a business sense. But with the archaic laws prohibiting homosexuality, she could not risk letting the others know. Especially Evelyn. She'd probably shop them to the police as soon as she walked out of the room. 'And this Francis Coulson bought the lease of this rather wonderful lodge and converted it into a hotel – well, perhaps that's a little bit of an overstatement, there's four bedrooms, but they also do afternoon tea for two shillings and sixpence.'

Clemmie looked at Angie. She could see the cogs whirring as Angie glanced over at Alberta. Her cakes and scones were the best she had ever tasted. 'By the sounds of it, the place is proving quite the success. He's calling it a "country house hotel".'

'A country house hotel,' Angie repeated, her mind buzzing with possibilities.

Evelyn made a guttural sound full of derision. 'But Cuthford is *hardly* Ullswater.'

Seeing the slightly deflated look on Angie's face, Lloyd jumped in. 'Perhaps so, but we're just a short drive away from Durham Cathedral and the castle.'

'Oh,' Clemmie added excitedly, 'and we've got more and more very rich American students paying to study at our prestigious university whose *moms and dads*,' she added in an American accent, 'come over to visit . . . God, they'd be falling over themselves to come and stay in a real *British* country house!' Now Clemmie was sounding almost as excited as Angie had been when she'd first arrived.

'Yes! I can just see the Americans loving it here,' Lloyd agreed, wanting to keep up Angie's spirits. This was the happiest he'd seen her since before Quentin died. *Bloody Evelyn.* Couldn't she just allow Angie to have this moment?

When everyone had gone to bed, Lloyd held back to chat with Mrs Jones, as had become his habit of late. They'd both settled in the chairs by the Aga, the dogs at their feet. Lloyd had a tumbler of whisky, Mrs Jones a cup of tea.

'Well, I think what we've just heard is very good news. Very hopeful. Promising,' Mrs Jones said.

'I agree,' said Lloyd, raising his glass and chinking it with her china teacup. 'And it was also really heartening to hear that Angie wants to involve the village in her plans.'

They both thought for a moment.

'Although it has to be said that it'll take a lot of planning,' Lloyd mused. 'It's not going to be easy – but it's just wonderful to hear Angie sounding so enthusiastic about the manor and the future. I just wish Evelyn would give Angie a break. The poor girl's trying – the last thing she needs is someone knocking her back and belittling her ideas.'

Mrs Jones nodded. 'I agree, but I think you underestimate Angie. She's stronger than you realise. And the way she feels about your wife, she's more likely to try her damnedest to prove her wrong.'

Lloyd looked at Mrs Jones. 'God, I hate it when you call her my *wife*.'

'But she is,' Mrs Jones said. 'There's no getting away from that.'

'Perhaps not,' Lloyd said. He didn't want to share his plans with Cora. It was something he just wanted to do and then tell her.

And then – *finally* – he could try and put right a lifetime's mistake.

Chapter Thirty-Five

As word spread about Angie's plans for Cuthford Manor, so did a sense of excitement and anticipation. It felt almost contagious as others were inspired to think of different ways the place might make money.

Thomas was the first to approach Angie with his idea, or rather, his family's idea.

'I was talking to my mam 'n dad last night – 'n my brothers,' he said to Angie when he caught her taking the dogs out for a walk. 'And they said, "What about fishing?" There's loads of places to fish for trout or go flyfishing. And the Tees has some of the best salmon in the country . . .'

'Great idea, Thomas!' Angie enthused, trying to hold back Winston and Bessie, who were eager to get to the gate, where they knew they'd be let off their leads.

'And my mam said they could bring their catch back to the manor 'n then Alberta could fry it up 'n they could eat it fer their supper!'

'Brilliant idea!' Angie said, finally losing the tug of war. 'Tell your family thank you! I must meet them – perhaps they can be involved with taking people out to the best spots. Maybe even teach them how to fish?'

Thomas's face lit up. 'Ah, they'd love that – especially my brothers. They know all the best spots.'

Angie knew they did – the legitimate as well as the illegitimate ones. Thomas's family were known poachers who were lucky to have been caught only a few times. Lloyd had told her that he had followed Leonard in turning a blind eye to the family's illegal hunting practices.

'There's plenty to go round,' he had told Angie, quoting his father.

Later that day, Danny relayed *his* idea to his sister, suggesting they could start giving horse-riding lessons.

'That's quite a good idea,' Angie said.

'Don't sound so surprised!' Danny laughed.

Angie looked at her brother, who was suddenly growing up fast. He was no longer skinny and was looking more muscular, which was hardly surprising as the moment he was uncaged from the classroom, he was busy in the stables or out riding.

'I'd have to be in charge, though,' he added.

Angie was going to say that he had school, but next year he could leave, and she knew there'd be no stopping him.

'Okay,' Angie said, much to her brother's surprise. 'Why don't you write out a plan of how it would work? What you'd do in the lessons, how long, how much – all that sort of thing. We haven't exactly got loads of horses, so would we need to get more? And would you be able to use Monty and Bomber?'

'Cor, Angie the businesswoman,' Danny said with a half-smile before running off to get his school jotter to start making notes. It was the first time he had ever willingly opened up a schoolbook, never mind had such an incentive.

Angie watched him as he ran off, full of the joys. *Angie the businesswoman*. His words rang in her ears. And she liked the sound of them.

Even Mrs Kwiatkowski, who had taken to sitting with Angie and Lloyd in what had become the 'back office' rather than the 'back parlour', had come up with a few ideas to throw into the pot.

'When Mrs Kwiatkowski was still living in Poland and lived in *her* manor house,' Stanislaw told them all over dinner one night, 'she said they used their spare fields to grow wheat and sugar beet. She suggested we might be able to do the same here.'

Angie was listening and felt a warmth radiate inside her when she heard Stanislaw say 'we'. She felt as though she had a growing team – her own squad of those willing to fight to save the manor.

'That's certainly an idea,' Lloyd said, 'but from what you've told me, two-thirds of Poland is very productive, very fertile flat land which gives bumper crops.'

'That's right,' Stanislaw said proudly,

'Unfortunately, the land around here is not such a match. It's mainly used for farm animals. For grazing. I could have a word with Bill and ask him what the soil's like in the fields we've got lying fallow. See if he thinks we could grow anything.'

'It could give Jake the work he needs to justify us keeping him on,' Angie said.

'And even if you don't decide to "plough the fields and scatter",' Clemmie chipped in, 'Jake could combine his chauffeuring duties with any other jobs that need doing as we transform Cuthford Manor into a *country house hotel*.'

'Agreed,' Angie said, smiling at Clemmie, who had been finding out about the legalities of changing a place of residence into a hotel.

'*I've* also been thinking,' Evelyn announced.

The whole table fell quiet.

'It's an idea I suggested to you some time ago, Angela, for holding events – balls and the like – to raise money for charity.'

'Yes, I remember,' Angie said.

'But that's not going to make *us* any money, is it?' Marlene suddenly piped up, much to everyone's surprise.

'If I'm allowed to finish . . .' Evelyn reprimanded Marlene. 'I was going to say that we could charge for the use of Cuthford Manor and everything else that goes with it, and the charity sets the amount for each ticket and pays us out of what they make. But forgetting about charities for a moment,' she continued, 'we could hire out rooms for parties or events. I thought we could have Gertrude and Jeremy over sometime to discuss how it could be done.'

Angie was taken aback by Evelyn's enthusiasm. Perhaps, she hoped, her mother-in-law was changing. And they all might just be able to live in harmony. Or at least with a degree of conviviality.

'Yes, that sounds like a great idea,' Angie said. 'You organise it and I'll be there.' She glanced at Lloyd, who was looking as surprised as Angie felt.

'Of course, I will make sure I'm there too,' he said.

Heading back to her room in the West Wing, Evelyn felt like screaming. She had been undecided as to whether she should endorse what was happening to Cuthford Manor, but as she tried to work out how to get shot of Angie and her clan, she realised that it would be far more advantageous for her to appear to back the plan for a country house hotel, rather than let it be known how vehemently against it she was. For when she did work out her plan and put it into action, she did not want anyone suspecting her of foul play. If she came out in opposition to it now, it might prove her undoing later on.

Closing her bedroom door behind her, she walked over to her dressing table and looked at herself in the mirror. She could see the strain on her face, which came as no surprise. She was finding it increasingly difficult to keep her hatred for her son's widow under wraps. Everything had come so easily to this miner's daughter – whereas she, Evelyn Foxton-Clarke, had had to work long and hard for her place in society. And unlike the present widow of Cuthford Manor, Evelyn did not choose to wear her poverty-stricken upbringing like a badge of honour.

Nobody still living knew the real Evelyn Foxton-Clarke – or rather, the real Bethany Browne – who had been born and brought up in the slums of Shoreditch in London. An upbringing that was not only dirt poor but shrouded in darkness – for her mother and father's cruelty had known no bounds. She'd seen from a young age the pleasure they derived from inflicting pain on her – whether that be with their words or their hands – and in other ways too.

But she had survived her childhood. Her parents had died and she had lived. Their death had been the first sign of lightness in her life. The leaking gas that had been unwittingly sucked into their lungs while they slept had proved an elixir for the young Bethany Browne, as the gas board paid out a substantial amount in compensation and, as an only child, Bethany received the lot. Not only had she been set free from the hellish existence she had endured, she had also got to keep the pot of gold at the other end of that rainbow, making sure that every penny went towards making her dream a reality.

As a child, she'd imagined herself as a rich princess who wore beautiful clothes and lived in a wonderful castle. As a mature fifteen-year-old, she exchanged this fantasy for one that was more realistic. She would marry a rich man who had a huge estate, and she would live a completely different life from the one she'd been born into.

One of the first things she had done was change her name from Bethany to Evelyn – a name she felt was more in keeping with the upper-class background she was fabricating. She worked hard at losing her cockney accent, immersed herself in the arts and popular culture and educated herself to cover her fictious boarding-school education, then sent herself to a finishing school – fine-tuning every part of herself so that she would blend in effortlessly with the middle and upper classes.

And as she clawed her way out of the East End and infiltrated the higher echelons of society, she erased her old life and created a richer one – in all ways.

She'd kept herself up to date on wealthy, available young men, not just in London but in the whole of the country. She kept a close eye on the obituary pages as she needed someone who did not have a big family. More relatives meant more complications. She also kept an eye out for any articles concerning the gentry. It was an article about Leonard Foxton-Clarke donating a work of art to one of the London galleries that led Evelyn to discover more about the Foxton-Clarke family, Leonard's wife's untimely death from TB, and their only child, a son, who was neither married nor engaged.

Further research led her to a photograph of Cuthford Manor and that was when she had fallen in love. The manor in the north-east of England was almost identical to the one she had once seen in a dog-eared children's book. This was, without a shadow of a doubt, her destiny.

She'd prepared well for her initial meeting with Lloyd at the first ball of the Season, to which she had been invited by her friend from finishing school. She'd done her homework and knew Lloyd would be there. She'd played her part well and, helped by her naturally blonde hair and good looks, had caught his eye and carefully reeled him in.

Lloyd had been a walkover. He'd believed everything she'd told him – how she'd had a wonderful upbringing marred by the tragically early death of her parents in a car accident. After that, they'd conducted a chaste courtship and she had worked her charms. She'd had Lloyd eating out of her hand and proposing to her within just two months, when he took her for a weekend visit to Cuthford Manor.

Seeing the magnificent, magical manor house for real, she wanted it even more, if that were possible.

After a relatively short engagement, they'd married in style in St Cuthbert's Church in the village and then she'd set about getting pregnant as quickly as possible, knowing that would secure her future. Only then could she be sure Cuthford Manor was hers. She'd thanked her lucky stars when she'd fallen within a few months and gave birth to a boy within the first year of their marriage. She'd done what was necessary, although she had no intention of telling her husband that there would be no more children.

For the first ten years or so of their marriage, Evelyn simply luxuriated in living at the manor. She was happy – truly happy – for the first time in her life.

Despite the rumblings of discontent caused by Leonard's will, her life had soon been back on track once she'd realised the status quo would remain unchanged.

It had not been easy keeping up her lies – loving someone and being the person her husband wanted her to be – but it had been worth it.

Which was why she was now determined she would never let a coalminer's daughter take from her something for which she had worked so hard.

It might take time, but she was determined that she would reclaim Cuthford Manor as her own.

Chapter Thirty-Six

Saturday, 4 November

Despite the excitement stirred up by the many plans to transform Cuthford Manor into a moneymaking business, a sense of unease crept into the house in the days leading up to the first anniversary of Quentin's death. Everyone knew it was coming, but no one mentioned it. Until the day itself, when it had to be acknowledged.

Waking up, Angie enjoyed those precious moments of mental oblivion before the mind plays catch-up with reality, when all she was aware of was the warmth and comfort of her bed. But as the residue of sleep slipped away, her heart contracted as she recalled the significance of the day. The wash of grief hit her along with a feeling of nausea. She didn't fight it, though, but instead allowed the grief to triumph and the tears to flow. She cried for a good while, not able to stop, and not wanting to. Perhaps, like Evelyn following Quentin's death, she was trying to 'expunge' her grief – although, unlike her mother-in-law, Angie's reasons were altruistic. She didn't want the children to see her upset. She wanted them to see that today should be acknowledged, but it didn't mean the day should also be mournful.

Splashing her face with ice-cold water to try and reduce the puffiness, Angie got ready and headed down for breakfast. After they'd eaten their bacon sandwiches, she looked round at the children. As always, her way of dealing with tough subjects was head-on.

'So,' she said. 'It's exactly a year since we lost Quentin . . . How are you all feeling?'

No one spoke. Alberta made her excuses and went out for a smoke.

Bonnie looked at Jemima for guidance, but she, along with Bertie, had turned to look at the eldest two.

'We're all right,' Marlene said. 'Actually, we were going to ask if *you* were okay? We loved Quentin, but he was your husband. The love of your life.'

Angie gave her sister a smile. 'Quentin *was* the love of my life,' she said, 'and I'm sad. Obviously, very sad. But I'm learning to adjust.' Angie didn't just want to brush off their concern with a simple 'I'm fine.' She wanted them to know that she really *was* fine.

'And I think Quentin would be annoyed with me if I was still being miserable and not getting on with life, don't you?'

They nodded.

'Do you think you'll ever love again?' Marlene suddenly blurted out.

This, Angie had not expected. What could she say? *No. Never. I'll never love anyone like I did Quentin*? But that was not a very good example of being *fine*. Or of *adjusting*.

'One thing I've learnt this past year,' Angie said instead, 'is that you never know what's around the corner. And even if I don't "love again" in the same way, that doesn't mean I don't have love in my life. I've got all of you lot.'

She leant forward and ruffled Bonnie's hair. It still hurt that her daughter would never know her father. Or have any memories of him.

'And, of course, Mrs Kwiatkowski,' Angie added.

'And you've got Lloyd,' Danny said.

'And Clemmie,' Bertie chirped up.

'And Mrs Jones,' said Jemima.

Just then, Stanislaw walked into the kitchen, bringing a blast of bracing air. Seeing their earnest expressions, he started to back out. 'Sorry, looks like I'm interrupting something.'

'No, you're not,' Marlene said, giving him her best Judy Garland smile. 'We were just checking that Angie's going to be all right today.'

'With it being Quentin's first anniversary,' Danny said, getting up and clearing the table of their plates and the remnants of their bacon sandwiches.

'Marlene just asked Angie if she will love again,' Jemima said.

'Oh, really?' Stanislaw looked at Angie with amused eyes.

'She said no,' Bonnie informed him, shaking her head with great seriousness.

'She didn't *say* no,' Jemima corrected her.

Marlene sighed theatrically. 'She said you never know what's around the corner and it doesn't matter as she has all of us to love, so, yes, she did kind of say no.'

Angie stood up. Her talk to her siblings had not gone as planned.

'Right, come on then. I'm sure Stanislaw doesn't need to hear every cough and spit of our conversation.'

Stanislaw laughed. 'Oh, I don't know. It sounds very interesting.'

'Right, on with the day,' Angie ordered. 'But what I wanted to say, before you all turned the conversation around to me, was that if you do feel funny, sad, upset, it's perfectly normal. Just come and see me. I'm going to be around all day.'

They all nodded with solemn faces.

When Angie walked into the back office, she found Lloyd waiting for her.

'I was thinking of taking the day off,' he told her. 'But only if I know you don't need me.'

Angie shook her head. 'No, I'm fine, Lloyd . . . But how about you? How are you feeling?'

Lloyd sighed. 'I'll be okay when the day's been and gone . . . Are you sure you don't need me?'

'Honestly, I'd say, but I really am fine. Don't worry about me,' Angie reassured him.

'You're a strong woman, Angie. I'm proud to have you as my daughter-in-law,' Lloyd said, his voice breaking with emotion.

Angie watched as he wandered off down the corridor, feeling choked herself. His words had touched her. It was the kind of thing Quentin would have said. Like father, like son.

Angie took a deep breath and forced herself to start doing some work, but it was hard to concentrate and she felt unusually lacking in motivation.

Just before midday, Wilfred knocked on Angie's open door and stepped into the office. He'd come to tell her that her mother-in-law had gone out for the day.

'She said to tell you not to worry about her, that she's "seeking solace on this awful day" with Mrs Fontaine-Smith in Durham,' Wilfred relayed.

'Thanks, Wilfred. Why don't you have the day off?' Angie said as she shuffled papers together and returned them to their file.

'I'd rather keep busy, if that's all right by you, miss?'

Angie got up and squeezed Wilfred's arm. This was a sad day for everyone at Cuthford Manor. Wilfred, Mrs Jones and Alberta had known Quentin since he was a baby.

'That's fine by me, Wilfred,' she said. 'I think I might have a break, though – get some fresh air and give the dogs a walk.'

Five minutes later, Angie had put on her warm walking clothes and wellies and was out the back door, being pulled across the cobbles by an overeager Winston and Bessie.

Seeing her on her way out, Stanislaw had a quick word with Thomas and grabbed his jacket. Pulling it on, he jogged up alongside her. 'Fancy a bit of company? I could do with stretching my legs.'

Angie's first reaction was to say no, she was fine on her own, but she found herself hesitating.

'I'll take that as a yes, then,' Stanislaw said, taking Winston's lead.

'Heel!' he commanded. Winston stopped pulling and did as he was told.

Bessie, realising that she was still attached to Angie, started to pull again.

'I really need to learn how to do that,' Angie sighed. 'They do as they're told when I'm in the house, but as soon as we're outside, they have minds of their own.'

Stanislaw chuckled. 'I think it helps to have a deep voice.'

They walked to the gate and then let them both go. Winston tore off just a little ahead of Bessie, through the muddy field. Suddenly, they changed direction. They'd got a scent and were off at a right angle.

Angie and Stanislaw followed their tracks across the field, trying to avoid the more boggy areas. They saw the dogs disappear into woodland, which was where they always ended up in their fruitless attempts to catch some furry animal that was far quicker than they were.

'How are you feeling?' Stanislaw asked.

They walked on for a while as Angie considered her answer.

'I think I feel all right,' she said. 'I had a good blub this morning, and then I decided enough was enough. I was telling the children before you came into the kitchen that Quentin wouldn't want us to be miserable, and I really believe that.'

'That's good.' Stanislaw nodded.

'How do you manage these strange anniversary days?' Angie asked, wiping her nose with the sleeve of her waxed cotton jacket.

'Well, I think I now do see it as an *anniversary*. I force myself to think of the happy times I had with Adrianna. I realised that for years I was letting the Russians destroy the life we had before they killed her, and I couldn't let them do that. So now I remember her face, her smile, her funny ways. And so it becomes about remembrance, not mourning. About the love we shared, rather than about her loss.'

'That is such a wonderful way of thinking.' Angie nodded. 'Perhaps I should try and do the same.'

They both avoided a large, muddy puddle.

'Do you think the children will be all right today?' Stanislaw asked.

Angie nodded. 'Yes, I think they will. They've had a lot to deal with in their lives. They're tough.'

'I heard that their mother abandoned them,' he said.

'Yes. She did that. Ran off with some young bloke she reckoned she was in love with.'

Stanislaw hesitated. He wanted to say he could not understand how a mother could just desert her children. But it was not his place to judge.

'And their dad didn't want them either,' Angie added. 'I wrote a few times, asking Dad if he wanted to see his children, even offered to take them to him, but he never replied. Although, if I'm totally honest, I was glad. By the time we all came here, Dad was drinking more and more – if he wasn't down the mine, he was in the pub.'

Again, as someone who would have dearly loved to have been a father, Stanislaw could not understand how a man could be so indifferent to, so lacking in love for his own flesh and blood.

'It was a wonderful thing you did,' he said. 'Taking them under your wing and bringing them here – giving them the love they weren't getting at home.'

Angie stepped over a log, keeping her eye on the dogs, who were presently sniffing around the bottom of a large oak tree. 'I couldn't have done anything else,' she said. 'My conscience would never have let me leave them there when I was going off to live in a huge manor house.'

'And you brought Mrs Kwiatkowski too – that was incredibly kind-hearted of you,' Stanislaw said, his tone full of admiration.

Winston and Bessie sped off again as Angie and Stanislaw drew near, just in case they were about to put them back on their leads.

'It's strange you say that,' Angie said, 'because I was just thinking today how everything seems to have turned around.'

'How come?' Stanislaw asked, looking at Angie and thinking how naturally pretty she was.

'Well, initially it might seem that I was the one who saved the children – and Mrs Kwiatkowski – but actually, they've been the ones to pull me out of the mire.'

Stanislaw was clearly interested in what she was saying, so Angie continued. 'They forced me to carry on after Quentin died. I couldn't just give up. And they've been brilliant with Bonnie. She's become their little sister. The same goes for Mrs Kwiatkowski. She's always been there for the children – from when we first came here.'

Stanislaw nodded.

'She was like a ready-made grandmother to them. It helped me out no end. Especially when Bonnie came along.'

'It is as the proverb says,' Stanislaw said. 'Kindness begets kindness.'

They came to a five-bar gate and Angie climbed over and jumped down into the adjoining field. Stanislaw followed, his long legs making the process much easier and quicker.

'Actually, that's also a bit like your soldier bear, Wojtek,' Angie said. 'You and your fellow soldiers took him in and saved him, but he ended up giving you all so much more in return. And I don't just mean carrying heavy artillery.'

'He certainly did,' Stanislaw agreed. 'Perhaps when I go and see him next, you and the children might want to accompany me.'

'I'd like that,' Angie said. She chuckled. 'We can take him a bottle of beer.'

'And a cigarette!' Stanislaw added.

They were halfway across the field when Angie realised that she couldn't see the dogs any more. Looking around the long grass they were wading through, she put her thumb and finger in her mouth and whistled. There was a rustling sound before their two big, furry heads could be seen bobbing up and down above the grass as they raced back to their mistress.

Stanislaw laughed.

'Something I learnt in the shipyards,' Angie explained.

Stanislaw's smile was wide. 'You are a unique woman, Angie Foxton-Clarke.'

Angie didn't know what to say. She felt herself blush, which annoyed her.

'Come on, we'd better get these dogs back. God knows what they've been eating or rolling in while we've been chatting.'

Chapter Thirty-Seven

Contrary to what she'd told Wilfred, Evelyn had not chosen to spend the day with her friend Gertrude 'seeking solace' on the anniversary of her son's death, but was instead with her lover, Desmond Pyburn.

Desmond had lasted longer than most of Evelyn's paramours, although this was not down to any overwhelming feelings of love – or even affection – for the man, nor because of his 'dashing' looks, which, it had to be said, were fading with age, his black hair now losing its battle with grey, and his once muscular physique giving way to a pot belly. The reason Evelyn had earmarked Desmond as her bedfellow and had kept him for so long was because he worked for Farrell & Sons, the family's law firm, and was not averse to providing Evelyn with confidential information.

The practicalities of their affair were made easier and discretion maintained by Desmond having his own pied-à-terre in Durham's South Street for when he was 'working late' and wouldn't be driving back to his family home in the market town of Bishop Auckland.

Sitting up in Desmond's plush double bed in a small Georgian terrace that boasted views of Durham Cathedral, Evelyn accepted one of her lover's Sobranie cigarettes. She hadn't smoked in the past, but had got into the habit when she'd started her liaison with Desmond.

'You know, it's all coming back to me today – this awful anniversary. I keep thinking of Quentin and how it still seems so unfair that my son has died and this woman, this miner's daughter, who he'd really only been with all of ten minutes, has inherited the whole lot,' Evelyn said, taking another long drag and exhaling slowly.

'By the "whole lot", you mean Cuthford Manor?' Desmond asked.

'Yes, of course *Cuthford Manor*,' Evelyn snapped. She was not worried about anything else her son might have left his wife, which, due to the government's greed, was very little. She thanked her lucky stars that a former lover, a very astute financier, had advised her to create a bank account solely in her name, so that she could siphon money away. Her financier had rubberstamped the application which had been 'signed' by Lloyd, as required by law if a married woman wanted to open a bank account.

Evelyn had also rented a safety-deposit box with the bank, which she was slowly filling up with jewellery and other small but very valuable antiques she knew neither Lloyd nor Angie would miss. Thankfully, her daughter-in-law was not a great one for jewellery. Evelyn knew Angie treasured her diamond engagement ring, though not because it was big and expensive, but rather because there was some kind of sentimental story behind it involving Quentin and her friend Dorothy.

If anything happened to Lloyd, the tax man would not get his sticky fingers on what Evelyn had stashed away.

Desmond took a sip of the cognac he allowed himself on afternoons like this. He checked the time. He'd said he was out on a long lunch with a possible client, so he didn't have to get back to the office until late afternoon.

'So, Desi, darling,' Evelyn ran her hand up his hairy chest, 'are you any nearer working out how I can legally claim the manor as mine – or rather, mine and Lloyd's?'

'I'm afraid the only way you and your husband will be lord and lady of the manor – or should I say lady and lord of the manor – is if Mrs Angela Foxton-Clarke were to die.' Desmond put out his cigarette. 'Cuthford Manor might go to the daughter, but you and Lloyd would be trustees of the pile until Bonnie were to come of age.'

Which would not be a problem, Evelyn thought. She'd ship Bonnie off to boarding school and send the rest of Angie's 'tribe' down under to live with their older sister.

'You just want to make sure your husband never finds out about our little shenanigans – or any others you might have had. Because then you wouldn't be allowed within a mile of the place.'

Evelyn bristled. *Lloyd would never divorce her. Would he?*

'I hate to say this, Evelyn.' Desmond took a swig of his brandy. 'But the only way that manor is ever going to be truly yours is if, *God forbid*, everyone were to perish in some awful tragedy.'

'Dear God, I can't even bear the *thought*,' Evelyn said, trying to sound sincere.

Desmond sighed.

'Why don't you,' he said, folding her in his arms, 'forget all about Cuthford Manor, leave that dull husband of yours and run off with me?'

'Mmm,' Evelyn said, giving in to his advances. 'I wonder what your wife, three children and business partners would think of that?'

Chapter Thirty-Eight

After his walk with Angie, Stanislaw worked until late, which was his habit. His *mama* and *tata* had instilled in him his strong work ethic. They were honest, hard-working people, never flush with money but still able to put food on the table and live a comfortable life. It helped that they had only had the one child, although Stanislaw had known his mama would have liked more, especially as she was a devout Catholic, but she'd accepted her lot and told those who asked that it was God's wish. When both his parents died of 'dust pneumonia', caused by working the land and getting dust and grit on their lungs, Stanislaw had been distraught as they were still relatively young. But now he was glad they were not alive to see what had happened to their precious Polska – a country destroyed beyond recognition.

Stanislaw would never forget the devastation he'd seen with his own eyes. Beautiful churches reduced to rubble; parks dotted with the bare mounds of hurried graves; trees tossed in the air with the violence of an explosion, their roots exposed as if they'd been plucked by a giant hand and tossed aside. But it was the smell that would never leave him – the stench of human putrefaction.

By working the hours he did at Cuthford Manor, only turning in for the night when he was dropping with exhaustion or after accompanying Mrs Kwiatkowski to dinner, Stanislaw was able to keep these images and memories at bay. To live each day as it was given to him. And when each day was done, he needed to be physically exhausted to ensure the respite of sleep. Not that sleep always gave him such a reprieve, as his dreams were often filled with the horrors of war or the gulag.

Lately, though, his more pleasant dreams had started to include Angie. He tried to rationalise that this was simply because Angie had become part of his life – but, if that was the case, why didn't he also dream of Lloyd and Thomas and everyone else at Cuthford Manor? *Why was it just Angie?*

He had a strong suspicion, but he wouldn't allow himself to go down that path. For it could never be. Life didn't give you second chances at love. He had always believed that. And he could tell that Angie believed it too. But more importantly, he knew that she didn't *want* another chance at love.

Which was not how he felt. Not any more. It had been eleven years since Adrianna was taken from him. They had been young when they'd met, just fifteen, and had been engaged at seventeen, married at eighteen – and would have had a family before they'd both reached twenty had it not been for the war. Much had happened since then. But in all that time, he had never *wanted* to be with another woman. Had never *met* another woman he wanted to be with.

Until now.

Chapter Thirty-Nine

Sunday, 5 November

Guy Fawkes Night

When Angie woke the next day, she felt relieved that she had got through the anniversary of Quentin's death. Having survived its passing, she somehow felt stronger.

Last night in bed, she had recalled what Stanislaw had said, that no one could take away the good times. She had to remember Quentin's life rather than his death. So, as she'd lain awake and had felt grief descend, she'd stopped it in its tracks and in place of the sorrow, she'd made herself go through the highlights of her life with Quentin. The day she'd first met him; their dates, which had been few and far between because of the war; Quentin's proposal at the Christmas Extravaganza; their unconventional but wonderful wedding; their married life here at Cuthford Manor; the excitement when she'd found out she was pregnant with Bonnie, and how their love had deepened in a way she hadn't expected when Bonnie was born.

And so, this morning, when Angie drew back the curtains and looked out at the emerging orange and yellow glow radiating across the horizon, she made the decision that today was going to be a happy day – and that this year they would celebrate Guy Fawkes Night. She would not let it be forever tainted by Quentin's passing.

After quickly getting dressed, she headed down for breakfast. Entering the warm kitchen, she saw the children were already sitting around the kitchen table, eating their porridge, and Alberta was at the sink, washing up pans. At the arrival of their mistress, Winston and Bessie nearly knocked Alberta over in their enthusiasm to get to her first.

'Them two'll be the death of me,' the cook grumbled, but Angie knew she loved having the dogs' company as she went about her work and spoilt them rotten.

'Morning all.' Angie sat down at the kitchen table and poured herself a cup of tea. Alberta disappeared into the pantry and the dogs flopped back down in front of the Aga.

'Listen to this!' Marlene said.

Angie was overjoyed to see that Marlene was actually reading a newspaper. They had the *Daily Mirror* and the *Northern Echo* delivered and she was always on at them to read the papers and find out what was happening.

'We're all ears,' Angie said, pouring a little milk into her cup and giving it a stir.

'Well . . .' Marlene looked up with wide, scandalised eyes. 'It says here that Errol Flynn "committed an offence" in a locked cabin on his yacht with a sixteen-year-old girl.'

Angie rolled her eyes. 'And there was me thinking you were going to tell us something of interest. Is there any real news in that rag?'

Bertie took the newspaper from Marlene and nudged his spectacles up the bridge of his nose. 'The main story is about the war in Korea,' he said, skimming through the article while the rest of his siblings carried on eating their porridge. 'It looks like there's "a major battle raging in north-west Korea. The UN forces were forced to withdraw after the Communists made a counter-attack. The spokesman would not say if Chinese troops have joined in the fighting."'

Marlene made a show of yawning. Angie threw her a look of reprimand.

As Bertie relayed how new British reinforcements had reached the south-eastern port of Pusan in the troopship *Empress of Australia*, Angie thought of the British men who had been called up to fight and wondered how many would die before the year was out. She thanked God that Danny was too young to do his national service and prayed that when the time came, the country wouldn't be involved in a war which had nothing to do with them.

'Thank you, Bertie,' Angie said. 'I'm glad one of you is interested in what's happening in the world.'

Alberta reappeared from the pantry. The dogs raised their heads and sniffed to see if it was worth getting up for. As it was only potatoes, turnips and carrots, they didn't bother.

'So,' Angie said when they'd all finished breakfast, 'who wants to go to the village bonfire and fireworks display this evening?'

The reaction was as expected.

'Me! Me! Me!' Bertie, Jemima and Bonnie chorused.

Marlene nodded her head enthusiastically. 'Can I invite Belinda?'

'Yes, of course,' Angie said. 'Tell her she can stay over if she wants.'

Marlene's face lit up. She was just about to speak when Angie beat her to it.

'Yes, you can use the phone – but make it short.' Angie knew she was wasting her breath. Marlene and Belinda could talk until the cows came home.

Marlene dashed off.

Angie looked at Danny, who looked less enthusiastic. 'It's not that I don't want to go, but I want to stay here – see the horses are all right.'

'Are you sure? I can ask Stanislaw or Thomas to watch over them?'

Danny shook his head. 'I'd rather do it myself.'

Angie knew why. It was Ghost he was particularly worried about.

Much as she might want today to be free of thoughts of death, it was inevitable that there would still be shadows. It was Guy Fawkes Night, after all, and it seemed highly likely the loud bang that had spooked Ghost a year ago had been made by a firework.

By the time everyone walked into the village for the display, the temperature had dropped, but it was a wonderfully clear evening, a perfect backdrop for the fireworks. For a change, the rain had kept away, so it was just the cold to contend with – and they were all well used to that. Hats, woollen scarves, thick winter coats and boots were the required attire, although Marlene and Belinda had added a good layer of make-up and had optimistically curled their hair. Angie put on a disapproving air, but it wasn't very convincing and she couldn't help smiling when they weren't looking as they reminded her so much of herself and Dorothy in younger days.

As Angie and the children arrived at the field behind the nursery where the display was to take place, she thought it looked as though the entire village was there.

It had been agreed that Stanislaw would bring Mrs Kwiatkowski in the car. As much as Mrs Kwiatkowski liked her walks, it was cold, and in Angie's words, 'there wasn't a pickin' on her'.

Lloyd had reluctantly agreed to accompany Evelyn, who had surprised everyone with her enthusiasm. She had even persuaded Gertrude and Jeremy to come along.

As Angie watched Bertie, Jemima and Bonnie race over to watch the bonfire being lit, she looked around for any other familiar faces. Seeing a few of the mams from the nursery arriving, she waved to them. Angie now knew, or at least recognised, most of the locals. Dr Wright was there with his wife and family. And there was the landlord of the Farmer's Arms, Donald Grey, and the barmaid who had given Angie a mug of tea and a double brandy on the day she'd broken down in tears after giving Quentin's clothes to the Travellers. She hadn't realised that the barmaid was married to Donald, and although his wife was a lovely woman, Angie felt embarrassed whenever she saw her.

'Excuse me . . . Sorry . . . If I can just squeeze through, please . . .'

Angie immediately recognised the voice. She turned round to see Stanislaw stooping slightly as he guided Mrs Kwiatkowski towards her.

'Ah, you made it!' Angie said, surprised by how uplifted she felt on seeing them both.

'We did!' Stanislaw said. 'What is that expression? *We would not miss it for the world.*'

Mrs Kwiatkowski smiled and spoke in Polish as she positioned herself to Angie's left to allow the two to chat.

'Looks like Ted and Eugene are here with their girlfriends.' Stanislaw looked over at the other side of the bonfire, which was now starting to roar.

'And Marlene and Belinda seem to have found Thomas and his friends,' Angie said through clenched teeth.

'Don't worry, I've already had a word with Thomas,' Stanislaw said.

If anyone had been eavesdropping, they would have thought they were earwigging on the concerned conversation of parents worried about their wayward daughter.

'Thank you,' Angie mouthed. Thomas would never do anything to cross Stanislaw. If only he could do the same to all the other boys Marlene might set her sights on.

'Did you see Danny before you left?' she asked.

Stanislaw nodded and rubbed his hands together. 'He loves that horse, doesn't he?'

'He does,' Angie agreed. 'I just wish I'd never sold him. He was as miserable as sin afterwards and *I* felt as guilty as sin. If I'd kept him, I'd have saved us a lot of unhappiness and remorse.'

'But, selfishly, I'm very glad you did sell, as otherwise I'd not have become part of your lives,' Stanislaw said, glancing down at Angie, whose face he could only just make out due to the thick bobble hat pulled down to her eyebrows and the woollen scarf wrapped around her neck and pulled up to her bottom lip.

'And *I'm* glad you're a part of our lives too,' Angie said. 'You've helped a lot – and I don't just mean with work, but with the children.' She paused. 'And me.' She looked up at him. 'You've helped me, too. I feel I have gained a good friend. Someone who understands.'

Stanislaw felt his heart lift and then plummet in the space of a second. The sudden high of being told how much he was wanted, how happy she was to have him here, followed by the nosedive from hearing the word 'friend'.

As the bonfire started to reach Guy Fawkes' stockinged feet, Bertie, Jemima and Bonnie came back with red noses and roses in their cheeks.

Jemima went to nestle up to Mrs Kwiatkowski, who put her arm around her and pulled her close. Bonnie put her hands up, showing her mum she wanted to be picked up. Angie acquiesced, knowing her daughter wouldn't see much otherwise.

'Here,' Stanislaw said, seeing Bertie looking a little lost. 'Do you want to go on my shoulders?'

Bertie nodded a little apprehensively.

Angie watched as Stanislaw took hold of her brother as if he was as light as the stuffed Guy Fawkes and popped him over his head and onto his shoulders. He took hold of Bertie's mittened hands in his own to help him keep his balance.

Bertie looked as pleased as punch to have a bird's-eye view of the entire event.

Angie smiled. She was glad Stanislaw was making a fuss of Bertie. He was the middle child and the quietest, and therefore the one who got the least attention.

More people arrived as the time neared for the start of the firework display and Angie felt herself being squashed up against Stanislaw.

'I feel like a sardine in a can,' she joked.

'Sorry – do you want me to make some more room?' Stanislaw looked around.

'No, don't worry,' Angie said, jigging Bonnie up on her hip, 'I don't mind. It's keeping me warm.'

Just then the first firework exploded, the bright white sparks looking like a scattering of stars high in the blue-black sky. There was a collective '*Aah*'. As more explosions followed, Angie felt a tap on her shoulder and turned to see Clemmie, who took the opportunity to wedge herself between her friend and Stanislaw. She couldn't help herself. It had irked her seeing them so close to each other – *and so blummin' comfortable with being so bloody close.*

Clemmie looked up at Stanislaw and Bertie and said hello in Polish, then leant forward to give the same greeting to Mrs Kwiatkowski and Jemima.

Jemima smiled, but Clemmie thought Mrs Kwiatkowski didn't look like she was enjoying the display very much, as she was frowning.

Clemmie was right. Mrs Kwiatkowski was not enjoying the display. She had instinctively pulled Jemima closer, more to protect her than to keep her warm. Jemima's pale little face was staring up in awe at all the pretty colours bursting to life against the coal-black sky, but she had her hands pressed against her ears. Had Mrs Kwiatkowski not had her arms wrapped around Jemima, she, too, would also have liked to mute the sudden loud bangs and explosions. She didn't like it. It reminded her of something that was not good – not good at all – but she was damned if she could recall what it was.

Chapter Forty

When the display was over, they all made their way back to the manor. As they walked down the driveway, Angie saw their home as she had not seen it for a long time. The outside lights were on and there was already a frost forming on the lawns as well as on the Welsh-slate roof and tapered turrets. Smoke was billowing out of the chimneys, which, together with the sudden descent of freezing fog, gave it a magical feel.

The beauty and surrealness of the manor took Angie's breath away – as it had the first time she saw it when Quentin had driven them down this very driveway.

As they neared the house, Angie saw the front door begin to open. She smiled as Winston and Bessie bulldozed Wilfred out of the way before he had time to open it properly. The dogs came racing out to greet everyone.

Pulling the door wide open, Wilfred smiled as everyone hurried towards the warmth. The children charged in first, flinging off their hats, coats and boots before running to the dining room, where Alberta had laid out her Guy Fawkes banquet.

Angie and Clemmie were the next over the threshold, followed by Marlene and Belinda, who were chattering away excitedly. Angie guessed their high spirits were not down to the actual firework display but to the gang of young village lads she'd seen them talking to. Angie had almost felt sorry for Thomas and his friend, who had looked on with woebegone expressions.

Next to arrive were Stanislaw and Mrs Kwiatkowski in the Morris Minor, then Lloyd in the Bentley with Evelyn, Gertrude and Jeremy.

Lloyd was pleased to be back, and as he walked into the dining room, he saw Angie, Clemmie and Stanislaw all happily chatting away. They looked frozen to the bone and hungry as they devoured Alberta's warm sausage rolls.

Making his way to the drinks cabinet to get Evelyn and Gertrude their vodka tonics, he saw Danny hurry in and head straight to Stanislaw. He knew Danny had stayed back to keep an eye on the horses and that Stanislaw had been teaching him some techniques to keep horses calm.

After giving Evelyn and Gertrude their drinks, Lloyd left them to it. He had no doubt they would be plotting their own banquets and charity events for the county's 'crème de la crème'. He knew this as Evelyn had been saying as much while they sat in the Bentley and watched the fireworks. At the display, Lloyd would have given anything to get out of the car and join Angie and everyone else from Cuthford Manor, but sometimes he had to fulfil his role of husband. It was one he was becoming increasingly loathe to play, and he knew the time was approaching for him to stop the charade.

'So, the horses were all fine,' Danny was saying as Lloyd and Jeremy joined Angie, Clemmie and Stanislaw.

'I would have thought half a mile would muffle the sound,' Jeremy chipped in, in a clear bid to ingratiate himself with Angie. His nose had been out of joint ever since Stanislaw had appeared on the scene. Tonight, more than any other time he'd seen Stanislaw and Angie together, you could almost feel their chemistry.

'Yeah, the distance helped, but they were still on alert,' Danny said through a mouthful of pastry and sausage meat. 'Starling and the shires weren't so bad – and of course Lucky was oblivious.' They all smiled. They knew there was very little that could spook a pit pony. 'But Ghost's ears kept twitching. And I could see he was unsettled. He got that look in his eyes.' This was said to Stanislaw, who nodded. 'So, I did that thing you taught me,' Danny said, his voice full of pride. 'And it worked. It really worked!'

'That's good,' Stanislaw said.

Naturally, everyone wanted to know what the technique was.

'You explain,' Stanislaw said, glancing over at Mrs Kwiatkowski, who was sitting on one of the dining-room chairs with Bonnie on her lap and Jemima next to her. They were sharing a large slice of parkin and chatting away. Bonnie and Jemima were licking their fingers, which were sticky from the cake. Stanislaw was beginning to think that the two might be starting to understand Polish. It wouldn't surprise him.

*

Seeing Dr Wright arrive with his wife and three children, Angie went over to greet them. They were followed by Thomas and his friend, and Ted and Eugene with their partners, who looked a little overawed as this was the first time they'd been inside the manor. Angie had invited the mams from the nursery, and although she was disappointed they hadn't come, she thought it just as well as the dining room was now full to bursting and the bonfire buffet was quickly disappearing.

Spotting Mrs Jones dressed in a rather chic cobalt-blue dress, Angie hurried over to her.

'You look lovely,' she said, feeling underdressed in her slacks and short-sleeved cashmere jumper. Glancing around, she realised that all the other women were wearing pretty dresses, at least a little make-up, and they all had styled their hair into updos, like Mrs Jones, or curled and let loose, like the groundsmen's girlfriends.

Angie was just about to introduce Mrs Jones to those she didn't know when Lloyd appeared at her side and took over. Angie watched them disappear into the crowded room, the air a mix of perfume, cigarette smoke and the smell of the village bonfire. She caught her reflection in one of the large gilt-framed mirrors adorning the oak-panelled walls and got a jolt. Her hair needed a cut, she hadn't a scrap of make-up on and quite frankly, as her mam used to say, she looked like 'something the cat's dragged in'. She thought of Stanislaw and how he had called her 'unique'.

Well, she was certainly that.

*

Mrs Kwiatkowski was playing cards with Bonnie and Jemima at the dining table when suddenly she froze.

She had remembered what it was she'd been trying to recall while they were watching the firework display. And with that remembrance came the same shock she'd felt when she had heard it the first time.

It was so shocking that had she not heard it with her own ears that night, she would never have believed it.

Placing her cards on the table, she told the two girls to carry on playing without her. They seemed to understand and put her cards at the bottom of the pile.

Feeling panicked that she might forget what it was she needed to tell Angie, Mrs Kwiatkowski scanned the smoky, crowded room. Finally, she spotted her. She got up and weaved through the throng of chatting and laughing guests to reach Angie, who was standing on her own, looking lost in her own thoughts.

Angie jumped as she felt someone grip her arm. Looking round, she saw it was Mrs Kwiatkowski, who immediately started speaking to her in Polish.

Straight away Angie could see that she was upset.

'What is it?' she asked, feeling a pull on her heart. Dr Wright had warned her this might happen. Angie took Mrs Kwiatkowski's hand and squeezed it. 'Let me find Stanislaw.'

Surveying the room, she spotted Stanislaw, whose height put him a good few inches above the second-tallest person in the room, which was a toss-up between Jeremy and Lloyd. She waved to catch his attention.

Stanislaw quickly made his way over. 'Is everything all right?' he asked.

Mrs Kwiatkowski put a hand on his arm, gripped it tightly and started talking – fast and frantically.

After a minute, he turned to Angie. 'It's hard to make out what she's trying to say – I'm only picking up bits and pieces. She seems very anxious. Can we go into a quieter room?'

'Of course,' Angie said. 'Follow me.'

Stanislaw and Mrs Kwiatkowski, who was now as white as a sheet and still talking, followed Angie into the front lounge. Thankfully, the room was empty apart from Winston and Bessie, who were lying stretched out in front of the fire. They didn't move a muscle, which was their way when they were somewhere they weren't supposed to be, as though by remaining perfectly still they might avoid detection.

Angie sat Mrs Kwiatkowski down on the sofa and settled next to her. Stanislaw perched on the edge of the armchair, leaning forward, his focus on Mrs Kwiatkowski.

'What is it, Mrs Kwiatkowski?' Angie asked gently. 'What's bothering you?'

And so Mrs Kwiatkowski started to talk. Her face full of anguish. Her words spilling out, hands clasping and unclasping her thick woollen skirt.

Stanislaw listened, his face becoming graver by the second.

Angie felt the stirrings of concern. Something was wrong.

Stanislaw asked a few questions in Polish and listened intently to Mrs Kwiatkowski's response. When Mrs

Kwiatkowski finished, Angie wasn't sure who out of the two of them now looked more angst-ridden.

'Well, come on, tell me. Honestly, it's times like this I really wish I'd at least tried to learn Polish,' she said, trying to lighten the atmosphere.

When Angie asked Stanislaw to translate what Mrs Kwiatkowski had just told him, he didn't know what to say. He knew he couldn't tell her the truth. Not yet, anyway. He hated lying – even white lies – but this was a situation where it was imperative. And where he had to make it convincing. Standing up, he told Angie that he would tell her after he'd taken Mrs Kwiatkowski upstairs to her room. Turning so that Mrs Kwiatkowski couldn't hear, he said in barely a whisper, 'She's a bit confused.'

As he took Mrs Kwiatkowski up to her room, he told her that he understood why she was so desperate. That he knew her memory was failing her and that it must feel like a switch which could flick on and off within a very short period of time. She nodded, glad of the understanding. This was something Stanislaw told her now on an almost daily basis – and it seemed to bring her comfort.

He also told Mrs Kwiatkowski that he needed to tell Angie this shocking, abhorrent news when she was on her own, and Angie's old neighbour nodded sagely and said she was going to bed, but she would be here if Angie wanted to talk further.

'I will tell her,' Stanislaw promised. 'But you needn't worry about it any more. Now that I know, I will deal with it.'

Of course, there was no way he could tell Angie what Mrs Kwiatkowski had divulged, not until he'd had time to think it over, and also to find out if it was true – that what Mrs Kwiatkowski had heard that night at the Travellers' camp was right.

He also knew that by the time Mrs Kwiatkowski had gone through her evening ablutions, changed into her dressing gown and climbed into bed, she was likely to have forgotten what she had told him that had caused her so much distress. It was why Stanislaw had made the suggestion that he tell Angie on her own.

After going back down to the lounge, he found Angie sitting on the floor, stroking the dogs, her face red with the heat from the fire. She'd confessed to him that she couldn't tell them off for being in here because she let them sneak in when she came here of an evening with her cup of tea before going to bed. Stanislaw smiled. Dogs – and bears – he thought, were life's angels. They were always there for you and loved you unconditionally.

Luckily, when he explained that Mrs Kwiatkowski had been worried about something that had happened when she was a young girl in Poland, Angie did not pick up that he was lying, which pained him. He felt terrible for deceiving her, even though he knew it was for the best.

After saying goodnight to Angie, who looked in no rush to go back to the party, he went to his room. He needed to be up early and wanted to be on his own to take on board the seriousness of Mrs Kwiatkowski's accusations.

He had to find a way to prove them before repeating what she'd said. If it was just her word, there was a good chance she'd be dismissed.

But if he had proof from those who had been involved, however unwittingly, then he would tell Angie.

He felt his jaws clench. How would she react?

This was going to blow her whole world apart – for the second time.

Chapter Forty-One

Monday, 6 November

When Stanislaw woke at the crack of dawn, he got changed and headed straight out to the stables. As he chatted to Ghost while saddling him up, he heard the back door open and clash shut and looked up to see Danny clomping over the cobbles in unlaced boots, a big coat over his pyjamas.

'You're out early – you going somewhere?' Danny asked.

'I thought I'd have a ride up to Sherburn Hill – see if the Travellers are still there.' Stanislaw tried to keep it as vague as possible.

'Ah, let me come!' Danny begged.

Stanislaw immediately rued the fact he'd told the truth.

'Another time,' he said, putting his foot into the stirrup and mounting Ghost. 'Besides, you've got school.'

Seeing the disappointment on Danny's face, he softened his tone. 'I promise, another time, and we can stay longer. You can get to know their horses.' He let out a short bark of laughter. 'You'll want to bring them all back here, though, and give them a good wash and groom.'

Danny nodded and smiled. He'd seen the Travellers' horses with their matted manes and muddy coats. 'Enjoy!' he shouted out as horse and rider left. 'You've got a beautiful morning for it.'

Stanislaw put up a hand to wave his farewell. The boy was right. This morning the sky could be mistaken for a celestial volcano that had spilled its crimson and yellow lava across the horizon. And yet Stanislaw's mind remained firmly set on the task in hand. A task that would have to be carried out very carefully if he wanted to verify what Mrs Kwiatkowski had said. He hoped against hope that she was wrong – that there had been some misunderstanding. But he had lain awake half the night, putting the pieces of the jigsaw together, and the picture that had formed led him to conclude it could well be true.

Once away from the manor, Stanislaw let Ghost have free rein, horse and rider both relishing the unbridled freedom. Stanislaw understood exactly why Angie loved to go out riding on her own. It was the ultimate escape from everything and everyone.

As they neared the camp, Stanislaw gently pulled Ghost back into a loping canter and then a gentle trot. He suspected that the Travellers' first reaction would be to lie – to deny what Mrs Kwiatkowski had heard that evening she had spent with them. The young lad and his elders had obviously not realised that the confused old woman they had found wandering across fields in the dark in just her dress and cardigan, speaking in a language they didn't know, could understand English.

Stanislaw had himself been amazed that Mrs Kwiatkowski had understood their accent. When he said this to her, she had told him there had been a small Irish community in Sunderland and one of her friends who belonged to it came from Cork and had shared the same melodic dialect.

Approaching the camp, Stanislaw could see that there were already a number of people up and about. The fire looked as though it had been stoked up, as its flames were robust and tall and were flicking around the large cauldron hanging over it.

The dogs came scampering up to greet him, giving the stranger a few cursory warning growls and barks.

'Good dogs, good dogs,' Stanislaw said, knowing they might recognise his voice, and that even if they didn't, his tone would subdue them, which it did.

The Travellers' horses could be seen behind the caravans, grazing on a patch of green. They raised their heads when they saw the newcomers, watching from their spot, knowing the ropes that tied them would not allow them to fraternise.

A few of the men, cigarettes hanging off their lips, stared as Stanislaw dismounted and walked towards them with Ghost.

'Hello there, I'm Stanislaw Nowak – you might recognise me from a few weeks back when you took in an old Polish woman. I'm trying to find the woman with the long curly red hair who is with child, and her young lad, who is about this tall . . .' Stanislaw put his hand out to show them the boy's height. 'I really need to talk to them both.'

The men remained silent.

'Come o' here!'

Stanislaw turned to see the old woman with the lined face and pigtails on the top step of her colourful caravan. He walked over with Ghost.

''Tis a beautiful horse yer have yerself tere,' she said through a cloud of smoke, her rolled cigarette between two nicotine-stained fingers. She pointed to a wooden pole next to her caravan where he could hook Ghost's reins, then turned and disappeared through the drawn velvet curtain.

As soon as Stanislaw walked into the caravan, he was hit by the colour and the warmth. The place was cluttered, cosy and clean. At the far end was a raised sleeping area, the bed covered in a beautiful hand-made quilt and a mound of cushions. It was sectioned off by a pair of red drapes tied loosely back with gold-coloured cord. In the middle of the living area, there was a small round table covered in a lace cloth and two wooden stools. To the side, a black stove and cushioned seating.

'Sit yerself down,' Clodagh ordered. She turned to the small log burner, on top of which there was a pot of tea keeping warm. She poured a cup and handed it to Stanislaw.

'Thank you,' he said, glad of the warm china cup in his hands.

Tentative footsteps could be heard on the wooden steps outside, then the pretty, red-haired woman appeared, her son by her side, half hidden in the folds of his ma's long skirt.

The first time Stanislaw had come to the camp with Angie, he'd seen them standing and staring as they had driven away with Mrs Kwiatkowski. The second time, he had been puzzled as to why the boy's mother had been so loathe to let him go to the car to fetch the clothes and food Angie had brought them.

Looking at them both now, as Clodagh motioned for the woman to sit on the stool next to her own, he realised why they had looked at Angie the way they had. He'd thought he had seen fear and guilt in their expressions, but had dismissed it as they'd had no dealings with Angie before.

Now he knew his gut feeling had been right. And although they had not had direct dealings with Angie before, they had with someone else from Cuthford Manor. And those dealings accounted for the look of guilt in their eyes – and their fear of what the repercussions might be.

He was sure that everything Mrs Kwiatkowski had told him was true, but he needed to hear it with his own ears. Whether they would admit to their involvement – however unintentional – was another matter.

After returning from the camp, Stanislaw spent the rest of the day on his own in the paddock, fixing the fencing and checking all the jumps. It didn't matter that it was bitterly cold. He'd known worse. In any case, he was distracted by trying to work out what to do next. He'd been surprised that the woman and child hadn't denied what had happened and what the young boy had been asked to do. But they were adamant they knew nothing of the malevolence that lay behind it.

'He'd been told tat it was a prank,' the woman had said, adding the boy had not used his head and wondered why he was being paid so much for a simple, harmless task. She had thrown the young lad a look that told Stanislaw the boy had already been punished for his mistake. 'Shan here was blinded by the *airgead*. The money. 'Tis true tat money is the root of all evil.'

Now he was back at the manor, Stanislaw needed to think without any distractions. He needed to know that whatever he did next was the right thing to do.

By teatime, he still wasn't sure. He'd hoped that Mrs Kwiatkowski would not want to dine with everyone this evening. That she would be too tired, having been in the kitchen most of the day, teaching the younger ones how to make bread and helping Alberta prepare a traditional Polish stroganoff. But Bonnie and Jemima had demanded that she have dinner with them all.

And so Stanislaw found himself accompanying Mrs Kwiatkowski to the dining room to eat his evening meal with Angie, Evelyn, Lloyd and the children. As everyone sat down and Marlene brought in the big serving bowl of stew, followed by Jemima and Bonnie with the two loaves of bread they had helped to bake, Stanislaw tried not to feel on edge. His main concern was for Angie and how what he'd discovered would affect her. He still hadn't made up his mind if he could even tell her, despite eight hours fixing fences in the bitter cold.

'So, Stanislaw,' Angie said as she ladled out the stew, 'Danny says you went up to the camp early this morning on Ghost.'

Stanislaw felt himself momentarily freeze.

'Um, yes, I did,' he said, passing the bowl to Bertie, who in turn passed it to Mrs Kwiatkowski.

He looked at Mrs Kwiatkowski to see if she would react – or rather, remember – but she was concentrating on keeping a steady hand as she put her bowl down in front of her.

'Why would you go there?' Evelyn snapped.

Lloyd looked at his wife as he put her stew on her placemat. She normally didn't acknowledge Stanislaw's presence, never mind ask him a question.

'Oh, I just needed to see someone,' Stanislaw said.

'You're gonna take me up there soon, aren't you?' Danny said, taking another bowl and passing it to Lloyd. 'They've got loads of horses, haven't they?' He looked to Stanislaw for validation. 'They might want to sell a few. You know, for the riding school?'

'Mmm,' Angie said, trying not to dampen her brother's enthusiasm. 'Perhaps get to know them, but no buying until the New Year, when we're more sorted.' Putting in place their plans to change Cuthford Manor was taking longer than anticipated. Lloyd had helped her to apply for a loan from the bank so they could start the work, as well as fix the roof, but the bank manager seemed to be taking forever and a day to make up his mind.

'I can't believe you're fraternising with them!' Evelyn exclaimed, staring at Stanislaw. She wasn't even trying to hold back her outrage. 'Never mind agreeing to take the boy to see their flea-ridden nags!'

Angie looked from Stanislaw to her mother-in-law. The atmosphere had suddenly become as frosty inside as it was outside.

Stanislaw didn't say anything. His look said it all.

'Right,' Angie said, checking that they all had a bowl of stroganoff in front of them. 'Tuck in, everybody.'

After the rather stilted dinner, everyone seemed keen to go to their own rooms. Angie had wanted to catch Stanislaw for a quick chat as she sensed something was worrying him but she had no idea what. He'd been working out in the paddock most of the day and hadn't come in for his usual cuppa when the children got back from school. In all the time he'd been at Cuthford Manor, she'd never seen him like this. She'd wanted to suggest he join her for a cup of tea in the lounge, but as soon as they'd all finished their desserts, he'd made his excuses, said his goodnights along with Mrs Kwiatkowski and they'd both headed off upstairs. Evelyn had been the next to make a speedy exit, declaring she felt one of her 'heads' coming on. And then Lloyd had sloped off to the study. Angie felt that everyone had something on their mind.

The only reason the children hadn't jumped up and left was because it was their night for clearing up after dinner. Because of their private education and the fact that their friends were all from wealthy backgrounds, Angie was worried her siblings and her daughter risked growing up spoilt and with a sense of entitlement. She could see it was already happening with Marlene.

When Angie had told the scullery maid, Mabel, that she could leave early every Monday, she'd looked worried, which Angie realised was because she'd thought her hours were being cut due to the manor struggling financially. She'd been reassured when Angie told her the truth about why she was giving her the evening off – and that she would still be getting paid.

'You can view it as a kind of bonus for all the hard work you do,' Angie had told her.

Angie had no concerns about Danny getting all uppity. His early years had already shaped him. He knew nothing got handed to you on a plate in this life and that you had to work for what you wanted. Which was exactly what he was doing now. He was working hard in the stables every spare moment he got – and was champing at the bit to put school behind him and get on with what he called 'real life'.

Marlene, however, despite being just a year and a half younger than her brother, seemed to have developed complete amnesia regarding her past life in Sunderland and was behaving as though she really was 'to the manor born'. Angie understood why. Marlene had had a tough time growing up and had been expected to look after the younger ones, cook tea and clean almost as soon as she could walk. The same had been expected of Angie and her older sister, Liz. But still, that didn't excuse Marlene's behaviour. Angie wasn't going to stand back and let her sister become a mini Evelyn.

The younger ones, Bertie, Jemima and Bonnie, were, in the cook's words, 'all smashers'. So far, they were not the least bit snobby or spoilt – and she wanted them to stay that way. Hence the Monday chores and the hour every weekend spent cleaning and tidying their own rooms.

Angie helped Jemima and Bonnie clear the table while Danny, Marlene and Bertie went to the kitchen and argued over whose turn it was to wash, dry and put away, all the while contending with Winston and Bessie nudging up to them with pleading eyes for any leftovers.

When everything was done, Angie made them each a mug of Horlicks before they trundled off upstairs to their rooms. As usual, the dogs gave Angie their 'please don't make me' look when she tried to coax them outdoors, and as usual, Angie gave up and muttered to them that they must have cast-iron bladders. She didn't blame them, though. The weather was awful. It was raining and the windows had started to rattle, which meant the wind was getting up.

After she had given the dogs a pat goodnight, she switched off the lights and shut the kitchen door. As she made her way along the short corridor to the main entrance, she heard the front door shut and Lloyd's voice from the study calling, 'Come in, Cora, come and join me for a nightcap,' followed by the swish of a coat being taken off and the sound of heels on the tiled flooring.

By the time Angie reached the foyer, the door to the study had been closed.

Chapter Forty-Two

'How was the play?' Lloyd asked as Mrs Jones took off her high heels. With the wet weather, she was worried about treading dirt into the oriental rug.

Seeing her in the doorway, Lloyd had to stop himself from exclaiming how stunning she looked in her blue dress. Instead, he smiled at her as she padded barefoot across the room and sat in the red-leather tub chair.

'Brandy?' Lloyd asked.

'Go on,' Mrs Jones said. 'I think I need it.'

'The play was that good?' Lloyd knew that she had been to see a play called *The Gioconda Smile* by Aldous Huxley.

'It was good,' Mrs Jones said as she watched Lloyd take the cranberry iridised-glass bird decanter. It always made her smile. Leonard's taste had been most unusual.

Lloyd pulled up the silver bird's head embedded with two rubies for eyes and poured a good-sized measure of cognac into a brandy glass.

'But,' Mrs Jones added, 'it has to be said, it wasn't exacting uplifting.'

'What was it about?' Lloyd asked, genuinely interested. He enjoyed hearing about Cora's theatre trips with her friend Izzy. He was not a great theatregoer himself, but he enjoyed learning about the latest plays – especially when it was Cora who was doing the educating.

'Well . . .' she said, reaching out and taking the brandy. She watched as Lloyd pulled his seat out from behind the desk and dragged it to the side so there was no longer a barrier between them. He sat down and stretched out his legs.

'It was a rather dark tale about a man who remarries after his invalid wife dies, but is sentenced to be hanged after it's discovered the wife was poisoned.'

Lloyd laughed. 'Oh dear, don't be giving me ideas!'

Mrs Jones tutted and took a sip of her brandy. She glanced at the log fire, which was keeping the study snug and warm. It had started to dwindle, but was being whipped back into action by the occasional gust of wind billowing down the chimney breast.

'How's *your* evening been?' she asked, letting her hair free of the tight French knot she had put it in this evening. She was amazed it had stayed intact despite the weather.

Lloyd watched as her thick chestnut-coloured hair, which was just starting to show a shimmer of silver, fell around her face. It wasn't often he saw her with her hair down, but whenever he did, it took his breath away.

'Well, it was a bit of a strange one, actually,' Lloyd said, forcing himself not to stare at the woman he loved, at her loose hair, bare feet and her face that might be showing the first telltale signs of age, but which, nonetheless, he found as beautiful as when she was a teenager.

Lloyd took a drink of his Scotch and then proceeded to tell her of the rather tense evening meal. 'Evelyn practically bit the poor man's head off when she heard he'd been up at the camp. And then when Danny said that Stanislaw was going to take him there to look at the horses, Evelyn looked as though she was going to have an apoplectic fit.'

'And how did Stanislaw react?' Mrs Jones asked.

'Well, he didn't say anything, but he didn't have to.'

'Mmm,' Mrs Jones mused, stretching out her legs, careful not to touch Lloyd's stockinged feet. 'It sounds as though Stanislaw was fed up with her blatant prejudice.'

'Perhaps,' Lloyd said with the beginnings of a frown.

They sat in thoughtful silence for a while. The wind whipped up and a slight whistling had started to come down the chimney. Lloyd was thinking about Evelyn and her behaviour over dinner. Normally, like Stanislaw, he would have ignored Evelyn's bigotry, but perhaps he too had taken as much as he could stomach. It was time for change. A change that was far too late in coming. *God, was it possible to have any more regrets than he had already?*

He looked across at the woman he loved and found her watching him.

'What are you thinking?' Mrs Jones asked.

Lloyd let out a deep, forlorn sigh.

'That bad?' she asked, a gentle smile playing on her lips.

He returned her smile. A loving but sad one.

'I feel as though I'm being buried in regrets,' he confessed.

'You know what they say,' Mrs Jones said, 'to regret the past is to forfeit the future.'

'That's precisely it,' Lloyd said, sitting up a little in his chair. 'I don't want all these regrets to sap the oxygen from the future. But I don't know how to stop having them, and to be honest, they seem to be mounting up by the day.'

'Well, let's look at that growing list,' Mrs Jones said.

'Okay.' Lloyd put his glass tumbler on the edge of the desk and knotted his hands together. 'I keep thinking about Quentin, and all the ways I failed him as his father. And I keep thinking about his wedding and how I didn't go to it. I feel so angry at myself.' He shook his head in disgust. 'But do you know the real reason I didn't go?'

Mrs Jones shook her head.

'I knew if I insisted on going, Evelyn would have come, as she'd have been worried about what people would think if I just turned up there on my own. And if she had come, she would have spoilt it with some drama or other. Of that I have no doubt.' Lloyd sat back, his face mournful.

'But why would you regret that?' Mrs Jones said. 'You sacrificed your own desire to see your son married for *his* sake – and Angie's. You were right to do so.' She paused. 'And Quentin and Angie had such a happy wedding day. Angie's spoken of it so many times. I don't know many couples who had their reception in a shipyard on VE Day.'

They both chuckled.

'Oh, I wish I'd been able to see it,' Lloyd said, taking a sip of his drink.

Mrs Jones waited as she knew Lloyd was struggling with his emotions.

'You know,' he said, 'I was so pleased when Quentin told me he was marrying Angie.' He paused, not knowing if he should say what he wanted to say next.

'It made me think of us,' he said, unable to hold back. 'Thank God my son didn't repeat my mistakes . . . His falling in love with Angie mirrored our lives – or rather, what could have been our lives. If only I'd had more gumption.'

Mrs Jones was quiet. This was a subject they had often skirted around but had never spoken of directly.

'If only I'd followed my heart.' Now Lloyd had started, he couldn't stop. 'If only I'd had the courage to take you in my arms all those years ago and tell you that yes, of course I'd marry you. That I wanted to be with you for ever. That I wanted you as my wife. But I didn't. And I have spent my whole life regretting that.' He made a sound of despair. 'Instead, I married a woman whom I forced myself to believe I loved because I was heartbroken that you had met someone else . . . God, I'll never forget that feeling.'

Mrs Jones sat up, surprised at the sudden outburst. Although she shouldn't have been. Since Quentin's death, Lloyd had changed. She reached forward and took his hand, squeezing it tightly.

'Oh, Lloyd, you can't beat yourself up . . . I am as much to blame as you for what happened. I was young and impulsive. My parents had drummed it into my head that if I ever became involved with you, it would end in tragedy.'

Lloyd remembered Cora had used that same word 'tragedy' all those years ago.

'My parents were forever on about Leonard – and how people like him with money liked to appear radical and unconventional, but when it came down to it, they reverted to form. Leonard, they said, would allow his son to "play around" with a poor girl from the village, but when it came to a serious relationship, and certainly marriage, then you'd have to "get back in line". Any relationship with you would only lead to "problems, heartache and misfortune".' Mrs Jones sighed at the memory. 'Mine, not yours, of course.' She gave a slightly bitter laugh. 'Because the rich don't suffer any of these things. My parents believed that money meant you got to live a carefree, untroubled existence.'

Lloyd shook his head. 'God, there are so many different types of prejudice in this world, aren't there? You know, my father was not as your parents envisioned. He was genuinely – naturally – unconventional. I don't think he could have been anything else even if he'd tried.'

'I know, I know,' Mrs Jones agreed. 'I really got to know Leonard during his last years.'

Lloyd nodded. He knew the two had become close after Cora had become more of a nurse to his father than a housekeeper. It was why Leonard had stipulated that she be allowed to live at the manor for as long as she so desired.

'He used to talk to me a lot,' Mrs Jones continued. 'He said one day that he could never understand why you and I never courted. Especially as he could see how we felt about each other.' She gave a sad sigh. 'That's when I realised just how wrong my parents were. It's so easy to look back with hindsight and see the truth, but it's difficult when you're young – and your own parents are as narrow-minded as people like Evelyn. But I was young when we realised we had feelings for each other. I'd only just turned sixteen. I believed my parents. And because of that I gave you that ultimatum, which was so ludicrous. No wonder I had you running for the hills. No wonder you weren't sure . . . After all, we had only exchanged the one kiss.'

A kiss Lloyd could still remember to this day.

Mrs Jones continued. 'And because I didn't follow my heart, I ended up marrying a man I liked a lot – but didn't truly love. I often wonder, if he hadn't died of pneumonia, how long I could have kept up the pretence.'

They looked at each other.

'You know you were *my* one true love, don't you?' Lloyd said, his eyes fixed on her, wanting to read her reaction to his words. 'And always have been. What's tragic is that it's now too late.'

Mrs Jones hesitated for a second. She opened her mouth to speak – but was interrupted by a loud crash.

'What on earth is that?' Lloyd exclaimed. He jumped up and rushed out of the study.

The crashing sound was a stone gargoyle that had become dislodged from its vantage point on one of the castellated turrets. The grotesque stone face had smashed into one of the lion statues that sat just outside the study window. Dozens of tiles from the roof of the East Wing had followed. Wrenched free by the gale, they'd rained down on the front lawn.

The crashing and smashing was enough to wake the entire manor. Stanislaw was first on the scene. He kept his face impassive on seeing Mrs Jones leave the study with her shoes in her hand. Lloyd and Stanislaw surveyed the damage, but concluded that there was nothing they could do until morning, by which time hopefully the winds would have run out of steam. There was now no putting off the roof repairs, they both agreed, before reassuring those who had been woken that everything was fine.

Knowing that Mrs Jones had retired to the East Wing, Lloyd ached to go there and do what he should have done all those moons ago – take her in his arms.

But she had not reciprocated his declaration of love.

She hadn't had time, thanks to the damned wind.

When Lloyd climbed into his own cold bed in the West Wing, he did not sleep. Which was also the case for Mrs Jones. Both were replaying the words that had been said. Words that had remained unspoken for such a very long time.

Lloyd realised that he'd been able to tell Cora how he felt because, in a perverse way, losing his son had liberated him from Evelyn. Emotionally, at any rate. Now he had to start liberating himself practically. He thought of the play Cora had seen. How easy it would be to poison someone. But he was no killer. And so he would have to take the lengthier and more torturous route of navigating his way through the divorce courts.

Chapter Forty-Three

Tuesday, 7 November

Stanislaw had also spent most of the night tossing and turning, unable to sleep. But his reasons for doing so were very different. He knew deep down that he had to tell Angie. Yet still he tried to argue the case against it. *It was not his position to meddle. He was simply an employee. This was not his business. He should let sleeping dogs lie.* But these were unworthy arguments. They were the coward's way out.

The only reasoning that held any kind of sway was his genuine concern for the devastation the truth would cause Angie. And he truly did not want to cause her any more heartache. She had been through so much already – and now here he was, about to dump more on her.

As the sun started to rise, Stanislaw stopped playing devil's advocate and forced himself to face the dragon and look at how best to tell her. Which was fruitless, as there was no best way. There was no way of telling her what he had to tell her that would in any way lessen the blow.

And so, Stanislaw got up and got ready.

After forcing down some breakfast before anyone else stirred, he went out to see the horses. He would do what he had to do after he'd taken Ghost out for a ride. Then he would come back and tell Angie – when the children had gone off to school and Bonnie had been dropped off at the nursery.

As he trooped outside into the yard, he barely noticed the debris caused by last night's wind, mumbling to himself that he wished he'd stayed in Scotland and never ventured across the border. Saddling up Ghost, whose dark eyes were looking at him as though sensing his unrest, Stanislaw admonished himself. Who was he kidding? He didn't really feel that. He wouldn't change how his life had progressed since moving to the north-east, because if he hadn't, he'd never have met the woman who had brought his heart back to life.

He just hoped to God that Angie did not feel like shooting the messenger when he delivered the news that would shatter her world – as well as the lives of those around her.

After coming back from his ride, Stanislaw procrastinated for another hour until he saw Alberta come out of the back door and head to the allotment to see Bill for her ten o'clock cigarette break. It was time.

'Can you take Lucky for a walk around the paddock?' Stanislaw asked Thomas.

'Course, boss,' Thomas said. 'I think that stuff you've been giving her has really helped with the wheezing.' Like most pit ponies, Lucky suffered due to the coal dust on her lungs.

'Good, good,' Stanislaw said.

'Do yer think it'll work on our Stubby?' Thomas asked.

Stanislaw knew that the lurcher cross, which was owned by Thomas's elder brother and wasn't just the family pet but a working dog – if poaching could be classed as working – was getting older. His wheezing was probably more to do with old age and being out in all weathers for long periods of time.

'It's worth a try,' Stanislaw said as he gave himself a brush-down, something he always did before going indoors. 'It's just a mix of ginger, rosehip and blueberries. I'll sort some out for you before home time.'

'Yer all right?' Thomas asked. His boss seemed unusually nervous and distracted.

'Yes, yes, I'm fine,' Stanislaw said, but his demeanour belied his words.

When Stanislaw walked into the kitchen, he found Mabel carefully manoeuvring the vacuum cleaner out of the scullery where it was kept. Mabel had told anyone who would listen that the new grey Hoover, which had been bought shortly before the manor's purse strings had been pulled tight, was a 'gift from the gods'. Although she'd added that it would also give her arms like Popeye as it was so heavy.

Stanislaw held the kitchen door open as she pushed it through the doorway.

'Thanks, Stan, yer a sweetheart,' she said, as she headed down the corridor to the staff staircase that led up to the West Wing.

Guessing that Angie would be in the back office, Stanislaw made his way there. Walking down the corridor, he noticed the door was half open. He couldn't see Angie, but could hear her talking to Lloyd.

'Ah, Stanislaw, this is a surprise!' Lloyd exclaimed on seeing him. 'Everything all right? No more damage after last night's high winds?'

Stanislaw had to smile at the way the people here downplayed the weather. Last night's 'high winds' would have been viewed as a gale anywhere else.

'No, no,' Stanislaw reassured him.

He looked across to Angie. She was smiling at him. His heart sank. She looked the most content he'd seen her since he'd started work here. *Do diaska!* he cursed inwardly.

'Are you all right, Stanislaw?' Angie asked, concerned.

'Yes, yes, I'm fine,' he lied. 'I was just wondering if I could have a word with you in private, please?' He looked at Lloyd. 'No offence.'

'None taken,' Lloyd said, getting up. 'I'll be in the study if I'm needed.'

Stanislaw smiled his thanks as Lloyd left, closing the door behind him.

'Blimey,' Angie said, looking at Stanislaw's ashen face. 'What's up? Come and sit down.'

Stanislaw did as he was told and took a seat on the small two-seater leather sofa next to Angie's desk.

He leant forward, his hands clasped as though in prayer, which in a way they were.

And then he told Angie everything.

And he watched with a wretched heart as a myriad of emotions showed on Angie's face – each as dark and as dire as the one before.

Angie sat for a long time, saying very little. Every now and again, she'd ask a question before once again falling silent.

'Right,' she said after a while. 'I'm going to go to the camp to speak to Clodagh, and the woman and her little boy.' She looked at Stanislaw. 'It's not that I don't believe you. I just need to hear it with my own ears.'

She stood up.

'Are you going now?' Stanislaw asked.

Angie nodded. 'Can you get Thomas to saddle up Starling, please?'

'You want to ride there?' Stanislaw asked. He'd thought she'd just jump in the car and drive to the camp.

'I need to,' Angie said, her face scarily impassive. 'I might implode if I don't.'

Stanislaw understood. 'I'll wait for you outside,' he said, getting up and opening the door.

There was no discussion as to whether or not he would go with her. And Angie knew there was no point arguing. Stanislaw would go with her whether she wanted him to or not.

This time, though, she *did* want him by her side.

The two horses galloped across the fields, one nudging ahead of the other every now and again. Ghost was naturally the faster of the two, but, encouraged by Angie, Starling was not only keeping up but occasionally taking the lead.

When they reached the turn-off for the camp, they dropped down to a canter, then a trot. The steaming breath of the horses mingled with that of their riders. Angie stood up in her stirrups when they reached the part of the hill that gave a view of the camp – or rather, of where the camp *had* been.

'Damn it!' Angie sat back into the saddle. 'I don't believe it! They've gone.'

Swinging herself off Starling and taking the reins, she walked to the area where the Travellers had made their home.

Stanislaw followed suit and dismounted. Walking Ghost over to the fire, he put his hand over the embers and felt the warmth. They were not long gone. He should have guessed they would not want to be around for the inevitable fallout.

Nor the wrath of the widow should she turn her anger on them.

Chapter Forty-Four

Over the next couple of days, Stanislaw tried to keep a close eye on Angie, which was not easy as she spent most of her time in the office while he was outside with the horses or working with Ted and Eugene on fixing up the barn, which had also taken a battering on the night of the gale.

He had managed on a few occasions to catch Angie on her own and ask her how she was feeling. Each time, she simply said she was 'fine' and not to worry about her. But he knew she *wasn't* fine. No one could be after what she had learnt. And he *was* worried about her – worried sick, if he was honest. Stanislaw wished more than anything that she would confide in him. He wanted to help her. As her friend. The woman he could no longer deny he was falling in love with.

On the third day after their visit to the deserted camp, he managed to collar Angie when she was coming back after dropping Bonnie off at the nursery. It was chucking it down, but she wasn't hurrying to keep dry and seemed oblivious to the rain and the wind pushing its way in from the North Sea. He jogged up the gravel and reached her as she arrived at the slight bend halfway down the driveway. This time he didn't ask how she was, knowing what her answer would be. Instead, he walked with her a short while, without saying anything. He sneaked a look at her and thought she seemed almost in a trance.

'Angie?' he asked gently.

She turned and looked at him. He'd seen that look before, during the war. A mix of anger and sorrow. He took the arm of her gabardine, which was now dripping wet, and squeezed gently.

'Talk to me,' he said. 'I'm worried about you. I want to help you any way I can.'

She turned to look at him, and as she did so, he felt his heart lift a little.

'I know,' she said. 'But this is something I have to work out for myself.'

They walked around the house and Stanislaw was surprised that Angie didn't go straight indoors to dry off, but instead went to the stables to see the horses. He watched her from outside, sensing she needed to be alone. Now he too was oblivious to the weather as he watched her blurred image through the waterfall cascading down from the pitched roof.

He looked on as she went to Lucky and then the two shires, Monty and Bomber, talking to them and kissing their muzzles. Starling rubbed her face against Angie's wet coat as a show of love, causing her to stagger back a little. She stroked the filly's forelock and whispered to her, which Stanislaw knew would be words of love.

He held his breath as she walked over to Ghost's stall, hoping against hope that she would show him the same love. Or at the very least stroke him. Something she had not done since her husband's death. Stanislaw wanted her to open her heart to Ghost, as much for the horse's sake as her own. Some might mock him for thinking he saw hurt in Ghost's deep brown eyes when Angie ignored him, but Stanislaw knew what he saw.

He watched with bated breath as Angie approached Ghost's stall. She stood within touching distance and looked at the gelding, who also stood quite still. Stanislaw's heart beat faster as he saw Angie move. For a fraction of a second, he thought she was going to step forward and for the first time in over a year show Ghost the same love she showed his stablemates.

But she didn't.

The movement she made was to turn and walk away.

Stanislaw felt tears sting his eyes.

She would never let herself love Ghost.

Just as he was sure she would never let herself love another man.

Leaving the stables, Angie beckoned Stanislaw to follow her out of the rain and into the kitchen. She had planned what she wanted to do with military precision over the past few days – days that didn't seem real – and it was time. She had considered all the pros and cons of her possible actions, knowing that no matter what she did, it would never bring Quentin back. If she had been on her own, with no dependents, no daughter, no siblings, no manor, she might well have decided on a different plan of action, but she wasn't. And so she had settled on what she was about to do.

'Will you make yourself available at around six o'clock, please?' she asked.

'Of course,' Stanislaw said. *Didn't she realise he would do anything for her?*

After that, Angie spent the rest of the day making phone calls and giving the staff instructions, which she did in hushed tones. None of them had seen their employer like this before. So deathly serious. So earnest.

When Angie went to pick up Bonnie, she had to force herself to concentrate while chatting to Rebecca, Jill and Hilda about the plans for the survival of both the village and the manor, their fates now entwined. Normally, she'd have stayed longer as there was excitement about how the local shops and tradespeople would be involved in converting Cuthford Manor into a country house hotel and then providing it with local produce when it was up and running. They all had their fingers crossed that the bank loan Angie had applied for would be given the thumbs up.

Walking back home as Bonnie regaled her with snippets of her day, Angie thought how happy she would have been in normal circumstances – before she'd learnt the facts that had turned her world upside down.

When the children got back from school, they were given an early dinner in the kitchen, as Alberta had been instructed, and afterwards were told they had to go to their rooms and do their homework. Danny was allowed to go to the stables.

'If you behave yourselves,' Angie had bribed them, 'then you'll have a treat later on.'

The children weren't fooled, though. They knew their sister well and they could tell something was afoot. They would do as she said, but they'd be keeping an eye out for anything unusual happening with the adults.

Even the dogs sensed the slight change in atmosphere and routine, and although they were hogging the heat of the Aga, their ears twitched every so often, and their eyes surveyed those coming in and out of the kitchen.

By the time the grandfather clock struck six, everyone who had been asked had gathered in the front sitting room. Lloyd was standing by the window, looking out. He had a dull ache in the pit of his stomach – a physical sense that news of something terrible was coming. Which it was.

Clemmie sat on one end of the sofa with the dogs at her feet. The fire had been well stacked with both coal and logs and had settled to a comfortable heat.

Seeing Stanislaw standing near the door, Angie told him, 'Make yourself comfortable – this might take a little while.' He gave her a look as he went to sit down, but Angie avoided eye contact. She needed to focus. She needed to stay strong and hard. And Stanislaw had a way of making her feel a little soft.

Mrs Jones arrived, accompanied by Mrs Kwiatkowski. They joined Clemmie on the sofa. Angie was too nervous and too angry to sit and was walking around the room, occasionally moving an ornament or brushing some invisible dust off the furniture. She looked at her watch, then glanced around the room.

'We're waiting for one more person,' she said. Just then the lights from the Bentley could be seen as the car drove slowly up the driveway.

Lloyd watched from the window as his wife waited for Jake to jump out and open her door. She was not in a good mood, judging by the look on her face. He could hear her reprimanding Jake for being 'so tardy'.

Wilfred was waiting at the door, having expected Evelyn back from town, where she had been shopping – or at least that was what she'd claimed to be doing.

'Ma'am,' Wilfred said as she stepped into the house.

'I don't know what the world's coming to,' Evelyn said, turning her back to him so that he could help her out of her coat.

'Punctuality!' she said, shooting a look at Jake, who had wisely stayed by the car. 'Seems to be a foreign word these days!'

Wilfred hung up the coat and walked over to the front reception room.

'The mistress of the house has requested you join her, ma'am,' Wilfred said, opening the door.

As soon as Evelyn stepped into the room, Wilfred, as instructed, shut the door behind her.

Walking into the lounge, Evelyn found herself staring at six upturned faces – eight if you included the dogs.

'Goodness me,' she exclaimed, heading straight for the drinks cabinet and pouring herself a vodka tonic. 'I'm guessing you've called another one of your "powwows", Angela?'

'Not so much a powwow –' Angie could feel her heart thumping in her chest. ' – more of a disclosure.'

'Oh,' Evelyn said, walking over to the empty armchair and sitting down. 'This sounds intriguing.' She took a sip of her drink and glanced across at her husband.

'That's not a word I would use,' Angie said, the mix of anger and adrenalin making her feel a little breathless.

'What word would you use?' Evelyn jibed.

Angie didn't answer, but instead inhaled deeply and said, *'I know what you did, Evelyn.'*

Evelyn pulled a puzzled expression. She looked around at the others. 'My dear, what *are* you talking about?'

'I'm going to give you the chance to confess,' Angie said. 'To tell everyone here what you did.'

She waited, giving her mother-in-law time. The room was still. Angie glanced at Mrs Jones, Clemmie and Lloyd, and wondered what their reaction would be when they heard the truth.

'Are you going to tell them, Evelyn, or am I?' Angie's voice was low and so cold it felt as though the temperature in the room had dropped a few degrees.

Lloyd stepped forward, away from his spot near the bay window. He stood as still as a statue, his attention focused on his wife.

'Angela, I have no idea what you are talking about. And I've got better things to do than be gawped at and told to confess to something you seem to believe I have done.' She took a quick sip of her drink. 'So, if you don't mind, I'm going to leave you and your followers to it.'

Before Evelyn had a chance to stand up, Angie began.

'When Mrs Kwiatkowski was rescued by the Travellers after her walkabout, there was much discussion over what to do with the *gorger* who didn't speak English.' Angie looked at her old neighbour, who sat on the sofa, back straight, her light blue eyes alert. 'They presumed, of course, that if the old woman they'd found wandering around alone in a field didn't speak English, then she also didn't understand it.'

Angie fixed Evelyn with a look as arctic as her tone.

'This was their mistake – and for you, one that has proved fatal because, as we all know, Mrs Kwiatkowski understands English perfectly well.'

Angie saw Mrs Jones take the old woman's hand.

'And what did they say?' Clemmie asked, her eyes going from Angie to Evelyn and back again.

'Well, now that's where it gets interesting . . .' Angie looked at Clemmie and around the room before settling her attention back on her mother-in-law. 'After Stanislaw told them where the old Polish woman lived and that he'd be back as soon as he could with someone to take her home, a little boy and his mother came to the caravan where Mrs Kwiatkowski was keeping warm. The woman whose caravan it was listened as the little boy explained that "the big house" – the one which was "like a castle" – was the place where he had been paid to go and "play that prank". A prank which had caused the little boy and his mother sleepless nights when they found it had ended up causing the death of the man who lived in the "castle".'

'What *are* you going on about, Angela?' Evelyn asked, her face a picture of confusion. Angie was surprised how convincing her mother-in-law was. If she didn't know better, she'd have thought she really was confused.

'The bang,' Lloyd said, his face showing the beginnings of understanding. An understanding so abhorrent that he was already feeling nauseous.

'That's right,' Angie said. 'The little boy had been paid to play a prank up at the big house the day before Bonfire Night. A prank that had to be perfectly timed. A prank that involved letting off a firework within moments of hearing the clash of the stall door. A stall door which has clashed shut for as long as we can all remember.'

Angie inhaled deeply. 'I asked Quentin about it once and he'd said it had always been like that – and he laughed . . .' She paused for a moment to keep her emotions in check. 'He said Ghost had got used to it and it had been decided to let it be. That it would probably spook him if it *didn't* bang shut.'

Angie trained her eyes on Evelyn. 'And that was when you told the young lad to let off the firework – knowing that the sudden loud bang would spook Ghost at the exact same time that I was fetching your scarf. A scarf you had purposely left there.'

'You're talking nonsense!' Evelyn exclaimed.

'Now I know why you were so forgetful every time you went out for a ride. If it wasn't your gloves, it was something else. You were making it seem a common occurrence so that on the day before Bonfire Night – the day you'd planned the "accident", it would not seem unusual that you'd left your scarf there.'

Angie walked over to the drinks cabinet and poured herself a glass of water. Her mouth was dry.

'How dare you!' cried Evelyn. 'You have no idea the guilt I've felt over that damned scarf. But it was an accident. My son's death was an *accident*!'

Angie took another mouthful of water and put the glass down. 'You knew the size of the stall. You knew exactly how Ghost – all sixty-two stone of him – would react if he heard a sudden loud noise. He'd rear up. You knew that being in that stall – being next to the stone wall where you left your scarf – would be fatal for anyone who was in there.'

She paused.

'Whoever went into that stall was not going to walk out alive.'

'This is ridiculous!' Evelyn looked around her with a look of pure incredulity. 'You don't believe her, do you?'

No one spoke.

'My God, Angela, I think you've been reading too many of those murder mysteries you're so keen on!'

'Remember at the inquest,' Angie continued, 'when we sat there, listening to the coroner tell us that Quentin's accident wasn't that unusual and several months previously there had been a similar one where a jockey was crushed to death because his horse reared after getting spooked in the starting stalls? I'm guessing that you already knew about it. And that was what gave you the idea.'

'Angela, I do believe you have lost your mind!' Evelyn blustered.

Angie ignored her mother-in-law and continued. 'On New Year's Eve, when you were talking about the new Travellers' camp which had set up not far from us, you made a point of saying that the children should avoid the Travellers at all costs. At the time, I thought you were being your usual snobby self – just like when I went to take them clothes and food to thank them for helping Mrs Kwiatkowski, and then again, when you heard Stanislaw had been to see them and Danny wanted to go – you were angry, but you weren't really, were you? No, in reality, you were terrified that if I – or the children, or anyone else – got talking to the people there, we might find out what you had asked that boy to do.'

'You're delusional!' Evelyn spat the words out.

'No plan is ever foolproof, is it, Evelyn? No matter how meticulously it's mapped out. You couldn't have foreseen Quentin coming back from work early. Or Mrs Kwiatkowski suddenly deciding to go on one of her impromptu walks, so that it was your son who went to fetch your scarf and not me. You wanted rid of me – didn't you? But you ended up killing your only son.' Angie shook her head. 'How you have lived with that knowledge, I do not know.'

Angie continued in an uncharacteristically dispassionate tone. 'You're obsessed with this manor – you desperately wanted it for yourself, which you knew would happen if I was no longer in the land of the living. By rights, it would fall to Bonnie, but Quentin and I had written in my will that if I died first, then Quentin would take the children to Liz in

Australia. You knew his intention was to let you and Lloyd stay here. Cuthford Manor would, for all intents and purposes, be yours.'

'Well, I've never heard such complete and utter rubbish!' Evelyn exclaimed.

Angie had not finished. 'That was why you kept blaming me for Quentin's death. I remember thinking it was just your grief making you say those things. But you really *did* blame me for his death – as *I* was the one who should have died. It explains why you were at pains to make me feel like I didn't belong here. You wanted me gone. Your son's death could not be in vain.'

Evelyn looked at Lloyd. 'You don't believe this, do you?' she asked.

Unable to speak, Lloyd looked at his wife.

'You can deny it all you want, Evelyn, but I have the proof,' Angie said. 'You see, Stanislaw went to the camp after Mrs Kwiatkowski told him what she had heard that evening – and everything was confirmed by the Travellers, who by all accounts were afraid they might in some way be held responsible for Quentin's death. Stanislaw reassured them that this would not happen, and they agreed to give evidence should it be necessary.'

Angie caught Stanislaw looking at her, as this last part was not true.

'I've heard enough,' Evelyn said. '*I'm going.*'

'Yes, you are,' Angie said. 'Straight out the front door – and you're not coming back. The Bentley's waiting for you. I've had your belongings packed up into suitcases which are now in the boot of the car. Jake will take you straight to the train station, where he will give you a one-way ticket to London.'

Evelyn looked in disbelief at Angie – then at her husband.

'Lloyd!' she demanded, as though bringing a dog to heel.

Lloyd's face had turned grey. Angie thought her father-in-law had aged during the short time he had been in this room – all the life had been sucked out of him. Slowly, he walked over to his wife, looking at her as though she were the devil in human form.

'You killed my son,' he said, his voice shaking. *'My loving, kind-hearted, gentle boy.'*

The room was eerily quiet.

Tears formed in Lloyd's eyes, but his inner fury still shone through.

'God, I could strangle the living daylights out of you—' His fists were clenched, and it was clear it was taking all his willpower not to do as he wished. 'May you rot in hell for what you've done.'

Turning away, he walked across the room and yanked the door open. He looked at his wife one more time.

'God help you if I ever set eyes on you again.'

And with that, he left.

His footsteps could be heard on the foyer's tiled floor, the sound becoming softer as he made his way up the carpeted stairs to his room.

Evelyn's mouth twitched. She looked on the verge of saying something, but didn't. The looks on all the faces of those staring at her told her to be quiet, as they might just lynch her.

'I'm not going to tell the authorities what you did,' Angie said.

'Of course not, because this is all pure fabrication!' Evelyn raised her voice.

'I'm not going to tell the authorities,' Angie repeated, 'because I don't think they would trust the word of an Irish Traveller and an elderly woman whose memory isn't as good as it used to be.' She walked over to the lounge door.

'You can't throw me out of my own home!' Evelyn gasped.

'I can,' Angie said, pulling the door wide open. 'And I'm sure I don't have to tell you that I also never want to set eyes on you again for as long as I live. *Now get out of here.*'

Evelyn slammed her drink down on the coffee table, then walked over to Angie. For a moment, Angie thought her mother-in-law was going to hit her. Instead, she leant towards her and hissed in her ear.

'You're right. It should have been you. This place does not belong to you.'

Angie felt a cold shiver run down her spine.

She looked at Evelyn, whose face was twisted, unveiling her inner malignancy, and thought her almost unrecognisable.

As Evelyn walked out of the room, she passed Danny, Marlene, Bertie and Jemima, who stood staring at her, wide-eyed. Like Wilfred, they had been listening to everything that had been said with their ears pressed against the door.

Wilfred was now positioned by the open front door, holding out Evelyn's coat. She snatched it and stormed out of Cuthford Manor – a place that was so much a part of her it was in her very blood.

Wilfred and the children were joined by Angie, Clemmie, Mrs Jones and Mrs Kwiatkowski.

Winston and Bessie pushed to the front and stood stock-still on the steps.

They all watched in stunned silence as the red lights of the Bentley turned at the top of the driveway and disappeared from sight.

Chapter Forty-Five

In the weeks following the shocking revelations about Quentin's death and Evelyn's expulsion down south, an air of stunned disbelief pervaded Cuthford Manor. But despite the shellshock of finding out the abominable truth about her husband's tragic death, Angie did not feel buried in the rubble of the aftermath – as she had done immediately after Quentin had died. The worst had already happened – she had lost her husband. Finding out what Evelyn had done might have shocked her to the core, but it didn't equate to the crippling devastation of losing Quentin.

And she had the support of everyone around her, as well as Dorothy, who was 'always and forever' there for her, at the end of the phone any time of the day or night. She also had her former workmates in Sunderland, and now she had Clemmie, who was coming over every day to check on her.

Clemmie had initially made no bones about the fact that she thought Angie should tell the police and bring Evelyn to justice.

'It would just drag on and on,' Angie explained. 'It would be hanging over us like a spectre – and then, after all the time and trouble and interviews and the investigation, the chances are she'd get off. I think it would be impossible to prove. And I really don't think people would believe that someone of Evelyn's standing would be capable of putting such a plan into action.'

'I think perhaps I just want retribution for Quentin – and, if I'm honest, for myself,' Clemmie eventually conceded.

The children were naturally Angie's primary concern. Bonnie was too young to understand that her father had died in a carefully orchestrated accident, but Angie kept a close eye on her siblings to make sure they came through this as unscathed as possible. A week after the revelations, Angie caught her brothers and sisters when they came in from school. Mrs Kwiatkowski had made some of her Polish pastries, which Angie knew would keep them there for as long as she needed to have her 'chat'.

'I think it's important,' she told them when they were all settled around the kitchen table eating jam-filled *kołaczki*, the two eldest with cups of tea and the two youngest with their hot chocolate, 'that we remember all the good times we had with Quentin. I know you're all probably feeling angry, but that will subside.'

Danny slammed down his mug, causing tea to lap over the edge and onto the wooden top. 'My anger won't *subside*!' he said. He was already in his jodhpurs and thick woollen jumper, ready to go out for a ride on Ghost.

'It will,' Angie said sternly. 'And that's the point I want to make. Do you really think that Quentin would want you to be angry and obsess about who was responsible for his death?'

Suddenly, Marlene burst out crying, which shocked Angie. She leant forward and put her hand on her sister's arm and squeezed it.

'Oh, Marlene, it's all right to cry,' she said, feeling almost relieved that her younger sister, who was normally not at all forthcoming about her feelings, was allowing herself this show of emotion.

'I'm not crying because I'm sad,' Marlene said through the tears.

'What is it?' Angie asked, shuffling her chair nearer and giving Marlene a cuddle.

This seemed to make Marlene sob even more. 'I . . . I feel so *guilty*,' she blurted out, tears now spilling down her cheeks.

'Why do you feel guilty?' Angie asked. She looked at Danny, Bertie and Jemima. They too had tears in their eyes.

'Because,' Marlene blurted out, 'all I can think is, "Thank God it wasn't you."' More heart-wrenching sobs followed. 'How horrible to be relieved that it was Quentin – and not you.'

Angie forced herself to stay strong and blinked back her own tears.

Jemima had started to cry now, and Bertie had a few lone tears making their way down his pale face. Danny, she could see, was desperately holding back his emotions.

'Well,' Angie said, giving Marlene a big squeeze and lightening her voice, 'it's good to know you still love me, despite me being "a right old bossyboots".'

Marlene heard the smile in her sister's voice and let out a half-cry, half-laugh.

'I don't know what we'd do without you.'

Angie's heart melted a little. Bringing up her siblings had been far from easy, especially this past year without Quentin, but those few words meant the world.

She looked at Danny, Bertie and Jemima.

'It's normal to think that. To be relieved it was Quentin and not me. I'm your sister. You've grown up with me. I've become a bit of a stand-in mam since our own skedaddled off with her fancy man.' She took a breath. 'But you're *not* to feel guilty. Do you hear me? I won't have that . . . There's only one person who needs to feel guilt. You understand?'

Marlene nodded and wiped away her tears.

Jemima shuffled off the kitchen bench and walked towards Angie with outstretched arms and a tearful, scrunched-up face.

Angie took her in her arms and gave her a big cuddle.

'No more guilty feelings? Okay?' she said. 'Promise?'

They all nodded.

Angie worked hard at following her own advice to remember the happy times with Quentin. She batted away any guilt that it should have been her who had died that day in the stables. It helped that she kept hearing Quentin's voice in her head, reassuring her it was right that she was still here. Bonnie needed her, as did Angie's siblings, now more than ever. When Angie told Stanislaw about her imaginary conversations with Quentin, he nodded vigorously.

'It's good you think that way,' he said.

Since Evelyn's banishment, Angie and Stanislaw had taken to having a cup of tea together before it was time to turn in for the night. Stanislaw was thankful that it hadn't turned out to be a case of 'shooting the messenger', but actually quite the reverse. The awful truth about Quentin's death had brought them closer.

For Stanislaw, though, this growing closeness was a double-edged sword. In one way, it felt so wonderful, so natural; it made him feel so incredibly happy, which he knew was not very appropriate, considering the circumstances, but still, he could not help the way he felt. He was in love with Angie. There was no trying to convince himself otherwise. And not just in love with her, he also loved her. The person she was. The woman she was.

'I think you are very resilient,' Stanislaw told her one evening while they drank their tea in front of the open fire in the lounge with the dogs.

Angie let out a short laugh. 'I don't think I've got a choice.'

'Well, choice or not, I feel a great admiration for you. You've suffered your fair share in this life, and you've battled on.'

The other side of the sword, however, the one that was sharp and caused extreme pain, was that Angie appeared to view him simply as a friend. And nothing more.

And therein lay the problem.

How long could he stay here – working and living in such close proximity – if her feelings were purely platonic, and his were not?

*

Mrs Jones had been a godsend, not just for Angie, but for Lloyd, who, after going to his room at the end of that terrible day, stayed there for some time. Mrs Jones kept an eye on him, taking him cups of tea and sandwiches, which invariably went untouched, and popping into his room to check on him throughout the day. She worried that he might do something stupid, so, at night, unbeknownst to anyone else, she slept in his room in the armchair by the window, looking out at the night sky. Sometimes they would talk late into the night, going over the heinous revelations.

Mrs Jones had also gone to the Durham office of the *Northern Echo* and asked if she could riffle through their archives. She was allowed and it didn't take her long to find the article about the poor jockey who had lost his life when his horse had reared up in a starting stall. The story had been printed in the local paper shortly before Evelyn had decided she wanted to return to Cuthford Manor.

Mrs Jones showed the article to Lloyd. She felt it important that he see it.

She didn't tell him, though, what Evelyn had said to Angie before being forced to leave. It worried Mrs Jones that Evelyn had not shown any kind of remorse. Far from it. She had a niggling feeling that they might not have heard the last of her. But not wanting to cause unnecessary worry, she kept her thoughts to herself.

Chapter Forty-Six

Having been driven to the train station by Jake in the Bentley, Evelyn had done as she'd been told and boarded the London-bound train. But when the train stopped at Darlington, she'd disembarked and got a taxi to the County Hotel, where she'd checked in under a false name. Evelyn would have preferred to book into the hotel's most lavish suite, as she would have done in normal circumstances, but she didn't want to draw too much attention to herself, so she had settled for the next best suite, which was still very sumptuous. As soon as she had tipped the porter and the door was closed, she'd gone straight to the drinks cabinet, in need of something to calm her down. She was so angry she felt as though she would explode.

'How bloody dare she!' Evelyn murmured to herself, kicking off her shoes and pouring herself a vodka and tonic. 'Who the bloody hell does she think she is? The little upstart.' She took a rather unladylike gulp. 'Ordering me to leave! *Me!* It should be *her* leaving – *her* being given her marching orders.'

Evelyn, of course, had not considered for one moment the possibility that she might do well to simply follow orders and go to London. Instead, her banishment seemed to make her even more determined to reclaim Cuthford Manor.

She was not going to give up now.

It had taken her a long time to work out how to do it, but an idea had formed when Desmond had shown her a copy of her son's will and – more importantly – a copy of her daughter-in-law's. She had wondered if she could do something so extreme, but every time she saw her son's wife – *in charge* – at Cuthford Manor, it strengthened her resolve. *It was her manor.* Her mind was made up.

When she'd read the article on the jockey who had been crushed to death by his own horse, she'd almost jumped for joy. She'd known exactly what she was going to do. And how to prepare for it. She'd told Lloyd that she wanted to go back to be nearer her son and daughter-in-law, and, of course, their granddaughter – and Lloyd had agreed. As she knew he would. He'd always done what she wanted.

Then she'd heard the gypsies were back in town and she'd got the Traveller boy to do her bidding, making out that this was a little prank she wanted to play. Mind you, she could have said anything. As soon as she showed him the five-pound note, she knew he'd do whatever she wanted.

With Angie out of the equation, her son, as stipulated in his wife's will, would assume guardianship of the children and take them to Australia.

And Cuthford Manor would once again be hers.

But her plan had gone disastrously wrong.

She had spent a long time after Quentin's death convincing herself that it was not her fault her son had died, but Angie's words and Lloyd's ire had left her once again having to rewrite the truth. Yes, looking at the facts, it might appear that her actions had led to her son's death, but she simply could not accept it was *her* fault. *It was the fault of the miner's daughter.*

Quentin would still be alive were it not for her.

In the days that followed, Evelyn kept a low profile, rarely going out in case anyone recognised her, while she considered what to do next. Her ideas were many and all were extreme. If she had confided her thoughts to any sane person, they would have seen straight away that Evelyn was losing her grip on reality. Even more than she already had.

After a week festering in her hotel room, Evelyn called Gertrude, then packed her bags, checked out and boarded a train back to Durham. As soon as she stepped out of the carriage, she was met by Jeremy, who ushered his mother's friend quickly and discreetly into his car, enjoying all the subterfuge.

Fifteen minutes later, Jeremy was pulling up at the family's country mansion, where Evelyn intended to stay until she was ready to put her plan into action. A plan she had no intention of disclosing to Gertrude. Or to anyone, for that matter. Her friend was, unwittingly, giving Evelyn what she was calling in her head her 'cover story'. Should she need one. Which, if all went well, she hoped she wouldn't.

'Oh, darling.' Gertrude opened her arms to embrace her friend. 'How are you feeling?' She shook her head. 'A ridiculous question, I know. I can barely imagine.' She shooed Jeremy away. 'Let's go into the drawing room and have a stiff drink. I jolly well think you need it.'

Evelyn looked at her friend with sorrowful eyes. 'What would I do without you, Gertrude. I've never felt such despair in my entire life.'

When they were both settled in front of the fire, Evelyn began her fictional tale of woe.

'He said he wanted – no, *needed* – some time to himself,' Evelyn began her well-rehearsed script. 'He's still struggling with Quentin's death.' She stopped and looked down, as though trying her hardest to control her emotions. 'Which of course we all are.'

Gertrude leant forward and tapped her friend's hand. Neither woman was particularly tactile.

Evelyn looked up with watery eyes. 'And it's not just Lloyd and me who are suffering, but poor Angela. Quentin was my son, but he was her husband. And despite the differences in their upbringings, I do believe they loved one another.'

Gertrude had to keep the look of shock from her face as this must have been the first time her friend had ever uttered a good word about her daughter-in-law. 'Yes, yes, of course,' she said, 'but by all accounts, she does seem to be soldiering on, even if she's still not making much effort with her appearance. I can't remember the last time I saw her in anything but trousers and a jumper.'

Evelyn refrained from making a bitchy comment. She needed Gertrude to see – and to be able to tell others if it came down to it – that she had no quarrel with her daughter-in-law, that, in fact, she was quite empathetic towards her.

'This is why I wanted to come here,' Evelyn continued, taking a sip of her brandy. She'd have preferred a vodka and tonic, but brandy seemed more appropriate for someone who was in shock at being separated from her husband.

Gertrude gave her friend a quizzical look. She'd only been told the bare minimum over the phone as Evelyn had been worried about people listening in.

'You see,' Evelyn explained, 'I want to keep an eye on Lloyd from afar, make sure he's all right.' She took another sip of the expensive cognac, which was not bad at all.

'And, like you've just said, you just need to *look* at Angela to see she's struggling to cope. And then there's little Bonnie, my poor granddaughter, having to grow up with no father.' Evelyn swallowed hard, as if trying to hold back the tears.

'Oh, Evelyn, I think that's a wonderful thing to do. You can stay here as long as you want,' Gertrude said.

'And you'll be able to keep an eye on them for me too, won't you?' Evelyn asked in her most gentle tone. 'So if there's anything amiss – if any of them need my help – I'm here.'

'Of course I will,' Gertrude said, thinking the more she and Jeremy visited Cuthford Manor, the more chance there was that her son might turn Angela's head. 'Jeremy and I shall up our visits there on the pretext that we need to get going with helping to make Cuthford Manor a viable business.'

'What an excellent idea,' Evelyn said. It was one she had been going to suggest if her friend hadn't.

Gertrude raised her brandy glass.

'Here's to getting you all back together again,' she said.

Evelyn forced a smile.

'Oh, I do hope so,' she said.

Chapter Forty-Seven

As the weeks passed, Angie started to worry that her father-in-law still hadn't come out of his deep depression. She was concerned for his sake as well as her own. She could not single-handedly do all the work that was essential if she stood any chance of transforming Cuthford Manor into a country house hotel. Everyone seemed to need her attention or thoughts or ideas. Gertrude and Jeremy had become regular visitors, spreading out their sheets of forecasted expenditure and lists of possible organisations to whom they could rent out rooms for conferences and social events. Angie was glad they were helping in this way, but wished that perhaps they wouldn't stay so long, chatting and asking to see certain rooms to decide which would be most suitable for possible future events.

Mrs Jones could see the increasing strain Angie was under and knew she had to try and pull Lloyd back into the light. She could well understand his feeling of despair after learning the chilling revelations about his son's death. *His own wife had caused the death of his cherished son.* But it was time for the man she loved to come back into the real world. And so, towards the end of the third week of Lloyd being cooped up in his room, Cora decided to speak to him when she brought in his tea tray and toast.

'It's time to stop,' she said, putting the wooden tray onto the desk and pouring out two cups. 'This might sound harsh, but you've got to step back into the real world. People need you. Angie in particular. You're not a selfish person – far from it – but if you continue to isolate yourself like this, that's exactly what you will be. Selfish.' She knew her words would hurt – could see they had by the look on his face – but needs must. 'People who love and care for you are worried, and after what's happened, they don't need any more worry or stress in their lives. Angie can't do this on her own. And it's not fair to let her.'

Lloyd took the cup of tea and nodded.

Cora sat down next to him on the cushioned window seat. 'Don't let this be another regret to add to your list.'

Lloyd took her hand and held it tightly. He knew deep down that she was right. He would pull himself together as best he could.

It took some doing, but he managed to drag himself back into the world of the living.

And as December got going, so did Lloyd.

When Angie walked into the office and saw Lloyd at his desk for the first time in weeks, she could have cried with relief. The burden of single-handedly managing the estate and worrying about the children was taking its toll.

She had told herself that she mustn't fuss over her siblings too much, or spoil Bonnie, but it was difficult not to. It took all her restraint to hold back, but she was glad that she did when she realised that she learnt more about how they were all coping by standing back a little and observing.

Jemima and Bertie seemed happy – at school as well as when they were at home, where they loved being with Mrs Kwiatkowski, Alberta and the dogs in the warm kitchen. Jemima loved to help with the cooking and baking and had started writing down recipes in a little blue jotter. Bertie would sit at the kitchen table and do his homework, stopping every now and again to listen to Mrs Kwiatkowski chatter in her native tongue and make notes on new words he was learning. When his homework was done, he'd read up on what he could about Poland, information he usually gleaned from the daily papers. He'd then impart what knowledge he'd acquired to Angie, who then relayed it to Stanislaw.

'Bertie was telling me they say over a million Poles have been displaced by the war,' she told him one day when they were out riding.

'That doesn't surprise me,' Stanislaw said. 'You've got all the armed forces, prisoners of war, refugees and survivors of forced labour and concentration camps. None of them can go back to the homeland.'

'Although,' Angie added, looking out at the miles of open countryside, 'Bertie said that most Polish people have gone to America or Canada.' Which didn't surprise her, knowing how the British Government had turned its back on the Poles in favour of kowtowing to Stalin.

As they carried on across the moors, Angie wondered if Stanislaw would settle here permanently and felt a stab of panic at the thought that he too might decide to travel somewhere else. It made her realise how close they had become and how much she enjoyed his company.

Other times they'd talk about the children and had agreed that Danny was happy *if* he was outside with the horses, and unhappy when he was at school. His moans and groans about the time he was wasting sitting in a classroom learning about 'nothing of any worth' continued, but those moans and groans were ebbing the nearer he edged towards the day he was legally allowed to leave school. It had been agreed with the headmaster that Danny could leave when the school broke for the May bank holiday.

Stanislaw had taken Angie into the tack room in the first week of December and shown her the whitewashed wall on which Danny had scrawled the date *Friday 4th May 1951*. Underneath, he'd nailed a calendar into the wall and was crossing off the days until the date of his liberation. They'd both chuckled.

'You've done well to keep him at school this long,' Stanislaw said. 'You need a pat on the back.'

Angie dismissed his praise, but still it made her feel good. Danny, as the oldest, had been the most difficult to bring up – although, it had to be said, Marlene was slowly edging her way towards the top spot. After the revelations about Evelyn, Angie's younger sister had pulled up her emotional drawbridge and was back to her feisty self.

In keeping with her decision not to stifle her siblings, Angie tried to engage Marlene in general chit-chat whenever the opportunity arose, which was infrequent. Marlene had joined a few after-school clubs, and most weekends were spent either at a friend's house or going into town or to the cinema. If her schoolmates came home with her, they'd all squirrel themselves away in Marlene's room, playing records and chatting as if they themselves had been injected with a gramophone needle.

Still, Angie told Mrs Jones, in whom she confided her worries, this was normal behaviour for girls of Marlene's age. Wasn't it? Angie and Mrs Jones had been looking for jobs when they were Marlene's age, but, as Mrs Jones said, 'times are changing', and from what she could gather, she thought Marlene's behaviour was normal nowadays. Or normal for well-heeled girls who went to schools that charged £210 a term.

In the weeks leading up to Christmas, Angie realised how much the removal of Evelyn had caused a shift in the way the manor functioned. Without Evelyn around to put down the staff and take up their time with endless chores and errands, the atmosphere was more cheerful, and much more got done.

Mrs Jones now had dinner with everyone. It had been suggested by Angie and wholeheartedly agreed to by Lloyd, who wished it had been his suggestion. Mrs Jones had taken on more duties in order to help Angie concentrate on the work that needed to be done to save Cuthford Manor. As a result, she had unintentionally become the head of the house, which was something no one seemed to mind – least of all Angie, who was massively relieved that she could leave that side of the manor to someone else who could be totally trusted and had a way of getting the most out of the staff – both indoors and outdoors.

Mrs Kwiatkowski was no longer trying to head off to meet Janusz at five o'clock, thanks to Alberta's very wise suggestion of 'creating a distraction' every afternoon at that hour. This involved them baking around the time Mrs Kwiatkowski tended to go on her walkabouts. Angie was relieved as her old neighbour was becoming too frail to go out for walks. Ambling around the manor was exercise enough.

All the staff who hadn't been privy to the scene in the lounge six weeks ago were simply told that Mrs Foxton-Clarke had gone to London to see an ailing relative and was expected to be away for quite some time. This, Angie knew, would filter through to the villagers. Angie repeated the same line to the mams from the nursery – and anyone else who enquired.

Wilfred, Jake and Alberta were the only ones who knew the truth and they had been sworn to secrecy – promising never to tell another living soul the terrible truth about Quentin's death.

Clemmie practically lived at the manor when she wasn't teaching, now she no longer had to worry about locking verbal horns with Evelyn. She admitted to Angie that she loved being part of 'this large, unconventional and dysfunctional family'. She felt she fitted right in. Something she'd never felt before, her boyish traits and sexuality having made her an outsider all her life. No one at Cuthford Manor judged her. Far from it. Everyone seemed to like her and enjoy her company. The children treated her as an eccentric but lovable aunty, and Clemmie, in turn, revelled in her relationship with them all.

She only wished her crush on Angie would fade away, as crushes often do, but it hadn't – it had actually grown stronger. She'd been down this road before – why couldn't she learn? There were many nights when she promised herself that she would go to the small, discreet club she'd heard about in the city centre. But she always chickened out.

The draw of dinner at Cuthford Manor had the greater pull.

Chapter Forty-Eight

Thanks to Gertrude and Jeremy's regular visits to Cuthford Manor, Evelyn got to know just about everything that was going on, which both pleased and incensed her.

It had made her blood boil to hear that Mrs Jones now seemed to be in charge, a role Gertrude said she thought had practically been foisted upon her by Angie, who was obsessed with Cuthford Manor's conversion. Especially now a loan had been approved. It wasn't a huge amount, but it was enough to set the wheels in motion.

Evelyn had wanted to tell them that the miner's daughter was wasting her time, for as soon as Cuthford Manor was hers, she'd be slamming the brakes on any work to be done and keeping the place a home. *Her* home.

She forced herself to keep shtum as she knew how excited Gertrude was about the possibility of the place becoming a hotel and about all the events she would be organising. She'd never seen her friend so full of energy and life. Evelyn suspected Gertrude had deluded herself that her son might marry Angie into the bargain. It seemed that a mother's love really was blind. She was certainly oblivious to the fact that her son batted for the other side. Something, she knew full well, Angie was aware of.

Gertrude might be partially sighted when it came to her son, but she was not blind to the closeness shared by Mrs Jones and Lloyd. She'd often wondered about the two. They'd been good friends when they were younger and there'd been whispers that the two had been sweethearts, but not much more was known. Gertrude pondered whether, with Evelyn gone, it might be a case of while the cat's away, the mice will play.

When giving Evelyn her reports on Lloyd, Gertrude had to downplay how well he seemed to be doing. Initially, they'd not seen him for weeks and Angie had always been very evasive when asked about him. Then, at the start of December, he'd suddenly reappeared, looking drawn and pasty, but he seemed to be on the mend now.

Most evenings, Gertrude and Evelyn would sit and enjoy a few drinks together, during which time Evelyn would be sure to talk lovingly about Lloyd.

'Oh, darling, when we first met it was like something you see in the movies,' Evelyn relayed. 'Our eyes locked across a crowded room at some terribly debonair party in London and that was it. There was no looking back. I wouldn't have cared if Lloyd had been penniless – I was in love,' she said. 'But it was the cherry on the cake when he took me home to meet his darling father, Leonard, and—'

'And you saw he was far from penniless!' Gertrude butted in with a chuckle.

'Yes,' Evelyn sighed. 'It was everything I'd dreamed of as a child. My handsome prince who lived in a beautiful castle.'

This part of the story, at least, was true.

Chapter Forty-Nine

1951

It was only after the festive season had passed and they'd entered a new year that Angie realised she felt happy. A feeling of happiness that was often marred by the clinging residue of guilt. *How could she be happy when Quentin was dead?* But whenever it came, she repeated her mantra that Quentin would want her to be happy. His philosophy had always been to enjoy life as 'none of us knows when it might be whipped away'. Like anyone who had lived through a world war, Angie knew how quickly and easily a life could be snuffed out. Quentin's death had shown her that this was not just specific to times of conflict. It was simply life.

It was a philosophy shared by Stanislaw.

'I know it's – what do you call it? – a cliché,' he said. 'But none of us knows what the future holds.' They'd been chatting while driving back from a meeting with a builder Angie was considering hiring. She'd given up going by herself or with Lloyd to chat to workmen they needed as they never took either of them seriously, Angie because of her gender and Lloyd because he was a 'toff' who they thought had bags of money and was an easy target to rip off.

Stanislaw had told her repeatedly that it would help if he accompanied her as he was male and also 'one of them' – a working-class man. Angie had finally acquiesced. And after taking Stanislaw to chat to a plasterer and a carpenter, she'd conceded he'd been right. She also noted they treated him with even more warmth and respect if they got chatting about which regiment they had served with during the war.

Angie had to admit she was glad of Stanislaw's support and company during these frequent trips. They'd chat about Mrs Kwiatkowski, Angie's siblings and Bonnie, whom Angie had just enrolled in the preparatory school at Durham High School for the start of the new academic year. She found herself opening up about her life, including her upbringing and her lack of any real kind of schooling, and how thankful she was that Bonnie and her own siblings were being afforded a top-notch education. One that would save Danny and Bertie from following their father down the mines and give her daughter and two younger sisters choices in life other than 'baking and breeding', as Dorothy was wont to say.

Occasionally, Angie would talk about Quentin, and Stanislaw would mention Adrianna – but when they did, it was more about how their loss had changed the course of their lives.

'I think life gives us burdens,' Stanislaw said, thinking not just about the loss of his wife and unborn child and the horrors of war, but the torturous enforced labour he had endured alongside other emaciated and starving prisoners of war working on the Trans-Siberian Railway. 'And we must be strong and carry those burdens.'

'But what if that burden is too much?' Angie said as they drove to Framwellgate Moor, a village to the north of Durham, to meet with a roofer. 'And it ends up grinding you down?'

'Well,' Stanislaw mused, 'I guess that's when those who are stronger must step in and help – shoulder some of the weight until that person is strong enough to get up and carry on.'

Angie thought about this as they slowed down for a horse and cart trotting ahead of them.

'Like Mrs Jones did with Lloyd,' Angie mused.

Stanislaw nodded. They had agreed during one of their previous trips out that Mrs Jones had saved Lloyd's life. She'd managed to pull him out of the mire of a deep depression and got him back to terra firma, where he'd been able to gain a secure foothold once more.

Angie was aware that in many ways Stanislaw had helped her to carry her burden of loss and that by sharing their experiences it had lightened her load.

Just as Stanislaw knew that Angie had alleviated his own burdens simply by coming into his life.

And not just that – Angie had reignited the fire in his heart and made him feel love. Something he'd never expected to experience again.

His only concern was that this love he was feeling might not be requited.

It hadn't escaped Clemmie's notice how Stanislaw talked to and looked at Angie. It would have been hard to miss, as she was looking at a mirror image of her own feelings. *Her* concern, though, was that the love Stanislaw clearly had for Angie *would* be requited.

Clemmie hated the way it made her feel to see someone else love the woman she wanted. A woman she knew deep down she could never have. But her heart continued to deceive her mind. Some days it succeeded, others it failed.

One evening, when she and Angie were going over costings for the East Wing, she couldn't help but tentatively test the water. 'So, how's Stanislaw getting on?' she asked.

'He's doing really well,' Angie said. 'He's been a great help. I don't know what I'd do without him.' She looked up and met Clemmie's gaze. 'I don't know what I'd do without any of you.'

Clemmie smiled. Inwardly, she was already feeling guilty for what she was about to say – or rather infer – in order to poke a stick in the fast-moving wheel of Angie and Stanislaw's burgeoning friendship. A friendship she was sure was destined to become much more. She could see the want in Stanislaw – just as she had also seen the same want in Angie, although she was sure Angie was in denial about her feelings.

Since his arrival back at the beginning of October last year, Clemmie had seen how much Stanislaw had helped Angie cope with everything that had been tossed at her, but selfishly she still desperately wanted to keep the two apart. It was an awful thing to wish for. But she couldn't help herself.

'I think Stanislaw cuts a tragic figure, don't you think?' Clemmie asked, drawing Angie's attention away from the business plans.

'Tragic in what way?' Angie asked, surprised.

'Well,' Clemmie began, 'it's just that I've heard him talk to Mrs Kwiatkowski about his life before the war and it's clear that his wife was the love of his life.' Clemmie sighed. 'I see him as one of those tragic Shakespearean characters, whose life is forever blighted by the loss of their one true love.'

'That could be me you're talking about,' Angie blustered, eyeing Clemmie.

'No, *you*, my dear, *will* love again – it's in the stars.' Clemmie waved a hand towards the window, where they could see the sky was actually dark and cloudy, with not one star on show.

Angie shook her head. 'You are such a drama queen, Clemmie. Just like Dor. God, I dread the day you two finally meet.'

Clemmie chuckled. She liked being compared to Dorothy. If Clemmie could reach the same lofty heights in Angie's feelings, she would be a happy woman. But not as happy as if she managed to make Angie see her as more than just a friend.

Later on, when Angie was having her late-night cup of tea with Stanislaw, and the dogs were settled at their feet, Clemmie's words about Stanislaw and his wife came back to her.

Angie thought about Quentin and how he had been her one true love. But she had started to feel of late that the gaping wound he'd left behind was healing over. As she felt it had for Stanislaw.

Angie had been adamant in the months after Quentin had died that in this life you only got the chance of love once. And only then if you were very lucky. But lately, she'd not been so sure. She'd been told about other women in the village who had been madly in love with their beaus and husbands who had not come back from war, but, as time had gone on, they *had* found love again.

So much about her life and her thinking had changed these last fifteen months since Quentin had gone. In her mind, she had felt she had aged fifteen years, not months. Thinking of Stanislaw as someone who felt he could never love again made Angie feel a little sad, but also gave her another feeling she couldn't quite work out.

As Angie described her vision for the East Wing and how this part of the manor was perfect for converting into good-sized rooms for their future guests, with the bonus of views on to the terraced gardens and beyond, Stanislaw nodded and listened, occasionally bending over to stroke Bessie, who was nearest to him. His mind, though, was also wandering and only partly taking on board what Angie was saying. It was hard to keep his concentration on track after his conversation with Clemmie earlier in the day.

'The tragedy of Angie,' Clemmie had said, 'is that she will never love again.'

Stanislaw had been surprised. He'd thought that Angie's heart was healing. He'd been sure of it, but perhaps he was wrong.

He'd asked Clemmie why she thought this, as Angie was still young – not even thirty. 'She has the rest of her life to love again,' he'd said.

'Perhaps, but Angie is one of those women whose love was so great, no one would ever be able to match it.'

Stanislaw had felt his heart contract at the words. He had thought that perhaps Angie might have feelings for him. There was no denying they shared a bond. Certainly, a bond of friendship, but it went deeper than that. Didn't it? Or was he simply seeing what he wanted to see.

What his heart wanted him to see?

Chapter Fifty

February

Lloyd and Mrs Jones were walking around the East Wing, discussing how they would move everything over to the West Wing in preparation for the work starting over the next few weeks.

It had been three months since Lloyd had declared to Mrs Jones that he had always loved her and that 'what's tragic is that it's now too late'.

Cora's actions since then, he realised, had shown that she did love him. She had brought him back to life. And now he felt well again, he was not going to let her go. As they walked into the far bedroom, which had once been Leonard's, Lloyd suddenly stopped, turned to her and came straight out with it.

'I've started divorce proceedings.'

When he'd told the family solicitors, they'd been shocked, but had tried to remain professional and had explained the whole process.

Mrs Jones stared at Lloyd. 'Really?' she asked.

'You sound surprised,' Lloyd said as he walked across the room and sat down in the window seat. His father's room had been left empty since he'd died and was now in disrepair. There was rising damp and the wallpaper was peeling off.

'I know,' Mrs Jones said. 'I am, although I shouldn't be. It's just . . .' She didn't know what she wanted to say. *It's just I never thought it would happen. I never thought you'd be free of that awful woman. Free to love again. To love me again.*

Lloyd put his hand on the seat to beckon Cora to come and sit next to him. He'd been at the solicitors the entire morning and all he'd wanted to do when he came back was to see Cora and tell her. When Angie had asked if he could start sorting out the East Wing ready for the builders, who were due to start soon, he'd jumped at the chance and had asked Cora to come with him. She did, after all, live in the East Wing, along with Mrs Kwiatkowski and Stanislaw.

'And what did they say?' Mrs Jones asked as she walked over and sat next to him. She knew divorces could be complicated. Especially when dealing with a wife like Evelyn.

Lloyd smiled as she sat next to him. They were almost touching, and he could smell the familiar scent of her perfume.

'I don't think it's going to be the quickest divorce ever,' he said, 'but it's a start. The ball is rolling. They asked where she is now, which was a bit awkward. I told them she's in London. I guessed she'd gone to stay with a friend of hers who lives in Mayfair until she finds somewhere of her own. I gave them the friend's name and they went off and rang the number listed, but Juliette, the friend, said she hadn't heard from Evelyn "in ages".'

Mrs Jones listened.

'They have to find out where she is so they can serve her the divorce papers,' Lloyd explained.

'And what reasons are they going to give for the divorce?' Mrs Jones asked. Her theatre friend, Izzy, had gone through a divorce and she knew a little about the complex and long drawn-out process.

Lloyd let out a bitter laugh. 'Killing her own son.'

Mrs Jones instinctively took hold of his hand and could feel him relax.

'Sorry. I still get these spikes of murderous anger,' he said.

'I know. That's natural,' she said.

She just wished she didn't still have the nagging feeling that Evelyn hadn't gone from their lives for good.

Chapter Fifty-One

Evelyn had endured being confined to her secret residence at the Fontaine-Smiths' by sneaking out once a week to see Desmond in his little pied-à-terre in South Street. She had sworn him to secrecy, a promise she knew he would keep because despite his proclamations of love for Evelyn and his desire to ride off into sunset with her, he really didn't want to do any such thing and he certainly didn't want his wife to find out about his affair. She would not only divorce him, she'd likely keep his children from him too and strip him of every penny he had.

This afternoon they'd enjoyed their time together in the plush double bed and were sharing a cigarette when Desmond dropped the bombshell on Evelyn. He had known what her reaction would be, which was why he'd told her after they'd had their fun.

'*What?*' Evelyn sat bolt upright, smoke spiralling out of her mouth.

'Lloyd is going to divorce me?' she roared.

'I'm afraid so, my dear.' Desmond adjusted his air to one of concern while inside he was calculating how quickly he could get out of bed, washed, dressed and out of there.

'I heard it with my own ears,' he said, stubbing out his cigarette.

'But we were meant to be having a break,' she said, outraged. Part of her had actually started to believe her own lies.

'He seemed pretty definite,' Desmond said, getting out of bed. 'We had to ring your friend in Mayfair – some woman called Juliette.'

Evelyn let out a gasp of disbelief.

'And what did Juliette say?'

'That she hadn't seen you in quite some time,' Desmond said, noticing that Evelyn had become quite red in the face, and it was not because of their sexual antics.

'My God! How dare they check up on me!' Evelyn spat out the words. 'I'm being hounded!' Now not only was she spitting feathers about the divorce, she was also beside herself that they were trying to track her down in London. *Did the miner's daughter really think that she – Evelyn Foxton-Clarke – would do what she'd been ordered to do!*

Seeing that Evelyn was on the verge of exploding, and not wanting to become collateral damage, Desmond decided to skip the wash and instead quickly climbed back into his clothes.

'And this wasn't some idle, spur-of-the-moment threat?' asked Evelyn, needing to know that Lloyd was indeed serious about cutting her out of his life – and killing off any chance she had of getting her hands on Cuthford Manor. No marriage meant no manor.

'Well . . .' Desmond hesitated. 'I'm afraid, my dear, he did seem very earnest—'

Evelyn looked at Desmond, all her fury directed towards him.

Seeing the glint in her eye, Desmond grabbed his shoes.

'Sorry, Evelyn, but really, I'm going to have to dash. I've a scheduled meeting at half three.'

Evelyn glowered at him.

'Scheduled meeting my arse!' She looked around and seeing the glass ashtray, hurled it at him.

It thudded against the wall, missing Desmond by inches.

Seconds later, Evelyn heard the front door shut and footsteps on the cobbles.

When Evelyn got back to the Fontaine-Smiths', she'd made out to Gertrude that she had one of her heads coming on and needed to have a lie-down, which was not totally untrue. The news of the divorce had made her feel sick to the pit of her stomach. And her head was banging with a myriad of questions about what she should do.

Back in her room, she felt like throwing herself onto the bed, beating her fists and screaming into her pillows.

But she didn't. Instead, she snatched her cigarettes out of her bag and cracked open the window. She lit one and inhaled deeply.

She should have guessed that Lloyd would want to divorce her after what he'd found out, but she didn't think he'd go about it so quickly. The clock was now ticking.

And although he had to find her first before starting down the slow, dreary journey to a decree nisi, she knew she had to step up a gear. People would be looking for her. It was time to put the plan she had been formulating during her time here into action.

A plan that would leave the pathway for her return free.

A pathway free of interference from anyone.

And with all the insurance money she'd receive – and, of course, the money, jewellery and antiques she'd stashed away – she'd easily be able to do up Cuthford Manor the way she wanted and live the life she deserved.

She just needed to pick the right time for what she had to do.

Finding out about the divorce might have forced her hand and propelled her into action faster than she'd anticipated, but perhaps that wasn't so bad.

The sooner it was done, the sooner Cuthford Manor would be hers. *All hers.*

Chapter Fifty-Two

In the days leading up to Valentine's Day, there was much excitement in Cuthford Manor. This was mainly due to Marlene mentioning it whenever she got the chance and wondering aloud how all her admirers would be able to get their cards to her when she lived 'in the middle of nowhere'.

'They'll use the post like everyone else,' Danny had said with a shake of his head. He'd often wondered aloud if he and Marlene really were related and perhaps their mam had had a secret affair with some 'airhead toff'. Angie had heard her brother's words and said to Stanislaw out of the corner of her mouth, 'Many a true word spoken in jest.'

Marlene loved the idea she might be the love child of an 'airhead toff' – well, perhaps not the airhead bit, but certainly the toff – and had said she hoped she was.

Not one to let her older brother get away with anything, she also took great joy in ribbing Danny about who he was going to send a card to, and 'would it perhaps be the enigma that is Lucy from Roeburn Hall?'

'Those two have got it the wrong way round,' Angie told Stanislaw when they were heading out for a ride. Stanislaw was still hoping that one day Angie might suggest riding Ghost, but so far that day had not come.

'In what way?' Stanislaw asked.

'Well, Marlene has the hots for poor old Thomas – the working-class son of a poacher,' Angie laughed. 'Who, I hasten to add, is living in fear of your wrath should he respond to her flirtations.'

'More like *your* wrath,' Stanislaw countered.

'And Danny has clearly fallen for the charms of Lucy Stanton-Leigh – who has most definitely been born with a silver spoon in her mouth and comes from a line of blue-blooded local aristocracy.'

'Ah,' Stanislaw said, 'but she's a gifted horse rider, which I believe is the real attraction. And unlike some of the – what do you call them here? – the *hoity-toity*, she really loves her horses.'

Angie laughed. It had been a while since she'd heard that expression.

'Well, let's pray that the pair of them get cards. Especially Marlene. Life won't be worth living if she doesn't.'

Stanislaw glanced across at Angie as they pushed their respective horses into a slow canter. He wondered how Angie would react if she received an anonymous declaration of love. From the man who might love her from a distance – but was always close by.

That night, Stanislaw couldn't sleep. His feelings for Angie seemed to be growing stronger by the day, which was not surprising as they saw so much of each other. Even more so of late, because of all the planning and the hiring of tradesmen for the impending work on the manor.

When he had been with Angie in the tack room after their ride today, they'd practically been touching. He'd had to fight the urge to pull her towards him, wrap his arms around her and kiss her. Kiss her neck, her face, her lips. Did Angie also feel the charge between them?

But Clemmie's words kept coming back to him. That Angie believed in a person only having one love in their life. One true love. And for her that love had been Quentin.

Stanislaw knew he should feel blessed that he had such a close and caring friendship with Angie. The bond they'd forged made him feel part of her family. It had been the first time he had felt at home anywhere since he'd been forced to leave his beloved Poland. But he knew that happiness couldn't endure if they were to remain just friends. It would slowly sour if his love was not reciprocated – if he had to be with Angie, knowing her love for him was one of friendship and nothing more.

There was only one thing for it. Tomorrow was Valentine's Day. What better day to ask her.

And if she said no?

If she said no, then there would be only one course of action.

He would have to go.

He couldn't stay here if she didn't want him. He could not bear to be around her if she did not love him back. It wouldn't be right – for either of them. The pain would be too much.

As he looked out of the window, he prayed to a God he didn't believe in any more that she wanted him as much as he wanted her.

Chapter Fifty-Three

When the postman arrived on his bicycle the next morning, Marlene was not disappointed. She was handed three valentine cards.

Angie was handed three bills and groaned.

After the children had gone off to school and Bonnie had been taken to nursery, Angie had a cuppa with Stanislaw in the kitchen. Alberta was bustling about, making jam turnovers in the shape of hearts, and Mabel was humming a love song Angie vaguely recognised as she got her cleaning products together. Winston and Bessie had flumped down between Angie and Stanislaw as they'd been shooed out the way of the Aga by the cook.

Eyeing the vase of wild primroses and pale pink crocuses in the middle of the table – freshly picked flowers they guessed had come from Bill – Angie raised her eyebrows at Stanislaw.

'Love is in the air,' she said quietly.

'It certainly is,' Stanislaw said. 'And I do believe your brother might have also been struck by Cupid's bow.'

Angie furrowed her brow questioningly.

'He took Ghost out for an early-morning ride. A very early morning ride.'

Angie took a sip of her tea.

'Let me guess. A ride that might have taken him to Roeburn Hall?'

'I reckon so,' Stanislaw said.

'Well, she better not break his heart,' Angie said protectively. 'Any girl who has my brother's affections is a lucky girl indeed.'

Stanislaw chuckled at Angie's protectiveness. Like a lion with her cubs. It was yet another trait he loved her for.

'Right,' he said finishing his tea and getting up. 'I'd better get back to it.'

Angie watched him go and was just about to get up herself and head to the office when she heard the familiar ungainly thud of Clemmie's boots as she came down the corridor and into the kitchen.

'Happy Valentine's Day!' she declared as she burst into the kitchen, nearly colliding with Mabel, who was dragging the Hoover with one hand, her other carrying a steel bucket in which she'd put her scrubbing brush, cloths and polish.

Clemmie waved her through the door with an elaborate flourish of her hand, as though she was a ringmaster introducing an act.

'So, did the postman manage to get up the drive with his bag stuffed to overflowing with rose-scented cards declaring undying love from now to eternity?'

Angie eyed Clemmie. 'Honestly, Clemmie, you are a funny one.' Again, Angie was reminded of Dorothy, who used to be insufferable on Valentine's Day. She'd have to ring her and find out what Bobby had got her. Woe betide him if he hadn't rolled out the red carpet for his wife and booked a romantic meal for two at some high-class restaurant.

'Marlene received three,' Angie informed. 'Although I have a sneaking suspicion that two might have been from the same not-so-secret admirer.'

'An admirer whose name begins with T?' Clemmie asked.

Alberta tutted.

'Poor lad,' she mumbled.

'I think I have to agree with you there, Alberta,' said Angie.

'Right,' Clemmie declared, staring down at the dogs, who both had a look of anticipation as her arrival usually heralded 'walkies'. 'As I have found myself with a rare morning off my duties educating the country's next generation of the academic elite, shall we take the hounds of the Baskervilles out for a you-know-what? I need air. Fresh air.'

Five minutes later, Clemmie, Angie and the two 'hounds' were heading out.

'So, talking of valentine cards,' Angie asked gingerly, 'did you have any dropping on your mat this morning, or perhaps you sent your own?' She had been curious about Clemmie's love life – and if she had one.

Clemmie laughed loudly. 'I wish!'

'So, you've not got anyone special at the moment?' Angie asked.

'Mmm, that's a yes-and-no answer,' Clemmie said. 'There is someone special, but she doesn't know I have feelings for her.'

'Well, perhaps she should know,' Angie said, as they trudged across the field to the small patch of woodland the dogs loved.

'Perhaps,' Clemmie said without conviction. *Perhaps not.* 'Did you and Quentin used to do anything special for Valentine's Day?' she asked.

Angie felt her heart drop. Followed by the resurgence of guilt. She *had* thought about Quentin today – she thought about him every day. But today her mind hadn't kept wandering back to the past as often as it usually did.

'Oh, yes,' she stuttered, 'we did.'

'Sorry – that was insensitive of me,' Clemmie said. She meant it. She *was* sorry. It was just that her need to keep Angie and Stanislaw apart superseded everything else.

'Anyway, what about the young ones?' Clemmie said, changing the subject. 'I'm guessing today is only really important to Marlene and Danny.'

'Yes, thank goodness,' Angie said. 'Hopefully, it will be a good few years before Jemima and Bertie become all lovelorn. And Bonnie! God, I dread the day.'

After Clemmie had left and Angie was finally able to go to the back office and do some work, she was annoyed that she felt unable to concentrate. It didn't help that Lloyd was bobbing about like a yo-yo.

'You all right, Lloyd?' Angie asked.

'Yes, yes,' Lloyd said distractedly. 'Just organising. Making sure everyone's got a bed to sleep in tonight. You don't think Bertie, Jemima and Bonnie will mind sharing the spare bedroom, do you?' The 'spare bedroom' used to be Evelyn's, but Lloyd couldn't bear to even refer to her, never mind say her name.

'No, of course not – I think they're quite excited about us all being in the West Wing.'

Angie had to smile on hearing her words. There'd been a time when her siblings had all had to share a bed – never mind the wing of a manor.

What Angie didn't know was that Lloyd's slightly distracted, agitated manner was because he had his own plans this evening – on St Valentine's Day – and he was nervous.

Nervous and worried.

But he had to do it.

No more holding back.

No more regrets.

Chapter Fifty-Four

Evelyn had woken up with no idea it was Valentine's Day, so focused was she on putting her plan into action tonight.

She had covered all her bases and was particularly pleased that she'd managed to create leverage with the family solicitors – or, rather, with Desmond. When everything was done and dusted, and she emerged like a phoenix out of the rubble to claim Cuthford Manor as hers, Desmond would do everything she asked. He would do what needed to be done: get rid of Angie's 'tribe', put money into a trust for Bonnie for the next two decades, make sure the insurance was processed without any hiccups – particularly the 'joint' life insurance she'd taken out last year. It would all go ahead seamlessly. And *she* would become the new widow of Cuthford Manor.

No more miner's daughter lording it over her.

No more husband trying to divorce her.

She just wished she'd thought of this before.

Still, better late than never.

Chapter Fifty-Five

'Are you going out for a ride?' Stanislaw asked, seeing Angie come out of the back door dressed in jodhpurs.

'Silly question, I know,' he said, suddenly feeling self-conscious. This was his perfect opportunity. He had to take it. 'Do you fancy some company?'

'Yes, definitely,' she said.

Stanislaw's heart leapt as his body flooded with nerves.

Angie brought Starling out into the yard while Stanislaw saddled up Ghost. Within five minutes, they'd put Cuthford Manor behind them and were heading for the hills. They rode hard for twenty minutes, before coming to a stop at Angie's favourite place, where on a clear day the high land afforded a view of the city's skyline.

Today it was clear and fresh with just a touch of frost in the air.

Angie scissored her leg over and jumped down, allowing Starling to drop her head so she could munch on the grass. Stanislaw took a deep breath, dismounted and gave Ghost a pat. He kissed the side of Ghost's face and whispered in his ear, 'Wish me luck.'

He jogged to catch up with Angie, who was walking towards her favourite spot.

'God, I love it here,' she said, breathing in the cold, clean air. 'I never thought—' As she spoke, her foot hit a clump of grass and she went over on her ankle.

'Whoa.' Stanislaw instinctively reached out to grab her.

Not realising how light she was or how strong he was, Stanislaw found himself pulling Angie into his arms. He could feel her body pressing against his as she regained her footing.

'Nearly!' Stanislaw said, not taking his arms away but holding her tightly.

For the briefest of moments, they stood still, their bodies touching.

Stanislaw was so much taller than Angie, who only reached his chest. She looked up just as he was bending his head down.

'Dear me . . .' Angie took a step back. 'I can be such a clumsy clot.' Her face had reddened.

On the way back, Angie could think only of how it had felt being in Stanislaw's arms. She had thought how it might feel before and had chastised herself. Now she knew. It had felt so natural. But then she'd heard Clemmie's voice in her head, asking her about what she and Quentin used to do on Valentine's Day – and there it was again, the feeling of guilt and shame. It was okay to recover from the death of your husband – to be happy, even – but to fall in love with another man. No. That was *not* okay.

When they were back in the yard, Angie made up a lie about forgetting to tell Lloyd something in relation to the

East Wing move. Hurrying away from the man whose arms had felt so right around her, she felt abuzz. Her whole body felt alive in a way it hadn't for a very long time.

But as she pulled off her boots and shrugged off her jacket, she felt her spirits drop like a dead weight.

It was wrong to feel this way.

She was Judas, betraying the man she'd loved.

Watching Angie head back to the manor, Stanislaw was feeling a similar seesaw of emotions. It was the first time they had been so physically close – even though they had known each other and worked together for so many months. *How he yearned to have her back in his arms.*

But then Stanislaw felt angry at himself for not doing what he'd really wanted to do – drop his head lower and kiss her.

As Stanislaw groomed Ghost until his coat shone, he made his resolution.

He would tell her. This evening.

Chapter Fifty-Six

Dinner that evening was a rushed affair. Alberta and Mrs Kwiatkowski had made a goulash with Yorkshire puddings, which had gone down a treat, but no one wanted dessert.

Bertie, Jemima and Bonnie asked if they could have some Horlicks and one of the cook's heart-shaped jam tarts to take to their room. Angie said they could, knowing that they were itching to show Mrs Kwiatkowski their new quarters in the West Wing. The three children were excited about having to share a bedroom while the building work was done.

Marlene had been like a cat on a hot tin roof and as soon as she'd spooned up the last of her stew had asked to be excused.

'Yes,' Angie said, knowing exactly where she was headed, 'but only five minutes on the phone – tops!'

Marlene had rolled her eyes, knowing she could probably get away with ten.

Danny went off to check on the horses, as he always did before turning in for the night. He and Marlene were both glad there'd not been time to move them into the West Wing – it had been decided they'd move over the weekend, along with Mrs Jones, Mrs Kwiatkowski and Stanislaw.

When Angie returned to the dining room after making the children their hot drinks and saying goodnight, she was surprised to see that there was just Stanislaw left at the table.

'Lloyd and Mrs Jones said they wanted to check the children had everything they needed in their new quarters,' he explained, reading Angie's mind. 'I said I'd clear up.'

Angie smiled and tried to hide her nervousness. Something had changed between the two of them this afternoon and she didn't know how she felt about it. Or how to act.

'We'll do it together,' she said with a little too much enthusiasm.

Neither spoke much as they cleared the table and took everything through to the kitchen. Winston and Bessie jumped up and plodded over to their bowls, awaiting any leftovers.

Angie and Stanislaw had just finished washing and drying the dinner plates when they heard the click of the wrought-iron latch and Danny came in the back door.

'There's an amazing full moon tonight!' he said, kicking off his boots. 'Apparently, it's called a Snow Moon. It's the exact colour of Ghost's coat.'

'That's interesting,' Angie said.

Danny looked at his sister. She seemed awkward.

'Right, well, I'll leave you to it, but seriously, you need to see it,' he said, giving the dogs a quick pat.

'Night, then!'

'Night, Danny,' Angie and Stanislaw said in unison.

When the kitchen door closed, Stanislaw turned to Angie. 'Well, we better do as Danny says and have a look at this Snow Moon.'

They pulled on their boots and grabbed their jackets. Stanislaw opened the door and waited for Angie to go first.

Standing in the yard, they looked up to the dark sky and marvelled at the full moon, which was indeed the colour of Ghost's coat – a marbled, smoky grey.

'A time for change,' Stanislaw said as they both kept their eyes turned up to the starry sky.

Angie didn't say anything, but sensed Stanislaw turn towards her.

'Angie,' he said, his voice quiet in the still, calm air.

Turning her vision away from the night sky, Angie felt her heart thudding in her chest. She could feel the blood pumping, pulsating.

'I want to tell you something,' Stanislaw continued.

No, please don't! a voice in Angie's head screamed.

'I have to tell you how I feel. About you.' Stanislaw spoke slowly.

Angie looked at Stanislaw's face. A face she'd come to know so well. A face that appeared in her mind as she drifted off to sleep at night. She'd tried to fight it, replace his face with Quentin's, but it had been a losing battle.

'I have feelings for you,' Stanislaw said, his own thumping heart making him breathless. 'Feelings which are more than those of merely a friend.'

He looked at Angie's face, its paleness illuminated by the brightness of the moon.

'But . . . your wife?' Angie stuttered, remembering what Clemmie had said about Stanislaw talking about his wife all the time to Mrs Kwiatkowski. She had actually been jealous of Adrianna. How ridiculously stupid was that?

'Adrianna died many years ago,' Stanislaw said.

'But she was your one true love.' Angie repeated Clemmie's words.

'She was then. But now it is different. You are the first woman I have loved since Adrianna,' Stanislaw said.

Angie didn't reply. She didn't know what she wanted to say. It felt as though she were being pulled in opposite directions. One towards Quentin and the other towards Stanislaw. But every time it seemed as though the pull towards Stanislaw was winning, along came the awful feelings of guilt and betrayal.

Stanislaw shook his head. 'I'm sorry,' he said. 'I shouldn't have said what I did.'

He paused and Angie opened her mouth to speak.

To say, *I do feel the same!*

But the words didn't come.

It was as though she had been struck dumb. Something had frozen her being.

Fear? Love? Or was it guilt? Guilt because she was falling in love with another man. Another man who wasn't Quentin. *How could she!*

And so she simply stood, mute, looking at Stanislaw as he waited a fraction longer for her response before he turned to go.

Angie watched as he walked away, across the cobbled yard to the stables.

Every part of her cried out to go after him. To run to him. To kiss him. To tell him that she *did* love him – that she *did* desire him.

But she couldn't. She just couldn't.

Chapter Fifty-Seven

Evelyn wrote a note for Gertrude telling her that she had gone to London and would be back in a week or so. That she would call her once she had arrived and settled in. She kept it short, saying she just needed to get away.

Gertrude and Jeremy had gone to York for the day on a shopping trip for new furniture. It would seem the plans for Cuthford Manor had inspired them to redecorate their own country pad. Their absence had spurred Evelyn into action.

She'd spent the day packing her suitcase, then used Jeremy's car to drive to Darlington, where she had left her suitcase in a locker and bought a ticket to London for the early-morning train. She couldn't risk getting on at Durham, where she might be recognised. Darlington was a safer bet. She might have been a little rusty on the driving front as she made her way to the main road, but it was like riding a bike. By the time she'd hit the A1, her gear changes were smooth and she was motoring along at a steady 60 mph.

The round trip had taken her just under three hours and she'd done it as soon as it started to get dark and the maid and the cook had left for the day. There was no supper to prepare, so they'd gone by four. This had given Evelyn plenty of time to do the trip to Darlington, arriving back at the house just after seven. She'd then forced down a sandwich and a cup of tea, even though her nervous energy was keeping her hunger at bay.

Just before nine, she put on her evening's attire: black jodhpurs, black polo neck, a black overcoat and black woollen gloves and hat. She then carefully packed her black haversack with everything she needed.

Evelyn left it as late as she could before venturing out into the dark night. Gertrude and Jeremy would be dining in York and had planned to get the eight-thirty train back to Durham. So, shortly before ten, Evelyn crept out the back door, making sure her message about her sudden decision to go to London had been placed so it could be seen as soon as they walked through the door. She didn't want them panicking and sending out a search party.

Having ridden between Cuthford Manor and the Fontaine-Smiths' many times over the years, Evelyn had no problem navigating her way on foot in the dark with her torch. When she reached the small shepherd's hut on the border of the estate, she went inside and settled herself in the threadbare armchair next to the wood burner. She'd have loved to have got it going, but she couldn't risk anyone seeing the smoke.

Now she just needed to wait until all the lights went out.

Chapter Fifty-Eight

After his disastrous conversation with Angie, Stanislaw sought solace in the barn. The horses were his comfort. They understood. He checked them and gave them one last groom, all the time turning over what had happened.

By the time he headed back to his room, it was late. He'd deliberately left it so late in order not to bump into anybody. His heartbreak was there – emblazoned across his face – for everyone to see.

It was deathly quiet when he went back inside. Even the dogs barely moved. Creeping upstairs and along the East Wing, he could see there were no lights on, and he could hear the gentle sounds of sleep – the creak of bedsprings as Marlene turned over, a gentle snoring coming from Danny's room.

Reaching his own room, he switched on the side light and quickly packed his bag. It didn't take long as he was not one for keeping many possessions. But although his bag might have been relatively light, his heart was heavy. Heavy because he didn't want to leave, but knew he had to. He could not stay here and love Angie from afar. He knew it was best to leave now, quickly, just as he knew the pain in his heart would linger for a long time after.

There'd only ever be 'one true love' in Angie's life – and that was her husband. He'd thought he'd seen a shimmer of possibility in Angie's eyes while they stood under the light of the moon, but then he'd seen that look.

It broke his heart that Angie was not able to love again.

Chapter Fifty-Nine

Seeing the last light go out, Evelyn picked up her haversack and swung it over her shoulder. It was time.

She opened the door of the shepherd's hut and looked back to make sure she hadn't left anything behind. It was imperative there was no evidence – nothing whatsoever to bring the police sniffing at her door. She then strode out to the manor. *Her manor.* She was glad she'd kept in shape – horse riding and, of course, her time with Desmond had combined to keep her fit.

As she neared the West Wing, she had only one concern – that the casings on the small window in the basement hadn't been fixed and it could still be opened from the outside with a gentle nudge. Of all the things that needed doing to the place, this was probably one of the last on Angie's 'to do' list.

Tiptoeing the fifty or so yards down the steeply sloping walkway at the back of the manor, Evelyn came to a stop and crouched down on her haunches so that she was eye level with the basement window. It was small, but not so small that she couldn't slither through without too much hassle.

She took a deep breath and prayed the window had not been mended.

Placing both hands on the wooden frame, she pushed gently.

It didn't budge.

Panicked, she pushed harder.

Suddenly the window broke free and swung open, hitting the wall inside, but not loud enough for anyone but herself to hear.

Bingo! She breathed a sigh of relief.

Nothing was going to stop her now.

Chapter Sixty

When Stanislaw closed for the last time the back door that led out to the cobbled yard, he knew he had to say goodbye to the horses. He walked quietly over to the barn and slipped through the door, which was slightly ajar.

'Goodbye, old boy,' he said, stroking Ghost's forelock. 'You take care of Danny.'

Stanislaw felt terrible about leaving Danny. He knew the boy viewed him as a father figure. Just as he knew he would not understand why Stanislaw had had to leave. Perhaps when he was older and knew more of love, he might. Perhaps then he would forgive him.

'I hope one day she lets you back into her heart,' he said as Ghost nuzzled his shoulder. 'I think she will. In time.' Stanislaw could feel the sting of tears. He rarely cried, but leaving this place and everyone in it was so much harder than he'd thought. He needed to go without any fuss. He couldn't bear to say goodbye to Angie in person – to everyone at Cuthford Manor. He had grown so close to them all.

His only consolation was that he knew Angie would manage just fine without him. He'd never known such a strong woman. Such a survivor. And, of course, she had the support of her family and friends.

As Angie lay in bed, looking out of her window at the full moon, she kept going over the day's events in her head. And in particular the time she had spent with Stanislaw. She realised that whenever they were together her heart lifted and she felt a surge of happiness – even if it was just having a cuppa and discussing her siblings' romantic yearnings.

She felt herself blush as she relived the moment when they'd stopped at her favourite place while out riding and he'd grabbed her as she'd tripped.

How she felt when she'd found herself pressed up against him.

This evening, when Stanislaw had confessed his feelings as they'd gazed at the Snow Moon, she had wanted more than anything to say yes – to step towards him and feel his arms around her, as she had imagined doing many times before.

But something in her still wasn't ready. The sense that she was betraying Quentin every time she imagined Stanislaw as anything but a friend was too overwhelming. She knew that Dorothy would tell her she was a fool – that she should allow herself this chance of a second love. But whenever she thought about it, the guilt stopped her. She could not act on her feelings. She didn't know if she ever could.

She thought back to Stanislaw's reaction when she hadn't reciprocated his words of love – and the sadness in his eyes.

There had been something else in his expression too – what was it?

And then it came to her.

He's going to leave!

Of course, it seemed obvious now that he would not stay there after declaring his love for her.

Suddenly, Angie felt terrified that he might leave tonight.

Surely he wouldn't go so soon, *would he*?

Lloyd woke with a start. For a moment, he thought his evening with Cora had been all a dream. He breathed a sigh of relief when he felt the warmth of her naked body next to his. He turned gently so as not to wake her, smoothing her long chestnut hair away from her face.

He need not have been so jittery and nervous as their evening together had felt so natural. So right. The strangest feeling of coming home.

Finally, after all these years, they had been able to show the love they had for one another.

They had so much lost time to make up for, but that was fine.

They had the rest of their lives.

Stanislaw shut the barn door quietly behind him. As he did so, he smelled a faint whiff of smoke. The last of one of the many fires that were always lit in the house, he presumed.

He smiled. Angie always insisted the house was warm. It was one of her idiosyncrasies. He wondered if that was because of her background. Even though she'd been the daughter of a coal miner, she'd told him that their home was always cold. She'd promised herself that when she had her own home, it would always be 'toasty'. Which must have been quite a challenge, living somewhere like Cuthford Manor, but she had succeeded. Every room always had a fire stacked and ready to be lit if need be.

Stanislaw walked past the terraced gardens, which he knew would soon be bursting to life with the colours of spring. He pushed away the memory of his first visit here. How he had walked past the gardens and been in awe at the beauty of the manor's grounds – although that had been nothing in comparison to what he felt for the manor's owner.

Angie couldn't sleep. As she lay in bed, wide-awake, she'd started to feel angry with herself. She should have said something. *Anything at all.* She should have told him to come back to the kitchen, made a cup of tea and explained how she was feeling. That she did have feelings, but she was scared. *Terrified* of them.

Sometimes she thought it wasn't just because of Quentin that she felt she couldn't love again, but because she was afraid that if she loved someone, they too might die – and she really didn't think she could endure that. Or survive it.

Instead, she'd just stood there like a great big lummox.

Her mind kept rebounding back to Stanislaw's reaction when they'd been in the yard. The sadness pooled in his eyes. Again, her gut told her that he intended to leave. And the more she thought about it, the more worried she became that Stanislaw might go tonight.

In the end, Angie tossed her bedclothes aside, put on her slippers and threw on her dressing gown. She just needed to put her mind at rest. Check that Stanislaw hadn't sneaked off into the depths of the night. She thought of Danny. He would never forgive her if she let Stanislaw go.

She would check the East Wing and reassure herself that Stanislaw was still there, and then she would come back to the West Wing and go to bed with the resolve to chat to Stanislaw tomorrow. Tell him how she really felt. That she just needed time to get her head and her heart in sync.

As she reached the bedroom door, she caught a faint smell of smoke.

Strange.

Perhaps Lloyd was up. He sometimes had a smoke or a cigar if he couldn't sleep.

She turned the doorknob, but it came off in her hand.

She stood for a moment, staring at it, before bending down and looking through the small hole where there should have been a metal rod attached to the doorknob on the other side. But it wasn't there.

She stood up and tried to prise the door open, her fingers gripping the edges, but it was no good. She couldn't open it.

She was trapped inside.

And that's when she saw the smoke beginning to snake under her door.

It took a moment for it to register before she bellowed as loud as she could:

'Fire!'

Chapter Sixty-One

Evelyn had carefully and quietly dismantled all three brass knobs on the doors of the main bedrooms in the West Wing. She had waited long enough after seeing the lights go out to ensure that everyone would be asleep. It was risky, but she'd practised for hours on her bedroom doorknob at the Fontaine-Smiths', which was the same as at the manor.

The idea for the fire had come to Evelyn while reading a book. She'd started to read lots of thrillers and whodunnits – not just because she'd been bored silly living at her friend's house, but because there were plenty of good ideas in the pages of some of these novels. The authors had done their research. When she'd read a novel in which the murderer sought revenge by making an arson attack appear to be an accidental electrical fire, Evelyn had her answer for what she would do.

She knew the layout of Cuthford Manor like the back of her hand. The children, Mrs Jones, the old woman and the Pole would be in the East Wing. She'd have been quite happy if Mrs Jones and Mrs Kwiatkowski had also been in the West Wing, but it didn't really matter.

As Evelyn crouched down on the landing, she got out her lighter and clicked it once, holding the flame over the small piece of charcoal briquette she'd got from her haversack. Carefully placing it next to an electrical socket, she waited a few moments to ensure it didn't go out, then she tiptoed back to the stairs used by the maids and crouched down.

And waited.

Evelyn had worked out that once the fire brigade was called, they would get there in time to stop the blaze before it razed the whole place to the ground, but not soon enough to free Angie and Lloyd from their burning bedrooms.

And by the time the fire was put out, there would be no telling that the doorknobs had been meddled with.

Evelyn watched from a safe distance as the smoke from the smouldering electrical socket thickened.

She jumped nervously as the first few sparks crackled.

Her eyes lit up when, a moment later, she saw the first proper flame licking up the wall and catching the wallpaper she had gently pulled away to feed the fire. The floral design went up in one fell swoop before gravity pulled it down and it landed on the threadbare rug, which, in turn, took only a few moments before it too caught alight.

Chapter Sixty-Two

Stanislaw had reached the top of the driveway. The ornate cast-iron gates were open, as always. He remembered that first day he had ridden through them on Ghost when he'd come to deliver the news that Mrs Kwiatkowski had been found. Had it only been four and a half months ago? It seemed longer somehow.

Tonight he had promised himself he would not look back. Life should be about going forward, but he couldn't leave without one last glance at the place that had brought so much love into his life.

And now so much heartache.

Taking a deep breath, he turned and took in Cuthford Manor for the final time. The place that had become his home.

But as he did so, a frown formed on his brow.

What was that?

He could see smoke drifting from the side of the West Wing. Dense smoke. He'd seen smoke like that in Warsaw when the Germans had bombed the city.

'*No! No! No!*' He panicked, seeing the first flickering of flames appear at one of the windows – *the window outside Angie's bedroom door.*

Stanislaw threw his holdall onto the gravel and sprinted as fast as he was able towards Cuthford Manor, his eyes glued to where he knew Angie to be – as well as Bertie, Jemima and Bonnie.

Stanislaw felt an anger unlike anything he had felt before – not since his wife's death.

Angie and those children would not die.

Even if it meant he had to sacrifice his own life to save them.

Chapter Sixty-Three

Between desperate shouts, Angie tried to kick the door, thinking it might just spring open, but again, it was hopeless. As the smoke started to billow through the gaps in the doorframe, she moved away and started banging on the wall.

'Bertie! Jemima! Bonnie! Wake up!' She put her ear to the wall, but couldn't hear anything, wasn't sure she'd be able to as it was a solid supporting wall.

All the same, she kept banging and shouting, 'There's a fire! Get out!'

As she continued to shout, she flung off her dressing gown and nightie and pulled on her trousers and a shirt she'd slung over the chair next to her bed. She grabbed her boots from under the chair and yanked them on, quickly tying the laces.

The room was now filling with smoke and her body was shaking with adrenalin caused by the sheer panic of not knowing if the children were awake, never mind aware there was a fire. Had the fumes knocked them out? Were they lying unconscious next door?

She stomped back to the door, feeling like a tiger trapped in a cage.

'Lloyd! Wake up!' she screamed. 'Fire!'

She held her breath and put her head to the wooden door, feeling the warmth emanating from the other side, but she couldn't hear a damned thing other than the gentle crackle of flames.

She turned away from the thick ash-coloured smoke edging its way into the room, trying to see anything that might help. She grabbed her dressing-table chair and banged it against the wall.

'*Wake up!*' she screamed.

And that's when she heard Jemima calling out her name.

'Get out of the room!' Angie bellowed at the wall.

She heard the children coughing.

And then Bertie's voice.

'We can't. The door won't open!'

And that's when she knew that what was happening was no accident.

This fire had been started deliberately.

Putting her hands to her head, she wanted to scream with anger and an overwhelming sense of impotence.

If both their rooms were locked, then so were everyone else's.

She ran to the window, knowing not to open it, having learnt about the effects of oxygen on fire during her years welding. She pressed her face against the pane of glass and looked out.

It was too high to jump.

There was no way out.

Turning away from the window, she heard the sickening sound of the whoosh of flames coming to life.

Just as Stanislaw reached the steps of Cuthford Manor, the front door swung open and he saw Wilfred standing in his pyjamas and dressing grown, a hankie over his face, smoke swirling behind him. His eyes were full of fear. He took the hankie away, causing him to start coughing. He pointed his finger to the staircase.

'They're up there,' he rasped.

Stanislaw made for the stairs just as Wilfred grabbed his arm. 'They're locked in . . . can't open . . . the doors.' His words were punctuated by more coughing.

Stanislaw hesitated, looking around – he'd need something to smash the doors open. His eye caught a glint from one of the suits of armour on either side of the fireplace. One suit had both hands resting on top of a long medieval sword. The other held a long-handled poleaxe.

Throwing off his coat, Stanislaw marched over to the knight and wrenched the poleaxe free, almost dropping it, it was so unexpectedly heavy.

'Have you rung the fire brigade?' Stanislaw shouted. The dogs were barking furiously, and he could hear muffled shouts from above, despite the crackling of the fire.

Wilfred nodded, but his expression betrayed his lack of hope they would get there in time.

'Get everyone out of the East Wing,' Stanislaw said, hauling his poleaxe up the stairs and disappearing into the fog of fire.

*

When Stanislaw reached the top of the stairs, he could barely see through the thick smoke, the only illumination coming from the flickering orange flames towards the end of the landing.

Angie's room.

Putting his arm over his mouth and dragging the heavy weapon in his wake, he charged through the choking smog towards the rapidly spreading fire, which had now caught the long velvet curtains. He could hear the shouts of the children, along with Mrs Jones's voice trying to calm them.

Reaching Angie's bedroom, he could see there was no door handle. He hoped to God that Angie hadn't opened the window, otherwise they'd be in trouble when he smashed the door down.

'Stand back!' he yelled.

Taking hold of the poleaxe halfway down, he used both hands so as to wield it like a wood chopping axe and stood a little to the side, aware of the flames licking just inches away from him. Then, using all his strength, he swung the heavy medieval weapon back and hacked into the middle of the door.

Pulling it out of the thick oak panels, he hauled it back again and swung at the door with all his might.

This time he splintered the wood.

He caught a glimpse of Angie on her haunches, a scarf covering her face.

Good, she was keeping low, taking in as little smoke as possible.

He gave the door one last blow. This time when he pulled out the axe, he took a wooden panel with it.

Dropping the weapon, he raised his foot to kick the rest of the door panels through, but as he did so his shirtsleeve caught alight.

'Damn it!' he cursed, patting out the flames.

The hole in the door was almost enough to get Angie through. He just needed one more almighty kick.

His foot smashed through, splinters of wood ripping into his leg.

'That's it! I can get through!' Angie shouted.

Stanislaw grabbed her hand and helped pull her through the ravaged door. He saw a sharp piece of wood cut into her arm, but her eyes didn't seem to register the pain. They were too full of panic.

'The children!' she screamed. 'Get the children!'

Stanislaw immediately grabbed the axe, pulled off the wooden panel and dragged it to the bedroom door where he knew the children to be. He swung the axe again. The fire was taking hold and he could feel pieces of burning plaster raining down on him as the flames wrapped themselves around the ceiling. Out of the corner of his eye, he saw Angie frantically trying to get Lloyd's door open. Bashing into it with the side of her body.

He heard Mrs Jones's voice. She was with Lloyd and was trying to reassure the children in the next room.

'Help's coming!' she was shouting.

Stanislaw kept hacking at the door, his desperation increasing by the second as he could no longer hear the cries of the children.

He was almost there. One more swing and he managed to smash through one of the panels. Dropping the axe, he looked through the crack in the wood and, seeing the smoke-filled room, felt sheer panic.

Kicking at the loose door panel like a man possessed, he squeezed his tall frame through the hole he'd created.

The smoke was overwhelming.

Angie went to the battered door, the heat from the fire burning her face.

'Oh my God!' Angie felt her legs go weak. Jemima and Bonnie were lying unconscious on the floor. Bertie had managed to wet one of the bed sheets in the sink and was now wearing it like a cloak to cover the two girls.

Her view was momentarily blocked as Stanislaw strode over to Bertie, scooping him up with both hands and tramping back to the smashed door.

'Bertie! Come here!' Angie had her head through the gap in the door, her arms stretched out. Bertie's face was blackened with soot. He looked on the verge of collapse and was coughing. He stretched his arms out towards his big sister. Angie grabbed him and hauled him through the hole, falling backwards as she did so.

Hearing the crack of splintered wood, she glanced to her right to see Lloyd pushing his bedroom door open and tossing down the brass poker from the bedroom fireplace.

'I'll take him!' he hollered, grabbing Bertie from her. He then passed the little boy to Mrs Jones.

'Get him out of here,' he implored. 'And don't come back up.'

Angie watched as Mrs Jones and Bertie disappeared into the smoke, then looked back into the children's room to see that Stanislaw had both girls under his arms as though they were rolled-up rugs. Jemima was awake, but not Bonnie.

No, no, no! the voice in Angie's head screamed as Stanislaw passed her Bonnie's inert form through the hole.

'I'm here!' Lloyd was by her side. He reached for Bonnie. 'Give her here!' he commanded.

Angie handed over her daughter's still body.

'She'll be fine,' he tried to reassure her, seeing the look of sheer terror on Angie's face.

Snapping her attention back to the door, Angie saw Jemima reaching towards her.

'Angie!' she cried on seeing her big sister's face.

'Quick!' Stanislaw shouted.

Hearing the panic in his voice, Angie grabbed Jemima under the arms and yanked her through with all her might.

As she did so, she heard a rip-roaring sound as part of the ceiling in the children's bedroom caved in.

She stared through the door and all she could see was black dust and flames.

She felt Jemima being lifted from her. This time it was Danny. Thank God he was okay. She had no idea if the fire was anywhere else.

'Come on, Angie!' he ordered. Jemima was clinging to him, her legs wrapped around his waist, arms hooked around his neck. 'The entire West Wing's going to go up in flames!'

'Marlene?' Angie shouted. 'Where's Marlene and Mrs Kwiatkowski?'

'They're fine! They're safe! Come on!' Danny bellowed at her, before turning and disappearing with Jemima, whose terrified eyes were staring back at her sister.

'Stanislaw!' Angie screamed.

She couldn't see him or hear him.

'Stanislaw! Where are you!'

And then she saw him. Or rather, she saw his blackened and bloodied face behind the flames.

'Go, Angie!' he yelled back at her. 'Get out of here! Now!'

Angie stared at him.

'No! No!' She started to cry, tears streaking down her own soot-smeared face.

She couldn't leave him!

Stanislaw came as near to the flames as possible.

'Go, Angie!' he shouted. 'There's nothing you can do! The children need you! They can't have anyone else dying on them!'

Angie wanted to scream at him, *Neither can I!* But she didn't. She knew he was right.

She took one last look at the man she loved. The man she had not allowed herself to love. A man she would now never get the chance to love.

And then she left.

Chapter Sixty-Four

As Angie ran down the stairs, she heard another thud. *Another beam falling?* Reaching the main entrance, she ran as fast as she could out of the house, her chest burning, coughing, her throat feeling like sandpaper. Her fears now focused on her little girl.

Bonnie! Angie did not think she had ever felt so afraid in her life.

She gulped in the fresh night air as she ran down the stone steps.

Her vision was blurred and her eyes stinging with the after-effects of the acrid smoke, but she managed to make out Winston and Bessie charging towards her.

She blinked hard, her pace slowing as she saw everyone had gathered on the front lawn.

Feeling the dogs next to her, Angie's eyes scoured the faces staring back at her, everyone standing stock-still.

'She's here! Bonnie's here!'

Angie hardly recognised Mrs Jones's voice, it sounded so deep and hoarse.

'She's fine!' Mrs Jones nodded at Bonnie, who was on her hip, clinging to her like a koala bear to a tree.

Angie saw her daughter's big blue eyes looking at her.

Thank God! Thank God! She felt her legs go weak but forced herself to keep walking.

She saw Bertie with Lloyd and Wilfred, Jemima with Marlene, and Danny wrapping a blanket around Mrs Kwiatkowski.

'Everyone's fine,' Lloyd said.

'The fire brigade and ambulance are on their way,' Wilfred said, his voice shaky.

'Where's Stanislaw?' Danny demanded, looking behind in the hope of seeing him.

Angie didn't answer but stood there for a moment. *She couldn't just give up. She had to at least try.*

'Follow me!' she said, turning and jogging back towards the manor.

Danny raced after her, then Marlene, followed by Lloyd, who was struggling to walk as he'd wrenched his bad back.

They followed Angie down the side of the East Wing, past the Tuscan gardens to the rear of the manor.

Angie looked around feverishly.

'I need the ladders. The big ones,' she said, out of breath.

Danny ran off to the barn. Lloyd made to follow, but Marlene stopped him.

'I'll go,' she said, running off.

'He's stuck in the children's bedroom, isn't he?' Lloyd said, his tone betraying his belief that Stanislaw would be both the hero of this fire – and the only fatality.

'He is,' Angie said, as they both stared up at the window of the children's room.

'Got them!' Danny shouted as he and Marlene half walked, half jogged towards them with the wooden ladders. Not needing instructions, they heaved them up against the wall. The top rungs reached the window to the children's bedroom. But only just.

'Thank God,' Angie murmured.

Danny went to get on a ladder, but Angie pulled him back.

'I've got a better head for heights,' she said.

Lloyd, Marlene and Danny watched as Angie climbed up with speed and confidence.

'She used to operate one of the biggest cranes at Thompson's,' Marlene said, her eyes glued to her sister as she made her ascent.

'I heard,' Lloyd said, his heart in his mouth for both Angie and Stanislaw.

Stanislaw, for his life. Angie, for the life she would have to lead if Stanislaw died. For it had been clear as day that the two loved each other – even if they hadn't acknowledged it themselves.

'And not one of them cranes – ' Marlene kept talking '– that had steps like a staircase, but the ones where they're like huge metal ladders that go straight up. Ninety degrees to the ground.'

Lloyd and Danny nodded, their eyes raised to Angie.

As Angie neared the top of the ladder, she could see the smoke drifting out of the sash window. Stanislaw must have opened it slightly. Which meant he must be near the window, keeping as far away from the fire as he could, trying to take in air rather than smoke.

Angie felt the first stirrings of real hope. *Maybe she could get to him before the fire did.*

But just then she heard an explosion.

Instinctively, she pressed herself into the ladder and bowed her head. She heard the shattering of glass as the fire did its work, then felt a shower of sharp stings as the glass rained down on her.

Looking back up, she hauled herself up the last few rungs. Taking a deep breath, she surveyed the room.

'I've an idea,' Danny suddenly said to Marlene. 'Follow me.'

The pair ran off, leaving Lloyd holding the ladders steady.

Hearing the window shatter, Lloyd put his hands over his head and felt the splintered glass fall on him, sharp as bee stings. Brushing glass off himself, he looked up. *Thank God. Angie seemed all right*. He could see her top half leaning into the bedroom, flames on the ceiling and swirls of smoke.

He turned to see Danny and Marlene dragging something out of the barn.

When Angie looked over the bottom part of the window frame, her heart sank.

Stanislaw was slumped up against the wall. As she'd guessed, he'd cracked the window open and had positioned himself next to it to try to take in as much clean air as possible. She reached over to touch his dirt-smeared face. His skin, in contrast, looked ghostly white. *Deathly* white.

Her hand moved down to his neck to feel for a pulse. She had to know. She had to be certain before she left him there.

Holding her index and middle finger in the soft hollow next to his Adam's apple – as she'd been taught during her training at the yard – she pressed firmly down. And waited.

She tried to calm the rapid beating of her own heart so she could tell if the pulse she thought she was feeling was Stanislaw's – or her own.

Yes! There it is! It was faint, but it was a pulse.

'Stanislaw! Wake up!' she shouted into his ear.

Then she slapped his face hard.

There was a groan.

Followed by the flickering of his eyelids.

And then they opened.

When he saw Angie, his face came to life.

'Come on!' Angie shouted. 'Get up! There's a ladder here! Hurry!'

Angie's attention flickered around the room. The bunk beds were now alight, as was the dressing table. Looking up at the ceiling, her heart skipped a beat. What was left of it looked ready to cave in at any second.

'Now!' Angie screamed.

Stanislaw rolled over. He was clearly in agony. Angie noticed his right arm was badly burnt, and his left leg had a deep flesh wound and was also badly burnt.

He shuffled and stood up, his leg dragging behind him.

'Put your good leg over,' Angie barked orders. 'I'm right here behind you.'

Stanislaw managed to turn himself around to face the fierce heat of the fire and manoeuvred himself so that he could lower his good leg onto the ladder; he then pulled his injured leg over with his hand.

'That's brilliant!' Angie encouraged. She could see he was struggling and in excruciating pain. She saw the exposed burnt flesh and blood coming from his injured leg and winced.

'Okay, one rung at a time,' she said, tapping his good leg and guiding it onto the next rung.

Seconds later, Angie heard the crashing of timber as the entire ceiling came down. A puff of dirt and smoke came out the window, followed by giant tongues of fire trying greedily to consume everything within their reach.

Stanislaw had made it out with just seconds to spare.

Halfway down the ladder, Angie could see he was struggling.

'Nearly there,' she shouted.

But when she looked up, she saw his good leg give way, as though finally every last ounce of energy had left his body.

She heard Marlene scream as he fell like a dead weight to the ground.

Angie scrunched her eyes, unable to look around. Unable to live with the vision of Stanislaw's body splayed out on the cobbles – dead.

No! Angie pressed her forehead against the wooden rung, wanting to rage against the injustice. *He was almost there!*

'Angie!' It was Lloyd's voice. 'Come down!'

As she made her way to the bottom, only then did she look round and see Danny next to Stanislaw, who *was* splayed out – though not on the cobbles as she'd feared, but on a bed of hay.

'It's okay!' Danny shouted to her.

'He's alive!'

Chapter Sixty-Five

As fire engines sped through the gates, followed by an ambulance, Evelyn watched from her vantage point in the shepherd's hut.

It was heartbreaking to see the West Wing go up in flames, and the smoke damage elsewhere would be awful, but she'd have plenty of time to rebuild it. She'd already started to plan the design. The West Wing would be her project. It would enable her to put her stamp on the place. She would live in the East Wing until the work was done. And with the money she'd have available, she'd be able to pay the workers to do a speedy, top-notch job.

She couldn't wait to go shopping for wallpaper and new furniture. And new curtains. She'd always hated those stuffy Victorian velvet ones. She knew the perfect place in Durham, just down from the cathedral. She'd take Gertrude. *They'd have a ball!*

Wrapping her coat around herself to keep warm, Evelyn ventured out of the hut. She had to get a little nearer to check that Lloyd and Angie had not made it out.

She had watched from the side of the house as the fire took hold, knowing that Angie's bedroom would be the first to go up, then Lloyd's. She'd stayed there longer than planned as it had been rather mesmerising.

By the time she had made it back to the hut, she could see the outline of figures on the front lawn, on the furthest side away from the fire. But the smoke was drifting over, preventing Evelyn from seeing who they were. She just needed to check that Angie and Lloyd were not among the survivors and then she would go. It would be a half-hour walk cross-country to the local station, and then another half hour of a stop-start journey to Darlington.

Evelyn started to walk through the undergrowth to get to where she could see them more clearly. She wished she'd brought her binoculars. With her haversack securely on her back, she tentatively made her way through the thick foliage to get past the veil of smoke obstructing her view.

'Yes!' Finally, she'd made it to the perfect spot.

Her heart raced as her eyes surveyed those on the lawn. There was Mrs Jones. She was watching the arrival of the emergency services. She had Bonnie on her hip. The little girl had her head buried in the housekeeper's neck and she was sucking her thumb. Next to them was Mrs Kwiatkowski, a blanket wrapped around her. Jemima was by her side, clutching the old woman's hand. Next to her was Bertie. They looked like two little chimney sweeps, their faces black and their hair grey. Wilfred suddenly appeared behind them as he slowly and unsteadily got to his feet. Evelyn had known he would be the one to call the fire brigade, just as she knew his age would prevent him from any heroics. She caught movement and saw Danny and Marlene appear from the side of the manor.

A smile crept across Evelyn's face. Her plan couldn't have gone more smoothly.

They were all there – everyone apart from the miner's daughter and Lloyd.

Evelyn breathed out. A self-satisfied sigh.

She'd done it. Her plan had gone like clockwork.

She turned to head back to the shepherd's hut. Time to make herself scarce. She would ring Gertrude when she reached the railway station, tell her how sorry she was for ringing so late, but she just wanted to tell her she was in London and was fine. And then that would be her cast-iron alibi sorted.

As Evelyn started to walk through the undergrowth back towards the shepherd's hut, where she would squash through a gap in the hedge and be gone, she glanced up to the full moon and smiled. *She'd done it!*

She looked back down at the dense foliage, but it was too late to spot a small tree stump. She felt it, though, when her foot smacked into it and she went sprawling on all fours, face down into a bunch of dock leaves.

She cursed as she pushed herself back up.

Winston and Bessie had been in a state of high alert since smelling the smoke and hearing the panicked cries of the children. Now they were settled on the lawn, looking more like two regal lionesses, their big paws stretched out in front of them, their solid, muscular bodies taut, their hind legs tucked under but ready to spring into action if needed. They were on guard. Those they were protecting were behind them. Their heads were raised, their eyes intense, their floppy ears up, looking like bat wings.

The two fire engines were almost at the house when Winston and Bessie cocked their heads in unison. They'd heard something.

A second later, they were up and off. Their speed, just like a lioness's, was instant and fast.

They tore across the driveway, just missing being hit by the first fire engine. The two dogs flashed past before the driver managed to touch the brakes.

Winston was a muzzle ahead of Bessie as they made a beeline for their prey.

They'd heard the threat from their position on the lawn, the soft thud and the crack of dry branches underfoot.

Now they could see the intruder.

Evelyn had no idea her fall had been heard or noticed by anyone on the lawn. She was confident she couldn't be seen or heard from this distance away. She hadn't noticed the dogs, though. Their fawn-coloured coats and dark, almost black faces provided camouflage, along with their low-lying position and statuesque stillness.

She had no idea they were coming for her as, unlike most other dogs, their breed was stealthy, rarely making a noise until they were upon you.

The first she knew was when a ton weight dropped on her back and, for the second time, she found herself sprawling headlong into the undergrowth.

This time, though, her head did not have such a soft landing, but instead hit the sharp edge of a stone. She felt the jarring pain in her temple at the same time as she felt the air leave her lungs as the heavy weight continued to press down on her back.

And then she felt nothing, and her world went black.

Only when Evelyn was down and out did Bessie start to bark as she pranced around the dark figure in the undergrowth. Winston started sniffing Evelyn's head.

It took a few minutes for the children and Mrs Jones to make their way over to see what had caused the dogs to bolt. Their hearts had been in their mouths when Winston and Bessie had missed going under the wheels of the fire engine by a whisker.

On seeing them approach, Bessie bustled over, tail wagging, saliva drooling.

Winston stayed in position until Mrs Jones tapped her side for him to come to heel.

Then, with great caution, Mrs Jones approached the inert figure in black.

Crouching down, she looked at the body, unsure if it was a man or a woman.

Pushing back the straggles of hair that were obscuring the person's face, Mrs Jones let out a gasp.

'Oh my God,' she murmured.

She should have known.

Chapter Sixty-Six

As Evelyn had planned, the fire brigade arrived on time to save the manor – if not the West Wing. They were aided by the villagers, who had heard the sirens and rallied to help in any way they could. Gertrude and Jeremy, having also seen the flames and heard the sirens, had driven the half mile or so to Cuthford Manor. Gertrude had cried on seeing the devastation the fire had caused. Jeremy nearly cried, too, on hearing about Stanislaw's heroics.

Stanislaw was taken off in the ambulance. Angie followed after being reassured that the children really were all okay. Having driven to the Dryburn Hospital in Durham, she stayed until the early hours. The doctor had told her that Stanislaw wouldn't be coming home anytime soon, but he was alive and he would recover, albeit with some nasty scars from the third-degree burns he'd suffered on his arm and his leg.

Stanislaw had been heavily sedated to deal with the pain but had smiled when he saw Angie's face and she told him she'd come back to see him again later.

His smile had widened when she joked, her voice trembling slightly, tears glistening in her eyes, that she smelled like a bonfire and now looked 'like a coalminer, not a coalminer's daughter' with her soot-smeared face and blackened clothes.

She wanted to say more but didn't.

She didn't trust herself.

Mrs Jones didn't know if she felt relieved or disappointed when the medic declared that Evelyn was alive, although she was unconscious, which was probably just as well for Evelyn, as Mrs Jones didn't know what she might say or do had she come round.

Evelyn was also taken to the Dryburn Hospital and was seen first of all by the doctors, and then, when she had regained consciousness, by the police.

She, of course, claimed the bash to her head had caused her to suffer complete amnesia.

Together with Danny and Marlene, Thomas, who'd come as soon as he'd got wind about what had happened, brought the horses in from the paddock, where they had been taken earlier for fear the fire might reach the stables.

The three stayed for a good while, keeping the horses calm as they were understandably jittery with all the commotion – the shouts of the firemen, the sound of the hosepipe gushing out water, the crackling of the fire. Only Lucky was unperturbed and seemed glad to be back in her stall, where she hunkered down on her straw bed for the night, her short legs sticking out from her tubby little body.

Wilfred rang Clemmie, who came charging over in her little sports car. Hearing Angie was at the hospital with Stanislaw, she felt disappointed that the woman she loved wasn't here, but she'd had a stern word with herself that she should just be over the moon that Angie and everyone at Cuthford Manor had escaped with their lives. She'd then taken charge and converted the rooms downstairs into sleeping areas for when adrenalin levels dropped and people needed to crash out.

Once the children had been checked over by the ambulance staff, Clemmie took them to the kitchen, where she made sure they drank plenty of water and, of course, allowed them to eat biscuits and the week's ration of chocolate.

Dr Wright, who arrived shortly after the ambulance, had told Clemmie to ring him straight away if the children showed any signs of becoming unwell, although he was confident they were going to be fine and had probably been saved from breathing in too much smoke by Bertie's quick thinking in covering them in a wet bed sheet.

Lloyd was trying to be brave about the fact he could hardly move, never mind walk, but the pain on his face was impossible to mask. After bandaging a deep cut on his arm, Dr Wright gave him a shot of something, and Mrs Jones made up a makeshift bed on the sofa in the lounge.

Nobody made mention that Lloyd and Mrs Jones had been asleep in the same room when the fire broke out. There was no need. The way they looked at each other said it all.

As Mrs Jones sat in the armchair next to her lover, she heard Clemmie organising the little ones in the room next door, reassuring them that Stanislaw was going to be fine, even if he might have to stay in hospital for a while due to his burns. The children were comforted as Clemmie never sugar-coated anything. The dogs, of course, were with them.

Clemmie said she'd get Angie to come and see them as soon as she was back from the hospital, and after a short while, Mrs Jones heard the room go quiet. There was only the sound of gentle snoring, which she wasn't sure was the dogs or Clemmie. Probably a mixture of both.

Chapter Sixty-Seven

March

Life at Cuthford Manor was chaotic. Not that anyone seemed to mind. They were all alive and relatively unharmed. They would put up with just about anything, whether it was the constant stream of builders, trucks and lorries up and down the driveway or the comings and goings of officials from the insurance company and the council's planning department, and, of course, those investigating the fire.

It was accepted that the fire had been arson – and that the perpetrator was Evelyn Foxton-Clarke – but proving it was another matter. Although no one at Cuthford Manor should have been shocked that it was Evelyn – especially after what they knew about her part in Quentin's death – it was still difficult to take on board.

Clemmie said she believed Evelyn to be certifiably insane. It was the only explanation for what she had done. Or rather, tried to do.

It seemed that she was not the only one to come to this conclusion. While the police and the Crown Prosecution

Service decided how to proceed, Evelyn was taken to a psychiatric unit in Rampton Secure Hospital in Nottinghamshire.

Angie, Clemmie, Lloyd and Mrs Jones had speculated about what Evelyn had hoped to achieve – and agreed that her aim must have been to get rid of Angie and Lloyd, since they were the only obstacles to claiming Cuthford Manor as hers.

They had all listened in shocked silence as the senior investigating police officer told them that, after some digging into Evelyn's background, they had discovered that she had started life as Bethany Browne and had been raised in the slums of Shoreditch. Her parents had not died in a car accident, as she had claimed, but due to a gas leak that had been ruled the fault of the gas board, who had been made to pay out a considerable amount of compensation.

'Which enabled her to transform herself into a sophisticated, born-with-a-silver-spoon-in-her-mouth debutante,' Angie surmised when they went back over everything later.

The thought flitted through Lloyd's head that Evelyn might have been the one to cause the gas leak, but he dismissed it. She had been just fifteen when her parents died; she couldn't have done something with such malice aforethought. *Could she?*

Perhaps because Evelyn realised that she wasn't getting out of the secure psychiatric hospital, or perhaps because she just got bored of repeatedly claiming she had lost her memory, knowing she wasn't fooling anyone, she started to talk to her designated psychologist, Dr Claire Eris, and opened up about her upbringing. Like Lloyd, Dr Eris was also beginning to wonder if the death of Evelyn's parents had been accidental. Listening to the truly awful details of her patient's childhood might make many believe that the mother and father deserved it. Dr Eris was happy to keep working with her new patient, whom she found fascinating. As a result, it would take a while longer for the courts to decide if Evelyn was to remain at Rampton or be brought back to Durham to spend the rest of her life in a six-by-eight prison cell.

As Lloyd's wife – soon to be ex-wife – had been arrested and sectioned under the Mental Health Act, it meant that all her belongings, bank accounts and safety deposit boxes were given over to Lloyd, who was gobsmacked to learn how much money his wife had pilfered, as well as all the jewellery and valuable antiques she'd squirrelled away. He'd felt – yet again – a number-one fool for having been so ignorant of her true character and deviousness. But he had managed to see the silver lining in that the money enabled them to start work immediately on rebuilding and repairing the West Wing.

Chapter Sixty-Eight

Saturday, 17 March

Just over a month after the fire, Stanislaw was finally discharged from the burns unit.

Everyone was in high spirits. They'd been to see Stanislaw in hospital, but they'd never really been able to show him just how indebted they felt for being prepared to sacrifice his own life to save the children. Knowing this would be the case, Stanislaw had begged Angie to ask everyone not to make a fuss as he would only feel awkward and embarrassed.

'I just did what anyone would do,' he said. 'And besides, *I'm* indebted to *you* for saving *my* life.'

Angie had smiled and said she would try to persuade them not to go overboard, although she knew no one would pay her any heed.

When Angie brought Stanislaw back to Cuthford Manor on a lovely sunny afternoon, Stanislaw realised he'd been wasting his breath. For, as Angie drove down the long driveway, he saw that a huge home-made banner had been hung between the two pillars at the entrance declaring: 'WELCOME HOME!'

The words made him feel the pricking of tears. Especially one word – 'home'. This *was* his home. It had *become* his home.

He wondered if he would be able to leave it for a second time.

He was not sure.

Angie had not spoken of their conversation on the night of the fire. Her words and actions came from love, but he wasn't sure if the love he felt from her was because he had saved the children. Or whether it was bound up in more than that.

Having heard the car crunching its way down the driveway, everyone had piled out of the front door.

Winston and Bessie were very excited and were looking more portly as they had been spoilt rotten by Alberta for catching the culprit who had nearly got away with murder.

Just as the car pulled up, Stanislaw saw Danny appear with Ghost, who'd had his mane plaited so as to make him look his best.

Seeing the emotion on Stanislaw's face, Angie put her hand on his and squeezed it.

'Sorry,' she said. 'But as you know, no one ever does what I tell them.'

After being hugged and kissed, slobbered on by the dogs and nearly pushed over by Ghost, who'd nuzzled his chest in joy at seeing his master return, Stanislaw was ushered into the front room where there were more balloons and a buffet laid out on the sideboard, along with a beautifully decorated Polish cake, which was presented to him by Mrs Kwiatkowski, who was particularly pleased at having Stanislaw back as it felt a long time since she'd been able to have a good chat to someone in her native tongue. Clemmie had tried her best, but it was hard work.

Angie stood back and let everyone fuss and chat and force Stanislaw to sit down in the armchair, telling him he had to take it easy as he was still recovering.

Lloyd added to the excitement by popping open a bottle of champagne and making everyone jump and then laugh.

Marlene took Stanislaw his glass and gave him a kiss on the cheek.

'Thanks for saving the little ones,' she said. 'I think I might have died if anything had happened to them.'

Stanislaw saw her blink away the tears and knew she meant every word.

'Don't you dare repeat that, though,' she said, narrowing her eyes at him and then turning her attention to Bertie, Jemima and Bonnie, who'd sensed they were being talked about.

'The little terrors,' she said with a faux scowl.

All three stuck their tongues out at her in reply.

While everyone toasted and sipped their champagne or home-made lemonade and tucked into the buffet, the air was abuzz with chatter.

Danny, Stanislaw commented to Angie, looked particularly well and happy, which he guessed was down to the fact that he'd been allowed to leave school earlier than agreed so that he could take over the stables while Stanislaw recovered in hospital.

After everyone had made a dent in the buffet, Angie chinked her glass with a silver teaspoon to get their attention.

'Not only do we have Stanislaw back,' she said, her eyes twinkling, 'but I have some more wonderful news.'

Everyone fell silent.

'Just before I went to the hospital today, I nipped into town.' She looked around the room at all the puzzled faces. 'And I popped in to see Mr Day at Durham Estates.'

'The estate agent?' Danny asked, his face suddenly showing panic.

'That's right,' said Angie. 'The one who said it was unlikely we'd find a buyer for Cuthford Manor . . . *Well*, it looks like word has got around about what happened, and the rebuild, and the plan to make the manor into a country house hotel, and Mr Day said he was "over the moon" to tell me he'd found not one but *two* buyers, and with a little bidding he reckoned he'd get a very, *very* good price. Enough to buy the biggest and best house anyone could want – in Australia, or anywhere else for that matter – with a good amount to spare.'

Angie had to suppress a smile on seeing everyone's faces. She glanced at Stanislaw, who realised the sparkle in her eye was that of mischief.

'And *that's* the wonderful news?' Marlene said in disgust.

Angie looked at her younger sister, who was becoming a very beautiful young woman, and shook her head.

'No, that's not the wonderful news,' Angie said. 'The wonderful news is that I'd actually gone there to tell the estate agent that we're going nowhere. *We're staying put.* For good. No matter how many people want to buy our manor – no matter how much they might offer. This manor – which I have to stress is *our* manor – is our home for as long as everyone wants it to be.'

The children jumped up and down, Danny and Marlene started playing holy war with her for having them on so, and Lloyd and Mrs Jones laughed. They hadn't thought for one moment Angie would sell up.

'And,' Lloyd said, 'I have just heard that because of our grand plans for Cuthford Manor, which as you all know involves the whole village and businesses beyond it, an appeal has been lodged to remove Cuthford from the Category D list of villages – and it's fully expected that the appeal will be accepted. So, here's to an exciting future!' he declared, popping open another bottle of champagne.

'Here! Here!' Everyone raised their glasses.

As Lloyd gave everyone refills, Angie looked at them all – Lloyd and Mrs Jones, Danny and Marlene, Bertie, Jemima and Bonnie, Clemmie, Mrs Kwiatkowski, and, of course, Stanislaw. And not for the first time she realised just how lucky she was to have this very mixed, very unconventional, but very loving family.

Why she had worried about what would happen to her siblings and Bonnie should something happen to her, she did not know. This was their family right here.

Since the fire, Angie had been doing a lot of thinking. She'd been having trouble sleeping, so instead of tossing and turning, she'd get up and go and see Winston and Bessie in the kitchen and have a cuppa. When it got light, she'd often take the dogs for a walk. She'd always found being out in the countryside helped her sort through her jumble of thoughts.

She'd gone over the past year and a half since Quentin's death. At first, she'd believed that if she belonged at Cuthford Manor, it was purely due to her being Quentin's wife – and that had ended when her widowhood began. Lately, she had come to realise how much her grief had distorted her perspective for a long time after Quentin's death. Her sense of belonging had begun to bud after she'd started to be more involved in village life. She had gone from being the rarely seen mistress of the manor, a rich and privileged outsider, to an important part of the fabric of the village.

During one of her early-morning walks, as she watched Winston and Bessie charge after a squirrel through the woodland on the far side of the estate, her mind had wandered to something Quentin had told her when they'd gone to buy the dogs from a well-known breeder in Great Lumley. The Bullmastiff, he'd explained, had been developed as a guard dog back in the nineteenth century by cross-breeding the English Mastiff with the Old English Bulldog.

Thinking back to that conversation, Angie realised that she, too, had become a kind of mix. A social contradiction. She had been born and raised a miner's daughter, but had become the mistress of a manor. She was a round peg in a square hole. She didn't 'fit' properly into either social class any more, but had become a strange blend of the two.

But more than that, she realised that she belonged here because her heart belonged here, in this 'manor that had aspirations to be a castle'.

Just as she belonged with all the people here with her today.

She smiled as she remembered Jemima's recital of 'Home Is Where the Heart Is'. The answer had been there all along. She'd just refused to see it. Or perhaps grief had blinded her.

When the buffet had been eaten, the tea tray brought in and the cake sliced up, Stanislaw threw Angie a surreptitious look.

Clemmie caught the clandestine communication between the two – had been noticing the ease with which they interacted and, moreover, how they looked at each other. Once again, she felt the guilt that had afflicted her since she'd learnt that Stanislaw had been leaving on the night of the fire. No one had felt it appropriate to ask why, but Clemmie had speculated with Mrs Jones that he'd left because of Angie. Because she'd turned him down.

Clemmie had felt terrible thinking of her calculating and conniving attempts to put the mockers on any potential love affair between the two. But then again, if Stanislaw hadn't left, he'd have been in the East Wing and oblivious to the fire until it was too late.

'Why are you two looking so conspiratorial?' Bertie asked, his attention going to Angie, then Stanislaw and back to Angie.

Angie smiled. She had to agree with Clemmie that her younger brother's speech and use of language were incredibly advanced for his age.

'Never one to miss a trick,' Stanislaw said, reaching forward and gently messing with Bertie's thatch of thick dark hair.

Now Angie and Stanislaw also had Jemima and Bonnie's attention.

'Well, it sort of involves you,' he said, looking at the three of them. 'And, of course, Danny and Marlene, if you want to come.'

'Come where?' Jemima demanded.

'Well, I thought it was about time I went to see Wojtek at the zoo – and wondered if anyone else wanted to come?'

The three young ones exploded with shouts of 'Me! Me! Me!'

Stanislaw looked at Angie and they both smiled. It was just the reaction they had expected. And hoped for.

A weekend in Edinburgh, seeing a brave bear who enjoyed a beer and a cigarette with his fellow soldiers, would be a perfect tonic after the near-death drama and murderous revelations of late.

Chapter Sixty-Nine

Later on that evening, when Clemmie had gone back home and Angie and Stanislaw had been persuaded to take the dogs out for a walk with the children, Lloyd and Mrs Jones were sitting in the lounge, now cleared of plates and leftovers from the buffet, but still decorated with streamers and balloons.

'Well, that couldn't have gone off better, could it?' Lloyd said.

Mrs Jones nodded her agreement. 'I thought Stanislaw might feel a bit overwhelmed, but he managed the attention very well . . . Although, I think a glass or two of champagne helped.'

'He seems happy,' Lloyd mused. 'I do hope he doesn't decide to leave again.'

Mrs Jones took a sip of her tea. 'I think that will depend on Angie.'

Lloyd eased himself off the sofa and went to pour himself a Scotch. His back was still bad, but not anywhere near as painful as it had been in the first couple of weeks after the fire.

'When Angie went to see the estate agents today,' he said, 'before she went to the hospital, she dropped me off in town and I went to Farrell & Sons.'

'I wondered where you'd snuck off to,' Mrs Jones said. Lloyd would have normally told her where he was going.

'Well, I thought I'd see how the divorce was going and I am pleased to say, it has been pushed through post-haste, helped along by Evelyn being sectioned. I should have the decree nisi through any time soon.'

'Well, that's wonderful news,' Mrs Jones said.

'Then it's just a matter of weeks and the decree absolute will be sorted, and I will be a free man.'

Lloyd took a slightly nervous gulp of his whisky before he put the glass down on the coffee table.

'I know this might seem like I'm jumping the gun a little, but I couldn't wait, I'm afraid,' he said, delving into the inside pocket of his jacket.

'I should have done this when I was seventeen.' He pulled out from his pocket a very beautiful diamond ring. 'I should have followed my heart. But I didn't, and I have lived – and suffered – the consequences of that failure ever since. But I will not live the rest of this life in regret.'

Mrs Jones watched as Lloyd carefully lowered himself onto one knee. She could see the agony doing so caused him, but she understood he wanted to do this the way he wished he had all those years ago.

'I love you as much as any man can possibly love a woman,' Lloyd said. 'All I have to give you is my love. I want to marry you and spend the rest of my life with you. Is that something you want too, Cora? Will you marry me? Will you be my wife?'

'Oh, Lloyd, I've always loved you,' Mrs Jones said. 'I think you know that now. I love you regardless of any marriage vows or any gold band on my finger,' she said, her eyes glistening with emotion.

'Is that a yes?' Lloyd asked,

'That's a yes,' Cora said with a smile.

Lloyd pushed himself back up onto two feet, oblivious to the pain, and pulled the woman he adored towards him.

And they stood and kissed and held each other close.

Chapter Seventy

When Clemmie got back to Durham and walked through her front door, she didn't head for the kitchen to make herself a cuppa and listen to her favourite programmes on the wireless, as she normally would.

Instead, she headed upstairs to her bedroom, switched on the light and flung open her wardrobe doors.

It was time to change. And she wasn't thinking about her wardrobe – although that would certainly need changing – but herself. Her way of thinking. Her way of living.

Change, she realised more than ever, was scary. Very scary.

She had seen how hard it had been for Angie to make changes – and how brave she had been. Not just in dealing with Quentin's death and all the dramas that had ensued, but in changing her way of thinking about life – and love. She'd seen that earlier when Angie had been talking to Stanislaw. Angie had acknowledged her feelings for Stanislaw, although Clemmie guessed it would be a while before she felt able to act on them.

Riffling through her drab wardrobe to find something a little more fashionable, Clemmie sighed. Her skirts were something some spinster headteacher would wear. She resolved to go out shopping tomorrow and buy herself some slacks.

'This'll have to do,' she muttered to herself, pulling out a navy-blue A-line skirt.

Teaming it with her best cream-coloured silk blouse with a neckline that was as daring as she got and gave a hint of her substantial bosom, she slipped on her leather pumps with the modest heel and looked at herself in the free-standing mirror.

She was not happy with the image reflected back at her.

'No excuses,' she told the woman in the mirror. 'You're going out whether you want to or not.'

She gave herself another once-over. There was something missing.

A splash of colour.

The blue and cream were far too conservative. She needed at least one thing that would give a hint of who she really was.

'I know just the thing!' she said, her face lighting up.

Walking over to her dresser, she pulled out the top drawer and took out a lipstick Marlene had given her. It was siren red.

Looking in the mirror, she unscrewed the top and dabbed it onto her lips. She sighed again. Her lips seemed very dry and thin compared to the likes of Lauren Bacall or Hedy Lamarr. Still, the splash of crimson had done the trick. It would be her signature, she decided. Her nod to her feminine side.

Taking one last look at herself, Clemmie made her way downstairs, picked up her handbag, popped her lipstick inside and then walked out of her little terraced cottage.

Checking the door was shut properly, she turned and started out on her new venture.

Striding down the street in her sensible shoes, she headed towards a place that had existed for quite some time, and where she had wanted to go for quite some time, but which, until now, she had not had the courage to frequent.

But no longer.

Now she knew that she could not continue living her life chasing the unattainable, nor could she keep on punishing herself – because that, she realised, was what she had been doing her whole life. Punishing herself for being the person she was. How insane was that?

Now she knew it was time to allow herself to live a true life – a happy life – a life of acceptance, and, more importantly, a life where she allowed herself not just to love, but to love someone who could love her in return.

Five minutes later, she had turned into a narrow alleyway. Halfway down, she stopped. She'd reached her destination.

She looked at the small innocuous doorway that was the entrance to a women-only club called 'Urania' – it was the name of the Greek goddess of astronomy and stars, who was also symbolic of Universal Love.

Clemmie took a deep breath.

She then stepped forward and tugged on the brass Victorian bell pull to the side of the small arched black door.

Chapter Seventy-One

Angie had thought it was a lovely suggestion by the children that they all go for a walk together after Stanislaw's 'Welcome Home' party. So she was surprised when, halfway through the walk, they all suddenly remembered they had things to do. Danny needed to give Lucky her special potion to help with her breathing, Marlene had promised Belinda she'd ring and tell her how the party went, Bertie recalled that he had some homework to do, and Jemima and Bonnie that Alberta had promised they could share the last slice of cake if they helped her clear up. The five hurried off, with Winston and Bessie chasing after them, leaving Angie and Stanislaw alone.

Angie suddenly felt awkward. This was the first time they had been completely on their own since their chat before the fire. When she'd seen Stanislaw in hospital, she'd either had one of the children with her or, if she was on her own, other visitors were about or a nurse would be checking Stanislaw's temperature or blood pressure.

'Dear me,' Angie said, 'it feels so quiet all of a sudden.'

The light was fading and as they walked back, they could see the outline of Cuthford Manor silhouetted against the backdrop of the darkening sky.

'All of this death and tragedy over a load of old bricks and mortar,' she said, her tone showing her incredulity.

Stanislaw nodded and they walked in silence for a while. Angie desperately wanted to ask something. A question she'd wanted to ask him since the fire, but it had never seemed to be the right time. She'd realised there would never be a right time.

She just needed to bite the bullet.

'Are you going to stay?' she asked tentatively, trying hard not to show – or even admit to herself – how much her happiness depended on his answer. 'No running off in the middle of the night?'

Stanislaw stopped walking. They had just reached the paddock.

'Only if I'm wanted.'

His words were loaded with a deeper meaning.

Angie paused, feeling the intensity of the man who had become her good friend these past six months. More than a good friend.

She took a deep breath and returned his gaze.

'Yes,' she said. 'You're wanted.'

During this past month of sleepless nights, early-morning walks and drives to and from the hospital, Angie had been forced to concede that she loved Stanislaw. And not just as a friend who understood her, and with whom she shared many of life's experiences – and tragedies. It had always been more than that, but she had not allowed herself to feel it. She'd been grieving Quentin. The thought of loving another man had felt like a betrayal.

But recently she had understood that the love she felt for Stanislaw was different to the love she had felt for Quentin. They were such different men – and *she* was now different. She had changed since Quentin's death. And she'd come to understand these past four weeks that she had been given a second chance at love. *She and Stanislaw had both been given a chance of a second love.*

And they'd be fools to let it pass them by.

Angie felt Stanislaw take her hand. He looked into her eyes and she saw a myriad of emotions. He paused. 'Would it be amiss of me to say that I feel we belong together?'

Angie shook her head.

'No, it wouldn't be amiss.' For she understood that they had both found a sense of belonging here at Cuthford Manor – and also with each other.

'I *do* feel that we belong together,' she said.

Stanislaw felt his heart soar as high as the kites he loved to watch during days when the sky was clear. The smile that spread across his face was wide and his hazel eyes sparkled with joy. He kept hold of her hand, and Angie felt a sensation coursing through her body that she had not felt for a long time.

She wanted more than anything to kiss him, but she held back.

'But I need time, Stanislaw.' She looked at him. 'Can you wait?'

'Of course I will wait – for as long as it takes,' he said. 'I never thought I would ever love again until I came here and met you – so yes, I will wait, I will wait my whole life, as long as I can be close to you and know that you love me also.'

Angie smiled. She was not ready to say the words yet, but she knew he knew, and she knew Stanislaw understood why she couldn't speak her love, even though she felt it.

They walked on, around the perimeter of the paddock, their way accompanied by the lark's evensong.

As the stables came into view, suddenly Stanislaw took a breath, as though about to speak, but stopped himself.

'What?' Angie asked. 'What were you going to say?'

Stanislaw hesitated, unsure whether he should speak his mind.

'You have to be honest with me, Stanislaw – we have to be totally truthful with each other if we are to be together.'

Stanislaw's heart lifted again at Angie's words – *be together*.

'Okay . . . What I was thinking,' he said slowly. 'What I was wondering . . . was . . . as you have opened your heart a little to me, well, I thought perhaps you might also feel able to do the same with Ghost?'

He left the question hanging in the air.

Angie looked at the man with whom she had fallen in love – without even realising it. A man she had come to realise she loved because of his unselfishness and his capacity to keep on loving – despite the damage inflicted on his own heart.

She smiled.

'I think I might . . .'

And then she stopped walking and, standing on tiptoes, kissed Stanislaw – a loving and gentle kiss.

And when they parted, their eyes locked and they saw the true and deep love they felt for one another.

Chapter Seventy-Two

Sunday, 18 March

After a restless night, Angie was up at the crack of dawn, knowing exactly what she was going to do.

Opening her wardrobe doors, she pulled on her jodhpurs and riding gear and headed downstairs.

Not stopping for her usual cup of tea and piece of toast, she quickly bent down to give Winston and Bessie a pat, telling them to 'stay' before she slipped out of the back door.

Breathing in the fresh morning air, she walked with purpose to the stables.

Having heard her boots on the cobbles, the horses were on alert as Angie opened the barn doors, hooking them back.

She looked at Lucky, Bomber, Monty and Starling before her focus rested on Ghost.

Walking over to him, she dug around in her jacket pocket and pulled out a sugar cube.

Putting it on the open palm of her hand, she reached through the bars of the stable door to give him her offering.

Feeling the familiar soft velvety lips on her skin and the warmth of his breath, tears trickled down Angie's cheeks.

'I'm so sorry, Ghost,' she murmured.

Opening the door of the stall, she went to stroke his long, regal neck and as she did so, he gently put his head next to her own.

She had been forgiven.

Angie kissed the side of Ghost's handsome face, and as he nuzzled her, she felt the love he had for her. Still had for her, despite her neglect.

Riding Ghost after such a long time did not feel strange. Quite the reverse. It felt as though it had been only yesterday that she had felt the rhythm of his long stride and his confidence in jumping the hedged fence that divided the estate from the surrounding countryside.

Her tears dried as they cantered across the open landscape. Her sorrow replaced by the most amazing feeling of joy and freedom.

As they reached her favourite vantage point, Ghost knew to slow to a halt. The breath from horse and rider plumed out into the dewy early-morning air.

Looking to her left, where the shimmer of the North Sea twinkled, and to the right, where the tops of Durham's majestic cathedral and its magnificent castle were just visible, Angie thought about how the River Wear began high up in the Pennines, then wound its way down and wrapped itself around the city before flowing through the county to her home town and out to sea. The river might pass through many places, but it was always the River Wear. It simply changed shape as it adapted to the terrain it flowed through.

Stroking Ghost's thick pewter-coloured mane, Angie leant forward and felt the soft, moist hair of his neck. She breathed in the familiar smell of horse sweat – but there was something else there too. It took her a moment to realise that it was Stanislaw. She could smell him. She inhaled deeply.

Then she sat up and looked out at the dawn of a new day.

The beauty of the patchwork of green countryside contrasting with the burnished oranges and reds heralding the dawn of a new day took her breath away. Not just because of Nature's beauty – but because she realised that colour had returned to her life.

Her being felt older but lighter. Stronger of mind and of spirit.

It was not just the dawn of a new day – but of a new life.

Suddenly, Ghost shook his head and let out a melodic neighing sound, as though showing his approval of the change he sensed ahead.

Epilogue

July 1952

Angie hadn't wanted to get married in the local church. This was her second marriage, after all. Instead, she and Stanislaw were married at Durham Registry Office. Angie wore a wonderful citron-coloured silk dress designed by her friend Kate under her label Lily Rose. Kate was now quite the celebrity and caused quite a commotion when she came up from London to attend the wedding.

Afterwards, everyone went back to Cuthford Manor, where the entire ground floor had been decorated with streamers and balloons and a huge 'CONGRATULATIONS' banner. There were beautiful floral arrangements in all the rooms, a sumptuous buffet had been laid out in the dining room, and the library had been converted into a dance floor with live music.

All of Angie's old workmates from the shipyard came. Helen and Dr Parker, Gloria, Jack and Hope, who was now almost eleven years old. Polly and Tommy had their own 'tribe' of four children, all boys. Polly had whispered to Angie that she'd just found out she was pregnant again and was hoping against hope it would be a girl. Angie had a feeling it would be another boy, as that was the way of the world.

Martha, who was now head riveter at Thompson's, came with her trombone-playing colliery worker, Adam. They denied that they might be next to exchange vows.

Hannah and Olly had made it back from Korea, where they had been working alongside the American Red Cross to bring blood supplies to injured troops and helping to oversee the POWs. They would be returning after the wedding as peace talks earlier in the year had broken down and the Korean War looked set to continue.

Rosie and Detective Chief Superintendent Peter Miller came, along with Charlotte, who was now in the last year of her law degree. Her dream of becoming a prosecutor for the Crown was now within reach.

Angie was ecstatic when Dorothy and Bobby made the epic journey across the Atlantic on an ocean liner. Dorothy's trip had been paid for by the *New Yorker* as Dorothy had become their number-one columnist, helped by an even greater American fervour for the Brits since Elizabeth II had become queen in February, aged just twenty-five.

Of course, while regaling the guests with her best friend's love story, Dorothy claimed that she'd known all along that Angie would end up falling in love with Stanislaw. And he with her.

Clemmie was also beside herself at finally meeting Dorothy in the flesh. As Dorothy was Clemmie. It took some daring, but Clemmie also brought her new 'friend', Barbara, to the wedding.

Marlene, fifteen, brought her boyfriend, Geoffrey, who was seventeen and whom Angie didn't like one bit, but that's a whole other story.

Danny, who was now also seventeen, had invited Lucy Stanton-Leigh, but she'd had to go to Inverness for some relative's funeral. Both claimed to be just good friends, but Angie wasn't so sure.

Danny spent much of the celebrations out in the stables – he even managed to take Ghost out for a ride without anyone noticing.

And Winston and Bessie, having exhausted themselves after the initial excitement of everyone arriving at the manor, had retired to their favourite spot in front of the Aga.

Bertie, now eleven, Jemima, ten, and Bonnie, who was 'nearly six', were in charge of the music room, which they had helped convert into the children's party room, and where they had their own buffet of ham sandwiches, sausage rolls, cake and a little chocolate – but only a little, as this was *still* rationed.

Lloyd and Mrs Jones looked almost as happy as the newlyweds. They were now officially Mr and Mrs Foxton-Clarke, although Cora insisted people call her by her first name. It didn't take a genius to know why.

Evelyn, it had been decided by the law courts, should remain at Rampton Secure Hospital 'indefinitely'. A decision that had been made, coincidentally, on the same day that Lloyd and Mrs Jones finally said 'I do'.

All the villagers, including the nursery mams, Dr Wright and his family, the landlord of the Farmer's Arms and his wife, and the vicar, who was glad to attend simply as a guest as it meant he could indulge in the wonderful selection of vintage ports, were there, along with, of course, Wilfred, Alberta, Bill, Thomas, Jake, and Ted and Eugene with their plus-ones.

Gertrude and Jeremy had also been invited, along with the neighbouring landed gentry. Gertrude and Jeremy, having finally recovered from housing a murderer under their roof, were particularly pleased the wedding reception had taken place at Cuthford Manor as it gave them a chance to show off the rooms they had helped to design. Jeremy had even started his own small interior design company, which seemed to take his mind off his failed attempts at wooing Angie and allowed him to focus instead on the men he came into contact with who were like-minded and also drawn to the arts.

The only person missing was Mrs Kwiatkowski, who had passed away at the beginning of the year, peacefully in her sleep. She could finally go and meet Janusz. In her last days, she had talked about her husband a lot to Stanislaw.

As Cuthford Manor was by now a fully functioning country house hotel, there were plenty of rooms for the guests to stay.

And in each room, Angie had put a small framed poem that had been embroidered onto cloth by Jemima. Care had gone into every stitch, and Jemima had allowed Bonnie to help her.

The poem was special to them all.

It was called 'Home Is Where the Heart Is' by Mrs Mary Lambert.

Dear Reader,

The more historical fiction I write the more I realise how much of what happens in our lives today parallels that which happened to those who lived decades ago.

No matter the era in which we live, we still have to deal with all the ups and downs and disasters and death which form part of life.

I love the quote at the beginning of this book by Helen Keller. I do believe we have to be as courageous as we can in the face of change. Whatever that change might be. Whatever Fate has in store. If there is one constant in this life, then it is surely the unexpected!

So, dear reader, I wish you brave hearts during changing and challenging times – as well as the love, care and support of others.

Until next time.

With love,

Nancy x

Historical Notes

Badge of the 22nd Artillery Support Company of the 2nd Polish Corps.

Cuthford Manor is based on many such grandiose homes of that time which speckled the length and breadth of the country. Many were requisitioned during the war and fell into such disrepair they had to be demolished, others were forsaken because their owners simply could not afford the upkeep. Luckily there are still many magnificent country and stately homes left, many of which we can visit thanks to organisations such as the National Trust.

I'm also pleased to relay that the majority of the 114 villages in County Durham which were given Category D status by the then county council defied their anticipated fate and survive to this day.

The references to Poland and the Polish refugees who were unable to return to the homeland they had fought so hard to save, are all true. Sadly, the circumstances surrounding the death of Stanislaw's wife, Adrianna, are also true. It is a matter of historical record that on 24 September 1939, the Soviet Army killed forty-two staff and patients at a military hospital in the village of Grabowiec, near Zamość, in Poland.

But on a happier and more hopeful note, the story of Wojtek the soldier bear really is true!

Discover Nancy Revell's bestselling Shipyard Girls series

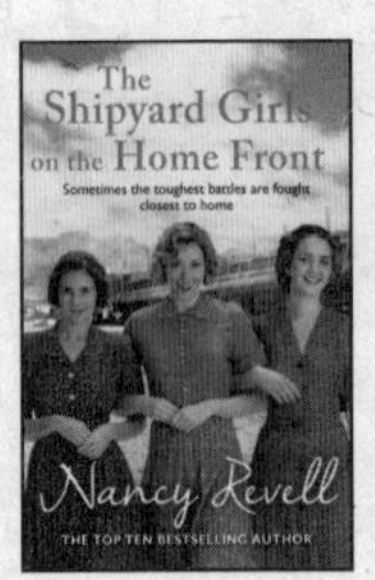

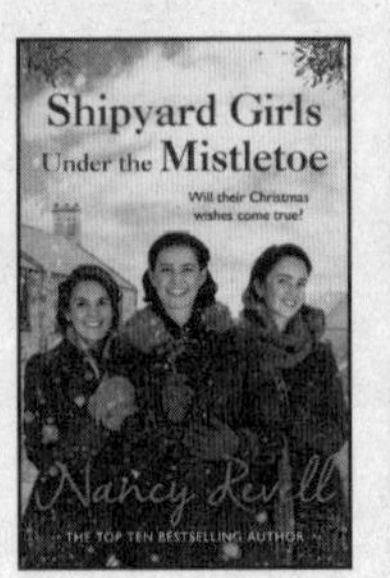

Have you read them all?

SIGN UP TO OUR SAGA NEWSLETTER

Penny Street

The home of heart-warming reads

Welcome to **Penny Street**, your **number one stop for emotional and heartfelt historical reads**. Meet casts of characters you'll never forget, memories you'll treasure as your own, and places that will forever stay with you long after the last page.

Join our online **community** bringing you the latest book deals, competitions and new saga series releases.

You can also find extra content, talk to your favourite authors and share your discoveries with other saga fans on Facebook.

Join today by visiting
www.penguin.co.uk/pennystreet

Follow us on Facebook
www.facebook.com/welcometopennystreet

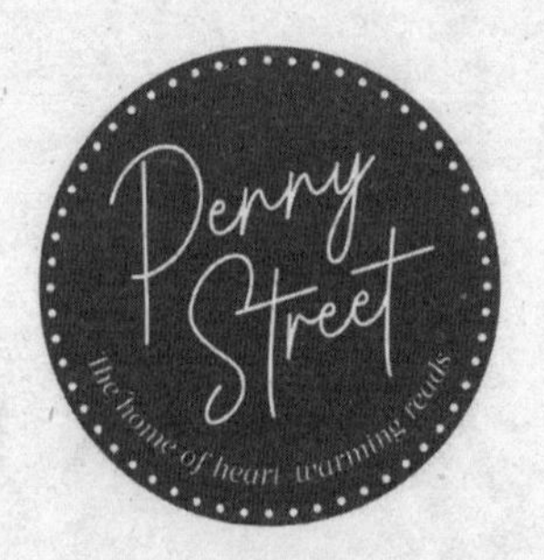